FLAME

Books by Judy Feiffer:

HOT PROPERTY

LOVE CRAZY

FLAME

FLAME

Judy Feiffer

DELACORTE PRESS/NEW YORK

Published by
Delacorte Press
1 Dag Hammarskjold Plaza
New York, N.Y. 10017

Manufactured in the United States of America

First printing

Library of Congress Cataloging in Publication Data

Feiffer, Judy.
  Flame.

  I. Title.
PS3556.E419R8   1986   813'.54
ISBN 0-385-29459-X
Library of Congress Catalog Card Number: 86-4270

for Kate Feiffer
with love

BOOK ONE

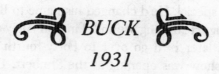

BUCK
1931

"Buck Herman! You're a goddamn Romeo!"

Baruch Herman stood in front of the bathroom mirror admiring himself. He was twenty years old with black hair, dark soulful eyes, and a dimple in his chin. Rose, his mother, called him her baby Valentino and he had to agree she was right. He lit a cigarette and puffed.

"A goddamn gift to the female race."

He had written a new song and he was feeling talented and self-assured. The song was throbbing in his head. He would sell it under his new name, Buck Herman. *That was a name. A winner's name.* He puffed, doused the cigarette, and splashed on some bay rum. Then he went down into the street.

There had been a heavy snowfall and Delancey Street was full of black mud. Hester, Essex, Forsyth—goddamn human sewers. Buck vowed that once he was out of this *fashtunkinah* hole, he'd never look back.

Across the street, an organ-grinder was playing "Embraceable You." Buck listened to the tune and watched the girls go by. Buck knew all about girls. He knew how to get a girl to love you and once she was stuck, how you stopped calling and she thought she would die. *Girls liked that—suffering. They thought it was life. The*

real thing. Dumb, girls were really dumb. At seventeen, Buck was a
Delancey Street Lothario. All the girls up and down millinery row
had necked, petted, or taken the long slide down with this hard-
boiled handsome guy who thought only of sex and being famous.

Today was special. He'd changed his name to Buck. He'd written a new song. He'd hang around Tin Pan Alley and make some
contacts, and later he'd go over to Forty-fourth Street. Glenda
Bruce's new show was opening at the Shubert. Everyone would
be there. Glenda was a goddamn great songwriter. She wrote the
tunes and she wrote the words. Pain. She was as good on pain as
Larry Hart, or Kern or Youmans. Some guy must of *shtupped* her
like crazy—some great fuck who made it feel like the most important thing in the world. And she'd gone all hysterical and
fluttery like some big frantic bird—yeah! Women were crazy!

That was Buck's talent—women! He knew how to make them
feel they were in front of a goddamn firing squad and he was the
guy with the gun.

Eight o'clock, and Forty-fourth was jammed with limousines
and men in tuxedos and women in diamonds and furs. Buck saw
Gershwin kissing Glenda Bruce and it tore his heart. Jed Harris
was there, and Fred and Adele Astaire, and one of those Gish
sisters, and, Christ, Noël Coward. The houselights blinked and
the crowd drifted into the theater. Boy oh boy. There was Mr.
Theater himself, David Belasco, kissing Glenda like a favorite
girl, and Glenda was mellow and cool and Buck loved her for it.
The crowd was gone now and it was as if God had planned it,
Glenda alone, and him.

Glenda was a good-looking blonde in a gold dress that wrapped
around her legs, and a white ermine jacket. Buck figured her for
forty-five. Buck's mother, Rose, was forty-five but she looked
sixty; the years of working in a sweatshop had left her wrinkled
and half blind. One day he'd make it up to her, everything, a
house filled with every vulgar *chachke* her big heart yearned for.

Rose's sensuous young prince stood on Shubert Alley that brisk
February night and Glenda Bruce, worldly, high-strung, and

gifted, watched him from the corner of her eye. Opening nights were a kind of death. A night to blot out. So when Buck Herman casually approached her, she realized this sexy kid in his cheap loud suit with the chiseled, strangely beautiful face, could distract her from the torment of three hours of living hell.

"I'm a great admirer of yours, Miss Bruce."

"Thanks."

"I guess opening nights are hard. I mean hard on the nerves."

"They're hell."

"I bet. I'm a songwriter too. I've written over a hundred songs."

"Then you certainly are a songwriter."

Glenda was superstitious. This intense young man with the dark dreamy eyes and sensuous lips was a dangerous type. She'd lived on the edge with dangerous men most of her life, but fifty minutes a day, five days a week with Dr. Sheftel had sublimated her need for dangerous men into her music, and her life was safe now except for the occasional night, like tonight. What did it matter if he was dangerous? He was young and beautiful, and the next three hours would be erased.

"What's your name?"

"Buck Herman."

"Well, Mr. Herman, how would you like to help a nervous songwriter through opening-night jitters with some Dom Pérignon?"

"Yes," said Buck. "I'd like it."

"Good. We'll go to my place. We'll be more comfortable there."

Her limousine cut through the park, and they got out at her apartment at Seventy-second and Fifth. Three short hours later a thousand electrified first-nighters cheered Glenda's new hit, but Glenda wasn't there to enjoy her triumph. She was naked on a white satin bed, in a white satin bedroom, drinking champagne with a boy who was making her unashamedly happy. Buck knew everything about Glenda Bruce. He knew her songs. He should. He had plagiarized her melodies. He knew the hunger in her body and how to fill the void. He was still a boy, but he was as sure about sex as any man who has made pleasure his business. He took Glenda from cool to a burning mass. He restrained his own pleasure until her heat was unbearable and she was begging for mercy. *Beg, you bitch!* His love was hard, his cock was shameless—his thrust slow, very strong and compelling. She kissed and caressed him. She clung to his body. She moaned. When he had her like this, spread wide and closed tight around his cock, he withdrew, very slowly, very sure, only to drive in harder. Her moans were different now, lower, sobs, the moans of a bitch in heat. "Now!" he ordered, "Now, baby." He burst into her and she flew into the sky. She sank into the earth. Buck lit the queen of torch songs into a human conflagration.

On the table beside her bed were framed silver pictures of Buck's heroes. *Love, Cole,* they read, or *I love you, George Gershwin,* or *All our love, Dick Rodgers and Larry Hart.* One day Buck's picture would stand there. He kissed her again, insuring she would want more.

"You're some hot kid," said Glenda.

"Whatever makes you happy!"

He pulled her toward him, growled, and got her going. Was he real? She touched his face. *He was real all right.* He let her kiss him like he was the last good meal before a fast, and then he really let her have it. Afterward, Glenda said, "You're a gift, Buck Herman, a goddamn gift from God." He knew then he was more important to her than the *Times* review, the opening-night party, and all her famous friends. He'd had her begging, begging for more, screaming for joy without drugs or booze. *It was enough happiness for the first time.* He got up from the bed and went into the bathroom to wash. He always washed himself after a fuck. When he finished, he came back to the bed.

"You're a dangerous young man."

"That's me. Mr. Danger from Delancey. You can handle it, Glenda."

"I have a bad track record with dangerous men."

"I'll teach you how to survive."

"What can I teach you?"

"I'm a poor illiterate kid from the Lower East Side. You can teach me how to get out."

Glenda introduced Buck to her friends and they said she was crazy. Who cared? She introduced him to caviar, bel canto, and Broadway, and he introduced her to love. It was afterward—his involuntary rushing to the bathroom to wash it off—that disturbed her. She excused it the first few times, but a week after they met there was a low table beside the bed. On the table was a bar of Guerlain soap and a silver bowl filled with water.

"What the hell's that for?" he asked.

"You'll see."

"Hey, Glen, in case you don't know, I hate surprises."

She didn't answer. *Well, what the hell. It was her bed, her place, her fame. She was calling the shots.* Buck gave her a hell of a fuck, and afterward, relaxed and peaceful, she reached over, took the soap, and sudsed his cock and balls. Then she dipped the washrag in the water, squeezed, and wiped him dry.

He grabbed the washrag from her hand and hurled it across the room.

"What the fuck you think you're doing?"

"What does it look like."

"You wanna play nurse? Find some other jerk."

"I don't want anyone but you."

"Believe me, baby, this ain't the way."

"You wash away my sex, Buck, that's how it feels."

He didn't answer. Instead, he grabbed her and gave it to her like some whore. She was a whore like everyone else, except she was a whore with talent. He fucked her until she screamed and he kept on. He felt her tears against his cheek and he kept on. He felt her shudder, her come, and he kept on. Glenda Bruce was a slut—a slut who'd been waiting for years for the obscene pleasure she now enjoyed. Her eyes were gooey as a dame in love. Buck pulled away. He went into the bathroom and turned on the shower spigot. Hot water drenched his body. He soaped himself the way he liked. He washed everything away.

The years passed in and out of Glenda's bed. Buck was
Glenda's last wild extravagance. This selfish yet alluring young
man whetted her appetite for the passion that was hers by in-
stinct. She looked at his body on the bed and softly said his name.
"Buck."
"Hmmm, Glen. Lemme sleep."
"How would you like to conduct your first show?"
"When?" He opened his eyes.
"You've been studying hard, Buck, making big progress. It's
time you took the plunge."
"Where?" Now his eyes were open and he was sitting up."
"Road company of *Lovers.* I'll fly out for weekends."
"Glen, thanks, but no."
"I see. Look here, Buck, I want to tell you something for your
own damned good. You're twenty-two years old and dying for
success. My success. Your own career . . ."
"No, Glen, it's not what I want."
She smiled at her greedy young lover. She would, of course,
get him whatever he wanted. She shrugged. "What *do* you want
then, darling?"
"Everything, baby! I want to write. I want to conduct. I want
your next Broadway show. Don't smile, Glen. I know I can do it."
"Would that make you happy?"
"Yeah."
"What else would make you happy?"
"This." And again, the springs sprang alive and Glenda felt the
shiver of youth slip over her soul and in a rumble of pleasure she
cried out and sank into that abyss of passion that kept her his
supplicant and slave.
In 1931, Winchell called Buck a wunderkind. He was twenty-
three years old and had conducted three Broadway shows—all
Glenda's, all hits. He was ambitious and talented, the passionate
lover of Broadway's most accomplished woman composer. Whatever you thought of this brash egomaniac, Winchell was right.
Buck Herman was Broadway's boy wonder.

"Hey, Glen, c'mere. One minute to play and those bastards are on the biggest winning streak in history."

Buck, sprawled on Glenda's white satin bed in a silk paisley bathrobe, was impatient. He walked to the bathroom to get her. It was misty with fumes. He opened the shower door.

"Hey, Buck, what in hell . . ."

He pulled her out, wrapped a towel around her, picked her up in his arms and carried her to bed.

"I want you with me."

The announcer was screaming, "There it is, ladies and gentlemen, a stunning upset. Victory turned into defeat on a single play with the final whistle one minute away. Trojans, sixteen. Notre Dame, fourteen. What a game!"

"A single play," said Buck. "A single fucking play."

He buried his mouth on her neck. The Delancey Street Lothario had come a long way since that cold February night three years ago. He had worked hard and used every opportunity. In his way, he had come to love Glenda. When it was over—and it would have to end—he'd do it like a gent. Glenda was a lady and he felt a peculiar gratitude.

That New Year's afternoon, as they lay side by side, the phone rang. Glenda picked it up.

"Hello, Max. Yes, darling, we heard it too." She paused. "Oh, Max, that's thrilling. No, Buck's right here. I want you to tell him yourself." She handed the receiver to Buck, covering it with her palm, "Max Sanford. President of Titan Pictures."

Buck put it to his ear.

"Hello, Mr. Sanford. Sure, I know who you are. Yes, sir, of course. Well, yes . . . of course I am, Mr. Sanford. Yes, sir, I'll come out there as soon as I can. Yes, of course. Glenda sends you her love too. Good-bye." He hung up. "Jeeeesssuss, Glenda!"

"That's what you *really* want."

"Oh, baby, you are the greatest dame in the whole fucking world."

"You big dope. You gave me the happiest years of my life. I've always known we were a limited run." She paused. "You'll be good, Buck, you'll be a big success."

Buck looked at his generous lover and felt sad, an emotion he had never before experienced.

"Hey, tough guy! Turning sentimental?"

"Just this once, Glen. One lousy time."

He didn't kiss or touch or fuck her. He looked into her eyes with love. That was the greatest gift he could have given her. Glenda understood—the hungry young animal who was her lover might never feel human again.

WANDA AND MISCHA
1936

Wanda Kahn watched while the other musicians, men without her Mischa's talent, men who would never amount to more than playing second fiddle, had the guts to leave their shabby life and gamble for the good life in Hollywood.

"We've got to think of the future, Mischa. We've got to be realistic. The future's in California."

"I'm not leaving Philadelphia. I'm not leaving Stokowski. My future's here. Period."

Wanda threw up her hands in a tragic gesture.

"What's that supposed to mean?"

"What does it look like it means?"

"You know what you want, Wanda? You want a slave. A nice henpecked schmuck who'll jump through your hoop. You want to go to California? Go! But me, I'm staying here."

"You really are a schmuck. When we get to Hollywood you can test for the part. Here I am, Mr. Zukor—Mischa Kahn. You don't have to audition any more schmucks."

"Very funny, Wanda. You've got a great sense of humor."

"If I didn't have my humor, I'd kill myself."

Mischa looked at his wife. Once, he'd wanted nothing more than to kiss her. But Wanda had passed from a sexy and hot-blooded girl he couldn't keep his hands off of, to an overweight, dissatisfied wife. Once, he had thought her kisses were love, and he had given up a Morgan heiress whose personal fortune would have bankrolled his career for Wanda's sweet hot kisses.

But Wanda's dream of the fame that would come with a world-famous violinist became the drab existence of an orchestra wife. God, she hated Philadelphia. The gray historic streets felt like a prison. At night the mansions in Rittenhouse Square were lit up, but Wanda's heart was bitter gall. Why else had she married this prodigy but to meet the great people, share the thunderous applause? Bask in the glory of his distinguished career? But no. She had married a fool. Shy, lacking imagination, happy to be invisible in a symphony orchestra. And suddenly this chance of a lifetime —this great new opportunity called Hollywood—and Wanda's hatred for her small, mean world became the central challenge of her life.

Through the walls of the apartment their five-year-old son, Nick, heard them fight.

"Music is my life, Wanda, can't you understand?"

"I understand this goddamn weather's killing me. I understand life is more than a lousy job with Stokowski. I understand you could be making a fortune. I understand you're an idiot!" She walked toward his music stand, tore away the music, and flung it to the floor. "Sure I understand. Your goddamn Beethoven will kill us."

She was sullen and full of anger. She cursed the soiled curtains that billowed in the breeze, the torn slipcovers, the worn linoleum, Stokowski. She cursed being poor. She was a broken record of invective. Until finally Mischa collapsed.

"We'll live in a palace, we'll have a maid and a swimming pool and a gardener. We'll have two cars. Oh, Mischa, I promise— you'll be the happiest man in the world!"

"We'll see," he said wearily.

Wanda flung her arms around him. She talked the way she had in the old days. "You're a genius, Mischa. You'll play in the studios and we'll have whatever we want. Give your Wanda a big kiss and tell me you're happy."

But Mischa turned away. He was over the kisses, the love, over everything. He could hardly bear to touch her. All right. They would go. He would work in the studios and finally Wanda would shut up.

On a warm June night in 1936, Mischa played under Stokowski for the last time. The lion with the flowing mane looked into the eyes of his men, lifted the baton, and swung it down. The doom-filled opening movement of the *Eroica* seemed an omen and Mischa felt suddenly frightened. His life was music. It was Beethoven and Bach, Schubert and Mozart, and on those afternoons and evenings in the Academy of Music, playing under the Maestro, he was a happy man.

He was worn out with dreams. Human dreams had deceived him. *Does a man shatter the core and substance of his heart for some ephemeral dream of happiness?* The hot glare of the sun, a Spanish mansion near the sea. These were Wanda's dreams. *Why in God's name had he listened to her?* She'd have worn him down, flat as some sea-drenched stone. He thought of the future—the scent of orange blossoms, a well-paid job in a studio orchestra, an expensive house in a residential neighborhood. It sounded good, all right, the good life Wanda wanted. Yet it filled him with dread.

Then came the furious beat of the second movement, the crash of drums, and again Mischa was a part of the music, one of the constellation of musicians forming a circuit of stars. Music! *That* was the sun. It was the moon overhead. Music was nature, and when Mischa played he felt himself to be part of the creation and he forgot, momentarily, the terrible fears that gnawed through muscle and bone and into his bowel.

ROSE
1936

A year after Buck moved to Los Angeles, he brought out his mother, Rose, his brother, Danny, and his kid sister, Zelda. Danny became his contractor at Titan. He hired and fired the musicians. Zelda studied typing and Gregg. If she didn't find a husband, there'd always be a job for her at the studio.

Since she had arrived in America at age fifteen, Rose had worked in a sweatshop on Hester Street. She worked twelve hours a day, six days a week. Her husband, Jake, before his stroke, had been a member of one of the hundreds of little congregations east of Broadway and south of Houston whose members came from different villages in Eastern Europe. Jake spent his days in the clubroom with the other men. They talked politics, studied the Talmud and Torah. It was Rose who worked to raise her family.

For Rose, that saint and paragon of virtue, Buck bought a mansion in the Hancock Park area, a neighborhood restricted to white Anglo-Saxon Protestants. Rose's house, on the outer fringe, was a Spanish Colonial with a sweeping driveway on an acre of land. She had a swimming pool and tennis court. She had a cleaning woman, a gardener, and a cook. For the first six months

Danny and Zelda lived with Rose. Then they found their own places, and Rose was alone.

Rose hired a decorator. She nagged the decorator to do her living room with a Chinese rug and antiques. The decorator wanted an Aubusson. She was fired, and replaced by a decorator who humored Rose. The house was filled with a thousand porcelain *chachke*s. Buck paid for everything. He made good his vow to give his mother her heart's desire. Rose was proud of her large house filled with expensive objects. She cleaned up after the housekeeper. *God forbid she should find a speck of dust.* One housekeeper was replaced by another. Rose's main activity was interviewing maids. The old days when Rose had worked from dawn to dusk, when she came home to cook, clean, and launder the clothes, laying her head on her pillow at night just grateful for rest, were over. Rose was a lady. She lived in a Spanish hacienda in the best part of town with three in help. But she was a victim of the Lower East Side who could barely write or read. She spoke with a hideous accent. Her neighbors despised her. She was a sore in their midst and worse—she was a Jew.

Rose was no dope. She understood that a woman who had come from Poland at the age of fourteen, who had worked in the stinking heat and filth of a dimly lit factory, was an untouchable wretch. She wanted to talk to her baby, Buck, but he was such a busy man these days, she poured out her woes to Danny. Danny, of course, told Buck, who knew he could give her everything but friends. Buck, Danny, and Rose held a family conference.

"The neighbors think I'm dreck."

"Lousy snobs."

"You worked hard, Mom, you raised a family. You got nothing to be ashamed of."

"God blessed me with two good sons."

"You're lonely, Momma. Danny and me will work something out."

"Find me some friends, Baruch."

"Buck, Ma, *Buck,*" Buck said, stiffening.

"Buck, my Buckelah. God bless my good boy Buck."

"Don't worry, Momma. You won't be lonely long."

Buck and Danny sat in the studio commissary and discussed Rose's situation. Buck lit a cigarette. He drummed his fingers on the table. A curvy blonde caught his eye. She smiled and waved at Danny.

"Cute," said Buck. "I like the way she's cut."

"Her name's Phoebe. I fucked her last week. Not half bad. Suppose I tell old Phoebe you'll give her a call."

"Ask her to call me at the office. You know how busy I am."

"Will do." Danny waved back and Phoebe moved on. "So what'll we do about Momma?"

Buck kept on drumming on the table. He lit another cigarette. "Suppose you tell your boys it would be nice, a courtesy, if their wives would call on Momma. Teach her cards. Gin. Bridge. Mah-jongg. Momma's always wanted to play mah-jongg. Mah-jongg would make Momma really happy."

"Orchestra wives! Jesus, Buck, I hate to admit it but you're a goddamn genius."

NICK
1936

The Santa Fe Super Chief began its early morning run toward the City of the Angels. Six-year-old Nick Kahn looked out in wonder at the streaks and cracks of dawn, the bleak stretch of desert with its black prickly cactus, the lines of telegraph poles, the flash of signs—San Bernardino—Glendora—Azusa—Alhambra—the convergence of silver shining rails, great smokestacks, clouds of dark billowing smoke, suburban tracts, and suddenly a large white sign, WELCOME TO LOS ANGELES, and below him the sluggish mudbank, the Los Angeles River. Then the porter was opening and slamming doors and shouting, "Last stop, Los Angeles, Los Angeles, last stop," and everyone was rushing around, hugging new friends and promising to stay in touch, grabbing small baggage and waving good-bye.

Only yesterday Old Chinatown and the shacks of the Chinese who had come across the sea to build the railways had stood here, but Chinatown was razed and in its place rose Union Station, a stucco building with a red tile roof and a 135-foot clock tower. Into this half-completed terminal daily roared the Southern Pacific, the Union Pacific, and the Atchison, Topeka and Santa Fe railroads with their carloads of new pilgrims.

Wanda took a deep breath of the sweet air. A new life, a good life, lay ahead. She put two fingers to her lips and blew a kiss. "Hello, Hollywood," she whispered, and it was like a prayer.

Mischa walked to the information desk. He arranged for a taxi to take them to the Bimini Bath Hotel.

Nick climbed onto an oversize wooden bench. It was like a burnished throne.

"I'm King Arthur."

Wanda laughed. "I'm Queen Guinevere." She sat beside him. In a minute Mischa joined them.

"I'm King Arthur," said Nick. "Who are you?"

"I'm Jascha Heifetz."

"That's not funny," said Wanda.

"So what is?"

"You know your problem? You love to be miserable. A millionaire and you'd be miserable. Greta Garbo for a girlfriend—you'd still be miserable. . . ."

Would it ever stop with Wanda? Mischa wondered, and turned away in disgust.

A porter piled their luggage into the trunk of the taxi, and Mischa, Wanda, and Nick climbed into the backseat.

Wherever you looked there were billboards. There were advertisements for high colonic irrigation, astrological and psychic readings, beauty shops, and funeral parlors.

Christ smiles and loves you at Forest Lawn, the Kingdom of Heaven at Hollywood Mortuary, What is good for Jesus is good for you. Die at the Celestial Funeral Home. "This isn't a city," said Mischa. "It's a landscape of death."

The cab pulled up to a two-story stucco building with a blinking neon sign. Inside, a big blond woman sat behind a counter. She was painting her nails. "Welcome to the Bimini Bath Hotel," she said. "I'm Mrs. Glass."

She banged on a silver school bell and a bent old man shuffled into the hall. Mischa signed the register and the old man took the bags. "Let me help," said Mischa, but the porter rushed ahead and up a flight of stairs.

Room 202 was beige and peeling. There were twin beds and a cot for Nick. There was a desk, a dresser, and a Gideon Bible. "Them's the baths," the porter said. "Still too early for swimmers, but another hour the place'll be full." He pointed to a glistening blue patch across the street. "It's plenty chlorinated so no one gets sick."

Mischa handed him a dollar. The porter mumbled thanks and shuffled away.

"Bathing suits. Bathing suits," said Wanda, rummaging through a suitcase. "I must've put them someplace."

"Maybe you forgot them."

"Forgot the suits? You think I'm crazy? That's the one thing we'll need." She pulled a pile of bathing suits from the packed valise, along with a white bathing cap.

"I'm not wearing a cap," said Nick.

"The pool is full of strangers. I don't want you picking up some disease."

"Take the cap," said Mischa wearily. "It makes your mother happy."

"Everything okay?" asked Mrs. Glass.

"Everything's fine."

"You'll need a car," said Mrs. Glass. "You can't live in Los Angeles without a car. When you've finished breakfast I'll run you over to Big Bill's. The most honest dealer in town." It was decided at breakfast that Mischa would get the car and join them later at the pool. He kissed Nick on the forehead and went into the hall. Mrs. Glass had changed into a sundress. She wore a straw panama with a feather and sunglasses in a tilted frame.

Driving along, she said to Mischa, "After a while you'll wonder how you lived any other place. Me, I'm from Salem, Oregon. It rains in Salem every day. I thought life was rain—until I hit L.A." She stretched out a nut-brown arm and a hand with red fingernails. "See that tan? I spend my life behind a desk, but five minutes of sun and it looks like I got nothing else to do."

"I like the rain," said Mischa.

"You'll get to love the sun." Mrs. Glass laughed, and her breasts shook. Mischa saw they were nut-brown too. "There's not much point in living if you don't."

Big Bill's banner was strung across the road and Mrs. Glass made a sharp left turn into his lot. She stepped from her car and Big Bill reached down and kissed her.

"Mr. Kahn just arrived from the East. The first thing you need, I says, is a car."

"Best buys in town," said Big Bill. He led them to a black Pontiac. "A bull could ram into this thing and you wouldn't feel it. You're Mrs. Glass's friend—it's yours for two hundred. Keep it twenty-four hours; if you're not satisfied, bring it back."

"I bring everyone to Bill," said Mrs. Glass. "And everyone is happy."

"Happy customers make happy dealers," said Big Bill.

Mischa took a checkbook from his pocket and wrote a check for two hundred dollars. He got into the car and turned on the ignition. Mrs. Glass leaned across the open window.

"Thank you," said Mischa. "You've been awfully nice."

"Forget it. Look, I'm free most nights—sometimes people need friends. I mean, you can be a nice sweet guy and still need a friend, if you get my point."

She turned away, waved to Big Bill, got into her car and followed Mischa back to the hotel.

"Pool's open!" cried Nick, and pulled Wanda from their room, across the street, and into the Bimini Baths.

"I need a swimming instructor," Wanda said to the bronzed lifeguard.

"Bob's very popular," he said, pointing to a muscular body doing laps. "He'll have your boy swimming in no time."

Wanda engaged Bob for the day, and Bob showed Nick how to breathe and kick and float. By afternoon, Nick could paddle along. The chlorine burned his eyes and when he swallowed, it stung his throat, but Nick didn't care—he was almost swimming!

At three o'clock Bob said he'd done enough for one day. They made arrangements to meet the following morning.

At dinner that night Wanda said, "We'll have a champion on our hands! Like that gold medal Olympic colored, Jesse Owens."

"Jesse Owens is a runner."

"I know he's a runner. The point is he's a champion."

That night in bed Nick practiced moving his arms up and down under the sheets. He inhaled and exhaled, he kicked his legs and made a bet with himself that one day he'd win a gold medal and his mother would be so happy, she would finally shut up.

Bob went over Nick's kick and his breathing, and showed him how to move his arms. He showed him the breaststroke and the crawl. At noon they stopped for a sandwich. Wanda was bored and went back to the hotel. Bob and Nick swam some more. There were hundreds of bodies in the water and it was hard to move. The water was foul. Nick's eyes were itching and red-veined. He hated the sting of the chlorine, but swimming was fun so he didn't complain—not about his eyes or the pounding, thudding thing in his head. Then the thudding got worse. Nick repeated his promise to himself about becoming a champion, but the fun was gone. All he felt was the pounding.

"You okay, kid?" asked Bob.

"Kinda tired. Guess I'd like to stop."

"Sure thing, Nick. See you tomorrow morning at ten."

"So long, Bob."

At dinner Mischa joked about the fifty-two funeral parlors he had counted, Wanda talked about the houses Miss Faye, the real estate agent, would show them, and how she was going to lose ten pounds and dye her hair blond, and Nick tried to keep alert.

"You got a headache, son?"

"I'm okay," said Nick. He'd be careful about complaining or his

mother would start a scene. After dinner he'd ask Mrs. Glass for
an aspirin and tomorrow he'd be fine.

"It's the sun," continued Mischa. "You stick him in a pool in
this goddamn heat and expect him to swim like a fish. Of course
he's got a headache. You'll come with us tomorrow."

"I'm fine, honest, I'm really okay."

Then Mischa was joking about the pretty girls and Wanda was
gabbing about the handsome men. Wanda was always going to
the movies and falling in love with some dumb actor. She'd write
away for a picture and send a quarter and she'd get an auto-
graphed glossy eight-by-ten. She had pictures of Clark Gable and
Robert Taylor and Errol Flynn. Nick wondered why she ever
married his father. Maybe Wanda would meet a real movie star
and fall in love and leave them alone.

Wanda gave Nick an aspirin, but his headache wasn't better.

"What's the matter, Nick? You're frowning."

"Just tired."

"Go to bed," said Mischa. "Tomorrow's a big day."

Nick wasn't sure why he didn't tell them about the terrible
pain. He lay on the bed and shut his eyes, his body burning and
his head pounding with a heavy dull thud. The thud was like a
hammer smashing into his skull, and he was shaking all over,
feeling cold and burning up at the same time. He felt like vomiting. He stumbled from bed to go to the bathroom, but his legs
buckled and he fell to the floor.

"Help," he gasped. "Someone help me. . . ."

When he opened his eyes, he saw a lot of machines and a
woman in a white uniform coming at him with a long needle.
Then he melted into the dark and there was only silence.

Nick woke up in a strange dark room. The woman in the white
uniform was standing by his bed.

"You've had nice long sleep," she said. "It's time to wake up."

"Where am I? What happened?"

She didn't answer at first. She changed the linen on his bed
and he saw one leg bound tightly in a splint. He couldn't move it.

She covered his body with a sheet. His toes stuck up, but a part of him between his hips and toes felt erased, as if the thing in splints weren't a leg at all.

"I can't feel my legs," cried Nick. "I can't feel them."

"You've been very sick," said the nurse. "But you're a lucky little boy. In a month we'll remove the splints, and you'll be up and about in no time."

The nurse's smile was like an ugly doll's.

"Where's my mother?" Nick asked excitedly. "Get my mother!"

"Your mother's with the doctor. I'll go and tell her you're awake."

In the late summer of 1936, victims of poliomyelitis, or infantile paralysis, reached epidemic numbers, particularly in children under ten years of age. There were warnings to avoid unnecessary contact with other children, or swimming in public pools, particularly in warm climates. But southern California, with its heat, its ocean, its open and contaminated pools, was an irresistible lure to the bored and restless children with nothing to do.

The hospitals were full.

After a period of isolation Nick was moved to a ward. There were twelve beds in the room, a wooden table beside each bed, and bedposts made of cast iron. The room was painted green. The children were sitting in bed or limping on crutches. When they saw that Nick was awake, they hobbled to his side.

A small blond girl stuck her tongue to the tip of her nose. Her face was like a rubber ball and she could do all sorts of tricks—punch out her cheek or suck it tight until she had half a face, wriggle her ears, roll one eye up and the other down—and each trick made the children roar.

"I'm Betty and I can make anyone laugh."

" 'Cept *them,* " the children cried, and pointed to two small girls on the far side of the room.

"Why don't they laugh?" asked Nick.

"They won't let my dog into the hospital," said one of the girls, named Judy. "His name is Biscuit. He shakes hands, he stands on his hind legs, and he lays on his back and plays dead. I give him a biscuit and he jumps up and licks me. I miss Biscuit!" And Judy began to sob.

The other girl stared at Nick through big dark eyes. "That's Judy. She's always crying. Her mother brought her to Hollywood to be a tap dancer in the movies. Her mother's so sad she'll never tap-dance, she never comes to see her."

"It's a lie," cried Judy. "She wants to come but she can't. . . . She's looking for a job. I know she is, she told me. . . ."

"Look at me," Nick said quickly. He raised his hands and moved his fingers and made shadows on the wall.

"Guess what this is."

"A dog," everyone shouted.

Nick moved his fingers back and forth.

"What's this?" he cried.

Everyone tried, but no one could guess.

"It's Judy," said Nick. "She's tap-dancing."

Judy laughed.

Nick's fingers flew up and did kicks and it was as if tap dancing was so much fun and Nick looked at the smiling children and thought, They're just like me. All they want is to be happy.

Mischa and Wanda walked toward Nick's bed. Wanda wore a pink sundress that showed the tops of her breasts. Men always looked at Wanda. Bob the lifeguard looked at Wanda. The doctor looked at Wanda. Only Mischa never looked at Wanda.

"How's my big boy?" asked Mischa.

"Okay."

"The doctor says he has children in the iron lung who can't even breathe," said Wanda. "But you'll walk again, Nick, you'll have a normal life."

"Mom, c'mon."

"And look who you've got as an example—our own great President Roosevelt! When I think of what that man has accomplished despite his affliction, it gives me hope. It gives us all hope, doesn't it, Mischa?"

But Mischa was looking at the sweet young children with withered limbs who had hopped and hobbled to Nick's bedside.

"Children," he said, "do you like music?"

"Oh, yes!"

"Then tomorrow I will bring my violin and I will play you some beautiful songs."

"Will you play 'Deep Purple'?"

Mischa smiled shyly. "I don't know 'Deep Purple,' but I promise the songs I play will make you happy."

The next day he brought his violin.

"This is a trout," he said. "You can hear it jump in and out of the water." His fingers slipped up and down the bow, and jumped from string to string. All the children agreed they could really hear the trout. Sometimes the song had no story. Mischa called it a Schubert or a Mozart or Brahms. Sometimes a song was so sad, it made Judy cry. Mischa looked at the forsaken little girl and it broke his heart. His fingers danced up and down the strings in a merry little song.

"There," said Mischa. "You're not crying anymore."

"I know," said Judy. "I feel better. You make me feel okay."

"It's not me," said Mischa. "It's the music. So just remember, when you're sick or you're lonely or sad, you can listen to music and music will take away the pain."

Mischa came regularly to play for the children. One day he announced, "Listen, everybody. I've got a job . . . I can't play for you anymore except on Saturday and Sunday, but when you are well, and you go to a movie, and you hear a violin go like this" —his finger gave a little trill—"remember, it's Mischa, playing for you."

The next Sunday, Mischa played the movie music for the children.

"This is vibrato," said Mischa. He pressed his fingers on a string in a short, jerky motion and he screwed up his nose in disgust.

"My boss likes vibrato. All day long he screams, 'Vibrato. Vibrato! Gimme vibrato!' " And Mischa played a vibrato and he screwed up his nose and the children laughed at Mischa making fun of the vibrato.

The weeks became months. During the day Nick underwent the hot baths and massages of the Sister Kenny method for treatment of polio.

Sometimes Nick heard a child crying in the dark. "It's not your fault," he wanted to scream. "Don't cry." However sad you felt, the only way to be crippled was to pretend you didn't care—you couldn't let it seem important . . . it wasn't your fault . . . crying made people feel sorry for you and that made things worse. . . . Why didn't the children understand? . . . He did . . . whatever happened, no one would see him cry. . . .

Finally, the splint was removed from his leg. Nick was fitted with an iron brace and discharged from the hospital. He hated the ugly metal brace. If he could wake his leg up from its long, silent sleep, then he could throw the brace away. He pinched his leg. He stuck a pin into it. The leg slept on—a dead thing attached to his hip . . . a leg that made him different . . . he wouldn't show that he cared. . . .

In the 1880s, in a big land boom, Mr. and Mrs. Horace Wilcox, prohibitionists and active members of the Methodist church, bought a large tract of land at the base of the Los Angeles foothills and christened it "Hollywood." Their pious, conservative, churchgoing community built adobe, stucco, and wooden bungalows, and tended their pretty gardens and lawns. The most exciting event of the day was the arrival of the stagecoach, lurching along an old dirt road.

Then, in 1911, the old Blondeau Tavern on Sunset and Gower —one of the very few saloons around—was bought and converted into a movie studio. The pious Methodists reeled in shock as cowboys in boots and spurs, comedians in baggy pants, and beautiful blondes paraded up and down their streets. Cheap hotels and boardinghouses sprang up like weeds while the new arrivals did what was necessary to stay alive.

America invaded Hollywood. Along with the dream came sin and scandal. Raging preachers filled the pulpits, but nothing could stop the growing mob. A young commercial artist named John D. Roche created a sign, HOLLYWOODLAND, fifty feet high and thirty feet wide, lit by four thousand light bulbs, and hauled up the mountain by a hundred Mexican laborers. It soared in the hills, a shimmering shrine that greeted the frenzied hordes in pursuit of overnight fame and fortune.

Mischa and Wanda's house was on Gower, above Beachwood. The house was on an incline surrounded by conifers, dwarf trees, and fragrant eucalyptus.

"It's a paradise, Mischa . . . as close as we can get."

Mischa was silent.

"It could have happened anywhere," said Wanda weakly. "Polio's a national epidemic."

Mischa remained silent.

"God damn it, *talk* to me, Mischa."

"What do you want me to say?"

"Anything. Tell me about your job."

"Buck Herman? The man's a lunatic. All he knows is vibrato. '*Vibrato!*' he screams. . . . I spend my life vibrating for some third-rate hack."

"He's your boss, Mischa. Your boss wants you to vibrate, so vibrate."

"Wanda, please."

"It's why he hired you."

"The reason he hired me is an old friend of mine from Philadelphia loses at poker to him and his brother."

"So *you'll* lose at poker too. Be a realist, Mischa. Nothing is free. We've got a beautiful home, a garden, two cars. For God's sake, losing at poker is a small price for paradise."

CASSIE
1940s

Blondes. Blondes. Blondes. The streets were full of pretty girls who had come to sing and dance and act their way into the movies. Love was a part of the act!

"You're a swell kid. You're absolutely terrific."

It was a casting director, an agent, a studio executive, complimenting the girl as she kissed, moaned, and peeled off her sheer black stockings. The casting couch became a metaphor for getting a job. It was a style of instant love, followed by a day's work, followed by silence, followed by months of haunting Central Casting. You had to be pretty—but more important, you had to have vitality. The men with power liked vitality. Vitality was to a pretty girl what vibrato was to a musician. Without vitality you might as well be dead.

Junipero Junior High was full of boys and girls stamped out of the blonde machine. The girls wore white peasant blouses that slipped off their shoulders, sandals called huaraches, Tangee lipstick, and Evening in Paris cologne sprayed between their budding breasts. Their talk was only of boys.

The boys were tanned and muscular. They were the athletes, the "Big Men on Campus." This was their finest hour.

It was a hot day. The sun made slanting patterns through the blinds. Nick sneaked a look at Cassie Castle. Her eyes were blue and her golden hair was rolled into an elaborate pompadour. A golden fraternity pin hung from her peasant blouse. Everything about her was golden: her face and hair and shapely legs. Cassie was a prepubescent golden girl who induced a mass hysteria among the boys of Junipero.

Mr. Godard, the history teacher, droned on, and Nick slipped into a favorite daydream. *He was mounted on his white charger. He rode toward Cassie waiting in the crowd. He swept her up and held her close. Everyone screamed "Nick" and Cassie trembled in his arms. . . .*

"Don't be frightened, Cassie. Men love a leader, and a crowd needs to acclaim. They know I only use my power for good. . . ."

The crack of Mr. Godard's ruler against the flat of his desk tore Nick from his daydream.

"Whatever you're thinking must be pretty interesting. Why not share it with the rest of us?"

"Nick's in love. The cripple loves Cassie."

"Who said that?" asked Godard.

The room went silent.

"Don't worry. Whoever you are I'll find you." And he would, because Mr. Godard had his spies. No one knew exactly who they were, but they were there, and loyal. At three o'clock the school bell rang and Mr. Godard said, "That's all, boys and girls. Oh, Nick, I'd like to see you a minute."

Nick watched Cassie from his seat. She swayed when she walked, as if the wind were carrying her along. She wore a perfume that wasn't Evening in Paris—it was something that came up from under her skin. She smiled her gorgeous smile and the boys fell on her like a pack in heat. When she was gone, it was like a void.

"There's more to life than girls like Cassie," said Mr. Godard.

"Is there?"

"Look, Nick, you're a smart boy. Maybe even brilliant. But

you're handicapped. I don't mean to be cruel, but it's a fact. You'll have to work hard for the girls you'll want. Girls like Cassie excite a man's imagination. . . ." He looked at Nick with a kind of amused affection. "When Eve dragged Adam from grace, she turned him crazy. The old scribes warned us, 'Thou shalt not suffer a witch to live'—a kind of insurance policy that man invented to protect himself from the Cassies of the world. Men called them 'witch' and burned them at the stake. They called them 'muse' and wrote them gorgeous love poems. But Cassie's an illusion—she can make a man destroy himself."

"I don't understand," Nick said.

"Men don't love girls like Cassie. They have passions for them. Cassie Worship. Man needs her in his weakness but he damns her in his heart. The Cassies of this world have repeated Eve's folly a million times and more. It's okay, Nick—you'll recover. If not, if she's your curse, you'll find another Cassie. She'll have a different name but she'll be a Cassie. And you'll be like the rest of mankind—dreaming of your ruling passion and running from its power."

"Not me. I'll never run away."

"Oh, no." Mr. Godard laughed. "Read your history, Nick. You'll see what fools men are. Merlin and Samson and old Henry the Eighth—there's always been a Cassie to put men in a trance. She changed the course of history. Governed men's lives." Mr. Godard stood up suddenly. He almost blushed. "Forgive me, Nick. I'm an old and failed romantic. You go on about your life. One day you'll understand. . . ."

Saturday afternoon, Nick went to one of the great movie palaces that stood like feudal castles on Hollywood Boulevard. There, in the dark, he met with love. The trembling lips, the quivering nostrils . . . He burned as the lovers of the screen leapt into love's flames. *Made for love, they were love's victims. Love was ruthless and cruel, exquisitely physical, given so randomly to those who abused it, while to Nick, who wanted it so desperately, it was denied.* He locked his feelings away like a terrible secret. At night he let them out. His fantasies of Cassie connected one night to another. He shaded the story—introduced variations, increased the dose, like a drug addict intent on pleasure. Cassie became a habit. A kind of bondage with which he lulled himself to sleep.

Beneath Gower, on Beachwood, was Cassie's house. From his bedroom window Nick could see the red maple in the yard and behind it a sort of shack or toolshed. The house was a Moorish castle that had fallen from grace. It was dilapidated, the paint peeling, broken shingles on the roof, a porch with broken slats. The yard was overgrown with weed and brush. Occasionally, a young man mowed it.

Weekends, in a white shirt and shorts, Cassie sat in the sun. She painted her toenails and wriggled her feet. Nick ached with desire. He knew he would do anything, except die, to win Cassie's love.

Cassie's mother, Mary, had been a showgirl in Earl Carroll's supper club, her father an out-of-work actor. When her father disappeared, he was succeeded by a parade of stuntmen, cowboys, and small-time hustlers. The men came and went, and Mary Castle, once a gorgeous showgirl, started drinking and turning to flab. Earl Carroll liked his showgirls young and firm. Mary Castle was fired. She got a job as a waitress in the Melody Lane, on Hollywood and Vine. Between Cassie and Mary, the rundown Beachwood place was in constant commotion with jalopies and roadsters, horns honking, brakes screeching, and motors racing.

The Castle women—mother and daughter—the noise, the men, the sin and sexuality, gave the ladies of Beachwood their chief activity—gossip. These old women's husbands had died, and the widows lived in small bungalows on dwindling pensions and savings.

—*Shameless hussies! Ought to be a law against women like that.*
—*But there isn't. There ain't nothing we can do.*
—*Women like that in a decent neighborhood—makes me sick.*
—*What can we do?*

—Wait and pray.
—And hope the good Lord hears us.
—Only He can help.

So the Beachwood ladies suffered the din and shock of the Castles' sin, and prayed daily for deliverance.

And like a miracle, it came.

John Aherne had been a carpenter at Earl Carroll's when Mary was a glamorous showgirl. He had fixed the revolving stages, and —from the wings—kept an eye on Mary Castle. But the long-legged flashy chorus girl had a lot of fancy actors hanging around her and didn't give John Aherne a second thought.

It was only a few years since Mary had dazzled her admirers, but a few years in the life of a showgirl is like twenty years in any normal woman's life. Mary didn't dazzle now. She was over-weight with a coarse look to her. When John Aherne walked into the Melody Lane one night and Mary took his order, he knew his time had come. *She is still beautiful,* he thought, *but she's ragged and worn, the way a sofa gets when it's been banged around. Needs reupholstering and the springs restrung.* When John saw Mary Castle he decided to fix her up like new.

"Remember me, Mary?"

"Sure I remember. You worked the stage at Earl Carroll's."

"If you don't think I'm fresh—I'd like to call you, Mary. I'd like to take you out to supper."

"That would be nice, John."

"I'm glad you remember my name, Mary. I wasn't sure you would."

"Of course I do."

"You didn't used to act it."

"Didn't I?"

"I looked you up in the phone book once. You still at that number?"

"Yes."

"I'll call you, Mary. We'll have a lot to talk over."

Sure Mary remembered this strong blond man. Back in the

days when men were fighting for her attention, when Mary was
waiting for someone important enough, she had felt John
Aherne's constant eye upon her and ignored it. He was just a
carpenter. But that wasn't the real reason. The real reason was
he scared her. . . . As if he could see beyond her peroxide and
mascara and into the core of her soul, as if he would twist her
and launder her like some soiled sheet he wanted made white—
that's the way he made her feel. So Mary had pretended indifference, let him think he wasn't good enough, what she wanted was
someone rich. *Well, that was yesterday. Today, at thirty-four, with
a kid to support—well, beggars aren't choosers.* She'd had enough
men to last her a lifetime. What was one man more? If she didn't
like John Aherne, she wouldn't see him again.

Saturday night, John took Mary to the Cocoanut Grove. There
was a floor show and dancing later and John held Mary close.
The following Sunday, Mary asked him over for supper. They
listened to Jack Benny, and afterward, over Walter Winchell, he
helped her do the dishes.

"There's no one like Winchell," said Mary. "Winchell knows
everything before it happens."

"A patriot, too. Winchell's a great American."

Cassie came home with her boyfriend in the middle of the
broadcast.

"Mighty pleased to meet you," said John Aherne.

"Me too," said Cassie. "Oh, this is Pete."

"Hello there, Pete."

"Oh, hi."

"There's chicken if you're hungry," said Mary.

"We already ate. Anyone call?"

"Harry called. And Jack—Jack's called three times. Poor Jack
doesn't know the meaning of no."

"Jack's such a jerk."

Mary and Cassie laughed over Jack the Jerk not knowing the
meaning of no, and Cassie and Pete went outside. Cassie thought
her mother's new boyfriend was kinda handsome, with his blond
hair and muscles, but there was something about him—she

wasn't sure what—just something odd. Like the school principal, who had you to his office when you were bad, and used a belt— you stayed out of his way.

Wednesday night John took Mary to see *Wuthering Heights* and when Mary started going crazy over this Heathcliff saying how gorgeous he was, John Aherne remembered all the years he had denied his dream of love, and how he hadn't had the courage to approach her. He despised himself for being a fool. That night, on the front porch of her house, he kissed her. She kissed like someone with a lot of experience. He asked her to turn off the porch light.

"Scared you'll shock the neighbors?" she joked.

"I like it better in the dark."

The following Saturday night they drove to Santa Monica. John parked his car on Ocean Avenue and they walked onto the pier. They ate in a place called The Wharf, and afterward they walked to the end of the pier. They leaned against the rail and watched the fishermen cast their lines. The sky was streaked with purple. In the distance, along the beach, a breeze lifted the palm fronds. John put his arm on Mary's shoulder.

"I love the gulls," said Mary. "I love to watch them lift up and fly."

"That's a beautiful thought, Mary." He leaned over and kissed her on the cheek.

"You're a big flirt, John Aherne!"

" 'Cept I'm not flirting. It's the way I feel!"

"Is it?"

"You know it is. It's how I've felt for years."

"I guess I do."

"There's something else you should know, Mary."

"What, John?"

"I used to watch all those guys giving you the rush—oh, I'm not criticizing, you were so damned pretty, but I always knew one day it'd be my turn. I love you, Mary. Guess I've always loved you, 'cept now I'm in a position to do something about it. Mary, I want you to marry me."

"Gosh. You hardly even know me."

"I've known you for over five years. You don't love me yet, but one day I promise you will. You'll come to love me more than anyone in the world."

Mary looked into his eyes and felt a mixture of fear and excitement. It was like a movie, this stranger telling her how much he loved her and how much she'd come to love him back. Then what was the feeling she sometimes felt—like wanting to shrink away and be invisible—secretly hoping he'd disappear? She was a fool. A man who loved you all the years John Aherne loved her—well, love was a habit. You said the words and after awhile you got to believe them. . . . She looked out at the sea, the gulls. There was a rush of wind, and John turned her toward him and he kissed her. His strong mouth on hers, his arms around her waist, the swell of him against her stomach . . . she closed her mind to fear. John Aherne was her last chance. She hardly dared admit it, but it was true. She had no choice. He was the investment she must make for the future.

"You're really sure you want to get married?" Mary asked.

"I'm sure."

"All right, John. We'll be married whenever you want."

John and Mary were married in the Methodist Church off Franklin, and all of Beachwood was there to celebrate. John had visited each of the ladies and personally invited them to the wedding and the reception afterward in Mary's house. Mary wore a white satin dress and a veil with seed pearls and Cassie wore a sky-blue dress. It made her blue eyes even brighter. The punch was spiked with champagne.

John put his hand on Mary's and guided the knife through the frosted wedding cake. Everyone clapped as Mrs. Feenie, the oldest Beachwood resident, raised her glass in a toast.

"God bless you, John and Mary! May you live happily ever after!"

All of Beachwood cheered. Deliverance had come.

For their honeymoon, John and Mary drove up to Lake Arrowhead. Mary looked forward to dinner and dancing in the big
hotel, and afterward, in their cabin, she would take off her new
red dress, and John would make love to her. *He'd be strong and
wonderfully kind, and she felt good about the bargain she'd made
with herself; security, a father for her child, and a man who loved
her.* She had faith she would come to love John too. He was
strong and good and handsome. He still made her feel odd, like a
part of her wanted to run away, but she pushed away the fear.
I'm a lucky woman, she repeated to herself, *I'm a lucky woman,*
and she thought about the hot mineral baths and how they would
soak in the tubs, and the fancy restaurants and the dancing. They
passed off Crestline Road into the Valley of the Moon. It was
spooky. A full moon and empty picnic grounds and deserted
cabins. A coyote wailed. Mary shuddered. She snuggled close to
John.

"I hate coyotes. They scare me so."

"I'm here to protect you."

"You're silly, John, big and strong and awful silly."

"I want to make you happy."

"You do, dearest. You make me real happy. Do I make *you*
happy, dearest?"

"You will."

"Don't I make you happy now?"

"Sure you make me happy. You're just going to make me happier. I'm going to be the happiest man alive."

John banked downward and Mary saw the lake. It shimmered
in the moonlight. John pulled into the driveway of a darkened
cabin. They got out of the car. She stood behind him as he
unlocked the cabin door. The moon, the wailing coyotes, the dark
and isolation. She felt a sudden fear.

"Why'd you ever pick a place so lonely?" she asked.

"It's our wedding night, honey. That's why."

Mary smiled. "Hey, aren't you going to carry me over the
threshold?"

He picked her up and carried her into the dark cabin. He

pushed aside the curtain. A ray of moonlight fell on the floor. *Of course, he'd want a private place. It was their first night of love together. He wanted it romantic. The same way she did. She was such a silly fool.*

John flicked on a light. He locked the door and put the key in his pocket. *How strangely he looked at her. The hard line of his mouth and that look in his eye, so queer and intense—like the way he used to look at her at Earl Carroll's.*

"Take off that dress," said John.

"Sure, honey." She took off her new red dress and got onto the bed. He stood there, fully dressed and watching.

"You embarrass me," said Mary. "You're staring so hard."

"You're still so pretty, Mary."

"Come on, honey. Come to bed," said Mary.

He didn't move. He put his hand in his pocket and pulled out some cord. He sat beside her on the bed. He took her hand. He slipped the cord around her wrist.

"Hey, what're you doing?"

He reached her arm toward the bedpost and looped the cord onto the pole.

"You're hurting me, John."

He reached across her, yanked her free hand upward, corded it, and tied it to the other bedpost.

"Let me go!" she screamed. "Let me out of here!"

John stood up. He unbuckled his belt and pulled it from his trousers. He stood near her. He started talking.

"I was hoping you'd reformed. Then, at your own wedding I saw you looking at the minister like he was a man of flesh instead of a man of God, and I knew you hadn't changed. You're still the same old Mary."

"What in hell are you talking about?"

"I'm talking about the men who soiled you, Mary, who turned you into a slut. I'm talking about how you smile and lead them on until they're helpless to stop themselves."

"You're crazy!"

"No, Mary, I'm your husband. And my first job is to teach you what that means."

She watched John Aherne roll up his sleeve to his elbow.

"When I punish you at home, I'll put a gag in your mouth. Tonight, I want to hear you scream."

"Don't hit me, John. I'll do anything you want."

"Other men have fucked you into a whore. If it takes me the rest of my life, I'm going to make you pure."

Mary watched him grip the belt, raise his arm, and strike. She bore the first stroke in silence, then the second and the third. Finally she screamed.

"Don't . . . Please, John, no more . . ."

"I want the name of every man you've slept with. So start in, Mary . . . start giving me names. . . ."

The strap bore down.

"Names, Mary . . ."

It bore down again.

"Enoch Johnson." She moaned.

It tore her flesh.

"Joe Serlina."

It cut her open.

"Oh, God . . . Sam Ritt."

She was sobbing violently when miraculously the strap stopped whipping into her skin. John Aherne was lying beside her and kissing her tear-soaked face and murmuring, "I don't like to hurt you, honey, but you're private property, see—no trespassing—no strangers near my woman . . ."

"I'll be good, John. I swear I'll be good. . . . Jus' don't hurt me anymore."

He took a mass of her bleached blond hair in his fingers and played with it and then he tightened his fingers into a fist.

"You gotta work at it harder than you ever worked at anything before. . . ."

"I'll work at it, John. I'll be so good . . ."

She was gasping for air and John felt the hiss of her breath and he let go of her hair and stood up. He looked down at the white curved body that was finally his. Then he struck her again.

"God," she moaned. "Oh, God . . ."

"That's right, Mary, pray for your sins. And thank the good Lord I've finally come along to keep you on the straight and narrow. And if you got any thoughts about running away . . ." And John's arm lifted and fell and Mary's screams fell away in the silent black night.

This was Mary's honeymoon. She came to understand John Aherne was her master and his belt cutting into her flesh was the price she had bargained for her security. It was over—everything. All her dreams and all her hopes . . . Then suddenly he stopped hurting her and the night was still except for her sobs. Now John was beside her holding her close and stroking her like a man terribly in love.

"Say you love me, Mary, tell me how much."

"I love you," she gasped. "Just you . . . no one else. You're the only one, John . . . I've been waiting for you all my life."

John Aherne stripped the peeling paint from the house. He painted it white. He fixed the porch slats, he mended the roof and shutters, and he planted a colorful garden. Mary tended the flowers and Cassie mowed the lawn.

Once, John Aherne had wanted to be a minister, but he didn't have the great calling. *He knew his lust for women was his weakness. He knew his strength, the Lord's bountiful gift, was in his powerful hands and body. He knew if he fixed Mary, a fallen beautiful sinner, he fixed his own sinning cock.*

He could fix a broken fence, mend a window, adjust a faulty wife. He could build a room, unclog a pipe or toilet. Whatever he touched he fixed. Yet something in Mary escaped fixing. When she went upstairs at night, when she unbuttoned her blouse, when she lifted her skirt and one by one pulled off her stockings, the part of John Aherne that lusted for Mary Castle from the first moment he saw her, half naked on the Earl Carroll stage, lusted even more. When he thought of the countless men before him, entering her body and taking his prize, it made him sick. John Aherne wanted all of Mary. He wanted her past, her present, and her future, but the past belonged to those other countless cocks, and John Aherne burned with jealousy and dread that his wife was still a slut.

Mary understood and feared his brooding jealousy. She must dress to suit him. No other man's eye must fall on her. She didn't realize she couldn't erase what was. She only knew she must please and satisfy his every need and look like a little brown mouse—or he would gag her and she must lift her skirt and fall on her knees and beg for mercy from the scourge of his jealous wrath.

Mary kept an immaculate house. She shopped and prepared his meals. She gardened and filled the house with bright flowers. Her only company, besides John and Cassie, was the Beachwood ladies, invited in for weekly tea. This was Mary Aherne's investment—this good-time blonde was rewired, refixed, and plugged into a husband insanely jealous of her past.

But Mary Aherne was a job half fixed. The other half was Cassie. John Aherne took immediate legal action to become Cassie's guardian. He didn't like that strut of hers, but it was God-given, like her mother's. He couldn't change the way she walked, but by God he could change her attitude. The white peasant blouses were torn up and replaced by starched white shirts, the huaraches with laced-up brown shoes. Cassie helped her mother with cooking, cleaning, and yard chores. Her grades must improve, she was warned. If she sulked or seemed fresh, she was marched to the shed at the back of the house. She opened the shed door and watched him shut it behind them, bolting it with the new iron bolt he'd installed.

"You know what's coming, so get ready."

Cassie knew and hated him all the more. It was like some terrible ritual. First would come his lecture, spoken softly and not at all a command, then his eyes would watch her as she lifted her skirt and pulled down her underpants. Then he would reach for the strap that was hanging from a nail; and she would lay herself across his lap—buttocks, thighs, and legs turned upward—and the strap would burn her skin, and, worse even than the pain, was that thing in his pants that began to rise up and push into her stomach. Sometimes she was told to bring her hairbrush from her room—and his hand held the brush, and stroke after stroke he hit her, and she felt that thing in his pants rising hard and strong, and the brush burned so bad she couldn't stand the pain and screamed out, "I'll be good . . . I promise . . . I'll be good."

But that wasn't what John Aherne wanted to hear. He wanted to hear the anguished wail of the penitent scourged of her sin. And John Aherne felt his task to be lifelong. *Penitence was a long, slow process and the task of redemption ceaseless before God.* And his hand with the strap or the brush bore heavily down and Cassie screamed until John Aherne gasped and moaned and the thing that was bursting into her lower stomach seemed to collapse, and John Aherne seemed finally at peace.

Mrs. Feenie needed John Aherne's help.

"Kitchen door won't shut proper," said Mrs. Feenie.

"Wood's still swollen from the last big rain." John Aherne opened his satchel full of tools. He removed the door from its hinge, shaved a fraction off the bottom, and replaced it. The door opened and easily closed.

"You're a mighty good neighbor, John. Don't know how we managed before you came into the neighborhood. You're a saint not taking any money and helping out so! Why, the ladies all agree the good Lord sent us his blessing when he sent us John Aherne."

"If you're thinking about my wife, Mary, if you're thinking about Cassie . . ."

Mrs. Feenie was suddenly flustered. "Why, we just think the Castles are mighty lucky women."

John's voice turned soft and almost confidential.

"I understand, Mrs. Feenie. I took a couple of sinners and turned them into decent folk."

"Yes, John."

"You know, Mrs. Feenie, a woman's looks can rule her life. Mary was too beautiful. Well, things just got out of her control. God sent Mary into my life, and God sent me into Mary's life because God knew Mary and me, together, would do His will."

"Bless you, John."

"If you really feel gratitude, you and your friends can make Mary feel like the good woman she is."

"We'll do that, John. And we'll be proud to be her friends."

"I knew I could count on you, Mrs. Feenie." He gave her a big warm smile, and Mrs. Feenie blushed. No one had ever caused her to blush, particularly not Mr. Feenie, and she felt a nervous excitement. In her heart she regretted *she* had never had a strong and loving man like John Aherne who would fix up her barren life as he fixed up Mary Castle's.

It was quiet on Beachwood Drive. The hideous roar of jalopies was gone. You could sit on your porch in the silence and hear the birdcalls and feel the sun on your face. Everyone agreed. *John had worked a miracle.* Beachwood rocked on its rocking chairs and congratulated itself on its good luck. And Sundays, in church, Beachwood looked approvingly at Mary. She wore muted dresses with no style. Her face, scrubbed of its sluttish makeup, seemed gentle and almost sad. Cassie, too, wore proper clothing. Mother and daughter looked almost angelic and Beachwood looked upon them with charity, and—for John's sake—it forgave them.

Late one afternoon Nick looked out of his window. Across the vacant lot with its stunted shrub, Cassie was tied to a maple tree in the center of the yard.

"Need help?" he cried out.

"No," she cried back. "It's okay. Thanks, Nick. I'm okay."

Within minutes John Aherne came into the yard. He untied the rope that connected Cassie to the tree. He shortened the tether to about three feet and led her, like a compliant dog, to the shed. He opened the shed door and pulled her inside. It was silent for a minute . . . then the air was filled with her wild, anguished sobs that turned to screams of pain.

Beachwood heard her wail and it was like the wail of music. John Aherne was a kind of evangelist who had been delivered to restore decency to their lives. *Cassie, at twelve, smoked cigarettes and exposed herself in those slut blouses. She fooled around with wild young men. Yes, the girl was a slut . . .* and John Aherne would whip it from her body. Those lonely women who had cut off their bodies from their souls rocked in their rockers and felt a small, mean pleasure.

When it was over, John Aherne stepped from the shed and walked toward the house. Minutes later, Cassie followed. She stood near the maple tree, paused, and looked up toward Nick's window.

"Are you okay?" he screamed.

He saw her nod. Then she waved. Her firm, curved, defiant body made him fall all the more in love. Cassie was so proud and brave and pretty. *He hates you for it,* Nick thought. *One day you'll really rouse him up, and then he'll try to break you.* And in that second he vowed to be her friend and protector—and that nothing would stand in his way.

The next afternoon he waited for her at Duane's, the drugstore at Franklin and Bronson. Nick was sure she'd stop in to look at the new movie magazines. She'd smile at Duane and Duane would let her read them . . . *Silver Screen, Photoplay, Modern Screen . . .* studying them as carefully as any movie historian.

"Listen," she'd read aloud. " 'Joan Bennett left the confines of a French convent at sixteen to marry a boy who loved her. All her life she had one recurring dream. Escape from loneliness.' God. Imagine Joan Bennett being lonely." Cassie put down the magazine. "Joan's so right," she said firmly. "When you're not happy, change your life."

"The day you're sixteen, honey, we'll elope," said Duane.

"Oh, Duane, you're already married."

"So it'll be some other nice guy."

But Cassie was already into the new *Silver Screen*.

"Listen to this. 'These stars pay income tax of more than a hundred thousand dollars: Harold Lloyd, Greta Garbo, Norma

Shearer, Constance Bennett.'" She caught her breath as if she were having trouble accepting this extraordinary information. "'Constance Bennett spends ten thousand dollars a year to maintain a Malibu house and a home in Beverly Hills. She denies she spends a quarter of a million on clothes.'" Cassie gasped. "I can't believe anyone could have that much money—much less spend it on clothes!"

"You're so pretty, Cassie. *You're* as pretty as any movie star."

Cassie smiled at Duane.

"Well, you are, honey. . . ."

"You're prettier than Constance Bennett," Nick said.

"I'm not."

"You are! Prettier than Jean Harlow or Betty Grable."

"Oh, Nick." Her smile was bewitching. "Well, if I ever do become a movie star, I'll always remember my old friends."

That was a week ago. After that, Cassie smiled at Nick whenever she saw him. One noon he tried to approach her.

"Not now, Nick. I'm not in the mood."

After school, Nick sat in Duane's facing the street, then he saw her, crossing Franklin, ignoring Duane's and walking up Bronson.

Nick put a nickel on the counter and limped outside. Cassie was up ahead, swaying her hips, stopping beside a parked gray roadster. The door opened and she got in. A man leaned over and kissed her. She put her arm around him and all Nick saw was her blond curls. She pulled away, laughed, opened the car door. Her foot reached down to the footboard. The man was talking hard, and her foot reached back into the car and they were kissing again. After the kisses Cassie looked into the car mirror and fussed with her hair. She opened the door and got out. The man raced the motor and zoomed off. Cassie waved to the moving car. She walked leisurely toward Nick. "I'm not mad at you," she said. "I just don't like to be spied on."

"I want to talk to you, Cassie."

"Can't talk now. I'm late."

Nick's fine speech about friendship seemed suddenly foolish.

"I wasn't spying. Honest, Cassie. When you passed Duane's I wanted to tell you I want to be your friend."

Cassie was walking fast, approaching Beachwood, and Nick hobbled behind. She turned suddenly. "You don't understand. Friends get me into trouble. I'm in more trouble than I know what to do with. So don't be my friend. And for God's sake don't follow me home."

It didn't matter. If she needed help, he would be there. He looked up Beachwood and her curvy body, the warm air, the fragrant orange blossoms, the cry of cicadas, made him ache with love. *He would never stop loving Cassie. Not even if he wanted to. She was rooted inside him and a part of his life.*

At school the next day Cassie was surrounded by boys. She wore a drab gray dress. When she saw Nick looking at her, she smiled. She left her admiring group and walked toward him.

"Yesterday you said you'd help me. Be my friend. You still mean it?"

"Yes."

"Most guys, well, they say they want to help, and then they kiss you and they think you're this slut. I know you want to kiss me but I know you'll help me too."

"Don't, Cassie, please."

"It's okay, Nick, it's okay." Her eyes got a faraway look. "If I had money I'd wear just blue. Blue's my lucky color. John can't stand it if I don't wear gray. They wear gray in reform school. I hate gray but it's what he wants. Money's the most important thing in the world, Nick. If my mother had some money she wouldn't have had to get married. Poor Mom . . . Money's what I want more than anything in the world. I'll do anything to get it." She paused. "Understand?"

"I think so."

"I like you, Nick, you're nice."

"You think I'm nice because I never tried to kiss you," said Nick.

"You never tried to kiss me because you're scared I'd say no— but if you did, you'd still be nice."

Nick wanted to take her in his arms and kiss her the way movie stars did, and she'd tell him it made her crazy, and he'd kiss her again and it would get even crazier . . . but at that second Tom Flanagan, an older guy and a fullback on the football team, came over.

"Hey, Cassie, how 'bout a date for the beach?"

"Dunno."

"I'll call you tonight."

"I can't go, Tom. Don't call me tonight."

"Hey, Cass, c'mon."

"Can't, Tom, honest. Can't go out for a week."

The way she handled Tom. The way she handled him. The way she talked about his not kissing her because he was scared—without pity, just like it was a fact. He was crippled and he was shy because of it. Even if she necked with older men like the guy in the gray car, Cassie was smart about guys. She was smart about guys' feelings. She was smart about not feeling sorry for herself. That's why he loved her. *She never made you feel you were different—she just turned up that flame till you wanted to grab her and love her with the whole of your heart.*

As Cassie got more and more detached from her friends, Nick became mysteriously visible. It started when Tom Flanagan came over one day at lunch.

"That bastard Brandt'll flunk me if I don't do well on the exam. My old man is going crazy."

"Brandt's a rotten teacher, Tom. Makes things seem harder than they are."

"It's *everything*, Nick. It's history. Science. I can't remember a goddamn thing."

"All right, Tom, I'll try to help."

"Thanks, Nick. I'm up for a football scholarship—I just got to get my grades up."

"I live on Gower, Tom. Come on over Saturday morning. We'll see what we can do."

Nick had a way of making things seem simple. The dates, the

math that twisted around in Tom's head. Nick taught Tom simple logic, and Tom began to figure things for himself.

"Son of a bitch—you did it, Nick. I got a B! A goddamn B. My old man almost fainted."

"That's swell, Tom."

"I'm celebrating on Saturday night. Buncha the guys. You better be there, Nick, my dad is dying to meet you."

Tom lived in a blue bungalow on Tamarind Street. The living room was furnished with a chintz-covered couch, a maple dining room set, and four wooden chairs. The most valuable possession in the house was Tom, his parents' future hope. When Nick walked in, Mrs. Flanagan got tears in her eyes. "I'm not sure what you done, Nick, but you've made Mr. Flanagan and me real proud and happy parents."

"She get it all outa her system?" Tom said afterward.

"Pretty much," Nick said, laughing.

It was a hot night and the boys and girls were drinking beer and dancing to "Tuxedo Junction." The front door opened and Cassie, in a demure white dress, stood there with John Aherne beside her. He took a careful look at the room and whispered in her ear. He looked again and left.

Before Cassie was halfway across the room, Tom grabbed her and dragged her into a dance. He held her close, dipped her, and twisted her out. Cassie was a great dancer. She danced like she was happy. She seemed so beautifully happy the boys began to itch from wanting to cut in on Tom. Tom and Cassie danced past Nick and she leaned over and whispered, "Get ready. You're next." No one cut in on Tom, but when the music was over Cassie walked over to Nick.

"Cassie, I can't dance."

"If you taught Tom math, you can dance."

"Cassie, c'mon."

"It's like the kiss, Nick. You're just shy." Cassie took his hand. "Moonlight Serenade" was playing and Cassie put her arms around Nick's shoulders. He held her close, like Tom had done, and they swayed backward and forward.

"Okay?" she said.

"Nice."

"Nice for me too."

"I didn't think you'd be here," said Nick.

"It's not jail," said Cassie. "Mostly it's a jail—but it's not a jail all the time. . . ."

"Must be awful," said Nick.

"You know how everyone's dying to come to Hollywood? Well, I'm dying to get away." Cassie paused. "You can be my friend if you want."

"I do."

"I need money."

"You're running away, aren't you?"

"Yes."

"All I've got is thirty dollars, Cassie. Wait—I know what to do. Tom will fix it so I can help the other guys with exams. It'll take some time but I'll get you the money."

"Thanks, Nick."

She pressed against him tight and Nick knew this was Cassie's way of making sure he'd stay her friend. It made him feel rotten. She didn't have to do it. He wanted her to do it because she wanted him, not because of the money. Then she tilted her head backward and closed her eyes and Nick bent toward her and kissed her. She kissed in a queer sweet way with her tongue and Nick told himself it was okay. It was the way things were. You did a favor for a girl and that's the way she kissed you. But it felt odd. Getting kissed like that for only being nice.

That night, lying in bed, Nick understood his shriveled leg was a trick of fate. He thought of Cassie using her mouth and body to get free of John Aherne. He thought of her mother, Mary, who used her mouth and body too, except it was too late. Fate had tricked Mary up. Sooner or later fate tricked everyone. It tricked up Nick earlier than most. Maybe it was a secret blessing. It gave Nick time to think up ways of tricking fate. How he had to be prepared to help others who couldn't help themselves. He wasn't sure how, but he was sure it

could be done, a way of deceiving fate, influencing fate, trick fate or
fate tricked you. It seemed, suddenly, the only way to live.

In southern California, there is an hour in the afternoon when
the sun crosses the meridian and life is dead and void. Human
hope is blotted out and suicide seems another leisure activity. It is
the hour of the death of the soul.

One afternoon at two o'clock an ambulance, its siren wailing,
turned up Beachwood and zoomed up the long straight road. It
stopped in front of John and Mary's house. Two orderlies in
white uniform got out and walked to the front door. They carried
a litter bed. John Aherne opened the front door and they entered
the house.

Beachwood Drive, sitting in its rocker in the sun, was restless
with curiosity.

—*Something wrong with Mary?*

—*Mary's okay. She stopped by yesterday with some peach pre-*
serves. She looked fine.

—*Must be the girl. . . . I don't trust that girl. She's made it her*
business to play John for a fool.

—*John's no fool.*

—*Maybe he isn't and maybe he is.*

—*The girl is all right. John's turned her into a God-fearing child.*

—*Maybe we ought to go over and see if something's wrong.*

—*If John needs us, he'll call us. He knows we're here.*

The front door opened. The orderlies emerged. The litter bed
bore a body that was covered with a blanket. John Aherne followed behind. The orderly opened the back door of the ambulance and the two men slid the bed inside. John Aherne swung
up behind it and they closed the door behind him. The orderlies
got into the front seat and the ambulance drove away.

Nick saw everything from his window. He ran from the house,
through the vacant lot, slid through a hole in the privet that
surrounded Cassie's house. The lawn was newly mown and it
smelled fresh and sweet. Gauzy curtains billowed in a breeze.
Nick limped up the planked steps onto the porch. He rang the

doorbell. He rang again. Cassie's face appeared in an upstairs window.

"Nick, you shouldn't be here."

"Open the door, Cassie, don't be scared."

"I'm not scared."

"Then let me in."

Her head disappeared from the frame and Nick heard the clack-clack of her heels on the staircase and through the half-moon window he saw her moving toward him. He saw how nervous she was and he wanted to touch her and reassure her. He knew something was terribly wrong and he must do whatever he could to help her through it.

"What's happened?" asked Nick. "Tell me what's happened."

"If I tell you the truth, you won't believe me," said Cassie.

"Tell me the truth."

"Oh, Nick, my mother's going to die," she whispered. "You don't know how it's been—how she hates him—he'll tell everyone it was something like food poisoning—but it's not so. She *wants* to die. Even if they save her, she'll try it again." There was a desperation in Cassie's voice. "Nick, run away with me. We'll take a bus to 'Frisco. I can wait tables or get into a show. You'll go to school . . ."

"I can't go with you, Cassie. I'll get you the money, but I can't go along."

"I thought you loved me, Nick."

"You know how much I love you."

She took hold of his arm and pulled him inside the house. She locked the door behind her. She stood up against him and kissed him hard. She pulled away. She took off her dress and stood before him naked.

"Jesus," he whispered. "Jesus."

She put her arms around him, her mouth kissing him with her tongue; it felt like he was thrown across the room. She pulled away and took his hand and they walked to the couch and she lay down like she was a movie star, smiling in a movie star way, her hair spread out in a movie star halo, and he moved toward the movie star face and kissed it again.

"Take off your pants."

Nick wanted to tell her he would get her the money but he couldn't go along, but he was hard, too hard, and then she was holding his cock and guiding it inside and he was pounding into her until it felt like being slammed into a wall and bursting apart.

"Ohhhhh," he moaned. "Oh, God."

"This is how it'll always be," she whispered in a movie star whisper.

"I can't go."

"You knew you wouldn't go the whole time you screwed me!" Suddenly, the movie star mask was gone. Cassie, in a fury, was screaming, "You lied to me, Nick—made me feel cheap! I'll never forgive you!"

"Oh, Cassie. We'd never get away and you know it. John Aherne would put the police on us so fast—there's no way they wouldn't find us."

"I don't want to hear. You're chicken, Nick, *chicken.*" She ran from the room and up the stairs.

Nick put on his pants. He walked to the staircase.

"Cassie!" he called. "I'm sorry."

"I hate you, you hear? I hate you!"

"I'm sorry," he whispered, "because I love you." He unlocked the front door and closed it quickly behind him.

It was hot and dry and Beachwood assembled on Mrs. Feenie's porch, fanning themselves, rocking, talking heatedly of Mary Aherne.

—*John came by last night. Said we must pray for poor Mary's soul.*

—*Burst appendix. One minute she was fine and the next minute she was doubled over in pain.*

—*Poor Mary.*

—*Poor John.*

—*Doctor's put her on morphine, pain's so bad.*

—She's a lucky woman to have a husband like John beside her.
—Mighty good man.
—God bless his soul. Amen.

Mrs. Feenie was hoping that John Aherne would pay another unexpected house call, so she ran around her little house, tidying, dusting, and sure enough—without warning, he knocked.

"I was hoping you'd stop by," said Mrs. Feenie. "Thought you'd be hungry, John. I baked an apple pie."

"Mighty thoughtful." John paused. "I've come with bad news. Mary died this afternoon. The doctors did all they could but nothing seemed to help."

"Poor Mary."

"She was so brave. You can't imagine the kinda pain she had, but she never cried. Never once."

"Your love helped make her brave, John."

John looked at Mrs. Feenie like an old and trusted friend who, under no circumstances, would reveal the secrets of his heart. "Mary was a beautiful woman and beauty was her curse," he said softly. "Beautiful women think it goes on forever. Oh, she knew how much I loved her back at Earl Carroll's, but I was just a carpenter. Well, the good Lord gave me patience. A woman's looks can change from one day to another, and I knew, one day, Mary Castle would be ready for me."

"And she was, John."

"Mary Castle felt my love. My love made her strong. She changed for me—because I loved her."

"She was a good woman, John."

"Saturday, noon, there'll be a church service. Mary would of liked it if her good new friends were there to mourn her."

"We'll be there to pray for Mary's soul."

"I guess I don't have to tell you how much I 'preciate your friendship, Mrs. Feenie, and all your help."

Mrs. Feenie felt a queer sort of thrill, like she was a young woman talking with a man she desired. She could barely look at John Aherne. If he saw any hint of her excitement, he hid it. He shook her hand and then he left.

The funeral service for Mary Aherne was held in the Methodist Church off Franklin and Beachwood and all the Beachwood ladies were there to mourn. The organ was playing an aria from the *Saint Matthew Passion,* and the contralto's rich velvet voice soared over the church.

> *Have mercy Lord, on me*
> *Regard my bitter weeping*
> *Look at me, heart and eyes*
> *Both weep to thee bitterly*
> *Have mercy Lord.*

The cry of mercy caught the ladies in its grip. They felt forgiveness toward the dead sinner in the wooden coffin and even toward Cassie, looking like an angel in her white dress and blazing golden hair.

The conspiracy of mourners turned its gaze to John Aherne, his muscles bulging against his dark blue suit, a strain of pious cruelty around his mouth, so deeply sensual and curiously exciting. John Aherne's dark virility, his puritanism, sprang these crones into life. And the victim of his fury, dead in her casket, satisfied their small mean unlived lives that found an outlet, finally, for their stifled sexuality. *The most beautiful of women had suffered deliverance at his hands.*

They vowed an absolute devotion to John Aherne.

Cassie missed school for the rest of the week. Monday morning, Nick watched as she walked down the school steps. John Aherne was waiting for her in front of his car. She got in and they drove off. Nick thought of Cassie cleaning his house and cooking his meals. *John would ask her who she talked to and what did she do. He would want to know everything—and then one day she'd run away. She'd find work as a waitress. Or meet some guy and get married. She'd have a couple of kids and her life would be over.* Nick wondered which was worse—rushing into a nothing life with some dumb jock, or the wretched life with John Aherne. He didn't know. He only knew he'd help her. He took the money he'd made tutoring—now over a hundred dollars, and to it he added twenty dollars in silver he kept in a cigar box. He put the money in a brown envelope and sealed it.

The next day Nick waited for her in the quad. When he saw her, Nick went to her side. It was the first time he'd spoken to her since the afternoon he'd screwed her and he felt embarrassed and shy. He wasn't sorry he'd done it, he was only sorry because he loved her and he wanted it to be different. *It was crazy to love a girl like Cassie. At least for Nick. But looking at her made him feel so crazy. Well, he would give her the money like he was her friend, and she could do whatever she wanted.* Nick handed the envelope to Cassie and she folded it in half and stuck it in her purse.

"Thanks, Nick." She paused. "Don't feel bad about the other afternoon."

"I don't feel bad," said Nick. "I just wish it hadn't happened like that."

She gave him her crazy grin.

"You're a liar, Nick. I know you're in love and I thought you'd jump at the chance to come along. Well, I was wrong."

"I do love you, Cassie, I just can't go."

Cassie laughed. "You're nice, Nick. Thanks for being nice."

"Let me know where you are and I'll send you all I can make."

Cassie paused again. "Give it to Mr. Godard, Nick. He'll see I get it. Hey, Nick?"

"Yeah?"

"Thanks." Without a word she turned and walked toward a group of goofy admirers. Nothing had changed. She was the prettiest girl in school and she still used it to her best advantage.

Cassie was in school the next day, but Wednesday afternoon she disappeared. At three o'clock the school bell rang. At three-fifteen, the schoolyard was empty except for John Aherne, standing by his car, waiting for his stepdaughter. He looked at his watch one final time. He walked up the steps to the principal's office. The administration officers had gone home. John Aherne searched the courtyard, the quad, and looked up and down the athletic field. He returned to his car and drove away.

The next day he returned. He talked to the principal and to all of Cassie's teachers. He talked to Tom Flanagan and the boys in Tom's crowd. When he left, the schoolyard buzzed with excitement.

—*Cassie's run away.*

—*Where'd she get the money?*

—*I loaned her five bucks a week ago.*

—*That bastard don't give her no money.*

—*Well, she got the money somewhere.*

—*Yeah, but where?*

After class, Mr. Godard motioned for Nick to stay on.

"Cassie told me how kind you've been," he said softly. "You know now how to get the money to her."

"Yes."

"I hope the poor child will be careful."

"Cassie'll be careful."

Mr. Godard leaned back in his wooden swivel chair. "You know, Nick, Mr. Aherne takes his family obligations very seriously. In the eyes of the law, Cassie's a runaway delinquent."

"She's too smart to get caught."

"I hope to God you're right." He paused. "An old man and a lonely boy aren't going to be much help if she's caught. Public opinion's with John Aherne. Considers Cassie a no-good kid who's lucky he's her guardian."

"You make it sound like she's a criminal."

"I know how you feel about Cassie, Nick, but take my advice and stay out of things."

"*You're* not staying out of things."

"I'm old, Nick. About to retire. It doesn't matter what I do. . . . Well, let's hope things work out. And just remember, I'm here if you want to talk."

"Please tell Cassie—well, just say I won't forget her."

"I'll tell her, Nick."

"Thanks."

John Aherne was asking everyone about Cassie. Late one afternoon, he climbed the steps of Nick's house. Wanda opened the door and invited him in.

"Guess you know the reason I'm here, Mrs. Kahn. I'd like to talk to Nick."

"Of course. Oh, Nick—Nick! Can you come down? Mr. Aherne would like to talk to you."

Nick was in his room. He went into the bathroom and drank a glass of water. He studied himself in the mirror and practiced looking dumb. *He must not, in any way, betray himself.* Then he went downstairs. The clunk of his uneven gait on the stairs caused John Aherne to look up and Nick knew he was thinking, This crippled kid's a waste of my time. It was what Nick wanted.

"I'm asking everyone if they heard something about Cassie. Some detail that may seem unimportant but could help."

"I heard she was sad about her mother."

"Of course she was sad," John Aherne said sharply.

"That's all I heard."

"The police think she had help."

"Maybe she's got a rich boyfriend."

The expression of jealousy that passed over John Aherne's face turned Nick cold.

"If you hear anything that would help the investigation, I'd appreciate your contacting me," Aherne said frostily.

"Yes, sir."

John Aherne stood and reached out his hand and Nick felt like he was shaking an iron claw.

"Thanks for your help, Nick." He turned to the door and Nick looked at his strong back and powerful arms and prayed Cassie was safe and far away.

Two weeks later the police found Cassie working as a waitress in the Foreign Club in Tijuana. She was making fat tips from American tourists. Someone remembered her pretty face from the newspaper and called the police, who brought her back to Los Angeles and John Aherne.

At school, Cassie was the center of attention. She talked about running away as if it had been a vacation, how she danced all night with handsome men and made great tips, and how no one believed she was only twelve, and how coming home was boring and school was boring and all she wanted was to live. . . .

"She makes it sound like a holiday," said Mr. Godard to Nick that afternoon after school.

"It's an act. Cassie's putting on a big fat act."

"Why do you say that, Nick?"

Nick hesitated.

"Go on, son, tell me."

"John Aherne's in love with her. He dresses her like an old maid so no one else will look at her. I'm not kidding, Mr. Godard, the guy's crazy with jealousy."

"Careful, Nick. That's a dangerous accusation."

"Maybe it is. All I know is, this guy acts like he owns her."

"Cassie's his stepdaughter. Legal kin. It's natural he's concerned about her. He's a strict man, maybe harsh, but you're accusing him of something more. Something abnormal . . . pathological."

"He's fooled you, Mr. Godard. He's fooled everyone around."

"Better keep those thoughts to yourself."

"Boy! Cassie's right about this place. About that sign up there —Hollywoodland—and everyone acting like it's a kind of church. She told me about this girl who came to Hollywood to be a movie star and nothing happened so she looked up at the sign and thought it's a bad joke and climbed on top of the *H* and jumped off. The big *H*. It's a curse. The curse of the big *H.*"

"Hollywood's a dream, Nick. A dream of human happiness. We're all human and we all have dreams. Dreams are part of being human."

Nick was silent. He wondered why dreams tore everyone apart. Cassie and Mary Castle, and Wanda and Mischa too. He wondered if his dream would bring him happiness—it will, he vowed, if only he could make everyone's dreams come true.

Mrs. Feenie was thinking about John Aherne. *She saw herself moving her hips in a bad way and moving her body as well. John*

Aherne pinned her arms against the bed and purged the sin from her body until she begged him to stop but he wouldn't, not until she almost couldn't bear it. She thought of that sin in the star-filled silence. Cassie's wail wrenched her into the present.

Nick leaned out of the window. He could see the shed. A pale light shone in the window. Nick heard Cassie scream. He rushed from his room and out of the house through the vacant lot with its bramble and brush, through a hole in the privet. The cries were louder now. There was a window on the side of the shed and Nick pressed his face against the pane.

Cassie was tied by her arms to a table. She was naked, face and breasts facing John Aherne who with shirt open and sleeves rolled, crouched above her. The flesh on her legs was ridged with red welts. John Aherne was whispering and touching her face with his hand.

Nick strained to hear:

"Oh, my darling Cassie. I look into your eyes and see Mary again, like she's coming back to haunt me, and I know it's fate, Mary coming back to me through you. I loved her from the first and I was patient and waited till she got the bad blood out of her system. And Mary came to love me as much as I loved her. I'm still patient. One day you'll love me too. . . . One day you'll take your mother Mary's place." He kissed and gripped her firmly. Then he stood up.

He took off his trousers. His full massive cock was brimming with sex. He lifted himself and moaned, "Cassie, Cassie." He plunged into her with a roar. Seconds later he sobbed, convulsed, and sprawled across her body. Then he raised himself and swung his legs onto the floor. He kissed her mouth and untied the rope that bound her to the table.

When he turned to put on his trousers, Cassie sprang off the table. She ran to the wall and took an ax from its nail. Some instinct made John turn around. He saw her hands clasped around the ax, the ax raised above her head, and he raised his hands to protect himself. She struck. The steel passed into his bone. He screamed. He clutched his shoulder and tottered forward. His face was twisted in pain. His shoulder spurted blood. Blood sprayed his shirt. It trickled onto the ground. He recovered his strength and lurched toward Cassie. She raised the ax and struck again.

"Don't!" he screamed.

The next blow smashed his skull. His hands went to his head. He toppled and fell to the floor. Cassie saw Nick looking through the window. She dropped the ax, opened the shed door, and ran toward the house. Nick followed behind.

"Cassie!"

"I had to do it, Nick."

"I know, he'd a killed you, Cassie."

"What'll I do, Nick. I'm scared."

"Follow me." He went up the stairs and into the house and she followed behind.

"Where's a suitcase?"

"Second floor. Where he slept."

He followed behind her and into John's bedroom. This is where it must have happened—where John made her do it and if she refused, beat her like hell. Now Nick knew why it got so quiet after Mary's death. Fear! Do whatever he wanted or his black heavy belt tore you apart. It made Nick sick.

"Did he have any money?"

"In that box. He kept it locked up."

Nick picked up a green tin box. He smashed it on the floor until it shattered. It contained sixty dollars in bills and change. "Here." He followed Cassie to the closet. She pulled a suitcase from the shelf and threw in some clothes.

Nick picked up the suitcase. He carried it downstairs. Outside, in the yard, he handed it to her.

Cassie held the car keys in her hand.

"What are we going to do with the body?"

"Don't worry," Nick said.

"Hell," she said, and leaned toward Nick and kissed him. She turned and walked toward the street. In a second the car door slammed, the motor caught, and Cassie was traveling down

Beachwood, toward the bright Hollywood lights, anonymous now, a part of the city.

Nick went back to the shed. John Aherne was a mutilated pulp, his head connected to his body by a muscular thread. Nick was sick. He wanted to vomit. He picked up the ax, turned off the light, and closed the shed door behind him. He went back to Gower. Between the houses was a hillside covered with wild bramble. Nick stumbled upward. At the top of the hill, he knelt. He tore away stones and thick clumps of dirt. When Nick finished digging, he put the ax in the hole. He packed the ground firm and covered it with twigs.

Nick entered his house from the back. He washed the soil from his hands. He scrubbed his fingernails. He went into his room and fell on the bed. Nick thought of Cassie's body when she danced. He thought of her hot wet mouth. He thought of her smile, her legs, her strut, and how she painted her toenails in the sunshine. The rest was a nightmare. No one would believe it. Nick lay in the dark and thought of how he loved her and how she made everyone fall in love. Then he covered his face with his hands and began to cry.

A few days passed. The Beachwood ladies were worried.

—*Maybe John got work out of town?*

—*He'd a said good-bye.*

—*Where's the girl?*

—*Something's wrong. It don't feel right.*

—*I say we go look an' see.*

The Beachwood ladies crossed the street. They walked up the flowered path and onto the porch. They rang the doorbell, but no one answered.

—*Door's locked.*

—*There's an open window. What's a window doing open?*

—*He keeps a ladder in the shed. We'll get it and bring it back and one of us can squeeze through.*

They marched to the shed. Mrs. Feenie opened the door. It took a second before she could see in the dark. She screamed. She fainted and fell to the floor.

The murder weapon was missing. There were no fingerprints. The police were baffled.

Mrs. Feenie gave an interview to the *Herald.*

She spoke slowly and precisely. "John Aherne was a saintly man. He brought back God to Beachwood." Her statement, with pictures of the mutilation, were spread across the morning newspaper. It was a thrilling mystery: A man without enemies murdered, and a runaway daughter. For a day or more, Los Angeles gorged itself on the lurid details. Then someone else was murdered and John Aherne was just another gruesome body in the morgue.

The orchestra wives were Rose's club. The cellist's wife, Joyce, suggested that Rose might like being read to. Rose, semiliterate, jumped at the idea. She lay on a divan in her bedroom and listened to Joyce begin *Anthony Adverse.* Joyce read with expression. Rose was thrilled and wanted more. After a week of reading to the old bitch, Joyce realized her folly. She called Rose and complained of a sore throat.

"Send someone else," said Rose.

"I'll send Millie. You'll like Millie. Millie's a great reader."

That afternoon Millie read to Rose.

"You don't read with feeling," Rose complained.

Millie attempted emotion. Rose was still unhappy. Millie was replaced by Jane. Jane read monotonously. Jane was replaced by Linda. Then came Sally and Grace. Rose waited for Joyce to return, but Joyce's sore throat was a chronic laryngitis. Meanwhile, Rose had her card games in the morning. In the afternoon, the orchestra wives rotated the reading.

But Rose wanted more than bridge partners and readers. Rose wanted friends. She wanted to reminisce about the old days in the sweatshop, and how tough life was, and how she had worked herself to the bone to bring up three kids.

"You're another Saint Teresa, Mrs. Herman."

"With a mother like you, how could Buck Herman not be a success?"

"Your children are very lucky, Mrs. Herman."

Rose's life under the yoke of poverty never wearied in the telling, and the women strained to hear every tragic detail. They were realists. Buck Herman was ruthless and a tyrant, but more important, he was their husbands' boss.

It was midnight. Rose couldn't sleep. She lay in the dark, bored, miserable, and lonely. She opened a box of chocolates and ate most of the contents. She turned on the radio. Finally, at 4:00 A.M., she fell asleep. The next morning while Millie was reading, she dozed. She missed Joyce's emotional delivery. The bitch had had the chutzpah to have a doctor call and say reading was too much of a strain on Joyce's voice. *A real* mumser, *that girl.* Rose brooded on Joyce's behavior. That night Rose listened to the radio. Her favorite shows were over by nine. She went to the phone and dialed.

"Hello."

"Hello, Joyce. Remember me? It's Rose. Buck's mother."

The voice coughed and fell into a whisper. "What a surprise. How nice of you to call."

"I've missed you, Joyce."

"I've missed you too. My voice is getting stronger, Mrs. Herman. I hope I'll be back real soon."

"The reason I'm calling, Joyce—well, an old lady gets lonely. Evenings you want someone to talk to."

"I know what you mean. We're all lonely, Mrs. Herman. Even married people get lonely."

"How long you married, Joyce?"

"Nearly ten years. Time flies, Mrs. Herman. Fred gets home at night bone-tired. Falls right asleep."

"Buck works the boys pretty hard."

"Oh, yes, he does, Mrs. Herman, but look at the result. Titan is the best orchestra in town."

"I'll tell Buck you said that."

"Everyone feels that way. . . . Gosh, we've been talking for almost an hour!"

"Time flies," said Rose. "Well, I enjoyed our conversation."

The women said good-bye and hung up. It was only ten o'clock. Rose turned on the radio. The comedy shows were over. She made a glass of hot chocolate. She tried to sleep. She lay in the dark wishing that one of the girls was there reading to her. She turned on the light. She peeled the polish from her nails and reapplied a darker shade. Finally, at four-thirty in the morning, she fell asleep.

The next day she fell asleep while listening to Chapter 21 of *Anthony Adverse*. She played badly at cards. By evening she was wide-awake. At nine-thirty she called Joyce.

"Hello." This time a man answered.

"Is Joyce there? This is Mrs. Herman."

Her husband passed the phone to Joyce. He shook his head in disbelief.

"Yes, Mrs. Herman."

"I enjoyed our talk last night. I wanted you to know that."

"Why, thank you, Mrs. Herman."

"Call me Rose, Joyce. It's less . . ."

"Formal."

They were both silent for a minute. "Guess what? I fell asleep in the middle of Millie's reading. Millie's a boring reader, Joyce. If you was reading to me I wouldn't fall asleep."

"Millie's doing her best, Mrs. Herman."

"I think reading bores you, Joyce."

"I love to read to you, Mrs. Herman. Didn't you get my doctor's call?"

"In the old days in the factory with a sore throat I worked fourteen hours a day. If I didn't work, I didn't get paid."

"I'm feeling much stronger, Mrs. Herman, I'll be back next week."

"Let's make it Monday. Next Monday, Joyce."

"I'll make it my business to be okay."

"Good. Oh, before you hang up, I want *you* to call *me* tomorrow night."

"Sure, Mrs. Herman, whatever you say."

"I'm glad you understand. I don't like to feel like a pest."

The next night Rose's phone was silent. Perhaps Joyce had forgotten. Rose decided to give her one last chance. The following night it was silent again. At ten, Rose called Buck.

Buck listened to his mother with amusement. Rose only wanted a friend. Was that a terrible crime? This Joyce made Rose feel like it was. His mother had sacrificed her life so that he would have the good life. Joyce's husband was one of those classical asshole snobs who came out of the big symphony orchestras. He would speak to Joyce himself.

The next morning, Buck's secretary called Joyce.

"This is Thelma, Mr. Herman's secretary. Mr. Herman is busy with rehearsal so he asked me to call. He wonders if you can come to his office for lunch."

"Is something wrong?"

"He said he'd like to discuss something with you. That you would understand."

"I see."

"One o'clock. I'll leave your name at the front gate."

Joyce was prompt. She had a neat little figure and soft brown hair. She wore a yellow dress.

"How about a drink, Joyce? You don't mind if I call you Joyce."

"Of course not. And thanks, but I don't drink."

Buck poured himself a tumbler of Scotch and drank it neat. "This is a little embarrassing, Joyce, but you've got to understand my mother sacrificed herself for her family, so we're naturally concerned."

"I understand."

"Older people get lonely, Joyce. Loneliness is a terrible thing. Is your mother still alive?"

"My mother's dead."

"I'm sorry." He paused and brightened. "Hey, my mother didn't tell me how pretty you are. No wonder she likes you so much." He lit a cigarette, puffed, and walked toward her. He lifted his cigarette to her mouth.

"Thanks. I don't smoke."

He doused the cigarette and walked very close. He put one

hand on her shoulder, the other around her waist. He pulled her close and kissed her. Joyce felt like a tramp, but she smiled and he pulled her even tighter. Then the hand on her waist slipped under her dress. The whole thing took just a few minutes and Joyce didn't feel as lousy as she had expected to, because Buck knew exactly what he wanted and exactly how to get it.

"You're a very exciting woman, Joyce."

"Thanks."

"You're a good sport. No, I mean it. I appreciate your trying to help. I mean with my mother."

"I'll help however I can. Well, I guess I better go."

Joyce slipped on her dress and left Buck's office feeling the crisis was over. She'd read to the old bitch and call her up occasionally and everything would be okay.

That was Monday. Tuesday, Joyce's husband, the cellist, was fired. He was told his vibrato was too soft for Titan but he could give Buck's name as a reference elsewhere. It was a lesson for them all. If Buck Herman was a tyrant and a bully, old Rose was a monster. She had proved her power was total and complete. Rose Herman was never lonely again.

By 1940 the unions were a force in California. Jimmy Petrillo, president of the Musicians' local 47, demanded time and a half after six o'clock, and if a session went past midnight, his men got double. The conductors worked the musicians like mules. Time was money, and woe unto him who spoiled a take.

There was tension and rivalry and jealousy between the men. You had to be a damned good musician. But just as important, you lost at poker with a good-natured smile, and you knew where the girls were. You weren't pimping; it was a simple act of friendship. You found your boss a pretty blonde and your boss chose you over your rival.

MISCHA
1940s

Mischa Kahn was shy, introverted, and not Buck Herman's style, but he had a luscious vibrato, a sound that created mystery, passion, and adventure. Mischa hated poker. He was no longer attracted to Wanda, but he didn't fuck around. He had learned by now to sublimate his sexual frustrations into his music. He trusted his talent. He thought it kept him safe. Once a week some old colleagues from the East came to his house to play quartets. Mozart, Beethoven, and Schubert filled the sweet night air. These were Mischa's precious hours and Mischa felt like a musician. His emotions, buried daily in the vaulted rehearsal hall of Titan, burst free and he was carried along on the sound of great music. In these precious hours he forgave Wanda, and was a happy man.

Nick sensed his father's misery. Mischa came home after work, closed the door to his room, played some Bach or Beethoven, repeating each phrase as if he were preparing for a concert, each note perfect, as though he could recover something irrevocably lost. He played until Wanda's voice floated up.

"Mischa. Your dinner's ready."

But Mischa was in his own world, surging higher and higher and unable to crash back to earth.

"Nick, go tell your father his food will get cold."

Nick knocked and opened the door.

"Dinner's ready."

"I'm not hungry." Mischa put the violin in its case. "Why in hell does she burden you with our problems?"

"It's okay, Dad."

Mischa patted his son on the shoulder and they both went down to eat.

"How was work?" asked Wanda during dinner.

"Lousy, thank you."

"I wish you'd give it a chance."

"I'm working for a bastard, Wanda, a son of a bitch who hates good music except to steal from. It's bad enough I have to play dreck all day, must I talk about it at home?"

"I'm your wife, Mischa. Who can you talk to if you can't talk to me?"

Mischa pushed his chair back from the table. He put his napkin in its ring. He went upstairs. There was the slam of his door and the sound of a violin. The sound was the sound of a man choking on his life. It swept out of the window and into the night. The melancholy strain reached as far as Beachwood.

Mrs. Feenie and her neighbors hated the sound. They put their heads together and decided to confront Wanda. A righteous body, they knocked on her door.

"We understand your husband is a musician, Mrs. Kahn, but music every night!"

"It's only nine o'clock."

"Nine o'clock is late for Beachwood."

"I'll see what I can do."

Wanda could do nothing. Mischa kept on playing. *He knew that if he didn't remember what music was or why he was a musician, he would die. Music kept him alive.*

The orchestra wives clamped the phone to their ears and listened wearily to Rose's litany of struggle, her pride in her wonderful son, and how he gave to the world the music of love. Rose didn't know Buck stole from Tchaikovsky and Rachmaninoff and Dvořák, with a half-dozen top arrangers to turn it into schmaltz. She talked of her younger son, Danny, who organized the orchestra into a big loving family and how good the family treated her.

The clarinetist's wife took her to the hairdresser. The violinist's wife took her to the masseur. The drummer's wife introduced her to the Santa Anita track. Rose put a hundred dollars on Cheapthrill and won seven to one. After that, *Anthony Adverse* was hastily replaced by the racing tabloids.

At night, the men in the orchestra drank, smoked, and lost good-naturedly at poker.

"Boy oh boy, this ain't my night. I pass."

"Hey, that's un-American!"

"Me, I'm a one hundred percent patriot, Danny."

"Breaking up a game like this—it's subversive."

The men laughed, the hours passed, and Buck and Danny, once again, had luck in their rear hip pocket.

It was Wanda Kahn's turn and she was admiring a small sculpture of a Chinese lady in a kimono.

"She's perfect," said Wanda.

"What it cost me, it should be perfect," said Rose. "My decorator says it's an investment."

"Must be very rare."

"Like a museum. You know what's *Han?* Han's old Chinese." Rose paused. "Your husband dies, right? They bury your statue near his body so he don't get lonely. Meshuga, the Chinese."

Wanda laughed. She asked Rose about the other antiques. She went to the library to track their source. A few days later she excitedly said, "Your sixteenth-century dining room table is English Renaissance. Henry the Eighth. I've found a book called *The Life and Loves of Henry the Eighth.* He married eight times."

The next month, Wanda read of the amorous king and Rose sat in rapt attention. Henry's passion for Anne Boleyn, his adulterous second wife whom he had beheaded after a thousand nights, particularly excited her. She had Wanda read it again.

That Sunday night over dinner, Rose told Buck about Henry and Anne.

"Such a love story, Buck. Such music my Buck could write."

Buck's cold heart swelled with pride. Old Rose, an illiterate peasant, was talking historical romance. The next day he told the studio president that Anne Boleyn would be a natural for Carole Lombard, who was on loan from Metro. It was a pass for Lombard but a go for Garbo. When Titan couldn't get Cary Grant for Henry the Eighth, the project was dropped. But Rose was credited with the idea and began to enjoy a certain notoriety.

The phone rang twice before Nick picked it up.

"Hello, Nick. It's me. Cassie."

"Where are you?"

"Here in Hollywood. I'm at Mr. Godard's."

"What's the address?"

"It's 165½ North Ivar. Top floor."

"Wait for me."

Nick stopped at a florist's shop on Franklin. He bought a dozen red roses. He walked south to Ivar and turned left. Mr. Godard lived in a brown Swiss chalet with an outdoor staircase. Nick limped up the wooden steps. He knocked on the latched screen door. He saw Cassie through the mesh. She was so pretty. She opened the door and Nick handed her the roses.

"Careful of thorns."

She smiled and said, "Come in quickly."

He latched the door behind him. Cassie smelled the roses. She wore bright red lipstick, a tight blue dress, and lots of mascara. Her eyes were very blue. She took the roses to the kitchen and put them into a vase. Then she went into the bedroom and Nick followed behind. She reached up behind her head to unzip the dress. She pulled it off and stood naked, chiseled and lean, with breasts that stuck out like tennis balls.

Nick wanted to screw her more than he had ever wanted anything before. He knew she had come back for that—come back to pay off a debt. It didn't matter why. She'd come back!

That's what mattered. She tilted her face and her bright blue eyes made him feel as if he were running a fever. She moved against him. The fever ran up his spine and into his head and made him crazy. She unfastened his belt. He was so full and hard and he moved up inside her, his rhythm strong and firm, his mouth kissing hers with a terrible hunger. The fever was near to die—near to break him apart in white heat flashes. He yelled with joy.

When he opened his eyes, he saw her eyes were wet with tears. He reached up and touched her face. Her eyes became hard. She pulled away and put on her dress.

"You didn't compliment me on my dress," she said. The tone in her voice was as hard as the look in her eyes.

"Cassie. What's happening?"

"Remember how I said blue's my lucky color and one day I'd be so rich I could buy whatever I want. You know how many dresses I got, Nick? Thirty-seven. I got dresses in every shade of blue ever invented. Dresses that cost so much it's almost a sin. Aren't you curious? How come Cassie's got so many blue dresses? Or maybe you don't want to know. Well, I'll tell you anyhow. I make more money than anyone you know—'cept a movie star. You can't imagine how popular I am. . . ."

Nick took her in his arms. He kissed her face.

"And each time I feel bad, so bad I can't stand it anymore, I buy another dress."

He felt her shiver in his arms. He felt her sobbing. He wrapped his arms around her. The sobs continued. He kept holding her. Finally she quieted down.

"My mascara's all runny," she said. "I must look a mess."

"You look beautiful."

"You're such a liar, Nick."

"You are," he repeated. "The most beautiful girl in the world."

"I'll start crying again." She wiped away a tear. "I'm smiling, Nick. Look, I'm smiling."

Nick was silent.

"I better go, I guess. Walk me to my car."

Nick followed her down the stairs to the street. She got into a gray Dodge. She rolled down the window.

"Good-bye, Nick."

"Write me, Cassie. Promise."

"I promise."

She started the motor. The car drove off. Nick looked after the car until it disappeared. Then he turned and walked in the other direction.

"I warn you, Wanda, that bitch will destroy you. She'll destroy us both."

"You attend to your job and I'll take care of mine. If you had played Buck Herman's game you could've been concert master."

"You're crazy, Wanda. I gave up a career so you could have your goddamn house, your car, the goddamn sun. You want the good life—okay, you got it. But it's not enough. *Nothing's* enough. What in hell are you doing to our lives?"

"Why don't you understand? I've got one life. I'm going to live it to the hilt. I'll fight for it with everything I've got. I can't stop. You're not going to stop me."

"I'm booked onto a one-way passage to hell."

"Stop being dramatic."

Mischa ran from the room and up the stairs. Wanda followed behind. He slammed the door to his study in her face. He locked it. In a second he started playing his violin, a crazy aching sound, his fingers going faster and faster, rushing from pain, blotting out fear, Mischa playing like one who is damned.

"Without me, Buck Herman would have fired you by now. He's sick of you, Mischa. It's me who's saved your job."

The music stopped.

"You're killing me," cried Mischa. "You and your insane ambition. I hear the men laughing behind my back, 'Poor Mischa,' they whisper, and they thank God it's not them! Don't you see what's happening, for God's sake?"

"Mischa! I'm keeping your job . . . that's what's happening."

Mischa opened the door. "You make me sick," he cried. "You

make me want to die from the shame!" He grabbed hold of her and pushed her away. Then he slammed the door.

Nick rushed upstairs. He turned the doorknob. He closed the door behind him. The shades were pulled. The room was dark. Nick saw his father's ravaged face.

"When I was sick, Dad. Remember what you told me."

"I don't remember anything."

"You told me about Beethoven's deafness. How he was cut off from the world. Alone. Without friends. Without sound. Without laughter."

"I hear them laughing behind my back, Nick." Mischa's face was strained and tight. He started crying. "Oh, God, I don't sleep. I sit there afraid I'll hit a wrong note and he'll go crazy. So mean. So cruel. Mischa Kahn!—once I was a prodigy. I played with Stokowski. I was an *artist.* Today I pray my fingers will act of their own free will, because there's nothing left in me to direct them."

"Dad. You told me one part of Beethoven was destroyed. But he found something else—an inner strength! Patience, you told me. Be patient."

"Nick. Nick."

Mischa picked up his violin. He began to play. The music was sensuous. It was spiritual. His fear passed away. For a second Mischa found his soul.

Buck's new passion was golf. He spent weekends at the Hillcrest Country Club, and to get in a game on Wednesday afternoons he let the concert master take the baton. In January the temperature dipped into the low forties. Everyone dragged out some old, unused overcoat and waited for the sun. The sudden chill dulled Buck's appetite for the game. But it was either golf or work. The thought of the men in the orchestra made him sick. The jazz guys were okay, but those musical snobs from the big symphony orchestras, they made him want to puke.

He thought of Joyce, the cellist's wife. He'd like to *shtup* her good, but the bitch would tell him to shove it. Screw her. For

every Joyce there were a dozen others. Take what's his name—
the zombie, Mischa Kahn. His wife was brown-nosing Rose like
her life depended on it. Well, as a matter of fact, it did. What tits!
Too much ass for Buck's taste, but she must have been a red-hot
number once upon a time. The zombie didn't give her half what
she needed was Buck's guess. And suddenly Buck knew how he'd
pass the cold winter spell. While his concert master drilled the
men he'd fuck the wives. He'd start with the zombie's wife. *At the
end of the afternoon she'd be grateful for a long hot* shtup. *She'd
thank God and Buck Herman, for delivering her from Rose.*

"Mrs. Herman," said Wanda, "I hate to do it but I've got to
cancel this afternoon. It's an emergency."

"What is?"

"I've got a terrible toothache, Mrs. Herman. I'm seeing a dentist at two o'clock. I didn't want to disappoint you, so I've talked
to Millie and she'll be there instead."

"So be here tomorrow."

"Of course. And thanks for being such a good sport."

"Just be here."

Wanda hung up and everything she'd denied erupted within
her. Mischa was right. She was Rose's slave. The old bitch didn't
care about anyone—"gimme gimme gimme." But more important
than that was the telephone call from Buck, in person, asking her
to come out to the studio to discuss something important. *That
meant one thing. Mischa. He was going to fire Mischa? Why would
he call her? It made no sense.* Well, another couple of hours and
she'd know. *Patience,* she told herself, *look pretty and be patient.*
She put on a white sweater and white pants. White was Wanda's
idea of glamor. *Well, Mr. Buck Herman, whatever your decision, I'll
meet it like a lady.*

Buck's secretary passed her right through.

Wanda had met Buck at Rose's house and she had sensed his
indifference, so she wasn't prepared for the big grin he flashed.
The bastard was attractive in his tan gabardine pants and tan
cashmere sweater. She found herself suddenly blushing. She
looked at the walls plastered with posters of Titan films. Mischa

had told Wanda that Buck was particularly proud of his score for *Anna Karenina,* having lifted the entire theme from Rachmaninoff's Second Piano Concerto.

"That was a beautiful score," said Wanda, pointing to the poster. "I mean even more beautiful than most."

"Glad you like it. I'm pretty proud of it myself." A framed picture of a good-looking blond woman was on Buck's desk. Buck caught Wanda's eye regarding it with curiosity.

"Glenda Bruce," said Buck. "A very good friend of mine."

"A great songwriter."

"A great lady." For a second, Buck Herman looked almost *human,* but the second passed, and all Wanda saw was trouble in cashmere.

Buck broke the silence. "You're wondering what this is all about, right?"

"Right."

"Then I'll be frank."

"Be frank, Mr. Herman."

"Call me Buck, Wanda."

"Yes, Mr. Herman. . . . Yes, Buck."

"That day at my mother's house. You remember?"

"Yes, I remember."

"I said to myself, 'That Wanda Kahn is one hell of a good-looking woman!' "

What in hell is he up to? thought Wanda, but she was glad she was wearing white.

"I'll get to the point, Wanda. I like hot women. You could say I like hot women more than anything on God's green earth. Please don't consider this an insult. It's a tribute. There are a thousand women I could have called, but I called you. Guess why I called you?"

He's crazy, thought Wanda, *and I'm crazy to be here.* But she was still glad she wore white.

"I wanted to make love to you since that afternoon," Buck continued. "Shocked?"

He wants to fuck me and I'm going to let it happen or Mischa will be fired, thought Wanda, and Buck's hand was suddenly inside her blouse, inside her bra, and pinching her nipple and despite herself she was wet.

Buck was right. Wanda was hot. Heat she had pushed away so long she couldn't even remember. Buck's mouth was kissing her as she hadn't been kissed for a long, long time, and she pushed away all thoughts of Mischa—Mischa who hardly ever touched her—pushed away everything except that she was saving Mischa's job, and she was wet between her legs, and the wet of her pussy and the wet of Buck's mouth, and his hand on her ass squeezing her close, pushed out everything else. Wanda pulled away. She took off the white sweater, the white bra, the white slacks and white panties. And Buck moved right in.

It seemed only seconds later and Wanda had her first orgasm in years. She hung around Buck's neck barely able to let go. He finally pulled away.

"I was right," Buck said slowly. "You are one hot piece of ass."

"Yes," Wanda said happily. "I am a very hot woman."

Buck gave her a very happy grin. "Put on your clothes, kid. I'll call you tomorrow."

Buck called during a five-minute break in rehearsal. Wanda called Rose to say her dentist had sent her to a periodontist for an extended gum treatment. Rose was grim. *What was this bitch trying to do? Wait until she told Buck.* After they hung up, Wanda smiled. She could hardly wait for old Rose to call up Buck and complain. Despite her guilt about Mischa she felt a glimmer of revenge.

Wanda's fear of Buck passed quickly into desire and desire quickly into love. Wanda fell in love with Buck so fast, it almost startled her. Not with Buck, exactly, but with Buck's cock. She was like an alcoholic who has stayed sober a good part of her life and has suddenly "slipped." She fell on Buck like a thirsty drunk and Buck felt great giving it to her as if she were a whore, whamming it up her hard and slow and long, and his comes, his comes were like murder. Murrr-der.

And then the sun came out, but Buck was having too much

fun. *This broad could take it however he gave it and the harder he gave it the more she could take.*

Then Wanda made her big mistake.

"You drive me crazy," she said. "You make me very crazy."

"Me too," Buck said happily.

"I think I'm falling in love."

Buck suddenly froze. Nothing turned him off as fast as some dame yapping about love. *Trouble. Trouble! He needed it like a hole in the head.*

"What's the matter, Buck, baby?"

"You better go."

"What's wrong? What did I do?"

"Nothing, kid. I got an orchestra to conduct, remember?"

"Sure, Buck, I remember."

"Be a good girl. I'll give you a call."

"Sure, Buck."

"And call my mother. She can't figure what's happening."

"Sure, honey."

"I'll call you tomorrow."

But Buck never called Wanda again. The sun was out and Buck was happily lifting his golf club and swinging at the ball.

And Buck was drilling his men like a sergeant, screaming about wrong notes, furious over nothing, making them repeat a passage again and again. "Your bowing's off," he'd scream, or "What the fuck is *that?*" or "That's a *vibrato?* I'll tell you what it is. It's *shit!*"

Mischa wondered how much he could take. He couldn't sleep. His mind wandered. He barely listened. He only felt the most heartbreaking pain. He wanted to scream out. But he couldn't. The pain was ticking away inside him like a time bomb.

The bastard was screaming again. The bastard was tapping the podium with his stick. The bastard was setting a snare—waiting for some dumb schmuck to *crrraaack* apart. Buck had cracked him apart before, but the last few weeks had been okay. Until the stick smashed on the podium and Buck was suddenly looking at him.

Buck looked at the gray schmuck violinist zombie whose wife

he'd fucked. A goddamn zombie in his orchestra. In the old days he'd been forced to look into those dead old eyes because his mother liked that Wanda. Well, Wanda was a terrific fuck, but she was a pain in the neck. He watched the zombie sitting there like the living dead and a terrible rage came over Buck. He couldn't look at that face one more minute. There were plenty of slaves around. Rose could have whoever she wanted. The zombie was hurting his orchestra. He smacked the baton again.

The room was silent as Buck continued to stare Mischa down. And then it happened. It happened in front of fine musicians, artists, and prodigies, men who once had wanted nothing more than to make beautiful music.

"If your wife Wanda wasn't licking my mother's ass," said Buck, "you wouldn't be sitting in my orchestra."

Crrraaack! Mischa was caught in the snare and cracked before their eyes. It could have happened to anyone. Thank God it was just Mischa.

Mischa stood, lifeless as a zombie. He put his violin in its case and walked away from Buck and the orchestra. The room was silent and still except for Mischa's footsteps. The baton cracked again and Mischa heard Buck's sarcastic voice. "Whenever you gentlemen are ready, I'd like to begin."

Mischa turned the key in the car ignition. He hit the green lights until Santa Monica, when the green light turned red. He kept on driving. No one stopped him. He felt the breeze on his face. He pushed hard on the gas. He was going very fast and the breeze felt very strong. The breeze would blow away the slime. Slime, sliding up his leg and onto his body and covering him, slime filling his ears and his nose and his mouth and burying him alive—dark and dirty, like shit, and then there was a roar and a rip and a tear of his skin and a jagged edge going into his eye and then the shit was gone and there was only darkness.

Mischa awoke in a strange white room. There was a woman he recognized beside his bed, and a boy. He smiled at the boy, for whom he felt love. "I am the greatest violinist in the world and I will never practice again," he said. "I am the greatest violinist in the world and I will never practice again. I am the greatest violinist in the world . . ."

Mischa was given electrical shock treatment and assigned to a therapist. Four months later he was allowed to go home. His violin sat in its case, untouched. An occasional colleague came to visit him. "I don't practice now," Mischa explained, "I am the greatest violinist in the world."

The men felt sorry for their lost mad friend, but in their hearts they were frightened that word of their visit might leak back to Buck. What happened to Mischa was unfortunate. Mischa wasn't strong enough. One needed strength to survive. Within months of his convalescence Mischa was alone.

Sedated and prematurely aged, stooped, his hair turning to gray, Mischa sat in the garden in the sunlight. He talked to the trees and the birds about his glorious career. His eyes were vacant. He smiled. Pain and purpose were gone from his life.

It was a clear bright day and Nick watched a moving van draw up to Cassie's house with a load of new furniture. Nick thought of Cassie, so greedy to live, breaking everyone's heart as she tripped merrily along, and he thought of John Aherne who raped her life and made her an outcast. He thought of Beachwood, the silent conspirator and witness, and that great lit sign, HOLLYWOODLAND, hanging over their lives with a reckless promise of fame and fortune. He thought of his gentle father, and of Buck Herman who had broken him. He thought of Buck's orchestra, where the law of the jungle was at work. Mischa and Mary and Cassie had had the bad luck of falling prey to brutal men who closed in on them like wolves.

Someone must be strong, *thought Nick. And Nick in that moment knew he was the one who would go among the lambs as a healer. Only one who had suffered could undertake such a task. He was the one. In that moment Nick knew what he had to do.*

Buck's doctor, on Buck's recommendation, offered Wanda a job as a receptionist. After work she studied typing and Gregg. She spent every spare hour perfecting her shorthand. She was tireless. Her fierce desire to survive turned her within months into a crackerjack secretary.

Her boss called up Buck to thank him and Buck gave Wanda a call.

"Dr. Rabin's office."

"Wanda. It's Buck Herman. Dr. Rabin's saying very nice things about you."

"Dr. Rabin's a saint to work for."

"Wanda."

"Yes, Mr. Herman."

"Look, I hope you understand—well, I feel bad about what happened."

"I know." Wanda stifled her long-suppressed fury. "But thanks for saying it."

"The reason I'm calling," said Buck, "well, one of the executives at Titan needs a good secretary. Someone capable. Someone discreet. The pay is good." Buck paused. "If it's difficult for you . . ."

"I've got a family to support," said Wanda. "The answer is yes. I am interested. And no, Mr. Herman, it wouldn't be difficult. I'd like to apply for the job."

Wanda replaced Mischa at Titan. She typed, took dictation—but most important, she protected her boss. His yen for blondes drove his wife half crazy and Wanda had a genius for calming her down. Why not? She had served her apprenticeship at the feet of a monster.

Within a year Wanda was an indispensable member of the Titan Pictures hierarchy.

Winter, summer, madness, and death were like a revolving door, and Nick passed his adolescence studying and taking care of Mischa. If Wanda was a part of the hungry pack, so be it. Her reckless ambition had brought them to this place. What Nick needed now was patience, and an infinite determination to reach his goals and his place among men.

At sixteen, Nick was chosen class valedictorian and was gradu-

ated with honors. Harvard, casting its net westward, awarded
him a scholarship.

"You make me proud," said Mr. Godard. He handed Nick a
package. Nick tore off the wrappings. He held three books.

"One's a biography of Spartacus," said Mr. Godard. "A slave
who led a band of rebels against the Roman Empire. Luther was
a monk who attacked the church and tried to change it. These
men had an inner strength. They inspired others. They created
change. That book of Nietzsche's, well, it's about the individual
and his struggle against evil."

"Thanks, Mr. Godard."

"One last thing, Nick."

"It's Cassie, isn't it?"

"Cassie's out there like a piece of wrecked humanity." He
paused. "You go out and help that kind of wreckage, Nick. And
I'll consider my work as a teacher to have been of some value."

BOOK TWO

BOOK TWO

NICK
1949

After a sun-drenched California adolescence, Harvard seemed a glorious vision of the great life ahead. Nick could have dressed like any of the smart young men in a tweed jacket and flannel pants, but he chose black: black sweaters and dark gray pants, a thin black cane. Black curls fell on his forehead and his deep gray eyes, his limp, his lean yet masculine body, his handsome face with its beautiful smile, gave him, at nineteen, a strangely sensual appearance. Girls watched him when he passed and felt pleasantly aroused.

It was October and the mornings were brisk and cool. Puffy clouds filled up the sky. A wind brought up the earth's sweet scent. Nick walked through Harvard Yard. He stood in front of Widener Library with its broad steps and stone portals. He burned with desire to learn and desire filled him with the greatest of plans. A chilly morning breeze swept him back into the present. He paused and he smiled at his dream of great achievement, but it was there and he longed for it with a fierce longing of the heart.

Nick studied while others slept. He never stopped, mercilessly pushing himself to learn more. The first year passed into the second, and Nick's desire for achievement grew ever more strong.

Nick lived in Wigglesworth House. The headmaster, Professor James, was impressed with Nick's self-discipline and his energy and ambition. Moreover, Nick gave himself to helping others whenever he could. Most important, however, was the way Nick used Widener Library, making extra money as a library assistant. He worked late into the night and returned to the dorm loaded with books. That spring Professor James spoke to Nick.

"I know you've got a scholarship, Nick, but you must be tight for extra money."

"Well, I work part-time at Widener."

"Can't bring in much money."

"Pays for an occasional movie."

"Look, Nick, I don't know if you're familiar with a fundamental academic law. Publish or perish. A lot of professors can't write —they're too dry—can't put it down on paper. They hire talented students to help organize research materials. Graduate students mostly but occasionally a gifted undergraduate to 'ghost' or write their papers. I think you could handle it, Nick."

"I'd sure like to try."

"Good. Your knowledge of Widener is critical—understanding source materials, organizing the information and restructuring it for them."

"This 'ghosting,' sir. What does it pay?"

"Thirty, thirty-five dollars a paper."

Nick whistled in amazement. He figured three papers would bring him in a hundred dollars. He could quit his part-time job. By next summer he could rent a summer place and bring Mischa east.

"I'm very interested, Dr. James."

"I thought you would be. I've got your first job all lined up."

Nick was suited to the job. He had a rapid-fire ability to absorb information. He used source materials well and he worked fast. Harvard is a small, tight community and word got around that Nick could deliver a publishable, even brilliant paper. Within a year he was almost supporting himself ghosting for important professors.

With money came a weekly ritual of a movie at the Brattle or an occasional drink at Cronin's bar. Afterward, Nick and a girl walked hand in hand along the shadowy street talking of serious things, but it was late and cold and the evening ended with furtive kisses on windy street corners and the awful frustration of nowhere to go.

Nick rented a room on Avon Street. Now the girls came to Nick's room for coffee, and the serious talk was replaced by serious screwing. Nick found out that once a girl said she loved you, things changed. You screwed a girl and you felt very happy and then she turned into an emotional swamp. A swamp with expectations of trading in her B.A. for an MRS. It was tough. The school year passed and the wintry gales melted away and it was spring. Nick stopped feeling guilty. He thought about the summer ahead.

Mr. Jones, a real estate agent on Martha's Vineyard, usually waited for prospective renters in his office. But this gorgeous spring day, with the scent of wild flowers and salt sea battering the senses, he stood on the wharf and watched the ferry slip into its landing. A half-dozen cars came off the ramp and some ill-assorted passengers. That handsome young man with the limp must be the Harvard kid.

"Nick Kahn? I'm Mr. Jones. I brought my car so we can start right off."

They drove up Main Street in Vinyard Haven with its white Federal houses and turned left onto a sloping road. There were farms with cows and horses, and shimmering glimpses of the sea. They climbed up Lambert's Cove, passed hills covered with pine forests, and small ponds with wild fowl. They passed old clapboard farmhouses, and Jones gave Nick a history of each house and how much it was worth on the market. "Heard of Emma Rand, the richest woman in the state—maybe the whole East?— this is hers. Down there, through the trees—her beach. She's leased it to the island and anyone who rents in the area can use it. The house I got in mind belongs to Mrs. Rand."

They stopped in front of a gray-shingled farmhouse. It stood on a pond. Wild geese scudded into the air and dropped into the water.

"Perfect," said Nick.

"I thought you'd like it. Everyone does."

"How much does she want?"

"Eight hundred dollars the season."

"That's a lot of money."

"Money's not the issue. Mrs. Rand's a very rich woman and that's the price of the house."

"Well, offer five anyway."

"She'll jus' laugh, son."

"Try it. Offer five hundred. . . . Okay, now why don't you show me the beach."

They walked along a wooded path. Wet leaves were pasted to the ground. They climbed up onto a sand dune. The air was crisp and sharp and the sky was full of fluttery birds. They overlooked a crescent cove. Sandpipers skittered along the shore and gulls dipped down and soared upward. On a rise of hill, not far away, a grand bleached-white castle rose into the air.

"That's her place. Rand's Head," Jones said proudly. "People come from all over the world just to look at it."

But Nick wasn't watching the mysterious castle, he was intent on a girl, very blond and very pretty, in a tight white sweater and shorts. She was with a group of boys who were throwing a disc. She leapt up, caught the disc, and ran. A powerful guy all rippling with muscles caught her legs and brought her down. She pushed him off, stood and waved the disc, grinned, dared them to take it from her, and the chase began anew. . . .

She saw Jones and Nick and she waved.

"That's Emma Rand's kid, Jeannie," said Jones. "One day she'll inherit this whole shebang. You'd think a girl like that would be kinda snooty, but not Jeannie. Nice as they come. Studies the violin with some big-shot violinist in Boston."

Nick watched Jeannie strut toward them and he thought of all the parades he'd ever seen and all the sexy blond cheerleaders leading the band.

"Hullo, Mr. Jones."

" 'Lo, Jeannie. This is Nick Kahn from Harvard. I'm showing him the house by the pond."

"No one's from Harvard," she said. "Where were you from before there?"

"I'm from California. Los Angeles."

"Oh my God."

"What's wrong with L.A.?"

"Nothing. It's great. Mountains and the sea and sun shining all the time." She grinned impishly. "And all those incredible things that can happen to you that can't seem to happen anywhere else."

"I lived there most of my life and nothing incredible happened."

"I hope you rent the house by the pond," she said, changing the subject. "It's a neat little house and everyone loves it."

"I hope I get it too," said Nick.

"I'll see you this summer, then."

"Sure," said Nick. "This summer."

As Jones had predicted, Nick's offer of five hundred dollars was refused. Then, curiously, Emma Rand changed her mind and accepted it.

"Beats me," said Jones. "No one's bargained with Emma Rand before. That is, bargained with Emma Rand and won. Sure beats me."

Wanda dared not admit she felt a wild excitement. Her job and new responsibilities took up all her time. Mischa's absence would give her a much-valued freedom. She would be free, finally, to live her life as she wanted and she intended to live it right up to the hilt.

Nick watched Mischa looking like a lost kid who has been set out on a strange journey and doesn't know why, and he thought of that monster behind it. Buck Herman. He pushed away the memory of Buck, but it was there, a merciless and unfinished business to be reckoned with one day. Then he walked toward his father and nothing else mattered and Mischa saw his son and the two men embraced.

"I've changed, Nick. I'm different."

"I know, Dad."

"It scares a lot of people."

"I love you, Dad. I've rented a great house and we're going to have a swell summer. You'll be glad you came east."

The first few weeks in July it rained. Mischa sat on the screened porch and watched the rain. In the mornings Nick worked as a "ghost." He thought about Jeannie Rand and how much he'd like to see her again, and when he finished work he walked down to the beach. A heavy fog hung over the bay. Nick walked toward the great white castle on the hill. Signs reading NO TRESPASSING were posted everywhere. Nick ignored them. At a cut in the beach, a deep stream of water separated him from Emma's castle. He looked up at it and wondered why it seemed so lonely and remote. Never a soul and never a sound except the mournful blast of the foghorn. Nick finally turned around and went home.

It continued to rain. Nick found a second-hand phonograph at a yard sale and brought it home. Mischa listened to the scratchy records. He remembered his youth. He remembered his hopes for a great career. The burst of music in a great symphony orchestra under the maestro's baton. He remembered Wanda's yearning for a glamorous life and the move to California. He remembered his studio job and Buck Herman's persecution. His colleagues laughing behind his back, the humiliation, the painful shame . . . ! Jumping up, he screamed, "Music killed me! Music killed me!" And Nick, working upstairs, rushed to his father and held him in his arms and comforted the frightened wretch.

Mischa needed help and Nick knew just who she was and where to find her.

That afternoon Nick walked through the woods to the beach. He ignored the NO TRESPASSING sign that stood as sentry to Rand's Head and stared up at the silent and ghostly place. It was as if Emma Rand had drawn a curtain between herself and the world. Nick rolled up his pants and crossed the brook.

He stood on the shore looking upward when he saw Jeannie on the marble terrace. She waved at him and disappeared. A moment later she appeared on the beach. She was wonderfully slender with a golden crown of hair and her face lit up with the loveliest smile. And her legs! It was her legs that got him the most.

"Well," she said. "I've been waiting for you for the longest darn time."

"So you saw me. . . ."

"Of course I did. Day after day standing in the rain."

"Or the fog."

"Not paying any attention to the signs. It's illegal, you know, and someone could have asked you to leave."

"But they didn't, did they?"

She laughed.

"Why didn't you come down?"

"I thought if he really wants to see me . . . really really . . . he'll cross the brook . . . and you finally did and here I am, just waiting to be saved."

"Funny, that's what I want too."

As she moved toward him her eyes closed to half-moons and her mouth curved into a crescent. Nick saw just the tip of her tongue. Her dreamy expression promised more than a kiss. Nick began to tremble.

"Not me," he said. "My father."

"What about your father?"

"My father needs saving."

"Oh, Nick . . . I've never saved anyone in my life."

"Well, this is your first big chance."

The sexy hot look disappeared from her face. Nick wondered if it had been his imagination.

"Why me?"

"Because you're the one who can do it. I wasn't sure before, but I am now. Just listen and see if I'm not right."

Nick told her about Mischa. He told her about Mischa's accident and about his fear of music. "Mr. Jones said you were a violinist. If you went to Mischa and asked him to help you—you see, he needs someone to need him—I'm sure he'd respond."

Jeannie nodded.

"Will you do it?"

"Of course." She seemed suddenly gentle. "I'll come tomorrow at three."

"Tomorrow," he repeated. "At three."

"See you, Nick."

Nick watched her walk away. He wanted to run after her and take her in his arms and watch her eyes close down and her mouth open for a kiss. He could almost feel the flick of her tongue. He had never been attracted to anyone so strongly. She's the one to help Mischa, he reminded himself, and his desire to make love to her was stronger than ever before.

When Jeannie arrived the next afternoon, Nick took her straight to Mischa, who was sitting on the porch. Mischa seemed lost in a private dream. Nick walked over to him and shook him gently.

"Dad, this is Jeannie Rand. Jeannie's mother owns our house."

"Hello," said Mischa.

"Hello, Mr. Kahn."

"Please call me Mischa."

"Mischa."

Mischa liked the pretty girl, with her sparkling eyes and the spray of freckles on her nose. He liked her fine young body. She would be a nice girl for Nick.

"Nick said you were a violinist and that you could help me."

Mischa stiffened. What had Nick said? The girl wanted something he couldn't give her. Something gone. Something dead.

"I study with Bukovsky. Joseph Bukovsky—he's with the symphony in Boston."

"Who's Bukovsky?" Mischa asked dully.

"My teacher. I go to Boston each week for a lesson."

"Be careful. Music kills."

She ignored him. "I've been studying the Bach chaconne. I practice and practice and I can't get it right. Bukovsky gets furious. He makes things worse. Nick said maybe you would help me, Mischa."

Before he answered she left his side. She returned with a violin. She put it under her chin and started to play. What came out was a ragged sound without passion or talent, yet her eyes were filled with human need.

"I'm scared," Jeannie said softly. "I need help."

"What frightens you, child?"

"What I do. The things I do. Oh, I don't hurt anyone, Mischa. Except myself. I hurt myself. When I saw Nick standing in the rain waiting, it was like some kind of sign. He's going to help me, I thought. I didn't know when or where, but now I do." She paused. "He brought me here to meet you. You're a musician. You can help me. Will you, Mischa?"

How could a wreck like himself help this beautiful girl, Mischa wondered. And music! Music destroyed him. No, it wasn't music that destroyed him. It was someone between him and the music. Music was beautiful. It was the light in his life.

"I am reading about Beethoven," said Mischa. "He was short and ugly and bad-tempered. He was deaf and despairing. A man who wanted to kill himself. And God looked down on his misery and led him from the dark. He showed him light. A flame. Within us all is a flame. Our own flame. Our own music."

Impulsively, Jeannie put her violin into Mischa's hand.

"Play for me, Mischa."

In that moment Mischa felt a darkness lift. He put the violin under his chin. He plucked the strings. He tuned the sound. He

lifted the bow and let it fall. It gave out a long clear note,
dropped an octave and hung suspended on air. A melody quivering on two notes—two beautiful notes—soaring from Mischa. He
stopped playing. His eyes glowed. "We are God's children too,
and he will lead us from the dark."

By August the sun was out. The island glittered in its hot light.
The beaches were filled with pale white bodies slopping oil and
waiting for tans.

Except for Jeannie and Mischa. The years of study, first with a
local teacher, then in Boston with Bukovsky, had not excited her
as Mischa did. He never touched the violin but he guided her
closely and the fiery heat that plagued her days—that shameless
bondage in which she struggled—seemed suddenly to lose its
force.

It had started years earlier. A look from a stranger, be he short
or tall or thin or fat, and it would begin. Jeannie tumbled with the
boys on the beach. She hurled herself against them as though
violence would quell it. But it was there, ever present and ready
to spring. She controlled the madness with a savage will. At night
she relieved the agony in prolonged masturbation. She was wak-
ened from sleep by its crude heat. She must destroy it, smash its
power. More important, she must lie. If her mother found her
out, she would lock her away for the rest of her life. Jeannie often
wondered if that wouldn't be for the best. No one who knew
what she really was could ever love her. So Jeannie lied. She
pretended innocence and virtue. It was how she protected herself from Emma's wrath, from Emma's fury at the world. If
Emma found out what Jeannie was, she would destroy her.

Jeannie was just fourteen when she went to study with Bukovsky, a short squat man with a body thickened from gluttony.
Bukovsky knew one law: the law of the senses. He lived for the
pleasure of food, a good cigar, music, and the pleasures of a
woman. When he saw Jeannie, heard her play, heard her animal
moans, sensed her loneliness, he moved. He unbuttoned her
blouse, slipped her brassiere from her breasts, removed her
pants. He touched her wetness, her sweat, and bent down and

kissed her heat. He whispered gently, then rudely, then roughly. He lied to her. He excited her, he laughed at her. She was just fourteen years old and he was forty-five, but who cared. What mattered was that within weeks she was in virtual bondage.

He lived on Newbury Street, off the Boston Common. An accomplished musician, this collector of second-rate art was clever enough to see that this rich heiress was suffering a pathological condition. He made her feel crude and unnatural—except for his presence. He made her dependent, a craven addict seeking relief. Afterward, he lit a fat and smelly cigar.

"I hate that smell."

"That's unfortunate, darling."

"You do it to disgust me."

"It gives me pleasure. Everything I do gives me pleasure."

"Like making me feel dirty."

"You are dirty, my dear, a very pretty, dirty little girl."

"You're vile, Bukovsky."

"Be generous, my darling—remember! I'm saving your life."

How she hated him. His bragging and foul breath. His stories of sexual conquest. Yet apart from him she was obsessed, a victim of desire, until night and the sweet relief of sleep. And even in sleep the torment of dreams. Was there no escape, no sanity?

Once Bukovsky punished a bowing mistake by refusing to touch her. She was so beautiful at his feet, wimpering and submitting to any indignity, telling him what he wanted most to hear, that, body and soul, she needed him, do with her what he would. He knew then he had her. He was the cat and she was a mouse within the circle of his paws. He forced her to finish her lesson and then gave himself over to gratifying the demons that tore her apart.

Now suddenly, through the care and kindness of this dear human being, the hunger that ruled Jeannie's life was connected to music. It flowed from her fingers onto the strings and her shameful sickness seemed temporarily at rest.

Mischa looked forward to Jeannie's daily lesson. Except, of course, the days she insisted on going to Boston.

"Surely you can take a vacation," he said.

"I wish I could, but Bukovsky expects me. I can't disappoint him, Mischa. He gave up his vacation just to work with me."

"He sounds like a devoted teacher."

"Oh, absolutely devoted. So you see I'm awfully lucky."

Bukovsky found it howlingly funny that Jeannie was studying with another teacher. "You don't need your lover now. Mischa's so kind and understanding. He'll give you all that you need."

"You're such a bastard."

Jeannie stepped out of her underpants. Another shameless debauch lay ahead, her connection to sanity. Who would ever want her, a sick, wretched human being. Who but Bukovsky. And he, reveling in her fear and dependence, teased her all the more, taunted her, drove her to the absolute edge until she was at his feet and crying for relief.

Nick watched Jeannie swinging along the path, holding her violin. She was like a beautiful butterfly, blond and radiant. Someday a man would catch her in his net, prick and mount her behind glass. Like an ornament, thought Nick. And Jeannie, in that instant, seemed to Nick as mysteriously vulnerable as Cassie Castle and he fell all the more in love.

What brought Jeannie to music? Mischa wondered. She had no particular talent. It had to be something else, a hidden inner fire, an emotion he helped release. He heard the sound in her music again and again.

"You hear it too," she said with eyes full of wonder.

"It's the beginning," said Mischa. "You are finding your voice, and having found it, you want to feel it again. You are beginning to make music, Jeannie. Now, let's take the next phrase."

It happened repeatedly: everything hidden and shameful was sublimated into her fingers and onto the strings. Jeannie had dreams. Everyone would have laughed and thought her crazy, but to Jeannie they meant escape. When she graduated from high school, she would go to Hollywood and play in the great movie orchestras. She had no desire to have a concert career or to play in the symphony. That was for the ambitious ones who dreamed only of fame and of glory. Jeannie had read all she could about Hollywood life and its unfettered sexual life-style. Out there she would seem normal. No one would ever know.

One more year! Then nothing would stand in her way. So Jeannie waited, secretly ached, thought herself a defective, and abandoned herself to the hateful Bukovsky. One more year and she would leave this world of New England puritanism and vanish into Sodom and sin. Each new Hollywood scandal brought her perverse pleasure and the hope that a new life would be had in the West.

After her lesson Nick walked her home and Jeannie thought him wildly handsome, a kind of sweetness mixed with a dark strain. His limp made him different. Nick was kind in the way a man who has suffered is kind and forgives suffering in others. She yearned to tell him about Bukovsky, to see if he would continue to like her or would turn away in disgust. Fear kept her guard up. Using every artifice she had, she smiled a smile of innocence.

But Nick saw through her mask. He saw her fear and it filled him with sadness. He put his arm around her shoulder. She shrugged it off.

"What's the matter?"

"Nothing, Nick."

"Don't you like me to touch you?"

Jeannie was silent.

"Tell me, Jeannie. For God's sake, what's wrong?"

How could she tell him she was a big whorish mass, that hunger nibbled at her womb until it was red and raw, that she was like a piece of meat to be thrown to a dog and chewed on? How could she tell him? Even Nick, so close a friend, would judge.

"Don't you trust anyone?" he asked.

"Yes. I trust you."

"Then tell me what's the matter."

She continued to be silent.

"I want to know."

"Okay." She took a long deep breath. "Bukovsky?"

"Yes."

"Bukovsky's my lover."

"Your lover!"

"You wanted to know. All right, now you know."

"You can't love Bukovsky."

"Love him! Bukovsky! I hate his guts."

"Then why?"

"You said I could trust you. Well, you've got to trust me too. If I could tell you, I would, but I can't."

"All right," said Nick. "You won't tell me but you've got to talk to someone. You've got to let someone help you. A good doctor . . ."

"Nick, you don't understand."

"What don't I understand?"

"About my mother, Emma Rand, the famous whore. Boston froze her out when Josiah died. Why do you think we live this way, alone, shut away without friends in that damned museum she thinks is revenge? They think she's a whore and she thinks they're right. In her head she's a whore. If she thought it was contagious, she'd lock me away."

"Jeannie. This is not the Middle Ages. You've got to tell your mother you're lonely and need help."

"And the moment the doctor knows who my mother is he'll be after her money for research. I thought about it, Nick. I've just got to get away. Someplace no one knows or cares about the great Rand fortune."

"I'm moving to a bigger place this fall. Mischa will be staying with me. You'll come to Mischa to study. Will you, Jeannie?"

"Oh, Nick."

"Well, will you?"

"All right."

"And you won't see Bukovsky. Promise me, Jeannie."

"Why, Nick. You're jealous."

"Okay, I'm jealous."

She told Nick about Bukovsky and he didn't call her a whore. His eyes, all bright and excited, were eyes of jealousy. Nick was jealous of her lover. He was jealous of Bukovsky. That meant Nick loved her. He loved her! No one had ever loved Jeannie before and she wanted to cry, all the tears of anguish and loneliness she'd denied for so long. She wanted to wrap her arms around Nick and kiss him long and tenderly. But then it started, sharp as an electric prod, and the joy of first love was replaced by the fear of judgment. She couldn't tell Nick what she was, not yet. When he loved her more, maybe. She couldn't risk losing Nick. . . .

"Well, will you promise?"

"I promise. I won't see him again."

Jeannie threw her arms around his neck and kissed him.

"Damn! I've got to get home. We're meeting with lawyers." A phony smile on her face, Jeannie blew another kiss, ran down the path, through the woods toward the sea and Rand's Head.

Everyone gave Wanda a lot of credit. She was a mensch. She'd taken a job. Supported a crazy husband. Her son had gone on to Harvard with honors. Wanda, for her part, had come to accept that the glamor that had lured her west was illusion. Yet being alone and being independent was better than marriage to an outcast, one whose presence was a reminder of what happened to the vulnerable and the weak.

One evening Wanda got a call from old Rose, inviting her to supper. Wanda said yes. She was no longer the monster's little slave. She was executive secretary to a senior vice-president at Titan. She could eat with Rose, and leave, a free woman.

It was a friendly evening. Wanda raved about her boss. She called Buck a musical genius.

"A Tchaikovsky of the movies," said Wanda. "The world sees the movies and hears the music and its heart is filled with happiness."

The following day she arrived home to find a dozen roses with a card: "Thanks for your kind words. You know how much Rose likes you. I hope you'll see her soon again. Buck."

She wrote him back: "You've got a wonderful mother, Buck. I look forward to seeing her soon." Within months she was invited back into a society that had ruthlessly shut her out. She was no longer contaminated.

One night, at a dinner party at Rose's, she met a widowed tax accountant. A month later, she filed for divorce.

That fall, on Saturday afternoons, Jeannie came to Nick's apartment. She brought Mischa seashells and fresh wild flowers. Mischa coaxed and coddled her like a baby and Jeannie thought herself momentarily safe. Mischa was her refuge, a protection against herself. She was no big talent. It didn't matter. What mattered was the music sending shivers through her body. She swayed back and forth, she sighed and groaned, and Mischa accepted her mannerisms as those of a romantic young girl influenced by movies and love stories.

After her lesson she went to Nick. He looked at her and he felt happy. Her lovely smile, her body, pale, with high round breasts, her slender hips—she was the prettiest girl he had ever seen. Nick was in love. He had fallen in love with a girl whose passion seemed to match his own.

Then gradually her responses began to trouble him. She dug her fingernails into his flesh until he bled. Her harsh breathing was like an animal's. He muffled her screams with his hand. No matter how intense his lovemaking, he couldn't satisfy her. She was insatiable. He felt at those moments there were two Jeannies. The sweet and tender girl whom he loved and a wild stranger who looked like Jeannie and smelled like Jeannie, but who fucked like a female fury.

Nick asked her to see a psychiatrist. Jeannie replied she wasn't sick. Nick said you didn't have to be sick to get help. Then why go, she replied.

Nick finally convinced her that her fear of doctors was irrational and Jeannie reluctantly started therapy with a psychiatrist on Park Street Place, just off the Common.

Jeannie liked to walk across the park. She liked men's eyes on her body, on her legs. She liked men trailing behind her. Only her doctor oppressed her. She told him her problems and fears, and he spoke to her of neurasthenia and sexual hyperesthesia. She felt isolated and alone. A textbook case. Sex with Nick had not, as Jeannie hoped, relieved her. On the contrary, she felt racked, hammers pounding in her womb, a craw opening and crunching its victim.

Fall became winter, and one January afternoon, a cold wind blowing her along, she heard someone call her name.

"Jeannie, Jeannie girl."

She looked around and saw Bukovsky. She quickened her pace. He caught up and took her arm.

"Have you forgotten your old lover, Jeannie, I still yearn for my darling girl."

"You disgust me."

"You're very rude, my love. One would have thought you were brought up in a gutter."

She marched on with Bukovsky clutching her arm.

"I adored you, Jeannie. I still adore you. Tell me one good reason we can't go on."

She stopped and faced him.

"Because I love someone else."

"Well, I suppose I should be jealous, Jeannie, darling, but I'm not. You were my greatest little fuck, and now I've got you again we'll be even better. I can't tell you how much better, my sweet." His voice dripped like soft butter. He loosened his grip and touched her face.

"I'm not coming back," she said defiantly.

Bukovsky laughed. "I know you, my girl, and this time I'm not going to lose you. You're mine, Jeannie, all of you, your ass, your sweet tits, and I'm yours, to give you what you want, what you need. Bukovsky knows you, my darling. . . ."

"You're vile!"

"I suppose I am, but so are you." His lips parted into the smile of the owner of a long-lost dog.

"Come, now, Jeannie. Wherever you're going, call him from my house and say you're ill."

This squat Don Juan, in a blue serge suit off the rack at Filene's, stingy, with a taste for the good life, guided her gently toward Newbury Street, toward his apartment, up the steps, through the door, onto the bed. Slowly he undressed her. His mouth was over her body, his tongue tasting it, each wretched pore opening to its touch. She was hot and needy, but Bukovsky took his time. He had her now the way he wanted, screaming from the heat that coursed her hot, runny womb. Hours seemed like minutes. Bukovsky leaned over and checked the time.

"That was the beginning," he said. "Next time I'll give you what you really need."

The next Saturday Jeannie went straight from Nick to Bukovsky. He was waiting for her at Newbury and Boylston. He linked his arm through hers. They walked along like an uncle and his favorite niece. Women greeted or looked at him queerly.

"Have you made love to every woman in Boston?"

"Women love artists, my dear. We're a terrific relief after the boredom of a dull good husband."

"What a cynic you are."

"Not a cynic, a realist. A man who understands what a woman needs."

They mounted the brownstone steps and entered his apartment. She hated the foul stench of his cigar. She had always hated it. It was in his mouth and on his breath. What did it matter. Nothing mattered except Bukovsky debauching her according to the dictates of his pleasure. There, on Newbury Street, in the pale afternoon light, she was victim of what she had hoped to destroy. And she was happy. Happy! She was soulless and unattached, snapped off from all emotion, and she gave of herself without dread.

"You're a perfect little mistress."

"Yes."

"Aren't you glad you've come back?"

"Yes."

"Shall Bukovsky forgive you for leaving him?"

"Yes."

"Shall he wring you out like a rag?"

"Yes."

"Then tell him how bad you were and you'll never do it again."

"I was bad to leave. I won't do it again."

"That's my good girl. Now get me a cigar and light it, please."

She got off the bed. She went to the dresser. She took a thick brown cigar from the humidor and put it in her mouth. She struck a match. She sucked on the cigar until it glowed. She handed it to Bukovsky and sat beside him. She knew what he was doing. He was offering servility to one who was damned. Yes, she was damned. A wanton slut and slave. All that mattered was Bukovsky, humiliating as he robbed her of will. She would slip from her life into his, and after he had her he would be brutal. He didn't love her. He never would. He was a hedonist and she was his sexual supplicant.

When she left him, she was as tired as any old scrubwoman. She slept on the bus. She slept on the ferry. She slept in her canopied bed in the great white castle by the sea.

Jeannie began leaving Nick earlier than usual. One Saturday morning she called Mischa and said she wasn't feeling well and would miss her lesson and could she talk to Nick.

"What's the matter?" he asked.

"Oh, I've got an awful cold."

"Shall I come to the island?"

"No . . ." She faltered. "I'm just going to try to sleep . . . thanks, though." She kissed him through the receiver and said she'd see him next week and hung up.

Nick couldn't figure why he didn't believe her. He walked over to Brattle Street, bought a newspaper, and had a cup of coffee. When he got back, he called Jeannie up.

"Is Jeannie there?"

"Miss Jeannie's in Boston."

"What time did she leave?"

"Who is this?"

"Nick."

"Oh, she went early, Mr. Nick. Long time ago."

Nick hung up the receiver. So she'd called him from Boston. Then it hit him. She'd gone back to Bukovsky!

Nick found Bukovsky's address in the phone book. He jotted it down on a pad. He dialed the listed number. It rang six times. Finally a man's voice answered. It was deep and musical. Nick hung up. He forced himself to read the paper. He made himself lunch but couldn't eat. He put on his coat and his hat and went down into the Harvard Square subway.

The ritual of selecting Bukovsky's cigar, drawing on it until it glowed, then sitting beside him while he smoked and bragged about his other women no longer humiliated Jeannie. It was part of a ritual in which she lent herself to his every whim if she was to be satisfied. She did all he demanded.

"Of course, dear girl," he'd said. "I can't insist on your coming. It's your decision, but do as I ask and I promise you won't be disappointed."

"And if I don't."

"Then, my dear, don't bother coming back."

"Please don't threaten me."

"I'm just saying that I miss you and I want you with me. If you don't come when I need you, then don't come at all."

So she canceled Nick and Mischa.

She wasn't disappointed. By late afternoon she was sated and at peace. She began to realize no matter how she loved Nick, Bukovsky's claim on her was stronger. Perhaps it was better like this. The kind of person she was, the humiliation she needed . . . She must sacrifice Nick's love. She had no choice.

Nick sat in a bar on Newbury Street. His table faced a window. He looked out on the street. It was three o'clock. Nick finished his drink and ordered another. He watched the afternoon crowd. It began to get dark. The crowd was thinning out. Nick saw Jeannie leave the building across the street. He paid for his drinks and went outside.

"Jeannie," he shouted. "Wait for me."

She turned around and saw him.

"You shouldn't be here, Nick."

"Wrong. I should be here and I am."

"This is none of your business."

"Wrong again. You're my business and what you do is my business."

"You're drunk."

Jeannie walked away. Nick caught up and grasped her arm. She pulled free of his grip.

"What's wrong? Why are you doing this?" he said.

She looked him straight in the eye.

"Because I'm garbage."

"Jeannie."

"I am. Bukovsky knows it and he doesn't care. I need him, Nick. I need the way he uses me. Do you understand. He doesn't care."

"Jeannie, I love you."

"You don't know me."

"I do and I love you."

"You mean it. You really do."

"Yes."

"Then stay my friend."

She reached up, kissed him, and ran to the corner. She flagged the first cab coming toward her.

EMMA
1930s

The great Rand name, the house on Beacon Hill, its comfort and luxury and servants, didn't bring what Emma yearned for, a place in that pinched and snobbish world of the high and mighty Brahmin. The Rands thought Emma a poison that had entered Josiah's body. Sooner or later he would wake from his thrall and see her for what she was: a whore. He would pay her what she wanted and return to his own.

The foolish Rands.

When Josiah saw the pretty girl that first cold night, when she undressed and sat naked on his lap, when she kissed and hugged him to her breast, and became so naughty, naughtier than he had ever dreamed, he fell head over heels in love. Josiah married Emma because he knew Emma would save his life.

In fact, they saved each other.

Josiah had been living out a dull and stultified life, and Emma was on her way to becoming a hardened whore. Josiah's fierce hot lunge at living, through Emma's lovely body, was brief. Five years passed. One night, after love, Josiah felt a streak of pain. His heart pounded. His breath winded. His eyes bulged. He looked at his pregnant Emma with the eye of death.

"They'll try to break you," said Josiah. "Try to take it all away.

Be strong, my darling. Promise." A final shuddering convulsion and it was over. The doctor found Emma crying, as though her tears would bring him back.

Josiah was right.

A hundred years earlier, this daughter of sin would have been scourged, whipped at the whipping post, and hung from the gallows as a witch. But this was the twentieth century. The Rands—bankers, merchants, and pillars of society—revenged Josiah's weakness of the flesh by shunning Emma from their midst. In their minds, his witch was dead. A succubus returned to the devil.

If Emma had been weaker, they might have won. But she had spent too many lonely nights in this world. She was hardened by the whoring and now in her grief, memories of that earlier agony owned her. *If they viewed her as depraved, so be it. Her depravity would have them at her feet. One day, they would beg her for forgiveness. But how?*

By what they held most dear!

Emma sold her great house on Beacon Hill to a hungry real estate developer. She bought her land on Martha's Vineyard. She went to Europe. She sacked it. She robbed it of its greatest artworks. Monasteries, auction houses, and collectors were at the mercy of her money. She had a genius for ferreting out the impossible. She shipped everything to Rand's Head. And then she shut the door.

She ate with Botticelli and Carpaccio and Titian. She slept with Goya, Gauguin, and Van Gogh. Stories of her mysterious collection became a kind of folklore. She lived in isolation, in her museum, among terraced parks with rare trees and exotic flowers, indoor and outdoor swimming pools, with murals by Picasso engraved upon the floors.

The years passed. Emma continued to suffer the heartache of the outcast. She was shy, unaccustomed to people. Her business was done by phone, with an occasional visit from her lawyer or her doctor to break the oppressive silence of her life.

She amused herself by sailing. A reconstructed nineteenth-century schooner sat in the bay facing her palace. She owned sailboats, racers, and motorboats. In February's bluster or August's calm, she sailed. It was the one mad recklessness of her life. She measured her bravery against winter's lashing winds. Her knowledge of the tides and currents was that of a master seaman.

One fine spring night the millionaire recluse stood on the terrace that joined living room to bedroom. She viewed her gardens, the ocean, the moon, the cluster of islands lying beyond. Jeannie was playing a Bach suite and the music rolled through the night.

Emma looked up at the starry sky and the winding pines that ran into the sea. Sea and sky were silent, and Emma felt the dread and emptiness of her life. She felt a desire to live. She wanted to break the isolation that set her apart from the human race. She wanted to talk and laugh. Once she had wanted revenge. The price was relentless solitude. She had cheated herself of what she most desired. For the first time in years she did not blame the Rands. She blamed herself.

Jeannie would be leaving home soon, and Emma thought of the lonely years ahead, and felt a wrenching ache. *I am destroying my life,* she thought. *I must save what is left before it is too late.* She would share this lonely grandeur with others less fortunate than herself. She felt younger suddenly, less odd. She prayed it was still not too late. She prayed for the miracle of life.

She returned to the house and went to Jeannie's room. She wondered about her daughter, swaying and moaning as she played her violin.

"What's the matter, Momma? You look odd."

"I've gone odd, haven't I, Jeannie. I guess God didn't put me on earth to live as I do." The words poured out in torrents. "Jeannie, darling, let's have some music. Ask Bukovsky to organize a quartet, and I'll invite some neighbors."

"Bukovsky can't possibly come. He has concerts in the evenings, and there are matinees."

"Nonsense. Bukovsky can't play every night."

"Mother, please, listen."

"Tell him not to worry about expenses. I'll charter a plane. I'll pay whatever it costs."

"Listen to me, Mother."

"It's a wonderful idea. Music will change our lives." Emma was already planning the night. After quartets she would serve a supper of caviar, lobster, and champagne. The musicians would sleep on the island. The following morning a chartered plane would fly them back to Boston. "You'll be gone in less than a year," said Emma. "And I'll be all alone. Oh, darling, it's more than I can bear." Tears filled her eyes. "Please ask him, Jeannie. Your mother wants to be with kind and loving people."

The frown was gone from Emma's face. It was the first time Jeannie had seen her mother happy. She had no choice. "All right," said Jeannie. "I'll tell Bukovsky to arrange quartets."

Bukovsky agreed immediately to arrange an evening of music.

"Naturally I don't want any money, but the other musicians will want to be paid," he lied, knowing full well any musician in town would jump at the chance of playing at Rand's Head.

So it was arranged. Bukovsky and four colleagues boarded the six-seat twin Beechcraft one Sunday afternoon at three, and found themselves an hour later on Emma's marble terrace, sipping champagne and eating gray beluga caviar.

"You're a horticultural wonder, Mrs. Rand. In the great Italian tradition. Fiesole and Tivoli. Do you know the Tuscan countryside?" Bukovsky asked.

"Yes," Emma said modestly, reflecting on her raid upon Italy so many years ago.

"I'm a gardener myself—not in your class, of course, just a modest city gardener."

"Would you like to see my roses?" said Emma.

"You cannot imagine how much."

Emma led him through her rose gardens, the wild English gardens, the more formal French one, and Bukovsky's greedy heart pounded with joy. They strolled back into the house. A connoisseur by instinct, he gloried in her art. The masterpieces of painting, the Gothic sculpture, Renaissance chests, the ivory, gold, and burnished wood of antique furniture, the priceless art objects one would find in museums, left him breathless. The spellbinding luxury revealed to him the coarseness of his own existence. He was aware this was the life he yearned for. *Destiny had come to him in the guise of Jeannie, but it was to Emma he was fated.* He realized, suddenly, that in his choice of music he had planned a seduction; music that would cast a spell over the eccentric millionairess. Unconsciously, he hoped to lift Emma to an emotional intensity where the shroud over her life would lift and he would slip right in.

"We'll start with the lyrical Brahms A minor," he said. "We'll follow with the 'Kreutzer Sonata.' Do you know it, Mrs. Rand? Tolstoy said about the Kreutzer, 'Such music should be played only on important occasions.' This is such a night." He disregarded her shyness, her fingers twisting like a schoolgirl's. "We'll finish with the great Schubert C major quintet. God's music, Mrs. Rand."

In the radiant twilight, in her vast and magnificent palace, Emma seemed to Bukovsky a goddess. *To worship this goddess, to make her his; it was like moving close to God. A man of his talent was entitled to a godly life.* He would leave the symphony, form his own quartet, record the great works, play in the major cities on a magnificent Stradivarius. All his life he had been lazy, and poor as a result. Well, tonight he would cure himself of that ridiculous habit. *Patience,* he warned himself. *Go slowly.* But within minutes he knew she had no weapons of defense, so he prepared her as he had prepared so many unsuspecting women; he was charming and seductive as he spoke of music and God and art.

Emma said nothing. She blushed, listened, and allowed his vitality to wrap itself around her like a long-awaited caress. The part of her that had seemed so cut off and numb came alive, and Emma, so isolated and unused to feeling, gave way to his dissolute charm.

Bukovsky coveted the life ahead with an even greater zeal. There was only one danger: *Jeannie.* He thought of his young mistress whom he had so ruthlessly debauched and the inner voice said: *She is sick, and she is frightened of her mother. She will never reveal what went on between you. You run no risk of betrayal from Jeannie.*

What danger, then? What possible danger lay between him and Emma Rand? Only himself! The danger was his own shameless appetite, which included, suddenly, the desire for a farewell fuck with his young mistress. The great good years ahead with Emma Rand seemed an inevitable reality. *He had only to be patient, play his violin like an angel, and he would win her heart. Music, after all, was a union of souls.*

What he desired was to mesh the threads, mother and daughter, the consummation of one love as he seized another. One last rapturous fuck and he would give himself, body and soul, to Emma and the enchanted life ahead.

After years of denial, Emma felt a mysterious excitement. At each break in the music Bukovsky looked over at her. She was still good-looking. He recalled the gossip of her early years. He must remember that Emma Rand, despite her wealth, was once a little tart. He had had a lot of experience with whores, and he knew that this gloriously rich whore was no different than the others.

Emma leaned her head against the back of her chair and let the music possess her. A haunting melody that conjured up fantasy, the past, impressions of a life long gone. Her eyes caught Bukovsky's as the music carried her from her ivory tower to a state of romantic adolescence where dreams are real as life.

She was suddenly frightened, yet the music continued, a sensuous adagio, and at its end Bukovsky's eyes caught hers. He smiled as though to reassure her. *Yes, life must be lived. He was presenting her with a gift.* She felt like rushing to him and throwing her arms around him in gratitude, but she sat quietly, a peaceful smile on her face. The shroud had lifted. Emma was free of its oppressive hold. Bukovsky's amorous victory was fast and sweet. At dinner, by candlelight, Bukovsky's fantasy went wild. He thought of the priceless Stradivarius he would have, his collection matching hers, and he charmed her with a resource of anecdotes and famous names.

It was late when the visitors said good night, and the musicians finally retired. Jeannie kissed her mother, smiled at Bukovsky, and went to her room. The terrible itch burned in her womb. Even her dildo and a multiple orgasm didn't relieve the anguish. She took a cold shower. The fire burned on. She grabbed a towel, slipped from the room, and went out to the sea.

Emma and Bukovsky lingered in the vast living room. Emma was like a quivering middle-aged virgin. Bukovsky couldn't believe the ease of his conquest. But conquest alone was not what he sought. He was after the future. *This innocent woman might go to bed a victim of passion, but she must wake up in the same school-girl trance. That was his duty, to himself and his future.* The inner voice nagged caution, but his mission made him reckless. All he saw was a rich and rapturous woman on the edge of falling in love.

"Mrs. Rand, your feeling for music, your response, is a musician's dream come true."

"You're a wonderful violinist. My response is only human."

"Such kind words, Emma. May I call you Emma?"

"Please."

"Some wise old mystic called music the brandy of the damned. It's fools like us who get drunk on its beauty."

"Yes." She laughed. "It feels like being drunk."

He raised his hand and let it fall beside hers. He felt her skin. *Patience,* the inner voice urged, but he ignored it. He caught her around the waist. He laid his cheek on hers. He kissed her. It was so surprisingly easy, he almost felt alarmed. He looked into Emma's eyes and saw a woman falling in love. He had ignored the inner warning—he had gambled, and won. He forgot his schemes and ambition and gave himself over to the pure pleasure of seducing his future wife. Wordlessly, she stood up.

"It's late."

"I know."

"It's time to go to bed."

"Emma."

"Yes, Bukovsky."

"You are such a beautiful woman."

She smiled then, suddenly shy. She pressed her fingers to her lips and blew him a kiss. She walked toward her room. Bukovsky lit a cigar. He returned to the terrace. The moon was shining, the gardens pale and unearthly in its bright white light. He saw Jeannie swimming toward shore. She emerged from the water. Her body glistened. Bukovsky felt a thrill. She looked up toward him. Bukovsky waved. Jeannie waved back. Slowly she walked in his direction, her naked body as perfect as Emma's great sculptures. She disappeared. Bukovsky waited. *This last final hour together was ordained. They would slip off to his room and he would take her. Then he was Emma's, forever Emma's.* He doused his cigar.

Jeannie walked through the living room onto the terrace. She slipped her arms around his neck. Her heat was thrilling. She slipped down to her knees, unzipped his pants, and took him deep into her throat. He almost exploded.

"Not here," he whispered, "it's too dangerous."

She ignored him. Her tongue was working his cock, very slowly, licking the hood and just beneath its rim, her mouth hugging the flesh. Now her mouth slipped down to the base. Bukovsky's cock tingled with blood and excitement. He moaned and lifted her up. Jeannie, naked in his arms, looked across the way to see Emma standing on her balcony. Mother and daughter looked into one another's eyes while Bukovsky, unaware of Emma, pulled Jeannie toward him. She struggled in his arms and pounded his chest. When she looked back across the way, Emma was gone.

"Have you gone crazy?" he whispered.

"Yes," she said triumphantly. "But it's you who did it. You, Bukovsky. You turned me into what I've become."

She slipped out from his grasp and ran into the house.

Bukovsky turned and took a last look at the moon. All of them, crazy, he thought, all women are crazy. He took a long, deep breath of the sweet night air, went back into the house, and to his room. Within minutes he was in bed and snoring.

The next morning was warm with a drifting scent of sea and pine. Emma, Jeannie, and the four musicians ate breakfast in a round white room facing the sea. Emma was remote, anxious to avoid any eye contact. Bukovsky knew women as well as he knew his violin, and a woman like Emma was emotionally starved and very proud. He'd moved too fast. He should have listened to the voice. Well, it would take a little longer than he planned, but once he had her, pride mastered, flesh awakened and full of desire, he'd be master of Rand's Head. *In the meantime, patience.* So he sat quietly and planned his life and let the others talk.

Everyone waved good-bye except Bukovsky, who lingered behind.

"How can I thank you?" said Bukovsky. "Your hospitality. The privilege of seeing Rand's Head."

"You can come back," said Emma charmingly.

"Yes, I'd like to. But when?"

"Next week. The same time. I'll pick you up at the airport."

"I'll be there," he murmured.

"Good-bye, Bukovsky."

"Good-bye, Emma. I'll see you next week." Bukovsky took Emma's hand and pressed it to his mouth. He looked deep into her eyes.

Emma returned his gaze, but she saw only ambition, a covetous soul, and desire for everything she owned.

Emma stood in the road and waved good-bye. She stopped before a rosebush and plucked a rose off its stem. She crushed the petal in her fist and went inside.

Jeannie imagined Emma's fury. She imagined her mother thinking her daughter was a whore. A reminder of her own disgraceful past. Oh, God, no whore ever suffered as she suffered. No whore ever needed what she needed. A body. Any body. Ram-ram-ram—crushing the itch, pulverizing it. Emma mustn't suspect what she was. She must lie. If she didn't, she was lost . . . lost forever—lost.

The front door closed and Emma walked toward her.

"Are you still a virgin, Jeannie?"

"Listen, Mother, please."

"Answer my question."

"No."

Emma stood silent and grim-faced.

"I wanted to tell you, Momma, I wanted your help but I was so frightened."

"Tell me now."

"It was all right at first. Then, on my fourteenth birthday, he tried to kiss me. I said no. He pushed me on the bed. He scared me so."

"What did he do?"

Jeannie was silent. She bit her lip.

"Tell me, darling. What did he do?"

"He touched my breast, kissed me, and said if I told you you wouldn't believe it. He called you a whore and said it would make you crazy to think your daughter . . ."

Jeannie threw her arms around Emma's neck, but Emma pushed her away.

"Go on," she said coldly. "Tell me everything."

"He said you could pay for anything you wanted and if you thought your daughter was a slut, you'd lock me away and no one would know. Oh, Momma, say you forgive me. I was so scared."

Emma was silent, her eyes dead space. Once she had bartered herself for money. Then fate had brought her Josiah Rand. She was happy with a man she loved. Then fate had taken him away. But now she had money. Money. It brought loneliness and isolation. And scum like Bukovsky. He'd raped her child and now, with music and lies, he was going to rape her. Vile and monstrous man. Jeannie's tears, her pleas, her cry of innocence, touched Emma's heart. She reached out her hand and Jeannie threw herself into her arms.

"Forgive me, Momma."

"It's over now, darling. He'll never touch you again."

Emma repeated his name, as though the sound of those three

hated syllables "Bu-kov-sky" would keep her to her course. She looked at the gray mist separating her white palace from the sea, nestling in the sails of her schooner, floating through the acorn pines. She looked up into the sky and prayed the plane would penetrate the haze. Emma was tired. Long ago she had lost interest in her rare collections, catalogued and locked away. She cared for nothing and no one, except Jeannie, whose tears and confession had roused her to her own selfish ends. She had robbed her beloved child of a normal life. *Well, she would make it up to her. Her vast wealth, her land, her holdings—everything was Jeannie's.*

As for herself, she had dulled a monotonous existence with pills and sedation, until Bukovsky lifted her depression. For a moment, his kisses and flattery had been a romantic miracle and life seemed full of hope. His was a heartless betrayal and it reinforced what she already knew. She could trust no one. What good was her money, her land, her priceless collections, if, after Jeannie's graduation and departure, she would be alone with her pills and oppressive fortune.

The fog was blowing away. Emma saw Jeannie swimming the length and breadth of the cove. What a strange girl, rushing to the water's edge and plunging in naked. How strong she was, her firm stroke and powerful endurance, beating her arms into the water and pushing it back, until, exhausted, she crawled to shore.

Emma looked at her watch. Nearly three o'clock. Bukovsky would land in another half hour. She went outside, got into her jeep, turned on the ignition, and drove off. She stopped at the Alley's General Store for cigarettes, then continued to drive east. She parked in the nearly empty airport lot. The plane had already landed and Bukovsky was waiting in the modest terminal building.

"Sorry I'm late," Emma said.

"We arrived early." Bukovsky smiled agreeably and took her arm. They got into her car and she backed out of the lot and headed toward Oak Bluffs.

"I've got a surprise for you," she said.

"I can't wait."

"I thought you might enjoy a boat ride."

"Little cool for that, isn't it?"

"Boats are my only recreation. I go out every day. You won't be cold, I promise. There are heavy sweaters and slickers if you are."

Bukovsky hated all outdoor activity except looking at women's legs, but he swallowed his displeasure and kept on smiling. "I've got a surprise for you too." He opened his music case and took out a phonograph record.

"Bach concerto. I conduct the orchestra. On the other side the Bukovsky quartet plays Haydn."

"I didn't know you had your own quartet."

"Members of the orchestra," he said sheepishly, "the same boys I brought over with me last week."

"I see."

"Every musician prays for his own quartet. The recording. The concertizing. America. Europe. The Far East. The acclaim. The dining with royalty. Oh, Emma, what a life it could be."

Emma looked at him thoughtfully.

"What's the matter?" he asked.

"I can't imagine you praying."

"Figure of speech."

"That's good."

They were driving along the sea. An aluminum warehouse loomed up and Emma pulled into its driveway.

"We're here," she said.

They went inside. There were boats of every size and description.

"My favorite collection," she said offhandedly.

"They're not all yours?"

"The joy of being rich is, you can have whatever you want." She smiled at him, but now her smile was odd. Superior. She kept smiling at him. Her money made her superior. *Well, everything had a price. Particularly love of the sort he envisioned.* If Emma had turned into the devil at that moment, he would have gladly paid her price, but she did not. She just smiled that odd superior smile.

At the end of the pier sat a trim blue racer. A young blond boy jumped onto the pier and helped Emma and Bukovsky on board. He untwined the rope that connected the boat to its moorings, pushed them off, then watched as the boat glided away. Emma took her place behind the wheel. In an instant they were flying along, with Emma guiding the boat out to sea.

"Chilly," said Bukovsky.

"There's a heavy sweater in the cabin," Emma said.

"Thanks."

He went down into the passenger cabin. It was upholstered in red velour. He removed his blue serge jacket and put on the cable-stitch sweater. There was a bottle of Dom Pérignon, two fluted glasses, a chilled Limoges bowl with gray pearls of caviar. *This was it! A taste of the great life ahead.* A greedy child, he stuck his finger into the caviar and swallowed it in a gulp.

"Where are you?" yelled Emma.

"Shall I bring up the champagne?"

"It's for you. Everything's for you."

He placed the champagne, the glasses, and the caviar on a tray and carefully carried it up to the deck.

They were soaring along, cutting the water hard and fast. It was clear Emma loved the sea. Her face was drained of tension and Bukovsky thought her strikingly beautiful. He knew how she had captured old Josiah Rand. He stood beside her at the wheel.

"You're a beauty, Emma Rand."

"Once, perhaps. A long time ago."

"Still a beautiful woman."

"You're flirting with me, Bukovsky."

Bukovsky leaned over and kissed the nape of her neck.

"That tickles."

But he stayed there, brushing her flesh with his fingers, and kissing it.

"Do stop."

He paid no attention, hugging her close. She jerked herself free.

"I want to talk to you, Emma."

"Not now."

"Why not?" he asked.

"Because I'm taking this boat into the straits."

"It's cold and windy. Let's go back, Emma, please."

She ignored him. Her face glowed. Emma was heading toward the far shore, enjoying the speed, turning her face to the wind.

"You're going awfully fast," he said.

"Don't worry."

Buoys were bouncing all around them.

"Buoys," said Emma. "They mark the channel."

Bukovsky felt the loss of control. Emma neither listened to him nor seemed to take him seriously. The boat was plunging into choppy waters. The spray from the waves and driving wind depressed him. He shivered. He had come to Rand's Head with one thing on his mind, and here was Emma staring fixedly ahead, refusing his kisses, ignoring him completely.

"We're in rough waters now," said Emma. "Those buoys are a guide to keep us free of the shallows."

"I'm catching a cold," he whined.

"I haven't finished what I came out to do," said Emma calmly.

"What in hell are you talking about?"

"I'm tired, Bukovsky. I've lost all desire to live. And when I go you'll come with me."

They were moving through the swirling currents, the boat rocking from side to side.

"Say your prayers, Bukovsky. We're in the shallows now. If a rock rips the bottom, it's over. Everything."

"You're insane!" he cried.

He pushed her from the wheel and grabbed it. It was stiff in his hands. It seemed fixed. This was a nightmare. A terrible joke. He grabbed her arm and pulled her back to the wheel.

"For God's sake, get us out of here!" he begged.

"Your charm's run out, Bukovsky. You'll never have your quartet."

"You're fucking crazy," he screamed.

"Am I? What you did has made me crazy."

"What did *I* do, for God's sake?"

"You raped my child!" She stared into the wind.

"Raped Jeannie! My dear woman, Jeannie raped me!"

Bukovsky grabbed her, determined she should know the truth —as if truth were the straw to determine his fate. "Okay. I've been her lover. She started lessons at thirteen. She was *not* a virgin then. Do you understand what I'm saying? I was not her first lover. Jeannie is sick, Emma. She is a pathetic and pathological girl. . . ."

The boat struck a rock and the bottom ripped open. Bukovsky's words were lost in the roaring crash as the water rose up, a small stream breaking into a flow.

"Save us!" Bukovsky pleaded. "For chrissake, do something! Get us out!"

She saw his fear, his mounting terror, and his panic gave her joy. The water swirled about their feet and ankles until it reached their calves. The wind was bitterly cold. The water swelled up higher and higher and then the boat listed. She stood and faced Rand's Head, surveyed her small glorious sovereign state.

"Good-bye, my sweet beloved Jeannie. Bless you, my dearest child."

Bukovsky pulled at her arm. "Save us," he whimpered. "Please, Emma, I don't want to die."

She looked at him icily. "Say your prayers, Bukovsky. Only God can save you now."

Water poured up around them. Bukovsky stared at the rising swell, the waves twisting around his legs, mounting, beating against his thighs, touching his hips. Another few minutes and he would be sucked into the sea—unfathomable darkness and oblivion.

"No!" he screamed. "I won't die!"

He looked out to sea. The nearest buoy was fifty feet away. With luck he could reach it and hang from its perch. He grasped the ledge of the boat and pulled himself up. He dived. He started swimming. The tide was pulling him in the opposite direction. With all his strength he resisted, swimming toward the buoy.

Forty-five yards, forty, thirty-five. He was fighting for breath, his energy flagging, losing momentum. His arms were heavy and his legs unable to paddle. His clothes were a weight and the swells lifted him and swallowed him up. He swallowed the frigid water. He gasped and swallowed more. He struggled for air, but the icy black sea closed over his head. It rushed through his mouth and his nose and his ears. He heard an inner piercing shriek— screamed as the force of the water burst his ears. His lungs burst with a deafening roar—the last explosion before the dark.

In a room filled with nineteenth-century English antique furniture, Jeannie listened to her mother's lawyer, Mr. Falmouth, read aloud from Emma's will. Rand's Head, extending from Tisbury through West Tisbury, the mansion, its contents, the Botticelli, the Titian, the Goya, the Impressionist masters, all belonged to her. Emma's estate, stocks, bonds, and real estate, a net exceeding over twenty million dollars, was hers.

While he read, Mr. Falmouth's eyes flickered over the girl before him. *Scarcely a week since Emma's death,* and Jeannie was wearing the sort of dress, how could he put it, of a girl in a hurry to live, the lovely girl in a dress that unzipped your imagination, the way she looked at you through half-closed lids, the way she stuck out her lips, aroused him to a strange excitement, like a whore, the expensive kind that came to your hotel room in places like London or New York. He didn't want to think such a thought, but it was there, an echo of young Emma. It made no sense! Emma's death was senseless, and the fact that one week before she died she had revised her will, leaving everything to Jeannie. Ironclad and incontestable. He would supervise Emma's estate until Jeannie was eighteen, less than a year away, and then Jeannie would inherit all of Emma's wealth.

Jeannie looked out the window, across Boylston, onto Newbury, and remembered Bukovsky as he clutched her arm and guided her up the steps to his brownstone apartment. *Oh, Bukovsky, if only you had been satisfied with me. But you got greedy. Greed killed you and your greed killed Emma. No, it wasn't greed that killed her. . . . It was a lie. . . . My lie sent my mother to her death.* Jeannie shut her eyes. She dared not think of what she had done. She must think only of the life ahead.

"I suppose you'll be going home now, finishing school, preparing yourself for college," Falmouth said.

"I'm going to California."

"California! You'll be graduated in three months, Jeannie. You can't throw away your education."

Jeannie smiled. "I don't have to worry about that, do I, Mr. Falmouth. I mean, I'm rich, and I can do whatever I want."

"You won't be rich for six months, Jeannie."

"I'll get along," she said.

"You're making a big mistake, Jeannie."

"Am I?"

Falmouth paused. "You're young, you're inexperienced. You don't know about the world."

"You're worried a bunch of fortune hunters will want me for my money. No one will want me for that. Not for my money. I promise."

"Be careful, Jeannie."

She ignored his warning. "One last thing, Mr. Falmouth. My friend Nick Kahn and his father can use the house whenever they want. No one else."

"But the museums! The Metropolitan, the Modern. Museums from all over America. Not to mention collectors and dealers. . . ."

"Just Nick and his father."

"All right." He sighed. "Whatever you want."

Jeannie quit school, packed a suitcase, bought a one-way airplane ticket to Los Angeles. Nick drove her to the airport.

"Good-bye fire and brimstone," she sang out, "and New England sin and retribution."

"Jeannie . . ."

"What, Nick?"

"Good luck."

She hesitated. "You think I need luck, don't you?" She smiled that innocent smile of hers. "I thought you knew me by now. A one-woman amusement park—all lit up with lights and music. It's me, Nick, the way I am."

"You never know who's going to come along for the ride."

When she grinned, it tore his heart.

"If I need saving, I'll call you. . . . Oh, Nick, honey, don't worry. I've got all the money in the world to keep me out of trouble. So give me a big fat hug and say you're my friend. Hey, Nick, come back to the planet earth."

"I love you, you crazy girl."

"I know."

She lit a cigarette. A call for the passengers to board came over the loudspeaker. She reached up and kissed him. The itch was crawling up her leg.

"You're so damned sweet," she said.

She ran from Nick's arms, through the terminal door, into the night and up the ladder and onto the plane.

At first Jeannie wrote every week. Then her letters became infrequent, and after a while they stopped. Her last one read:

Guess what, darling. I've got a radio job. A three-hour rehearsal and the show and I'm making forty-eight dollars a week. I'm a working woman, Nick, and I love it! I'll be nineteen soon. Wish me a happy birthday. And, hey, do you still love me?

Jeannie.

Nick sent her a dozen red roses and a gold locket in the shape of a heart. She wrote thanking him and saying she carried his picture in the locket.

After that there was silence.

The years passed quickly. Harvard Medical School was followed with a residency at Massachusetts General Hospital. Nick threw a harness around his life and focused his attention on his work. He had a couple of girl friends who were nurses at the hospital. There was no time for a serious romance.

Mischa was feeling quiet. He was feeling very tired. It had been a long road, but the last few years had been peaceful ones. He went to the window and looked out at the sky. Once, long ago, he had played his violin in the night with the stars overhead and the moon shining bright. A sudden thrill passed through him —a renewed desire to feel the old ecstasy. He went to the violin case and opened it up. He picked up his violin—so long unused —and plucked the strings. Horrible. What did it matter? He put the violin under his chin and pulled the bow across the string. A long sweet note gave out onto the air. He shut his eyes and pulled the bow again. The feel of it, so sweet and so sensual, went through his body. He was lost to everything except himself as a part of the sound and the sound as a part of himself. The sound fell into the night and became a part of time and Mischa was one with the sound of the music and the time in which he lived. After a while he put the violin back in its case and he sat in the dark and he cried from the happiness.

It was late when Nick came home. Mischa had fallen asleep on the couch. Nick went over to see if he was all right. He picked up his father's hand and took his pulse. Mischa was dead. Nick sat down beside Mischa and looked at his face. He wanted to cry. After a while he got up. He went to the phone and picked up the receiver and he called Wanda.

Mischa's funeral was held on Martha's Vineyard, in an old cemetery near Rand's Head. A stricken Wanda flew east.

"I loved him, Nick. Do you believe me?"

"Of course."

"Did Mischa hate me?"

"No."

"I'm so tired. I wish he was here and I could explain."

"It's all right, Wanda."

"I didn't know what I wanted. I just wanted to live. I made him come west and take a job he hated. I had to live. You understand, don't you, Nick?"

Nick nodded.

Wanda was fighting back her tears. "When he left I met a man. It was all right. A lot of fun. I thought he would marry me. I wanted to live and it scared him. It didn't work. Nothing works anymore. I loved Mischa. I'm so ashamed."

"This is a sad day, Wanda. Go back to L.A. You'll live your life."

"I'll work. I'll forget my loneliness in work."

"Yes," said Nick. "You'll work."

"Forgive me, Nick."

"You did what you thought was right."

"Oh, Nick."

Wanda began crying and Nick gave her his handkerchief.

"I'm okay," said Wanda. She wiped away the tears.

"Time to go," he said. "I'll take you to the airport."

In 1960 Nick was twenty-nine years old. He had finished his residency. He was a psychiatrist. He was offered jobs at Massachusetts General Hospital, and, in New York City, at Montefiore and Mount Sinai. But it was Los Angeles, sprawled out and swollen, and all the creatures of childhood, grotesque and fantastic, that encouraged him to go back. Once they had haunted his boyhood dreams. They haunted him still. So one June morning, with the smell of green leaves fresh in the air, Nick got on the United noon flight and headed back toward home.

BOOK THREE

NICK
1960s

After World War II the population of Greater Los Angeles was three million. By 1960 it had jumped to over six million. All kinds of people from all over the world had gone west to take a last big fling at the American Dream. Forests of oak and eucalyptus were cut down. Freeways crisscrossed, interlocked, and connected an endless suburban tract into a huge megalopolis grid. It was an explosion of cars and houses and bodies. Incinerators and engines threw off a blue cloud of chemical smoke. The good sweet air was gone. Who cared! This was Hollywood, and fame and fortune were like popcorn, waiting to be gobbled up. So they came: youth and beauty and every drifter with a dream.

And with the dream came drugs and despair. Lives that sprang from nothingness were swallowed up in a void. Houses and careers were built in a day and sold in a day and the wrecking ball was banging.

It was ten years since Nick's return. He had thrown himself into work with a creative fervor, building his practice with the beautiful and bright talent who thought their psychiatrist was a cross between Svengali and God.

An early case was Lana Budd. Lana's mother, Monette, always wanted to be a movie star. She ended up as the wife of a shoe salesman and the mother of five girls. Nubile Lana was the eldest child and the one destined to fulfill Monette's unfulfilled dream. Monette shoved her into one beauty contest after another and the voluptuous twelve-year-old, who passed for fifteen, got the lead in a picture called *Kitten. Kitten* was followed by *Kitten at the Beach.* After that it was one skimpy bathing suit after another, until teenage boys all over the world were howling for her pussy.

There was just one problem. Lana hated the way she looked on the screen, her big breasts jiggling like melons. She lost five pounds, but it wasn't enough. After eating, she began a ritual of vomiting. "You're gonna turn into a scarecrow," whined Monette. Why couldn't Monette understand, skinny wasn't just beautiful, it showed discipline and control. The skinnier you were, the better. Lana lost another ten pounds, but she still didn't feel skinny. She felt alone, isolated from everyone in her fat, and the fat was like a poison. She rushed to vomit the poison out.

When he fired her, the director urged her to see Nick.

By the time Lana got to Nick it was a race against death. After two years of analysis with him, Lana's obsession with starvation to achieve a perfect body was gone. She began to accept herself as she was. She began to study acting. She began to work again as a respected young actress.

Cocaine comes from the fresh green leaves of the coca shrub in Peru and Bolivia. It is distilled into a white crystalline powder. Taken in moderation, it creates a sense of self-confidence and euphoria. Those addicted to larger doses suffer hallucination or delusion. Nick's old high school friend Tom Flanagan had become a cocaine addict.

After Tom was graduated from Hollywood High he went on to the Pasadena Playhouse to study acting. An important agent saw a future Flynn in Tom's easy charm and physique. Success came fast. Tom wasn't prepared. The old feelings from high school—that he wasn't smart enough or good enough—disturbed him. He sniffed cocaine. When he didn't feel like the star he now was, Tom sniffed more cocaine.

Then he ran into the bad luck of a couple of flop movies and Tom free-based cocaine to boost himself up. Within months he was a heavy addict.

One night Tom awakened from sleep. Worms were crawling under his skin. Tom couldn't pull them out, so he grabbed a long knife to slash them away. Blood dripped onto the floor. Tom screamed in agony. Somehow, he remembered Nick. They'd had dinner once when Nick first came back. Tom rushed to the phone. Nick's service took Tom's message. Within an hour Nick called him back.

Nick got Tom into a detoxification center. He got him to go to Alcoholics Anonymous, and he took Tom on as a patient. The prognosis for cocaine addiction is rarely favorable, but Nick gave Tom a fresh and positive feeling about himself. Nick suggested Tom audition for the part of the Chocolate Soldier in Shaw's *Arms and the Man* at an Equity showcase. Tom was a natural swashbuckler. He was offered the role of Captain Blood. *Captain Blood* grossed over fifty million dollars. Now every studio wanted to remake the old Flynn classics with Tom in the lead.

And every ambitious actor, writer, and director in Los Angeles wanted Nick to make the magic work for them. Only ten years— but Nick was Hollywood's guiding priest and counselor.

He made his patients feel special—precious lives with precious gifts.

There was more to it than that.

He made them feel part of a community in which they worked and he urged his community of patients to help one another in that bigger community called "The Industry." His patients were friends. They helped one another. And the greatest of Nick's stars was never lonely at the top.

If a critical part of therapy is submission, Nick's patients surrendered their lives. A celebrated wit called Nick the "Hollywood Messiah," but no one laughed. How could they when Nick was in them, a human god, at one with their dreams and their extravagant ambition.

His critics, and they were loud and vocal, called him a charlatan and a rogue.

And Nick replied, "My aim is to cure. To that end I use whatever method works."

He chose his patients carefully. Nick wanted pliant personalities who would lend their wills to Nick's unorthodox ways. He wanted to experiment and was prepared, if necessary, to fail. "Error," said Nick, "is as important as truth." No one knew of his failures, but Nick's successes were the bright shining stars of the Hollywood firmament.

The Italian stone villa with its great wrought-iron gate imported from Toledo and located on Bellagio, north of Sunset, was a masterpiece of Twenties Hollywood architecture.

A great silent star built it and then committed suicide. A notorious Hollywood madam took it over and gangsters and movie stars shared the beautiful girls. When the madam died, the mansion came on the market, a great white elephant no one in his right mind wanted. It languished until Nick came along and fell in love with it.

Slowly he began the expensive business of restoration. The cracked marble floors were repaired, the dome fixed, the gaudy wallpaper stripped from the walls, the rutted macadam road cemented over. Broken stained-glass windows were replaced, a circular staircase repaired, the man-made lake was drained and fixed. Nick had the interior painted white and filled it with wicker furniture. Once the great musicians had turned their back on Mischa. Now they flocked back, happy to be asked to play. On warm tropical nights Hollywood society drove their Mercedeses to Nick's stark palace to hear quartets.

Nick was a brilliant young doctor who seemed to achieve small miracles. His success and his fame seemed awash over the town. Hostesses plotted, mothers conspired, and beautiful and talented young women turned their arrows in his direction. But Nick was elusive. He had favorites but he didn't seem to fall in love. He didn't want to get married. It became clear after a while. Women came and women went. Only a gorgeous brunette actress named Clair kept hanging around.

"One day," said Clair, "some great sexy bitch is going to spread her legs and catch you."

"Don't talk like a whore."

"Why not?" said Clair. "I get a million dollars a picture to talk like a whore."

Nick laughed.

Clair pulled him over and he kissed her. She felt the kiss in her crotch.

Nick pulled away.

"I thought you liked me," said Clair.

"Sure I like you. But it's very late and I'm tired and I've got a seven-twenty patient."

"You may be Hollywood's great shrink but sometimes you're a shit."

Nick laughed again.

"Call me tomorrow," said Clair.

"I'll call you tomorrow," said Nick. And he did. He called Clair the next morning and he saw her that night and this time they made love. But he didn't fall in love. Not with Clair or the numerous beautiful and intelligent young women that came his way so easily.

JEANNIE
Late 1950s—Early 1960s

Buck Herman stalked his orchestra like a predatory beast. Some of the Titan musicians had abandoned music, others had had nervous breakdowns or took lesser paying jobs. The hard core who stayed on played by Buck's rules. They lost at poker, laughed at Buck's jokes, and found him girls. The orchestra wives faithfully attended old Rose.

It was a well-paid hell on earth. The unions protected the older musicians from the young turks who clamored for the prestigious Herman jobs. Everyone was tough. You had to be tough. Great musicians gave up what they once loved in this conspiracy to survive.

During World War II the men were drafted and Buck, 4F because of a heart murmur, had to hire women. After the war he let them go. The returning veterans reclaimed their seats and once again it was a man's orchestra. Except for a girl Buck met after his last marriage. Four goddamn wives! When Buck thought of what women cost him, he shuddered. What in hell made him do it? He knew, of course: the smoldering eyes, the sighs, the phony orgasms. The cosmic come was his greatest extravagance, and the last bitch he'd married had taken him to the cleaners.

Buck looked out over the orchestra and watched Jeannie in the back of the second section, so goddamn lovely it hurt. He'd take her to that new French restaurant in Malibu tonight and afterward he'd take her home. Whatta talent! It wasn't her lousy vibrato but the way she worked him over—teasing him, tormenting him—just driving him nuts. And when he couldn't take any more—when he was one hundred percent fucked out of his goddamned head, she'd pull out another orgasm. She was a goddamn jockey, racking him up like it was the sweepstakes and the fast money was on him. Well, if you had to meet your maker, *there were worse ways to go.* And that wasn't all. She actually *liked* Rose, so needless to say, Rose adored her. Christ, how Rose hated his wives. Not that he blamed her. They fawned and flattered her like a goddamned queen, but safely married, a diamond on the finger and an annuity for life, they acted like she was low-life, something to put up with on Christmas or for a birthday meal. The last bitch called Rose a spider. It was like a gunshot in his mother's heart. He should have broken her fucking neck. Instead he kicked her out. The thing about Jeannie—the best thing—was, she loved to fuck, and didn't want to get married. *Some girl. Worked all day. Rushed home to change, and it was like she spent the day resting up to make Buck happy. A guy should be so lucky! She must want something. All bitches did.*

"I swear, Buck. I don't want to get married."

"Yeah, yeah."

"I don't. Honey, honest."

"My first wife said that and then she got pregnant. My second was a frigid bitch."

Jeannie wasn't listening. Her mouth was open, her tongue wet and hot on the hood of his cock. He gasped but continued:

"The third had money, the fourth was a cunt."

What a mouth! Like there was no plumbing except for that tongue, and Buck looked down at this beautiful kid giving him the best blow job he'd ever had and said, "You musta learned to give head on the First, Second, and Sixth divisions of the United States armed forces."

She looked up at him with big blue innocent eyes.

"Talk about your wives. I like it."

"They screamed like hell," said Buck. " 'I'm coming!' they'd scream, 'I'm coming—I'm coming!' "

But Jeannie wasn't listening. She was flicking his cock with butterfly kisses and his balls were heavy with come and he turned her over and gave it to her deep and slow and got her wailing like a banshee and he was coming, coming, the come shooting out like a geyser.

Last night's picture of Jeannie giving him the best blow job of his life and the excitement of what she had in store for him tonight was going through Buck's head as he waved the baton. He looked out over at the second section and a smile flickered across his face, and the men in his orchestra, in one body, blessed Jeannie, for Buck seemed finally at peace.

Sunset hit Highway 101 and Buck turned north. He pulled into a parking lot, gave the blond attendant a buck, and took Jeannie's arm. *Some kid.* No babble-babble bullshit. Just that shiksa smile that got him in the *kishkas*. He forgot those bitches he'd married and how they'd bled him dry. Instead he looked into her virginal face masking one hundred percent pure depravity. Outside, gulls were circling. Inside, Buck's heart was pounding. He'd finally found a broad who'd keep him hard the rest of his life. Murder! She leaned forward, smiled, and he smelled Joy, the sweet hot scent she wore between her boobs. Later, she'd undress him—trousers, shirt, socks, and shoes. She'd whisper crude obscenities, and the Joy would fill his lungs.

"Remember, baby. You and me are going to see a lot of each other."

"I know, Buck."

"I'm going to make you so crazy you won't know what hit you."

"Bet you tell that to all your girl friends."

"Since I met you I haven't looked at another dame."

Jeannie was looking across the room at some dark-haired guy with a cane. The guy met her glance, and she smiled like an angel. The guy made an excuse to the dame he was with, and limped to Buck's table. The guy was good-looking—what dames call sensitive—with those soulful gray eyes and curly black hair, but what bothered Buck most was, Jeannie seemed so goddamn happy to see him. The guy was standing at their table, and Jeannie stood up and the guy kissed her. Buck felt a jealous spasm and he knew she had him by the balls. He wanted to kill this gimp kissing Jeannie. She never looked at Buck like that—that gaga look in her eyes like a dame in love.

"Buck," said Jeannie. "This is Nick Kahn. Nick's an old friend of mine from the East. We haven't seen each other for years."

"I know about Buck," Nick said softly. "My father once played in your orchestra. I'm sure you remember him—Mischa Kahn." Then, ignoring Buck completely, Nick turned to Jeannie. "When can I see you?"

"I'm in the Beverly Hills phone book."

"I'll call you tomorrow."

"Swell."

Nick took her hand, held it, then let it go. Buck watched him limp away.

"When he calls, say you're busy."

"Nick's an old friend. I can see my old friends."

"You're one of a few lucky dames who play in a studio orchestra, Jeannie. When I say don't see him, I expect you to dump him."

"You're tough, Buck. You're really tough."

"I know about this guy. He's a hot shot shrink who thinks I'm responsible for an accident his old man once had. Baby, he'll try and hurt us."

"Well, Buck, are you responsible?"

"No. The guy was having a nervous breakdown. Is that my fault?"

Why was he making excuses to a lousy violinist? Because she was queen of the fancy fucks. Even in Hollywood, where fancy fucking was as easy as ordering from a mail-order catalogue, Jeannie made Frederick's of Hollywood seem like Sears.

"Go on," he urged her, "say it. Tell me you won't see this guy again."

"Okay. I won't see him again."

"You won't be sorry, baby, I promise."

They sat in silence. Then Jeannie said:

"You've got a very jealous nature."

"You know why, don't ya, baby? Because you drive me absolutely wild."

Jeannie's absolutely gorgeous smile sent a shiver up Buck's spine. He'd make it up to her. He'd move Chasman out of the first section and he'd move Jeannie in. Chasman would squawk and call her a whore, but so what. Jeannie, playing with the best violinists in town, would be a dumb happy broad who'd never look at another guy. Then, when he worked her out of his system, he'd dump her. Until then she had him by the balls.

Studio jobs were almost impossible for a woman to get, particularly if she had no talent. Jeannie couldn't risk incurring Buck's anger. Working all day, screwing all night, were the exhausting ways she fought the demons that struggled to rule her life.

She was quickly addicting Buck to her ways: long marathon fucks broken by short naps. She'd gotten Buck hooked on what she needed and he thought of himself as Mr. Virility. *She needed Buck for sanity. Of course she'd see Nick, but quietly and on the sly.*

Nick and Jeannie arranged to meet that Sunday afternoon. Jeannie told Buck she was seeing an old girl friend from school.

Sunday, she lay in the bathtub and let the water soothe her body. Not that the irritation was gone. Rather, she had come to accept it, like a genetic defect she must endure. When it got unbearable, she got in her car, drove to a bar, sat with a drink and a cigarette.

It was as simple as:

"Want some company?"

"Be my guest."

"I will. Hey, you're a very pretty lady. I guess you hear that a lot."

"Now and then."

"Well, you are."

"Well, thanks."

Within minutes she'd be fucking a stranger in a strange dark room in a sleazy hotel. Once, she got pregnant. She told Buck the baby was his. After Buck's initial anger, when he saw it wasn't a setup to get married, he drove her to Redondo Beach. He managed to keep his hands off her for a day or so but then he fell on her like a hungry beast. Driving home, she thought about her baby. How a baby would make life normal. How she wanted lots of babies. Babies needed love and care and Jeannie would throw herself into being a mother. When Buck came home at night, she would be tired in a normal way. Who was she kidding? She wanted to be normal more than anything, but she feared she'd never be free of her sickness.

At 3:00 P.M., Jeannie arrived at Nick's. She wore white: a white sweater, white slacks, an ivory bracelet on her arm, every inch of her a white goddess. Bukovsky was a long way off and maybe Nick had forgotten. Nick mustn't suspect anything.

He took her arm but she broke free and flew up the steps. She waltzed from room to room. So much to be fixed, plastered, and painted. The place was like an old whore on her long slide down. Cosmetic improvement couldn't disguise the buckling walls and cracked marble floors and neglect. The greater the wreckage, the greater her joy, as if this derelict mansion symbolized what she was and what she could be. How often she'd wanted to call Nick, but pride, and the feeling she was damaged and beyond repair, certainly beyond love, had stopped her. But Nick loved her once and maybe he could love her again. Oh, if only she were free of the demons that rose up to torture her. Nick would understand. Nick would forgive her. Nick's love. Nick's babies. It was a chance she must take.

Jeannie heard his footsteps and turned toward him. She smiled her loveliest smile and she was more beautiful than ever, all golden and shining blond with her bright blue eyes and small waist and the curve of her shapely long legs beneath her pants, and Nick went toward her and saw in her eyes a shattering cry of *save me* and was helpless. Then she pulled him close and her mouth was like honey and her tongue sent shock waves through his body and Nick was filled with the same old desire.

When she pulled away, she said:

"I shouldn't be kissing you."

"Why not?"

"Because I'm getting married."

Nick hesitated before saying, "You're not marrying that bastard Buck Herman." And not knowing anything more than that he had found her again and he wasn't going to lose her, he pulled her into a kiss that told her what she had to know. When he pulled away, Jeannie knew it was the end of Buck.

"I've got to marry someone," she said.

"I suppose you do."

"Well, who, Nick? Who will I marry?"

"You dumb sweet bitch—you're marrying me."

When she smiled, Nick thought he would faint. He put his arms around her and kissed her as if he were making up for all the loveless fucks and he knew, finally and forever, Jeannie was the love of his life.

More than anything, Buck hated waiting. Especially in public, in La Scala, in his corner booth beneath the porcelain Madonna and the empty Chianti bottles strung out like laundry. Any dame but Jeannie and he'd tell her to take a flying fuck, but Jeannie was ecstasy, so what choice did he have but to sit like a goddamn jerk and wait. He nodded to the studio execs and their flunkies and dames—Christ! She'd fixed it so he couldn't look at anyone else.

She was twenty fucking minutes late. She made him sick. He fingered the box with the diamond ring. It cost him more than he'd ever lost at the track, and he wasn't sure he'd even need it except that jerk Nick made him uneasy. He couldn't afford to lose Jeannie. Buck was sixty-one years old, and while his friends were up to their balls in scrotum crisis, Jeannie was his insurance policy it wouldn't get him.

Twenty-six minutes late and in she walked. *Small tits. Small ass. Murder in the sack. She'd make it up to him with a thousand variations on fellatio, and then he'd give her the goddamn ring.* She was standing there like a goddamn waitress. Why didn't she sit down?

"Where the hell have you been?"

"I've been with Nick. He's asked me to marry him."

"Are you out of your fucking mind?" Buck was playing with the ring. The white bright diamond glistened in his hand. "If you see that cripple again, I'll break your goddamn ass."

"I said yes," said Jeannie. "I said yes, yes! I said yes!"

"You cunt!"

"I guess you can give Chasman back his seat now. I won't need it anymore. Good-bye, Buck."

She walked away, past the crowded red-leather booths full of studio guys watching in rapt fascination, out of La Scala and onto the street. It was dark and empty. She felt like yelling for joy. Nick was in love with her in a way that would only get better. She wanted to scream out "I feel good!" As if it were a national holiday. *If she felt good tonight, she would feel good tomorrow. It would become a habit, feeling good about yourself, feeling someone really loved you for yourself* . . . and out of nowhere the itch curved through her body—ugh! She got into her Porsche and shut her eyes. *What a fool. What a goddamn fool to even hope.* She turned the ignition and drove toward Western—to an anonymous bar, the jazz, a drink, a man, and a moment's relief from her suffering.

A month to the day she asked him to marry her, the *Los Angeles Times* carried an announcement of Jeannie and Nick's marriage. She'd hired a landscape consultant and a team of Japanese gardeners, who crawled about, digging and planting. The rose garden, with more than fifty strains, was equal to the one at Rand's Head. Behind the cottage Nick used as a laboratory, she'd planted a wild English garden, and along the driveway were the bigger pines and conifers, the chaparral and Joshua. In the mornings poppies glowed like fires. Afternoons there was the dizzy light of primrose. She combined cacti and lantana, juniper and jacaranda, and purple wisteria twisted over the house. The artificial lake was restored to its original grandeur and the gazebo replaced with a grandstand like the one of her youth in the town of Oak Bluffs.

After the marriage ceremony everyone came to celebrate. A few wise citizens reflected on this quirk of fate; how an ambitious cripple had gone on to fame and glory, and returned home to steal his boyhood sweetheart from the arms of a hated rival. It was like a fairy tale, the happy ending everyone wants. Everyone came. They danced, drank champagne, and cheered the man who made fairy tales come true.

Nick and Jeannie honeymooned at Rand's Head. The October air was brisk. A warm wind swept off the sound. The gardens burst in a frenzy of color before the winter frost. Nick and Jeannie walked along the beach holding hands.

"Happy?" asked Jeannie.

"Very."

"That's good." She pulled him close and kissed him.

"Not now."

"Don't be a prude."

"Later," said Nick.

"Later's hours away. Nick, it's my honeymoon."

Nick laughed and when she pulled him close he let it happen. He fucked her hard and deep, but it was not what she wanted. She wanted a drill, a striking hammer, an electrical apparatus sinking into her womb. She didn't need him, she needed a machine—ram, ram, ram. Then Jeannie was grinding against him and he burned hot and he thrust. She held him tight and moaned, moans more of pain than pleasure. Pain! When it was over, Nick could hardly bear to look at her face.

A few days later Nick woke up early. It was 6:00 A.M. Jeannie was gone from the bed. Nick put on a bathrobe and went into the kitchen. He made a cup of coffee and drank it. He went out on the balcony. He looked at the sea. It sparkled like diamonds. A hawk circled overhead. There were sparrows in the trees. Nick spotted a blue jay. He spotted a cardinal. Down below he saw two bodies on the ground. A man was on top. He saw a woman's blond curls. They were going at it hard. Nick felt sick. He wanted to scream. He thought of Bukovsky and Buck. He thought of Jeannie burning hot and moaning and the look of pain on her face. He'd called it a dark passion but knew it was worse—much worse. If only he didn't love her so. But he did. He always had. He always would.

He understood why he had resisted calling her when he returned to L.A. A part of him knew she was sick and couldn't accept it. Yet, when he had seen her again, felt her in his arms, seen that cry for help in her eyes—he'd known she needed him. She had known it, too, and came for his protection. He was her only refuge. The one who really loved her. He felt helpless for a moment, all twisted up. He walked away from the railing. He looked out at the sea. He thought of the two Jeannies, the strange sick girl and the laughing and gay nymph. He thought of how she'd helped Mischa. He thought of her sweetness, her kindness. He wasn't sure how long he'd been staring at the sea when Jeannie stood in the doorway.

"Hello, darling," she said cheerfully. "You're up early."

Nick was silent. He was thinking of the lovers, trespassing strangers, and how he'd assumed it was Jeannie. He must be crazy. A curious optimism came over him. Whatever Jeannie's sickness, she was curable.

Jeannie stood at the railing looking at the lovers.

"Look, Nick. We've got company."

"I know."

"They look so happy."

"Jeannie, come here."

She walked toward him. He put his arms around her waist.

"I love you so," he said. "You don't know how much."

She laughed. She seemed so very happy.

Later, that afternoon, Nick said to her: "When we get home I want you to see a doctor."

"You're a doctor."

"I'm your husband."

"Nick, why are you suddenly bringing this up?"

"Do you remember, when I found out about Bukovsky, how you answered me?"

"No."

"You said, 'I'm garbage.' "

"For God's sake, Nick, I was a kid with a crush on my teacher. Please, darling, don't start in on that."

"Jeannie, you've got to trust me."

She was silent. "All right," she said. "If you really want me to, I'll see one."

"Good."

"Nick?"

"What, Jeannie."

"Do you still love me?"

"Of course I love you."

"Then hold me, Nick."

"Oh, baby . . . baby." And Nick took her in his arms and held her like a child.

The great Rand collections were packed, crated, and shipped to California. On their return, Jeannie threw herself into remodeling the house. She talked to architects, and builders. She bossed the workers around. She bargained, haggled, and complained; finally everything was ready. The antique rugs were laid and the priceless treasures released from their crates. Jeannie seemed proud of her glorious home. She seemed, to the world, in charge of her life. She saw a psychiatrist two times a week. She told him about her childhood on the island. She talked about her early isolation. She said she'd had an affair with Bukovsky. She smiled and charmed and stalled. She came in late. She broke appointments. She apologized and said it wouldn't happen again.

Sunday nights, the crème of Hollywood, the men who wrote the checks, and the men who made the movies, sat in the moon-

light under the stars. The music rose into the air. It was perfect;
a life beyond desire; a seeming human paradise.

When her desire got sharp and almost unbearable, Jeannie got
into her car and drove south, past the slums and back streets of
Santa Monica and Venice, the steel rigs and oil fields rising from
the dunes; past Hermosa and Redondo beaches, into the Harbor
district with its freighters and fishing boats. Japanese, Mexican,
and Scandinavian sailors filled the streets and bars. Jeannie
parked and entered Whispering Joe's, or Shanghai Red's, or the
Silver Dollar Saloon. She sat on a barstool nursing a Scotch. She
puffed on a cigarette. In a minute a tall brawny man would come
over. She'd pay for her drink and they'd leave together. They'd
drive over to Mexican Beach or Happy Valley, shantytowns of
shacks where seamen slept between voyages. Hours later, Jeannie
would get into her car and drive home. Within three months of
her marriage, Jeannie was pregnant.

*Whose child was it? Was it Nick's? Or from a faceless and forgot-
ten man she'd picked up in a bar?* Jeannie didn't know. She
couldn't afford to. What counted was, she was pregnant. Growing ugly with a thickened body and swollen feet. Soon she'd have
her baby. When she stopped nursing, she'd get pregnant again.
Poor Nick. Surrounded by kids screaming for attention. She was
five months pregnant. The itch had been quiet for five whole
months. Jeannie finally thought she was safe. Then it struck.
Despite swelling breasts and bulging stomach, she drove to an
anonymous bar. She hated herself for what she was doing. What
she felt herself compelled to do. If Nick knew, he would hate her
too. She felt desperate in keeping his love.

"I wonder how long you'll love me," she said wistfully.

"Try forever."

Jeannie smiled.

"When I'm an old lady, will you love my gray hair?"

"I'll love every wrinkle."

"That's good, darling, because I'm scared of getting old." She
paused. "We're going to have a girl, Nick. I read it in a horoscope.

Nick, darling, let's call her Flame. For Mischa. Mischa would have liked it."

"Flame." Nick took her hand. He looked into her eyes. He reached over and kissed her. "Like her mother. Bright, hot, fierce, and passionate . . ."

"Oh, Nick, I didn't mean it like that."

Nick laughed. "I know how you meant it and I love you for it. Flame. I like it, Jeannie. She'll be Flame."

"Nick?"

"What, darling?"

"Did you really mean it when you said you'll love me when I'm old?"

He laughed, pulled her close, and kissed her.

Momentarily she felt safe. *Pray to God, her baby, all her future babies, would be the cage in which to hide. Let her pound and beat her fists, maternal bondage would protect her from herself.* Yet she feared reality. Submission to strangers in strange rooms, and she hadn't the will to stop it. No loving husband or beloved child could protect her from herself. *She was both prison, and prisoner, and she feared for her life.*

She gorged on food and became obscenely fat. She sat on barstools until her ninth month of pregnancy. She hired a beachboy to fuck her. He was calm and indifferent and good at his job. He never looked at her with pity. She paid him by the week.

Finally it was time. The monotonous throbs became torturous spasms. She yielded to the pain, as though it would cleanse her, blot out her disease. Nick was beside her. She wouldn't let him call the doctor until it was unbearable. He couldn't watch her suffering.

"I'm calling the doctor," Nick finally said.

"Not yet."

"It's time, darling."

Nick made the call and he drove her to the hospital. The moon rose overhead. She howled in pain. The moon went down. Pain seared her. She refused sedation. At 4:00 A.M. the doctor performed a cesarean section and Flame Kahn, six pounds and seven ounces, was pulled from her mother's stomach wailing a great war whoop of life.

A week later Nick brought Jeannie home from the hospital. It was morning. He watched Flame suckle on her mother's breast. Jeannie was radiant. The baby was beautiful, blue-eyed and blond, a perfect miniature of Jeannie. After Jeannie burped Flame, she handed her to Nick.

Nick held the baby. She was so small in his arms, so sweet. Nick made soft whispery sounds. He kissed her. He smelled her skin.

"She's incredible," he said.

"I know."

"She looks just like you."

Jeannie laughed.

Nick made more whispery sounds.

"We have a gorgeous baby."

"I know." She seemed so happy.

Nick handed Flame back to her mother.

"I'll call you later," he said.

"Kiss me, Nick."

Nick leaned over and kissed her. "Good-bye, beautiful." Then he turned and left the room. In a moment the car door slammed and he drove off.

For the first time in her life Jeannie was at peace. Motherhood brought a serenity she had never known. She seemed unable to let go of her baby, waving the nurse away and taking over herself. Nick woke up in the early dawn. Jeannie's side of the bed was empty. He went into the nursery and found her gazing at Flame.

"Shhh," she whispered. "Don't wake her."

She gave him a look of such sweet happiness that Nick dared to believe she was cured. They stood in silence, looking at each other, smiling at the baby. Finally she put the baby in its crib, and hand in hand Nick and Jeannie walked back to their room.

"My sweet angel, Mommy loves you more than anything in the world."

Flame smiled as if she understood every word.

"My Baby. My beautiful child . . ." Holding Flame, cuddling and nuzzling her, Jeannie suddenly felt the itch, moving like quicksilver up her groin and into her womb. Shocked and miserable, she called the nurse. She handed her the baby. She lay on the bed. She felt a low-grade nausea—*fury,* as it took over her body. She lay for hours resisting what she knew was her fate.

By afternoon she was unable to fight its mounting pressure. She got in her car and drove out to Santa Monica. She parked on Ocean Avenue. Her high heels clip-clopped on the cement boardwalk. She passed the pepper and palm trees, the afternoon bathers, assorted lovers, and vagrants sprawled on wooden benches. Ahead, a neon arc sprang into the afternoon sun. It was part of Ocean Park pier with its roller coaster, its shoot-the-chutes, its Ferris wheel tumbling through the sky. Men and women strolled along. Children screamed. Barkers in loud cheap suits yelled out their spiel. "Let Me Call You Sweetheart" floated up from the calliope. The air stank of fried food.

Jeannie's hips locked and unlocked like human machinery. Her ass swung along. She held her breasts high. She felt feverish and hot with sex. Up ahead, a gypsy woman was telling fortunes. The gypsy smiled at Jeannie. She beckoned with her hand. Jeannie gave the gypsy a dollar. The gypsy dealt her a card. The queen of spades—bad luck in love. A shiver went up her spine. The gypsy fingered the card. Her smile was gone. She replaced the card in the deck. She looked out, beyond Jeannie, into the crowd. "Futures," she chanted. "Look into the future for only a dollar."

Jeannie walked to the pier railing. The water was pitch-black. It made smacking sounds against the wooden piles. Catalina glistened in the distance. A small, muscular man with a battered nose and pockmarks on his face came up and stood beside her. His shirt was open. His chest was tattooed with interlocking hearts. One was red and one was black.

"Feel like company?"

"Why not."

"Mind if I smoke?"

"Go ahead."

He put a cigarette in his mouth and lit it. He offered one to her.

"No thanks."

"Feel like a ride?"

"Sure."

"You like the roller coaster?"

"The roller coaster scares me."

"How about the Ferris wheel?"

"Fine with me."

Jeannie smiled. She turned away from the rail and the muscular little man followed behind. He caught up to her and took her hand. At the Ferris wheel he said:

"Got a dollar?"

She took a dollar from her wallet. He bought two tickets. She got into the cage first. In a second he joined her. An attendant bolted the door. He lit another cigarette and puffed. He blew the smoke in her face.

"Don't do that."

"Just teasing."

"I don't like it."

"Okay, I won't tease you anymore."

The car jerked. It began its ascent. He took another puff on the cigarette. He blew a smoke ring that was perfect. He took the cigarette from his mouth, and threw it on the floor and stepped on it. They could see Santa Monica pier in the distance. They could see the whole of the Pacific coast and up to Malibu.

"Good legs," he said.

"Thanks."

"I like good legs."

He put his hand on her knee. She let it rest. He pushed up her skirt and put his hand on her thigh. She let it rest. He slid his hand under her underpants.

"You're wet," he said.

Jeannie was silent.

He fingered her clitoris.

"Tell me you like it," he said.

"It's okay."

"Okay's not an answer."

She was still silent.

"What else do you like?"

"Everything."

His hand left her leg and went to her breast. He squeezed the nipple. She moaned. He leaned over and kissed her hard. He put his hands around her neck.

"Hey, that hurts."

"No kidding."

"Just stop it!"

The cabin was swinging as it approached the top of the arc and began its descent. Jeannie reached up to take his hand from her neck. He sprang up and crouched above her. His hands were still on her throat, but now they were pressing in harder, his fingers like talons digging into the flesh.

"Ouch!" she screamed.

"Yeah," he said, and now his hands yoked onto her neck like a vise and she was choking, and she wanted to cry out but she had no sound, and the pressure of his hands was gagging her, and spit oozed from her mouth and dribbled down her chin, and the gagging, the nausea, the ooze, and his fingers like pincers—a terrible pain crashed in her eardrums.

Her neck was fractured. Her head rolled to the side. She looked like a huge broken doll. The pockmarked stranger listened to the calliope music. He smelled the fresh sea air and the fumes of frying fat. The cabin bounced into place. He reached his hand outside the grate and unbolted the door. He stepped out of the cabin into the crowd.

A laughing couple stepped up to the door.

"I haven't done this since I was a kid," the woman said. She stepped inside. Jeannie's body was slumped against the seat.

"Jesus!" the woman screamed. "There's a *dead thing* in this cage!"

Nick walked through the morgue, that filing cabinet for dead bodies. He watched as the attendant pulled out a drawer. He saw Jeannie, her neck twisted, her face a mess. He remembered how she could turn from a sweet little kitten purring against him to a Jeannie that was wild, bristling, staring at you with ferocious eyes, ready to leap at your face. A wildcat rushing through the streets like a demon who thought only of making love. It was always there, even at the start. Jeannie, in her baggy sweater and jockey cap, strutting toward him, so long ago, on the beach at Martha's Vineyard, and how, in that second, he had fallen in love with that highwire wildcat way that she moved. It came at you in a rush. It was in her smile, her walk, her eyes that could turn in a blink from purring pet to dangerous animal. He knew—had always known. Beneath the mask of sensual abandon was madness, and he wouldn't admit it. *I've helped her destroy herself,* he thought dully, *let her stumble toward death and stood blindly by.* He hated himself at that moment. Then he thought of Flame. No matter who her biological father is, she's my child. I'm her father now. Nick looked at Jeannie's swollen face and his eyes filled with tears. Forgive me, darling. Forgive me. He brushed away the tears and went outside into the sunshine.

Jeannie's murder was front-page news. Reporters bribed the Ferris wheel attendant for any lurid detail. They ripped at the seams of a perfect marriage. They haunted the pier, the bars, the ragtag concessions. No one remembered the lonely woman who drifted in and out of the night. Then the fortune teller came forth. "She picked the queen of spades. She had to die. It was fated." Her prophecy of Jeannie's death got a small headline. After that it was quiet, except for a giggling, gawking crowd who hung around the Ferris wheel, and soon got bored and disappeared.

BOOK FOUR

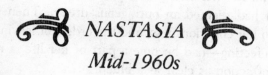

NASTASIA
Mid-1960s

Nastasia Rostov opened her eyes. Sunlight streamed into the room. For a moment she was happy, lulled into a sense of peace and security. She stretched out her long, lean, graceful body. As she lay there, feeling the sun, feeling alive, the precariousness of her situation was blotted out.

Then the first strong wave of morning nausea swept through her. She jumped from bed and ran to the bathroom. A faint stench of stale urine and disinfectant rose from the cracked enamel basin. *Did they never clean these awful toilets?* She stuck her finger into her throat. A thin white mucus discharge burst forth. She showered, dried herself, and returned to bed.

The Roosevelt Hotel, Hollywood, California. America.

A double bed, a cheap mahogany dresser with tarnished pulls, a rutted night table with an orange lamp, a framed Cézanne print of oranges, a Bible, a flowered rug; timeless dirt pressed into the pattern of a rose.

She closed her eyes. *It was not enough to be strong. She must have audacity and courage. Her plans were contingent upon it.*

Her thoughts drifted to last night's performance, her solo appearance at the Greek Theatre. How she had danced the pas de trois, not a strenuous piece, thank God, and how later Suvorin had come to her room and they had made the kind of love that sated and satisfied him. And how, finally, he had returned to his own bed just down the hall. Now, with just a few hours sleep, she must muster her energy and proceed with her plan.

Once it had seemed an outrageous dream. Then it had fastened onto her consciousness, and the ordeal of leaving Russia—bolting, defecting—had become a part of her life, a reality, and her plan of action as clear as a blueprint.

Nastasia was thirty years old. Another few years and she would be retired. She was obsessed with time, each day dragging her closer to that moment when her legs, so strong and reliable, would falter, and her dreams, her hopes and desires, would be wrenched away. She would be put on a small pension, or teach at the academy: training the new young dancers who sprang up like wild flowers. She would guide the strong young undisciplined bodies of other women's children when all her hopes were of having a child of her own. It would happen, but it must happen outside Russia, for Nastasia was not a true Russian, nor had she ever been. Her mother was a Jew.

Once she was out of Russia, the years of grinding effort would pass to her unborn child. She prayed for a girl—a future Anna Pavlova. Her Anna would be an offering to art, her life a life of discipline, of sacrifice; of total dedication to ballet. The ballet demanded a slavish devotion. The child within her body would electrify the world.

Nastasia had seen her first ballet at eight and from that moment on she wanted only to dance. At ten she was accepted at the Marinova school, a part of the Kirov Theater, in Leningrad. The years passed quickly. Upon graduation she was chosen for the Kirov corps. She graduated to small parts as a secondary principal.

Nastasia was a fanatic. She was merciless with herself, suffering any physical pain to prepare for the great parts, falling into bed at night like a wounded beast. Nothing mattered but body control, a mastery of movement, and technique. Her body ached and rebelled, but she kept on. *Dance was her life.* She was driven by an ambition that bordered on insanity.

The head of the Kirov corps was a former party official named Suvorin. Suvorin had had his eye on her since she entered the corps. She was a perfect Kirov ballerina, with a superb bearing and brilliant technique. She seemed to welcome physical pain, if only to overcome it. *She is an iron maiden,* he thought, and he was blind to everything except her sultry good looks and her dogged dedication to dance. It was inevitable that the iron maiden would become Suvorin's mistress. Her passion matched her beauty; she scratched and tore his flesh, and it was like a riptide tearing through him toward a furious orgasm.

He rewarded Nastasia with an occasional lead: Giselle, Cinderella, the Spectre de la Rose. But more important, Suvorin moved Nastasia from the noisy communal closet where she washed her feet in a washtub to a small comfortable room on Moika Street, not far from his place on the Fontanka Embankment. Privacy, bathing facilities, nylon stockings, jazz records, pretty shoes: Nastasia enjoyed all the luxuries her colleagues were denied. They smiled to her face. Behind her back they cursed her. *Who cared for their curses! As long as Suvorin was her lover she was safe.*

She was his lover for seven years. Her tireless and inventive lovemaking kept him faithful, and yearning for more. He came to her room three or four times a week. Afterward, more dead than alive, he dressed and returned to his wife and three children.

Alone in her room, she picked up a framed picture of Pavlova she kept beside the bed. She pressed the picture to her heart. She thought about the passing years, and shuddered. She knew—indeed had always known—no matter her self-discipline and drive for perfection, she would never leap into the air and hang there, never transcend space. She was a technician, on occasion brilliant, but that was all. *The miracle of genius was denied her. She would never fly.* She thought about the forthcoming tour to America. She would go, as always, because Suvorin was addicted to her lovemaking. And as she lay there, Pavlova's picture upon her breast, her future sprang before her in a big bold flash.

Andreyev!

The first time she had watched him dance was two years earlier at the graduation recital at the academy. *He flies!* she thought excitedly. *God flies through his body!*

From that time on, Andreyev felt her approving eye. He was flattered by her silent admiration. Her smile, her eyes, her startling beauty, seemed to tell him what he already knew; that he was half man, half bird. He didn't know he was flying; he just flew, shot up, lingered in the air, and landed in a perfect jeté. He flew higher and higher. Nastasia trembled. Her eyes sparkled. Her mouth sent him silent kisses.

The party officials cheered their brilliant virtuoso; all but Director Suvorin. Without understanding why, he felt threatened. He never mentioned it to Nastasia for fear she would laugh, but it was there, unwarranted and mysterious, a tense, hard band around his heart. He decided to have Andreyev watched.

He studied the weekly report on the prodigious dancer. The man was like a rabbit. Before rehearsals, after rehearsals, he flew from bed to bed. Bang! Bang! Bang! A human firecracker.

Suvorin despised himself for his jealousy, yet it was there, painful and humiliating, an obsession. His mind said *You're a fool, Suvorin,* and his heart replied, *A man in love's a fool.* So his watch over the dancing prodigy continued.

Nastasia was cautious. She never spoke to or danced with Andreyev, but he was always in her thoughts. He was erotic and sensual, losing himself in each part. He was all the great romantic heroes—Siegfried, Romeo, Petrouchka. She watched him leap and flash upward. She watched him float through the air and fly, and return to earth, to the fifth-floor studio of the Kirov, to Rossi Street—*and she knew! God danced through Andreyev and God would dance through her. Through Andreyev's sperm, God would dance through her unborn child.*

It would happen in America!

Suvorin was occupied with his official party meetings before the American tour, so Nastasia enjoyed a sudden freedom. *She must act at once.*

Rehearsals ended at five o'clock, and Andreyev walked down Rossi Street, his arm around a pretty ballerina. Nastasia approached him from the Nevsky Prospekt. She accidentally dropped her purse. He knelt and helped her collect her things. When he handed them to her, she slipped a note into his palm. Nastasia thanked him and hurried on. Andreyev put the folded paper in his pocket. He put his arm on the ballerina's shoulder.

"The Iron Maiden is flirting with you. Be careful, Andreyev."

"Don't be silly."

"She was flirting, Andreyev. That's the oldest trick in the world."

"Everyone flirts with me, including you." And he hugged the girl close and smiled so sweetly she forgot everything but his charm. *But Andreyev understood. The Iron Maiden had beckoned. It was impossible. Unthinkable. A terrible, ridiculous risk. The Iron Maiden belonged to Suvorin. He would read her note and destroy it. But he felt a delicious thrill.*

At Nevsky Prospekt he kissed the dancer good-bye and promised to see her that night. He watched her walk away. He pulled Nastasia's note from his pocket. *I live at 28 Moika. Come tonight at 7 o'clock. I will expect you.* He laughed, whistled a tune from *Petrouchka,* and thought about the great night ahead.

Nastasia's room, overlooking the Neva River, was comfortably fitted with a wardrobe, a bed, two straight-backed chairs, a small table, and a naked figure in bronze—a gift from Suvorin that pleased his voluptuous taste. A Sinatra record was on the phonograph.

"Women love Sinatra," said Andreyev. "He makes them feel romantic. I personally think Sinatra is overrated, but I understand how Sinatra makes women feel."

"Do you like jazz?" Nastasia asked.

"Outside of Sinatra, yes. Every spare ruble goes to my collection."

". . . Lover, I surrender . . ." Sinatra moaned.

"Rodgers and Hart. I've got Ella Fitzgerald's recording."

Nastasia came close to him. "We're safe," she whispered, "I hope you're not worried." He smiled so charmingly, she saw he was fearless.

"You have as much to lose as I do."

"I have much more to lose, I assure you."

"Then we're both safe." Andreyev paused. "I've waited for you a long time."

That was when she pressed her soft full mouth on his. They threw off their clothes and fell onto the bed. Her wet tongue, her hot kisses, the fit of her body, the way she clasped his cock in her womb; her sighs, her sharp cries, her trembling groin . . . Andreyev shivered, convulsed, and climaxed. Moments later he was sleeping like a child on her breast.

Then suddenly Nastasia was shaking him and pushing him away. She stood up. She picked up his clothes and handed them to him.

"Quickly. Before it's too late. Get dressed." Her voice was icy and detached.

"One more kiss, Nastasia, then I'll go."

"You'll come back soon. I'll kiss you then."

He reached to embrace her, but she pushed him away.

"Are you deaf? I said no. Now, go. Get out of here fast."

"I'm wondering," said Andreyev, "why you wanted me."

Nastasia smiled strangely. "You dance like a god. I wanted to know if you fuck like one too."

"Well?" he asked.

"I just told you. You dance like a god."

Nastasia didn't want to hurt Andreyev, but it was the only way. She turned her back on him. "Please go," she said. "Leave me alone." The door slammed behind him. Alone! She shut her eyes and wept.

Andreyev bounded down the steps. He turned from Moika onto Truda Square. He was angry and confused, unaware of footsteps behind him. *How he hated the teasing bitch! She was an Iron Maiden—inside and out. She would never be a great dancer— she was cold. A frigid cunt giving a performance of love. If she wasn't Suvorin's mistress, he would fuck her like a dog. That's all she deserved. Well, Suvorin was welcome to her. Wait! He wasn't through with the bitch. He'd get her so jealous, she'd be climbing the walls.* The cold night air stung Andreyev's cheek, but he felt only the sting of hurt pride. He hailed a taxi and climbed in. Minutes later he collapsed on his bed. He couldn't sleep. He spent the night raging against Nastasia and plotting a ridiculous romantic revenge.

Suvorin watched his mistress with cruel, sensual eyes.

"Don't lie to me, Nastasia. For God's sake, spare me your hysterical hypocrisy."

"I'm not lying. I swear I'm not. I heard a knock on the door and when I opened it Andreyev pushed his way in. I told him to leave. He said I was the only one who could help him, that I must convince you to let him come to America. I said I had no influence with you. He called me a liar. It was awful! I told him to go or I would report him. That's when he left. Suvorin, please, you've got to believe me!" She clung to his jacket and he could feel the curve of her breast through the fabric and he thought of her hardening nipples and the wet between her legs and he knew he was helpless before her heat.

"In the old days I would have you whipped," said Suvorin. "I would have you on the floor, at my feet, begging for mercy! You know I should cancel your tour as discipline."

But she was sliding down his pants leg and she was on her knees, unbuckling his belt, and her mouth, her wild wet tongue, was taking his cock and her hand was fondling his balls. And now her mouth, which knew his every crazy taste, was ruthlessly rousing him to a state of swoon, and he knew he had no choice. If he canceled her tour to America, he would deprive himself of an addictive pleasure, and he had gone through a great many women before finding one wanton as her. *Her real punishment would wait. Meanwhile, the pig Andreyev would be removed from the company and sent to Siberia. Let him dance on the icy steppes. Andreyev was finished. He would never dance to the great audiences or be heard of again.* Suvorin smiled bleakly.

"Forgive me, Suvorin. Forgive your Nastasia."

"You said I had nothing to forgive."

"Nothing. Nothing. But when I cause you pain, I deserve . . ."

"What does my frivolous Iron Maiden deserve? Tell your Suvorin."

"She deserves whatever her beloved wishes her to have."

And moving against him, took him long and deep and effortlessly into her mouth and into her throat, into a state of sublime excitement. If she had had the same enchanted gift in a tutu and toe shoes, she would have been a brilliant star.

Her ambitious plan demanded a disciplined body. It demanded the miracle of a pregnant woman dancing like a girl. Nastasia willed away all self-pity. She suffered the nausea and the pain. "I am in charge of my body. I won't permit it to take me over," she repeated again and again. She kept her weight to its chiseled leanness, continued her hectic schedule, and responded to Suvorin with an even greater ardor.

The moment had come.

She was in Hollywood, in America, in this nondescript room, the only unshared room in the troupe, and she prayed for strength. *Nastasia would finally be free—free of Suvorin, free of the party, free to raise her child as a great international dancer who would bring the world to its knees.*

She quickly dressed in a simple beige suit. She opened her purse and took out a wallet. She put it in a jacket pocket. She locked the door behind her and pushed the elevator button. She stepped inside. There was another passenger. She looked through him as though he were a stranger, but she thought, *He is KGB.* In the coffee shop he sat opposite her table. She caught his eye and smiled. He avoided her glance and sipped his coffee. He *was* one of them. She ordered toast and coffee. She sipped the coffee and opened her purse. "My wallet . . ." she murmured. She left her purse on the table and walked into the front hall.

Except for the pimpled desk clerk, it was empty. She sauntered to the front door as though to get a breath of fresh air. She saw a taxi approach. She moved quickly to the curb and ran toward it. She got inside. She looked through the window and saw the KGB agent waving her purse.

"Police!" she said excitedly. "Police!"

The taxi driver looked through his rearview mirror at the beautiful hysterical woman. She must be in some kind of trouble. He saw the man waving her purse and urging him to stop. He put his foot on the gas and zoomed off. Minutes later he pulled up to the Hollywood police station. The woman opened the door and ran up the steps of the white granite building. A uniformed cop was sitting at the desk. She looked back behind her. Through the open doorway she saw another taxi stopping.

"Nastasia Rostov. Kirov Ballet. I am pregnant. I want baby in America," she said in the few phrases she had memorized.

Within hours she was granted asylum.

The Kirov played to a frenzied roaring crowd. After the performance the dancers climbed into the bus and were driven back to the hotel. They spoke of Nastasia's defection.

Suvorin had written her a letter begging her to return. His letter went unanswered.

The next morning her story was on the front page of the *Express*. It read:

U.S. GRANTS ASYLUM TO PREGNANT RUSSKIE DANCER

Her statement to the press was read to Suvorin. "I want to have my baby in a free country."

Nastasia pregnant! Impossible! She was rehearsing and dancing until the moment they left Russia. She had danced the night before her defection! *It made no sense—none of it.* Then, slowly, the memory of that clandestine meeting between Nastasia and Andreyev flashed through his mind. He thought about Nastasia's ruthless ambition, and the way she had used him to advance her career. He remembered how she had whispered in his ear so many years ago, "Ah, Suvorin, if it is not to be me, then God grant me a child who will dance like Pavlova." And how he had answered, "You know I'm a married man. You know the party frowns on divorce," and how she had smiled so adoringly and said, "Forgive me, Suvorin. Sometimes I am unrealistic," and kissed away his fears. The pieces of the puzzle snapped together. *He had been blind! An imbecile! In her private room she had betrayed him, played him for a fool.*

The seriousness of his situation terrified him. How the party powers would respond when they were told Suvorin's Jewish girl friend had used him to defect. God almighty! They would throw him out like garbage. Banish him, along with Andreyev, to some remote Siberian gulag. Ignominy, ruin, and defeat lay ahead. Suvorin groaned. "God," he sobbed, "how can I bear it?" Then, wrenching free of his pain, he cried, "I curse you, Nastasia Rostov! I curse your unknown bastard child! I pray hell's furies rule its wretched life. For the rest of your life, may you know only suffering and grief!" and he fell on the bed and cried bitter tears.

Nastasia knew her pregnancy prevented any offers of work from the major ballet companies, but her instant celebrity assured her well-wishers and friends. She had no money, no possessions, no immediate hope of work, but she was not frightened. She had herself, her ruthless ambition, and an indomitable faith.

In the sixties, Americans turned to the Pill, nudity, and a drug culture that included excessive hair, communes, and free love. War polarized the country. There were ghetto disorders, campus rioting, and political assassination. A theological debate on God raged on—and *Time* magazine, on its cover, asked, "Is God Dead?"

"God is not dead!" murmured Prince Ivanov. *"God is restless, but He is certainly not dead."* His thoughts, of late, had been of Russia. Tsarist Russia. He thought of his first cousin, the pretty princess, and of the days when they stole kisses in the Church of the Resurrection, on the spot where Tsar Alexander was assassinated by the nihilists. What naughty children. The little princess would steal away to meet her favorite playmate and the two of

them would take a troika and the driver, in his heavy wadded gown, would whip the horses at great speed through the raw damp streets. They would stop to buy kvass from a street vendor, or a pastry called pirogi. Everyone was in a uniform: military officers, students, policemen, yard porters in short fur coats. Even the wet nurses wore bright costumes, blue gowns for boys and pink for girls.

The prince remembered the Kazan Cathedral where the royal family prayed, the kneeling communicants and the blazing candles and golden icons. The struggle for Russia's soul had not yet been fought, and the tsar was Russia's sovereign ruler. The Winter Palace burst with light, and on the nights of the great balls there were bewitching beautiful women, army officers in braided uniforms, princes, princesses, ladies-in-waiting, and scarlet-liveried footmen rushing about thick as bugs.

He remembered the eve of the revolution, and how he had sewn his jewels into the lining of his clothes and escaped from St. Petersburg, going from Finland to Shanghai, and finally to America. Before the revolution a handful of tsarist aristocracy had found refuge in Los Angeles, and Ivanov's good friend Prince Mdivani, once married to Pola Negri, wrote to Ivanov urging him to come west:

I am surrounded by self-styled imposters. They call themselves Georgian princes and have descended on Hollywood like locusts. The rich society women are crazy for titles—and "Georgian prince" has become synonymous with gigolo. Believe me, a real prince is treated like glittering royalty. There are so few of us in Hollywood. I need a friend. Come!

Prince Ivanov was gentle and dumb and beautiful. He spoke no English, but he looked glorious in a uniform. He found work as an extra in the extravaganza crowd scenes. One by one he sold his jewels. Rich women bargained for his treasures and he parted with them for a fraction of their worth. He had married a pretty actress, but she had died young.

When Prince Ivanov saw Nastasia on the evening TV news, he

longed to recapture the past. Nastasia was all he had lost, St. Petersburg, the glorious ballet. He called the television station and tracked her down.

So Nastasia found herself with an aging patron.

Prince Ivanov sold the last of his jewels. He rented a studio for Nastasia on Highland Avenue, a long room with floor-to-floor mirrors, an upright piano, a barre, and some wooden chairs. There were two smaller rooms and a kitchen. He bought a crib for the baby, and a bed and dresser for Nastasia. He framed a picture of Pavlova and hung it over the bed.

"You're a gift from God!" Nastasia cried happily.

"And you're my past—Petersburg, my youth . . . all I loved and held dear."

"I'll do everything I can to bring Russian ballet to America. And when Anna is born—yes, her name will be Anna—I will train new teachers before I resume my career."

The prince knew it was only the very great dancers who were invited into the good American ballet companies—that secondary dancers like Nastasia were doomed to a nondescript life of teaching or dancing in some Broadway road show, or vanished into a second-rate troupe, address unknown. But he was silent and Nastasia dreamed on.

About six weeks later, the Rostov School of Classical Ballet opened, and snobbish mothers from Pasadena to the Palisades rushed their daughters to Hollywood. Nastasia's school was based on a learning process combining dance technique with emotional motivation. It was part of the great ballet tradition and required a slavish dedication: *Dance is life, the very reason for existence. One lives only to dance, and life must be Spartan, and monastic.*

Nastasia wanted strong, supple bodies. She insisted her students restrict their diets to fish, chicken, and vegetables. She drilled them like a sergeant, walking back and forth, chanting, *"Elevez, s'il vous plaît! Elevez, élevez!"* She kneeled to correct a badly placed foot, clapped her hands in horror at an arm askew, and woe unto the hapless victim whose body refused to respond to the classical pose. She criticized and corrected, with never a smile or encouraging word. Just the strict old-fashioned ways she thought the only method of teaching classical ballet.

Within months, Nastasia despised these spoiled daughters of the rich whose main concern was popularity and a year-round tan. But if she hated these frivolous brats, they despised the Iron Mistress even more. The excitement of studying with a real Russian ballerina had become a nightmare. The girls begged their mothers to stop the hateful lessons.

"Your ways are old-fashioned, Nastasia," said Prince Ivanov. "These are modern American girls."

"Are you saying Russian ballet is old-fashioned? You should be ashamed."

"When you were young, ballet was art. One lived to serve art. It is different here."

"I was a fool to have left Russia. God is punishing me for my arrogance. Yes, Prince, this sad and lonely life is my punishment."

"You wanted Anna to be born free. You believed in the future. That's why you left Russia."

Ivanov took a handkerchief from his pocket and wiped away her tears. "Little Anna will dance and the world will forget, for an hour, the sadness of life."

"Oh, Prince!" Nastasia threw her arms around her benefactor, and in her shining eyes he once again saw hope.

Nastasia's celebrity was short-lived. She studied English at night. She ate with the prince. She sat at the window dreaming of the future. There was the glare of the sun, the sprawl of cars. A gray peeling yucca faced her window, the palm fronds drooping like wings of the swan—*The Dying Swan.* How she had yearned to dance it. She mastered the thirty-two fouettés, the high-speed turns, cut through the air like a knife, but the soaring emotion of the swan was not hers. *One day her Anna would soar up and hang, weightless, before sinking to the ground. One day the emotional charge of that moment would bring an audience to its feet—a thousand cheering fans.* It was this vision of Anna's future that kept Nastasia sane.

When Nastasia was in her eighth month of pregnancy, the Rostov School was unofficially closed. The class gave a sigh of relief. The Iron Maiden would have her baby, and they would be free. They would never come back. Only a handful of girls shared Nastasia's vision and waited impatiently for the moment they could resume their great work.

After a long, painful labor, a baby girl was born. Nastasia held little Anna to her breast. How she loved this baby with its dark eyes and coppery hair and skin the color of ivory! Anna smiled and Nastasia's cold heart thawed.

"You are more beautiful than I even dared to hope." She whispered to her baby. "God danced through your father and God, one day, will dance through you. I swear it, little Anna, I swear, on my life, it will be."

Nastasia reopened her school to a zealous few. Determined to turn them into dancers, she insisted they forgo junk food, build a barre on some unused wall at home, and practice. They must think ballet, talk ballet, see ballet. When a dance company came to Los Angeles, she took her brood of girls to see it. These were the future American ballerinas.

Baby Anna was a miracle of beauty. One year old and her legs were already shapely, her skin flawless, eyes so deep, you were caught in their depths. Nastasia hugged her baby close. She loved her Anna with so fierce an intensity it almost frightened her.

But mother love was for ordinary women with ordinary children. Her Anna was predestined to be a great dancer. She had sacrificed two men, Andreyev and Suvorin, to this vision of immortality. Now she must sacrifice herself.

She must deaden maternal feeling and when it appeared, pluck it out like a flower of evil. Love made a woman sentimental. It softened her. Anna would be raised in the tradition of the great Russian ballerinas, weaned and separated from a normal childhood. It would be hard to accomplish in America, but it was not impossible. With a ruthless discipline it could be had.

Nastasia knelt beside Anna's crib. Anna smiled at her pretty mother. Nastasia picked her baby up and covered her with kisses.

"Beloved Anitchka. After today you will have no mother to hug and hold you and comfort you with kisses. I am no longer your mother, my child. From this day forward, I am Madame."

It was such a loveless and bleak decision, the Iron Maiden wept tears of anguish. But she was strong. She had vowed her Anna would be a very great dancer. To that end she must renounce the normal joy of mother love.

Nastasia returned Anna to her crib. She looked into her dark and wonderful eyes. She called upon some higher power to provide the strength to keep her to her goal.

ANNA
1970s

There is no seasonal clock in southern California. Weeks became months and months years, and Anna was suddenly five years old. Nastasia started her at the barre. Anna learned the rudimentary exercises. Her legs grew strong. Her posture and control were amazing. When Anna was eight, Nastasia put her on toe. Now she could pirouette and do glissades and leap through the air in a sissonne and jump and beat her calves in an entrechat. Nastasia led her from entrechat one, a beating of the calves, to entrechat seven, the finishing position.

Even in sleep Anna heard the voice.

Point your toe! Watch your arm. Your hand, Anna. You're not listening to me. That critical voice demanding more of her body than it could give. She felt helpless before Madame's insistence on perfection.

She was not allowed to call her "Mommy." Nastasia was Madame. And what Madame wanted was law. Madame permitted no cookies, no candy or ice cream. Madame permitted no friends. No pets. No eating between meals. Food was so boring; boiled chicken or fish and a green and yellow vegetable. A potato every other day. After school Anna came directly home. She worked at the barre until Madame was satisfied. Then there was the stick.

"Raise your leg, higher, Anna."

"Yes, Madame."

"Your arm is crooked."

"Yes, Madame."

"Watch your foot."

"Yes, Madame."

"You dance from your feet," Nastasia criticized. "You must dance from your soul."

"I try."

"Try! You must feel. You must be. A beautiful bird that flies through the air."

A bird! Madame was crazy. Why didn't she understand she was just a girl who wanted friends and affection?

"You're not listening to me. You're daydreaming."

And day after day, the anger, criticism, the sharp sting of the stick on her leg. How she hated Madame. How she hated Madame's stick and her droning voice. But she couldn't cry. Ballerinas didn't cry. Madame's disgust with her when she cried was even worse than the stick. Anna looked at the shabby room, its paint peeling and pipes exposed, the upright little piano with its broken keys. She felt chained to a terrible life and a cold, unloving mother. No matter how hard she tried, she could never satisfy Madame. Her entrechats were never fast enough or clean enough. Her jumps never high enough.

"Owww," screamed Anna one awful afternoon.

"Ballerinas do not cry," Madame said coldly. "Wipe away your tears and we will start again."

"Yes, Madame." She sank into a plié. She rose into the air. She fell into place. She felt the stick snap against her leg.

"Try it again."

Another plié, another jump, another tingle of the stick.

Finally, Anna's body responded and Madame was satisfied.

In her cage on Highland Avenue the years passed quickly. At age thirteen Anna looked into the mirror. Reflected back was the face of a sad but beautiful young woman. She felt so hopeless now. If it weren't for her friend, the prince, life would be unbearable.

"She wants me to fly," Anna told him. "As though I had wings. I don't. I've got arms and legs like everyone else, and she beats me for it every day of my life."

"I'll talk to her, Anna. Perhaps I can make her understand."

"She won't listen to you."

"Nastasia's a difficult woman, but try to understand, she is guided by a dream."

"I hate it. It means I'm lonely and always being punished. Oh, Prince, she hates me so much."

"Nastasia's ways are old-fashioned, but she's your mother and she loves you."

"She doesn't!"

"I swear she loves you. I'll talk to her, Anna."

"If she loves me, ask her for a puppy. Tell her I won't be lonely with a pet, my own dog."

"I'll tell Nastasia it's important."

"Prince?"

"Yes, Anna darling."

"If she loves me she would cook me fried chicken . . . oh, not often, just once in a while."

"I'll tell her about the fried chicken."

"And ice cream. Just on Sunday."

"Ice cream on Sunday. Anything else?"

Anna was silent.

"Tell me, Anitchka. What are you thinking?"

"I was thinking that even if she buys me a dog, or lets me eat ice cream, I'll never be great. I won't, Prince, I won't, never, ever, as long as I live."

The prince took Nastasia for dinner at the Samovar, a favorite Russian restaurant. In the candle-lit room they faced one another.

"Buy her a dog," said the prince. "It would mean so much to her."

"What else does she want?"

"Fried chicken, occasionally. Ice cream."

"I cannot believe you, who know the ways of the classic ballet, are listening to a child."

"She's a human being."

"No," Nastasia said firmly. "She's a dancer, and a dancer sacrifices many things for her art."

"And this is not Petersburg and Anna is not Pavlova."

"The girl is skilled. Her body is supple and well trained but she is earthbound."

"You are too ambitious, Nastasia. Your ambition is dangerous. It is turning you into a shrew. It will destroy both you and your child."

"You dare to talk to me of ambition." Nastasia's voice was ice. "This child is the altar at which I sacrifice my life. She is the flame I place before God. Don't call it ambition, Prince, for God's sake."

But the prince understood this foolish, proud woman was caught in a tragic vision of immortality. Dance was God and Anna her sacrifice. She was like a religious fanatic and he dreaded the day when Anna would have enough of her and rebel.

The prince was old and frail, but he knew one day Anna would need him and he sought the strength to go on. He must live, find the strength, for his darling Anna's sake.

The prince's death was swift and unexpected. The candles burned in the chapel of the Russian Orthodox Church of the Holy Virgin Mary. A few decrepit survivors of the once glamorous Russian movie colony came to mourn. Among them the ambitious ballerina and her lovely daughter.

Nastasia sobbed in grief.

Anna yearned to put her arms around her mother, to comfort and hold her close. But Madame would surely repulse her. A rigid discipline, the stick, a vision of Anna dancing to a cheering crowd. That was Madame's love. Madame didn't love *her*. She loved the crowd leaping to its feet. Anna was her stand-in. Her legs a substitute for Madame's. Madame didn't want Anna to fly. Madame wanted to fly through Anna.

In the darkness of the chapel, the candles flickering low, the incense rising, Anna wept for the prince. A longing for love filled her heart. Longing and loneliness were a part of her life. They stole over her in sleep and in dreams. Anna glanced at Madame. Madame was crying. She was human, after all.

Anna closed her eyes and prayed:

"Please, God, send someone to love me and I promise, I'll forgive her."

To show God she was serious, she reached over and touched Madame's hand.

"Look, God, I forgive her!"

Nastasia's heart leapt with joy. In a church, facing death, Anna understood her great sacrifice.

Nastasia did not understand that Anna was consumed by a passion far more powerful than ambition. Anna longed for love and love ruled the whole of her heart.

And so, in the decaying splendor of the old Orthodox church, amid the icons and the massive gold cross, the last Russian prince lay at rest in a simple pine coffin.

A mother prayed for art.

Her daughter prayed for love.

A period in time was over.

Nastasia's rent was overdue. She had money for only the barest of necessities. She was desperate when she read in the newspaper that Antonio, the great flamenco dancer, was performing at the Hollywood Bowl. What insane impulse directed her to the box office she never knew, but that Sunday night, Nastasia and Anna sat high on a hill overlooking the crowd. The stage was dark. Then the trill of a guitar, and Antonio, in a tight black suit and tipped black hat, and his partner, in a black dress wearing her hair in a bun, moved into the spotlight. Their bodies were steel. They beat their heels on the wooden floor; they clicked the castanets; they advanced, retreated, twirled around one another; they swooped through the air as if they were shot out of an Andalusian cave. Antonio's rigid body defied gravity. He stamped. He yelled. He hurtled through space.

The crowd reeled. It was drunk. It threw flowers and screamed: *"bravo."* It was delirious and frenzied. Nastasia turned her head and watched Anna, breathtakingly lovely, and she thought, *This girl will take a crowd to the same drugged state.*

In certain moments human beings believe they can accomplish anything. Hours earlier, Nastasia was hungry and without hope. Now she watched the crowd and believed the world was hers.

Tonight the crowd belonged to Antonio.

Tomorrow it was Anna's!

The next morning Nastasia withdrew the last of their meager savings. She bought castanets and a tight-fitting black dress. She went to the library. She bought Carlos Montoya's records. Working from flamenco rhythms, books, and instruction as well as her imagination, she combined ballet movement with the harsh staccato of flamenco.

Nastasia got a job as a part-time instructor of ballet in one of the proliferating schools. She relaxed her teaching methods. What was crucial was money for food and rent. She pulled Anna out of school. She drilled her all day and into the night. Always a perfectionist, Nastasia flicked her switch and Anna stretched her lovely body and clicked the castanets and her heels crackled like a volley of bullets, but it was never good enough.

"Again," cried an exasperated Nastasia.

"No more. I'm too tired," said a weary Anna.

"I said again."

"I can't. I won't do it. I can't."

Nastasia walked toward Anna. She reached back her hand and landed a blow on Anna's face.

"Listen closely," she said intently. "It's time you understood. Once I saw that my career in Russia was restricted to second-rate parts, I made a decision. I would have a child. That child would have all the opportunity denied me. Nothing and no one would stop me." She paused. "I sacrificed two men. One was a party official, a functionary and unimportant in the history of ballet. The other was your father." She paused again. "You have asked me so often who your father was and I replied, 'A dancer who wouldn't defect,' and refused to discuss it further. Now I'll tell you."

Anna stood still and silent. She watched Nastasia closely. Nastasia was suddenly no longer the hateful Madame but a woman responsible for her fate. It was the closest she had ever come to feeling she had a mother.

"Who?" she said softly. "Who is my father?"

"Andreyev." Nastasia spoke with deadly calm. "The greatest dancer in the world. I sacrificed his life for yours. His career for yours. If I stopped now, before you danced for the world, it would be a crime against his genius . . . and my sacrifice would be for the devil."

"You're crazy!" screamed Anna.

In a fury, Nastasia lifted her switch and struck her.

"Don't call me that . . . ever!"

She shut her eyes and took a deep breath.

"All right," Madame said slowly. "We'll start again. And when we finish you will dance like a gypsy who has grown up dancing by the light of the camp fire."

Nastasia searched the town. She found a small Mexican night-club on Western Avenue called the Agua Caliente. The owner took one look at Anna and agreed to an audition. He sat in the dark and sucked his cigar and watched Anna roll her hips and wail. The kid was a knockout. He remembered seeing the Russian dame on television years ago. Now she was peddling her kid like a thousand Hollywood mothers. Life was sure funny.

When the kid stopped dancing, the owner said, "Your girl's got talent. I like her."

"Then you'll give her a job."

"Like I say, she's a talented kid, but there are laws in this state

against employing a minor. So you see, it's a risky proposition."
He paused. "Look, I'm going to take a chance."

"You will not be sorry. I promise you."

"Suppose I give you ten dollars a night."

"Ten dollars! That's an outrage."

"Like I say, Madame Rostov, the girl's a minor. If John Law
gets wind of what I'm up to . . ." The fat owner puffed on his
cigar. He smiled. "All right, I'll go for fifteen. Fifteen dollars a
night."

Now Nastasia smiled. "I speak poor English so you think I am
a fool. I am not a fool, señor."

"No one said you were. All I know is, I could lose my license
for breaking the law."

"And I say forty dollars for Saturday and Sunday night. And
you will not lose your license."

The Russian bitch was no dope.

The owner knew his crowd: the lower depths of the movie
business, small-time agents on the prowl, tired businessmen who
could barely get it up, actors who would fuck her and pass her on
to some studio executive. Yes, he knew his crowd, and he knew
this kid would pack 'em in and drive them crazy.

"I'll give you fifty dollars for a long weekend, that's Friday
through Sunday night. Fifty bucks is my limit. I'm taking the
risk."

"Yes. Yes. I understand. You are a smart man. It is a good
decision. You will not be sorry."

Nastasia was calculating how once they saw Anna she would
get a better offer. In the meantime, she had no choice. She must
take the offer and hold her tongue.

The owner watched mother and daughter disappear into the
street. He sat back in his chair and sucked his cigar. He'd out-
foxed that Russian bitch as easy as you take candy from a kid.
He'd have offered her double if she'd held out. *The kid was
dynamite. He'd never let this one get away.*

The fat owner stood up. He faced the audience.

"Ladies and gentlemen!" he cried, though there were only men in the crowd. "It's my pleasure to introduce, in her first public appearance, the beautiful and talented . . . Anna!"

Anna walked onstage. She bowed. She clicked the castanets. It sounded like crickets. She stamped her feet. Her coppery hair fell onto her shoulders. Her dark eyes blazed. She moved like a sizzling wire. Human sirens are few and far between, but that night, in a cheap café, a siren was born.

Anna was being thrown into life too fast. She had no choice. *The years of servitude, the discipline and training, had prepared her for whatever life demanded.* Her hips swayed, her feet stamped, her body rose and fell like a snake's. She was not yet fourteen. She moved with animal ease. She was danger. Excitement. It happened easily and fast, a body of bored men transformed into a howling pack. She was a thorn in their flesh. They screamed and cheered and their lust filled the air. Anna felt its heat. It thrilled her. It was all so simple. You moved like a cat, you threw back your head, you twirled, stamped, smiled, and it took them to a peak of madness—it came at you in waves, and the waves kept coming, and Anna felt its thrill, and knew she had a power to make men crazy. It was as close to love as she had come. The thrill of her own untapped sexuality, rising up like a geyser, was bringing her love.

Luis Delgado owned the Montezuma nightclub in Acapulco. He came regularly to Los Angeles, and always to the Agua Caliente. He smoked a cigar and watched Anna. The girl was fearless. She faced the hot-blooded crowd with exquisite self-confidence. Anna was perfect for his nightclub in the hills of Acapulco, where a full moon shone and the men were parched with desire. She was perfect for the slaves of Satan that lined his pockets with gold. He gave the waiter five dollars and found out what he needed to know.

Next morning he phoned Nastasia. She agreed to have lunch. It was noon in the Polo Lounge. High noon for the agents and executives talking their deals. Luis Delgado was already seated.

The maître d' led Nastasia to his booth. Luis stood up. He extended his hand. Nastasia's grip was as strong as a man's.

"Thank you for coming," said Delgado.

"Your proposal interests me." She waved a hand toward the diners. "Perhaps, we, too, will do business."

"I hope so, Madame Rostov. Your daughter has an interesting talent. I can use her in my club. Without undue modesty, the Montezuma is the best nightclub in Mexico. Perhaps in all of South America. In addition to her salary, I provide lodging in the Casa Azteca hotel and, of course, food."

"You neglect to tell me what you pay, señor."

"I will pay you in pesos the equivalent of one hundred dollars a week."

Nastasia's eyes were cold as gray flint. "Next you will tell me Anna is too young, and for another hundred dollars you can hire a more famous dancer. The reason you want Anna, señor, is because she is young. Last night you saw her dance. You saw her power over men—lowlife and bums. You saw her turn them into lovers. It is a mysterious talent, señor—a gift. She is still unknown, but once the world hears of her allure they will *run* to your club. You are right, Señor Delgado, Anna is 'interesting.' And for that she must be paid."

"I will pay what is fair."

"Good. She will start her engagement for two hundred and fifty dollars a week. After a month we will negotiate."

"Impossible."

"It is, nonetheless, my price."

Delgado was silent. She was right. For another hundred he could have a star—not the biggest, of course. But Delgado knew his audience: Mexico's jaded industrialists, the bloodthirsty military, movie stars, politicians, rich tourists, a ruthless bunch with big appetites.

"You drive a hard bargain, Señora Rostov."

"When we negotiate again, then I will drive a hard bargain. Meanwhile, you have hired a very good dancer. You saw her send the customers through the roof. She will do it again, señor. You will see this pitiful salary is nothing against what you will make."

Delgado looked at the money-mad bitch and thought, *What she needs is a hot young fuck to put juice in those loins.* You couldn't argue with a frigid bitch. He had just the boy to loosen her up.

"You'll have to learn Spanish, señora."

"We have already started studying. You see, Señor Delgado, I have been expecting your call for some time."

American Airlines flight 720 arrived in Acapulco in the late afternoon. A limousine was waiting. It drove along the airport road, past Pie del la Cuesta with its roaring surf. It passed Indians cursing their burros, bent old men, ragged children, and starving dogs. Women gathered corn, and men in white shirts sat in the cantinas, drinking mescal and waiting for night and the *putas* who would dance by candlelight. They passed the shimmering bay with its bathers and big yachts. They came to a hill on a ninety-degree slant, and the driver turned upward. They passed a white church. The homes were lavish now, with tropical plants and gaudy shrieking birds. Gnarled old trees lined the road.

At the top of the hill was the Casa Azteca, built in the seventeenth century and used as a fort. Its spectacular view had made it irresistible to land speculators, who bought and turned it into a hotel. Its two bedroom villas with private pools, its cuisine, a nine-hole golf course, tennis courts, saltwater swimming pool, the gardens, and finally the Montezuma, its luxurious nightclub, made Casa Azteca the most expensive resort in the world.

Inside the Montezuma entrance hung two famous murals by Diego Rivera. On one wall, Montezuma, the Aztec prince, sat surrounded by his chieftains. Opposite was a mural of Montezuma's harem. Beautiful girls, supervised by their duennas, wove and spun cloth for their master. Anna stopped and stared at the picture.

"It is very famous," the driver said. "People come from all over the world to see it."

"It is very beautiful," said Anna. But the grim duennas and the slave girls renewed her desire to be free.

Their cottage was in the rear of the hotel. It had a simply furnished living room, two bedrooms, a kitchen, and a bath. From the living room they saw smoke billowing up from a kitchen funnel. Behind the house was a patio with large gray cacti, and beyond, a curve of hill, a drop, and the bay. They unpacked, ordered a meal from the hotel, and fell asleep. They awakened refreshed and dressed for the long night ahead.

The stage of the Montezuma was dark. Two spotlights blazed onto the bodies of Nastasia and Anna. Behind them a guitarist plucked his strings. Nastasia was dressed like a man, her hair pulled up under a hat, her breasts pressed firm by a bolero. Anna wore a tight white dress. If fit like a second skin. They sprang to their place. They clicked their ebony castanets and clapped their hands and snapped their fingers. They were like two lovers—whirling around, teasing and taunting, wailing like demons. They soared, they leapt apart and came together. They ground their heels into the ground. Applause came up like thunder.

Starve an appetite and it shrinks. Release it, it explodes. Anna heard the roar of the crowd, and it was all the love denied her. It swept onto the stage and enveloped her. *Love: cherished love was finally hers . . .* or so she thought, confusing her romantic dreams with these devils of desire.

Word of her beauty spread like wildfire; the rich and the spoiled flocked to the Montezuma to see Anna dance. Nastasia, so ruthlessly protective of her property, began to fear this hungry mob. She was always at Anna's side. Between performances she locked the door of the dressing room. And Anna, confident that freedom was near and within her grasp, felt ever more resentful of being shackled to Madame.

Pepe Faro, Mexico's great bullfighter, loved nothing more than the conquest and killing of a great bull; the frenzied *olés* from a worshipful crowd, its roar when the chief official handed him the bull's ear and the crowd swept down into the arena and bore him off on their shoulders—he loved nothing more, except the conquest of a pretty woman.

Admiring cries of *"to-re-ro"* rolled through the Montezuma as Pepe, his *mozo de espada,* and a small, devoted retinue sat at Pepe's favored front table drinking champagne and laughing.

Pepe had a youthful face. He wore long sideburns and long combed-back hair. He was slender and very brave. They called him a *valiente*—a brave one. His body was scarred, and savagely marked. He had been badly punished by the bulls. Women adored him, and followed him idolatrously to bed, yet Pepe was proud that he had never been infected with "Casanova's disease," one of the occupational hazards of bullfighters. Pepe preferred virgins. He could fornicate without the nuisance of a prophylactic.

Now a white beam of light burned onto the stage and Anna, in a tight black dress and dancing alone, cracked the castanets. Outside it was a warm tropical night, but inside—lightning flashes and shots of thunder as the audience sprang to life!

Pepe couldn't believe his luck. Anna's drumming feet, her mysterious cry of pain, the roll of her heels, harder, harder, the clacking castanets—it all filled him with the same excitement he felt in the arena, in the last act, the *tercio de muerte,* when you kill the bull or the bull kills you.

Anna looked straight into his eyes. His heart was pounding. Pepe had had too many women to remember, but this one was special. He was thinking how he would take her, like a brave and indestructible bull. He thought of the bulls coming at him, closer and closer, and how no man could work so close to death and survive. But Pepe, defying death and mutilation, was very much alive. He watched Anna stamp her feet, and it was like the charge of the bull. He had prepared the bull for this final moment; worn it down, dominated it, until nothing was left but the kill. All the while he was working the bull and preparing it, he had whispered to it, the same lush sounds he made to a woman before the fuck, *ahhh, mira, ahhh, mira, mira, bonita, ahhh, ahhh,* and Anna's eyes caught Pepe's, and he whispered, *ahhh, mira, mira, mira, ahhh,* and in his head he saw her charge, splendid and straight, and he raised himself high and lowered his sword, and the sword entered into Anna's groin and Anna and Pepe were one. Again and again he thrust—he could take her in a thousand ways, but it was this single most primitive way that pleased him most. Women were as crazy as bulls. They wanted full surrender. As Pepe watched Anna dance, he played her agonized surrender over in his head. When the lights blazed up, Pepe Faro was hard with lust.

Anna smiled enchantedly. She bowed and stretched out her arms like an ancient goddess and Pepe signaled to the waiter.

"Ask the señorita to join me."

The waiter hesitated. He had been instructed by Madame to tell her which of the patrons had asked about Anna.

"Señor Faro, Señorita Anna has an old-fashioned mother who does not permit her daughter to meet strangers."

Pepe laughed. "A girl like that should be locked away from dangerous men. However, I am Pepe Faro." He slipped a thousand-peso bill into the waiter's hand. "Go and tell her I am here. That I am waiting."

Anna came out to the excited crowd and took another bow. The waiter went to Nastasia.

"Madame Rostov, Pepe Faro, our greatest matador, wishes to meet Señorita Anna."

Nastasia had watched Anna flirt with Pepe Faro. She had seen his retinue grow quiet when he was quiet, and laugh when he laughed, their sole aim in life to acclaim and be a part of his orbit. A smile from Pepe Faro and a girl grew wild with excitement. Anna had sent him an invisible signal, and now Pepe Faro had summoned her to his table. Nastasia entered the dressing room. She locked the door behind her. The key turning in the lock was a reminder she was in charge of Anna's life.

"Tell me the truth," she said coolly. "You danced for the bullfighter, Pepe Faro."

"I dance for anyone who pays."

"Don't lie to me, Anna."

"Why should I lie?"

"You saw those fools. *To-re-ro! To-re-ro!* They wanted to kiss the hem of his coat. I'm not blind, Anna. You danced to meet this Pepe."

"And does he want to meet me?"

"What do you think?"

"Then let him."

"You're acting like a star-struck adolescent."

She's my curse, thought Anna. *Pepe Faro is brave and strong. If Pepe Faro falls in love, he will help me escape. I need Pepe Faro's help.* Anna swallowed her anger. "Pepe Faro is the greatest bullfighter in the world. Of course I want to meet him! Oh, Madame, I know you want to protect me, but please, five minutes. I promise you can trust me."

"I do trust you, Anna. It is the men I don't trust. Do you know how they look at you? Like meat! They dream only of the conquest. It fills their animal souls." She paused. "I haven't raised you for that."

She's crazy, thought Anna. *Her ambition is sick.* And Anna's desire to escape Nastasia grew ever more strong.

"Five minutes," said Anna. "Stand by the side of the room if you want. But give me five minutes."

Madame knew there would be many men wanting five minutes, and if she denied Anna an occasional glamorous moment, Anna would grow rebellious. "All right," she said. "Meet the great matador. But be back in this room in five minutes."

Anna reached into Madame's pocket and took the key. She unlocked the door and walked straight to Pepe Faro's table. The girl was superb. He thought of the nights ahead, and how he would take her as he would a brave bull, and break her down, and he asked her to join him for champagne.

The following Sunday a black limousine drove Anna and Madame to the airport. The morning sun was strong. The blue sea glistened. There were goats, pigs, and dogs on the road, and the chauffeur honked his horn and cursed. In the mangrove forest

there were screaming birds and coyotes and wolves. The road
leveled off and became straight. The airport loomed up ahead.
The chauffeur parked and led them to a small chartered plane. A
pilot greeted them and helped them into the cockpit. The motor
hummed, and the plane lifted into the sky. In less than an hour
they were in Mexico City, where another limousine waited to
take them to the bullfight.

There are two bullfighting arenas in Mexico City. The older,
Gran Plaza de Toros, holds a crowd of twenty-six thousand. The
more recently built, Plaza Mexico, accommodates sixty thousand
people. It is here Pepe Faro would fight the bulls.

The rutted road was filled with burros, jalopies, and buses
crowded with peasants in sarapes who lived only for Sunday and
the bullfights. Afterward everyone would go to the cantinas and
restaurants on Avenida 16 de Septiembre: the agents and manag-
ers, the prostitutes, the matadors and their claque, whoever knew
that nothing mattered but the bullfight.

"Aficionados," said the chauffeur. "The scum of the earth, but
they have *afición*."

"What is *afición?*" asked Anna.

"The love of the bullfight. The aficionado's children will be
hungry, his wife will go without shoes, but he will watch Pepe
Faro kill the bull at the *corrida de toros*."

Anna shrugged in disgust. She did not understand how people
sacrificed their families to see a poor animal suffer and die. It was
vile! Nastasia, too, did not understand this brutal entertainment.
She looked at Anna and saw her wince. In an uncharacteristic
gesture Nastasia reached over to take her daughter's hand. Her
hand lifted. It hung in the air. Forgive me, it seemed to plead,
show me mercy.

How Anna wanted to reach over and take her mother's hand,
but her anger, so long repressed, prevented her. Anger and the
anguish of a life without friends. How often she had longed to
call this woman mother. It had been on the tip of her tongue
every day of her life, only to be swallowed and denied. Anna was

fourteen years old, but Anna was numb. She watched her mother wordlessly ask for forgiveness, and she forgot her deal with God.

In that second, Nastasia knew her ruthlessness had cost her her daughter. She wanted to scream, "I'm sorry." It was too late. She feared what lay ahead, Anna running from a hungry male pack. She prayed for Anna to be strong enough to survive those who would try to ravish and destroy her.

The driver passed steamy cars and screaming aficionados. He parked in a lot filled with Bentleys and Rolls. He led Anna and Nastasia into a tunnel. There were rooms on either side.

"This is the hospital," he said. "It is here they bring the wounded matadors. And there they keep the horses. In this chapel the matadors pray."

The tunnel was full of men, sword handlers, vendors of *cerveza*, photographers, and doctors. Matadors in gaudy uniform wore massive watch fobs and glittering jewelry. A wooden barricade, about five foot high and painted red, separated the *callejón* from the arena.

The chauffeur led Anna and Nastasia out into the sunlight. They walked past the lower row of seats into a reserved box in the pit.

"The aficionados sit here," said the driver. "Here one catches a torero's hat or is offered his cloak. It is a great honor." He tipped his hat and left them.

It was four o'clock. The sun was hot. The sunny side of the arena was full of holes, but the shady side was packed. Women waved fans. Men drank *cerveza* and smoked cigars. A bull escaped his corral. He charged into the ring and the crowd roared, *"Toro! Toro!"* Two boys jumped over the barricade. They jeered at the bull. A policeman and two men in red sarapes rushed into the ring, grabbed the boys, and pulled them to safety as the crowd applauded and laughed.

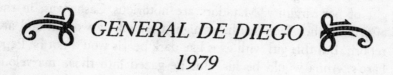

GENERAL DE DIEGO
1979

A military man blazing with gold medals entered the box. He was with a drab sad woman in a white dress. She wore a white mantilla. They sat down beside Anna and Nastasia.

He extended his hand.

"I am General de Diego," he said. "This is my wife, Señora de Diego."

"I am Nastasia Rostov. This is my daughter, Anna."

General de Diego was in his late forties. He was lean and compact, a wolf in the body of a man. His bright yellow eyes were sharp and hard. The flash of his gold medals and the glint of his eyes made him look like a devil. He looked very strong.

Señora de Diego seemed worn. Her makeup was waxen and white, and her face was like a mask. Except for her eyes; hard black dots in a deadened face.

General de Diego looked at Anna. He felt a queer little thrill. The girl must be Pepe Faro's guest, and the momma beside her, acting as chaperone, meant the girl was a virgin. This afternoon, Pepe Faro would be a *valiente,* a brave matador. Again and again he would offer his body to the bull and finally, despite the crowd's roar to go on, he would kill it. *El oficial* would present the dead bull's ear to Pepe Faro and he would offer it to the girl.

The crowd would cheer and lift him on their shoulders, and sweep him into the ring. Later, he would get rid of the sour-faced momma, more like a crow than a woman, and Pepe Faro would bed down the girl. She would honor this brave matador with the gift of her virginity. Matadors are notorious Casanovas; in the afternoon they face death; at night they take a woman and are reborn. But this girl with eyes like dark pearls would not be Pepe Faro's. Anna would be his. But he gazed into those marvelous eyes and felt a warning—a protest.

His hands were damp and nervous.

What was the matter with him, anyhow?

You fool! She makes you happy! And the general realized he had not been happy for a long time. He was out of the habit. It was time to feel happy again. His nerves were a sign that this alluring creature with the crazy eyes would make him happier than he had been in a long long time.

The passion of the general's life were his virgins. When he was young, he had sated his voluptuary taste in worldly women, but in recent years he had confined himself to the chaste sweet young flesh that confirmed his waning masculinity. His girls were trained with the same exciting care as his fine Thoroughbreds or his disciplined army.

Parents might struggle with their consciences, but they had no choice. De Diego called it a "transaction." It was in fact his command. His "young flesh," as he called them, were assigned apartments near his palace. They were guarded by duennas who recorded their every move on daily reports. If they misbehaved—that is, if they were insolent or rude, or resisted their chores—they were tied by their hair to a bedpost. After the tears and promises of repentance, Diego turned them loose. Then he taught them love—or, rather, love as he enjoyed it.

The general was a restless man. The girls fawned and tried to please him, but they soon found out he was easily bored. Then he released them. Not to hearth and home but into the ranks of his men. He was known as the "spoiler," a terror that stalked all beautiful girls, and, indeed, his morbid pleasures were a peril to all the virgins of the state.

General Diego de Diego served and was responsible to one man, one master, *El Presidente.* His sixth sense for brave men and fast horses, his fanatic loyalty, and his own fierce courage under impossible circumstances made him that ruler's most trusted ally. His army was strong. Dissenters and malcontents were stamped out and crushed. But for the fearless, for the brave and the obedient, there were rewards. Young men quickly became officers and officers prospered in their rank. They lived in handsome villas. The general's cast-off virgins became their mistresses and wives.

Through his mother, de Diego was a descendant of Princess Tecuichpo, Montezuma's youngest daughter. He was steeped in the superstitions of his savage ancestors. His appetite was that of a barbarian. His army could sweep into a crowd and take prisoners at random and throw them into dungeon-like prisons. De Diego's prisoners were accused of crimes against the state. He was a brilliant soldier. His army had once been a chaotic assortment of rival factions, and he had welded them into a single force. He scourged the subversive elements. He kept domestic order. *El Presidente* rewarded his cunning general with a palace, gold, and unlimited power. General de Diego was a brutal warrior in the dress of a modern soldier.

His wife, Marina, had been sold to him in marriage by her father, Jorge Alvarado, a shrewd industrialist who saw in the ambitious young soldier a pawn to represent his interests. He arranged for a consortium of powerful men to buy de Diego an influential position in the army. De Diego in turn would serve their best interests. Marina was a part of the deal. Marina and de Diego were married in the Cathedral of the Asunción de Maria Santism. They stood in front of the massive granite altar and took a vow to love one another, and the corrupt assembly that filled the cathedral knew the ruthless young bridegroom was theirs. De Diego was cold and calculating, a willing player in this conjugal game. His marriage to Marina assured him of their favor. *He*

would rise fast. He would have great wealth and power. He listened
to the marriage ceremony, the beautiful hymns rising toward
heaven, looked into the eyes of his boring young wife, and
thanked the Almighty for this blessed union.

Power, however, was not de Diego's only passion; he loved
pleasure as much and more. But power brought pleasure, im-
mense and unlimited, and as the years passed his pleasure became depravity. His father-in-law warned him, "Be careful,
Diego. I do not want my daughter, my daughter's children, or any
of my family hurt by public scandal."

The ambitious young soldier inwardly laughed. *This world of
rogues thought themselves his masters! So be it.* He would play out
the charade of slave and henchman, execute their victims, play
their dupe. But one day the ultimate power would be his. He
would wrench free, be his own man. In the meantime, his activities would be clandestine, covert. No one need know. *He would
work hard for personal gain, rising higher and higher, and then he
would throw off their yoke.*

He needed gold.

He needed power.

He needed public opinion to be on his side.

De Diego knew the world for what it was: wealth and power
were accepted as virtue, and virtue meant public acceptance. He
meant to rule Mexico in the way of his noble ancestor Montezuma. In the meantime he was responsible to those who bought
him: to *El Presidente,* and the great worshipful mass.

It happened as he had planned.

He exterminated *El Presidente*'s enemies, and then he turned
on his own. He waged a siege of terror until he was free, finally,
to live the life that he wanted. He wanted the pleasures of the
flesh, *young flesh, flesh he could educate to his barbarian tastes.* His
great wealth and power made his craving for virgins a simple
task. Obstinate parents saw what happened dare they refuse:
resistance, and a house was burned to the ground, a job mysteriously lost, an invisible persecution for an unknown crime.

"My tastes are primitive," he laughingly admitted. "Primitive as my ancient ancestors who seized the most beautiful virgins and sacrificed them to the gods. . . . But I am a modern man. My virgins are not hurled to a bloodcurdling death. They are destined for happy and respectable lives." And even the most frightened parent understood this plunder by the general was a simple barter that indulged his dissipated tastes and guaranteed their daughter a husband and money.

A suite of rooms in his palace was separate and sealed off from the family's quarters. It was here the mommas brought their young. The girls wore long-sleeved dresses and stockings, only their faces exposed. The general entered the room. He greeted them warmly, dismissed the mother, who was told to return in an hour. He appraised his new acquisition. Seemingly satisfied, he stood, asked her to follow him into a small adjacent room. The room was white. It contained a metal filing cabinet, an examination table, a wooden chair. It was like any modern gynecological examination room. The girl was asked to undress. The general held each article of clothing as she pulled it from her body.

A doctor in a white uniform entered the room. He measured her breasts, her hips, her waist, thighs, calves, and ankles. She was asked to mount the examination table and put her feet in the stirrups. Now the doctor took a silver probe and inserted it into her vagina. He measured the circumference of her virgin's mound, the labia minor with its small cockscomb form, her sensitive clitoris, her tight, constricted vagina.

Once it was established that coitus had not occurred, the doctor put his notations on a three- by five-inch lined card. The card was filed in a metal box. The doctor nodded mutely to the general and left the room. The general told the girl to dress. He sat passively, handing her one article of clothing at a time. Then he opened the door and led her into the lavish outer office. He asked her questions, which she answered. When momma returned, she was instructed on the time and place of the next assignation. Momma was told her duties as chaperone. On occasion, General de Diego smoked a cigarette. He did not drink or gamble. Virgins were his only vice.

The general had heard of Anna's power over her audience and he had stayed away. He wasn't sure why, except the coincidence of her dancing at the Montezuma with its red porous walls and low stoned ceiling, an iron eagle guarding the entrance like some prophetic omen. Yes, the general was superstitious, a man at war with a pagan strain within. Now, suddenly, unexpectedly, she was here beside him, watching the *corrida de toros,* where the glory of courage can triumph over the power of death—and the general felt his fate.

Nonsense! She is just another pretty virgin. The presence of her mother, a stern chaperone, was proof of that. The general felt reassured. He looked at the glorious girl and thought how he would ravage, possess, and finally discard her, and he smiled at his ridiculous fears.

"Would it disturb you if I smoke, Señora Rostov?"

"Of course not, General de Diego."

"And you, señorita, would my smoking disturb you?" Anna smiled. And the general saw an invitation to do what he wanted.

The general lit a cigarette. He liked the smell of tobacco blending in with the tacos, the pastry and *cerveza.* He liked the noisy crowd, the clapping of hands, the cheering—the laughter before death. The sound of laughter, a woman laughing in the dark. He couldn't keep his eyes off Anna. He imagined her laughing in the dark. Imagined her naked on his bed, and how he would lift himself, poise, and drive in, and how her laughter would change into a passionate howl. She excited and frightened him. She confused him. *She was too proud, too beautiful, too mysteriously sensual for someone so young.* He knew why he had not gone to Acapulco to see her dance. He was threatened. But of what? That she would scourge him, bleed him of his manhood? *Fool!* She was just another girl, young flesh, moist and tender.

He lifted the manicured hand holding the cigarette to his mouth. He puffed. It was hot. Ordinarily he loved the sun, but this was the heat of the blood. He felt irritable. He knew that destiny, mysterious and fated, had delivered Anna to him through Pepe Faro. He was overcome with desire. He cursed the bullfight, the crowd, his ugly wife. He cursed the long afternoon ahead.

A trumpet was blowing.

He turned to Nastasia and Anna. "A bullfight is a tragedy," he said. "There is danger for the man, but death, only death, for the bull."

Anna winced. A chill ran up his spine. He continued to talk.

"In the first act, the bull charges the picadors."

Anna watched the bull, snorting and pawing the sand, dive at the belly of the horse and tear it open. Guts, blood, and excrement fell out upon the sand. The stricken horse twitched and fell to the ground. The crowd cheered at the carnage. A fresh horse was brought out.

"I hate it!" said Anna.

"The wound is not fatal, señorita. The doctor will wash and sew up the hole, and the horse can be used again. Look! Here come the banderilleros. Act two belongs to them!"

The municipal officer made a signal, a cornet played the *suerte de banderilleros,* and two banderilleros, grasping sticks tipped with a barb, moved toward the bull. They lifted them and swooped down, planting the sticks in the toro's neck.

"The banderilleros tire the bull even further and slow his attack."

The crowd roared for fresh bloodshed. Anna shut her eyes, and turned her face.

"It is a drama, señorita. A tragedy in which a man faces his destiny and risks his bravery above death. Our friend Pepe Faro is fearless. A brave man who kills honorably. It is his genius."

Pepe Faro stepped into the sun. A drum was struck and rolled. The trumpets blared. The band played a song, and the crowd cheered their favorite matador.

"The *toque de muerte,* señorita, the signal of death."

Pepe Faro bowed before the official, who raised his hat, then Pepe Faro raised *his* hat. He walked toward Anna and placed it on the fence before her. He turned to face the bull.

How she hated it! The ravaging torture as the bull, gored and bleeding and poked with sticks, moved slowly to its death. She wanted to put her hands over her ears and shut out the frenzied crowd.

"It is a bad bull, señorita. Pepe Faro works bravely."

De Diego looked at her and Anna saw eyes of ownership and authority. A rush of fear went through her. She looked into the ring. The bull was charging Pepe Faro. The crowd screamed for blood and held their breath as Pepe Faro raised his sword. He stood in the line of the bull, dropped his red *muleta,* then waved it. The bull, with feet together and head bowed, charged—and Pepe Faro plunged his sword in. The bull swayed and buckled and collapsed to the ground. Now the band was playing a tango and the crowd threw their hats, their handkerchiefs, and their cigars into the ring.

The sun was hot and bright and Pepe Faro could feel it burning the back of his neck. His gold uniform was heavy. It had been a terrifying time. A bad black massive bull hurtling toward him. A second of fear, the left horn coming too hard and too fast, and the roar of the crowd turning to hoots and catcalls. Then his feet had miraculously led him away and the bull crashed past, flashing by his cape, and the hoots and jeers turned to cheers and *olé*s. After that the *olé*s never stopped. The official was handing him the ear of the bull, and Pepe turned and walked toward Anna.

Pepe Faro handed it to Anna. The general reached over and gave Anna his handkerchief and Anna held the ear. She wanted to vomit, to throw it into the sand and run from the shrieking mob, from the dead animal, the mournful music, the general, and the brave matador who stood before her.

"Congratulations, Pepe Faro. Perhaps you will honor my wife and myself with dinner." De Diego turned to Nastasia. "Señora Rostov, it would be a great honor if you and your daughter would join us too."

Pepe Faro saw the general's eyes as they gazed at Anna's lovely face, and he knew the afternoon was a terrible mistake. After a bullfight, he loved nothing more than to be with a woman—but this exquisite girl was not to be his. If he agreed to the general's invitation, he could find himself in a dark street, overpowered by thugs, trussed up, his ear cut off, his body dumped into the river. Yes, he had heard stories of those stupid enough to interfere with the general's pleasures, and he knew he could pass from this world, not as a brave matador on the horn of a bull, but as a bloated, discolored body. A fury possessed him, but he concealed his rage.

"General de Diego does Pepe Faro a great honor. Unfortunately, I have other plans for tonight." Without looking at Anna, he stepped back and into the screaming crowd, who rushed from the stadium into the ring, to bear the victorious hero on their shoulders.

"Do you know the Alhambra?" asked de Diego. "It is the best restaurant in Mexico. I think it will amuse you."

"I dance tonight," said Anna. "May I suggest General and Señora de Diego come to Acapulco and see me perform? It is less than an hour by plane."

The general was unaccustomed to women, any woman, challenging him. When he suggested the Alhambra, it was not a suggestion, it was a command! It amused him that Anna did not understand. She *would* understand, of course, this adorable creature would understand all his desires. Señora de Diego understood. She looked at her husband with a frosty complicitous smile.

"You must excuse me if I don't join you," said Marina. "The afternoon has tired me."

"Of course, my dear. Go home and sleep. Tomorrow you will be fine."

"Thank you, Diego."

"So, it's settled. We will go to Acapulco and I will finally see the famous Anna dance." And turning to Marina, he said, "I will be home late. If there is an emergency, you know how to reach me."

"*Sí*, Diego. Do not worry."

The general nodded. He watched the frenzied fans carrying

Pepe Faro away and he said, "Pepe Faro is very brave. He is a brave matador."

"Do brave matadors ever get killed?" asked Anna.

"Every year," the general said slowly, "many brave matadors die in Mexico City." His yellow eyes caught Anna's, and she remembered Pepe Faro drawing his sword and calling, *"Toro! Toro!"* Plunging it between the bull's shoulders—the bull spurting blood, the bull collapsing—and the general's ominous words ran through her head. *You kill the bull or the bull kills you,* and she knew. *Like Pepe Faro, she must be fearless and strong, a* valiente. *Her life depended upon it.*

It was a fast trip to Acapulco, with everyone caught up in their own thoughts.

The general, who took his women easily and cheaply as any pasha, felt confused. He would take Anna as he did the others— without consequence or feeling. That was how he lived. Then why did he feel so uneasy? Was it her luscious mouth, or those soft dark eyes, or her sweet smile? What was this feeling that disturbed him? *It must be happiness,* he thought. *Happiness was the capture and taming of a wild mustang. Happiness was wrenching an orgasm from a virgin's womb. Happiness was complete control.*

No woman had ever controlled the general's passions, except in the dark, brutal moment of orgasm. This fierce excitement made him feel odd and vulnerable. *Women are like horses,* he reminded himself. *You train and pace and break them in, you give them tending and care, and when you take them from the paddock, they fly into the wind. My fears are ridiculous!* Still, it disturbed him, as though he were in the harness and the girl in control. *Before I finish, she will run and rear high on command!* And he shut his eyes to fantasies of Anna, tethered in a satin paddock, waiting for his mount.

Nastasia looked into the dark. She knew something important had happened that death-filled afternoon. The general's influence extended to the president of the republic, to foreign heads of state. If he favored Anna, her rise would be swift. Thwarted dreams and postponed ambitions became a fresh reality. Fate was suddenly an ally. *Anna would have a great career. She would be a shining star.* Denied ambition suddenly sprang free.

And Anna understood her gift was to enchant and cast a spell over men. With the general's help, she would wrench free of the hated Madame. She would be unfettered, free. *Free!* She was young—blessedly young. *Whatever life was, it was finally hers or would be very soon.*

They landed on a private airstrip outside Acapulco. Sandoval, the general's chauffeur and bodyguard, had gone on ahead. He waited for the general and his guests in a limousine.

Sandoval gasped. There had been hundreds before Anna, girls pretty or prettier, girls who had passed from the general's bed into the ranks, and who, had he wanted, would have been his. But Sandoval preferred the hardened *putas* who sat in the cantinas and laughed, and were satisfied with a glass of tequila, and the crackle of the peso.

Some called Sandoval the general's faithful dog. Others said he was the poisonous fish that attends the shark. He was both. A brute and a bully from the town of Cholula, he had entered the army as a young man. Ambitious to advance, he had determined to become the general's aide. He had overheard a soldier critical of the general's taste for virgins. He engaged the culprit in a brawl and cut out his tongue. News of his violence reached the general, who had summoned Sandoval to the palace.

"I should cut out *your* tongue as a lesson to my overly ambitious soldiers."

"I protected the general's honor. I would do it again if I had to."

"Come now, Sandoval, you cut the man's tongue from his mouth so it would come to my attention."

"When a man, a soldier, insults his general's machismo, he deserves what he gets."

The general had laughed heartily. "I need brave men in my army, not violent fools."

"The general needs men who would sacrifice their lives for his safety." It was a warm bright day, and the windows were open.

Sandoval had walked toward them. Outside, a bee was buzzing on a flower. Sandoval reached out and caught it in his hand. He clenched his hand into a fist. The bee buzzed, vibrated, and stung its captor. Sandoval closed his eyes and squeezed his fist tighter. He opened his hand. It was red and full of welts. The bee was on its back, struggling for life. Sandoval pulled off its legs and wings.

"That is how I guard you from your enemies," he said.

The general had looked into the unsmiling eyes of this brute who, with senseless ease, destroyed animals or men, and hired him as his bodyguard.

What a beauty, thought Sandoval, looking at Anna. An unconscious smile lit up his brutish face.

"You are smiling, Sandoval. You have not smiled for years."

"I smile because I am a man, and it is natural that I admire a beautiful woman." Far better to tell the truth than find disfavor because of a stupid lie.

It amused the general that his cold-blooded henchman would smile at his woman. If it had not been Sandoval, he would have been disciplined and dismissed. But through the years this passionless thug had proved himself courageous and loyal, even throwing his body in front of a would-be assassin, taking a bullet in his groin instead of the general's. *He is human after all, a human beast,* thought the general, and forgave him his carnal weakness.

Anna danced that night as if he were the great Prince Montezuma and she a favored slave, and the general watched this glorious girl throw gold dust into the eyes of the infidels, and thought, *She's mine. I have only to take her.* But he did not feel a conqueror's joy. He felt anguish. A desire to own her and a need to destroy her. These conflicting emotions disturbed him. No woman had ever challenged his authority or ever would. But Anna made him feel vulnerable, and when her dance was over and she bowed and lifted her hands, the wild applause and cheers sent fear through his heart. It was midnight. De Diego signaled the waiter.

"Send the owner to my table."

"Pronto, General. I will get him immediately."

In a moment Delgado joined him. "I hope everything is satisfactory and that the General enjoys the show."

"Señorita Anna is tired."

"Oh, no, General, Anna is tireless. She is young, strong . . ."

"*I* say she is tired. She is done for the night."

"But, General, the audience . . . what will I tell them?"

"Say she is ill." The general smiled. "I will be here each weekend. And I don't like this table."

"Table number four is our best table. It belongs to the General."

"None sits there but me!"

"*Sí*, General." The sweating owner knew he had no choice. He must cancel Anna's last performance, and his best table, number four, was gone. "Your wishes are my commands, General de Diego."

"*Gracias.*"

"I am honored by your presence."

The general, followed by Sandoval, walked the women to their cottage. He took Nastasia's hand and kissed it. Then he took Anna's hand, the hand of a child, its flesh firm and unbroken by lines. The scent of youth filled his senses.

"*Buenas noches,* Señorita Anna."

"*Buenas noches,* General."

"I will come again on Friday. I look forward to seeing you then."

Anna smiled, and her beauty broke his heart. When the door closed behind them, the general and Sandoval walked to the limousine. In a minute they were speeding along. Sandoval watched his master through the rearview mirror. A man in control of emotion, his eyes reflected his confusion. *My savage master will get his comeuppance at the hands of that girl,* thought Sandoval. *Yes, even the general is human,* and for the first time the loyal thug felt superior to his master.

"Move them," said the general, breaking the silence. "Find something more suitable. You know my needs."

"*Sí*, General."

"I want complete luxury."

"I will make sure the General is satisfied."

That evening Anna flung herself onto the bed. She thought about the general, medals flashing on his chest, eyes faltering, and how he had fallen in love. Next week he would fall in love a little harder, and the week after, harder still. It had happened faster than she dared hope. *Madame's power was over. She was finally free.*

Early next morning, Anna was awakened by a knock on the door. She arose, threw on a robe, and ran to open it. Sandoval stood there with a porter.

"What's the matter, Sandoval? What's wrong?"

"The general is not satisfied with your quarters. Please get dressed. The porter will pack your clothes."

"Where will we go?"

"The general has rented a villa."

Anna smiled happily. Anything was possible if the general was your friend.

Anna's new home was an elegant villa behind a high mysterious wall. There was a living and dining room with antique furnishings, a kitchen, and up a circular stairway, an enormous bedroom overlooking the bay. A smaller cottage, in back, was for Nastasia. A swimming pool, tennis court, whirlpool bath, and brilliant garden completed the luxury.

"I can't believe it!" cried Anna.

"The general wants you comfortable. Two maids will serve you. Yolanda leaves at seven and Rosa stays on until she returns."

"We don't need two maids."

Sandoval ignored her protestations. "I will take you wherever you wish. When I am not on duty, José will be at your service."

Anna laughed. "It's like a fairy tale."

"Acapulco is full of strangers. The general wishes the señorita to have protection at all times."

"Well," said the general. "How is she?"

"She can't believe her luck. In the mornings she practices with the momma. Afternoons, I drive them to the beach. I took them shopping yesterday. She bought a dress. It is a splendid black dress, General."

"What about the men?"

"What about them? The girl is a beauty."

"Answer me!"

"She makes them loco."

"I see . . . and the bullfighter. Has he returned?"

"No, General."

"Good. If anyone—any man—makes trouble, I want him thrown out. Permanently."

"It will be done."

"Anything else of interest?"

"Nothing important."

The general fell silent. Everything in his life was done in the service of self-interest, everything a tribute to his superiority. Still, this first week apart from Anna he had suffered, a victim of love, as though an electric prod were attached to his genitals, and Anna had only to push a button and torment would rip him apart. He felt himself the lamb, a victim of his senses, and despised himself for it. *Anyone who threatened his pleasure must be rooted out and crushed. Anna was no exception.* They drove along. The general felt strange and vulnerable. He crushed the feeling as he crushed all human feeling, but it sprang into life despite its powerful master.

Sandoval, too, was silent. He did not say how, from a vantage point behind the foliage, he had watched Anna lying in the sun, rise, walk to the water's edge and dive in, a sublime figure, sharpening his senses. After all, he was a man and human. So he was silent, keeping guard for his master and rejoicing that Anna's precarious freedom was in his hands.

The maid Yolanda opened the door to Anna's bedroom.

"The general is here, Señorita Anna. He waits downstairs."

"Thank you, Yolanda."

Anna took a critical look in the mirror. Her lovely face, the deep dark eyes, gave an impression of mysterious calm. Who could guess her heart trembled with fear? The moment had arrived. She hovered a second—straightened her dress—and called on her courage.

"It is not wise to make him wait, señorita."

Anna smiled. "I'll be there in a minute. No, wait, I'm coming now." She took a last critical look, and went downstairs.

The general stood by the window. He gasped as she walked toward him. Part Spanish noble, part Aztec savage, he crossed himself in prayer as the barbarian within him crouched on its knees. He felt a real emotion, and it stunned him. *Wait until nightfall. Then he would bear down, and she would join that long procession of virgins fallen from their pedestals.* He would use her up, and once bored, throw her to his men. *Let her exalt in her radiance! Tonight she would learn some humility.*

"You are lovelier than ever," said de Diego.

"Thank you, General."

"Have you thought about me one little minute?"

"I thought about your kindness. Your generosity."

"You are charming, my dear Anna, a charming liar."

"Of course I've thought about you—wondered how I could ever thank you."

"You can thank me when you dance. There will be many others watching tonight, but I want you to dance for me."

"I will dance for you, and only you."

If the general wanted a pretty dancing doll—so be it. She would dance as she had never danced before; excite him even more than the others. Drive him wild. It seemed so easy in that second. How could Anna know de Diego's soul was of the ancient warrior, his altar the altar of the Aztec, stained with blood and human suffering. She only knew one thing: *escape.* She reckoned without the consequences of her sexuality and her blinding power over men.

That night, the mystery of the empty table, of which all Acapulco had been gossiping, was solved. Table number four belonged to General de Diego. Every head was turned in his direction.

A wise old cynic, and the dean of Acapulco gossip, whispered to his friends:

"The wolf has met his match."

"Shhh," they cautioned.

The Acapulco dean continued:

"The general is a sportsman. A lover of great horseflesh and young women. The girl is a Thoroughbred. The general will put a whip to her flanks. He will build her speed and endurance. He will teach her sexual strategy, and he will ignore the real danger."

"What is that?"

"The danger of love. The general will enjoy a momentary conquest but victory belongs to the girl."

"Impossible."

"I think not." The wise old gossip smiled. "He may be a military genius but he is a man. Look! How she excites him! Our fine soldier will attack and overcome her, but the girl's powers are as great as the sum of his experience. It will be an amusing winter, gentlemen. If the strong man gains a victory, which I doubt, or suffers a defeat, which I predict, we will not be bored."

That night, in the red satin bedroom, Anna prepared herself for the general as she prepared herself for the dance. Even in pain, a muscle strained, a tendon twisted, she submitted to the suffering only to overcome it. Madame's vision of dance was submission. Anna's lifelong discipline, the years of solitude, had developed a fierce inner strength. Tonight she would make love as if love were dance. So she faced the ordeal ahead with the same simple strength as she summoned for daily practice. One simply did what one must do.

The general looked into her eyes. He looked at her naked body and felt himself a supplicant before a goddess. He wanted to lay flowers at her feet, to throw his body before her and pray for mercy. He had experienced all of life's dissolute pleasures but none of its pain. He yearned for the experience of surrender, as though it were a weak link in his manhood. He must conquer it as he conquered all obstacles in the path of machismo. He raised himself, poised to attack, and bore down.

Anna screamed with pain. She remembered the general was no more than a strained muscle—one endured the agony and went on. She took a deep breath, opened her eyes, and smiled.

Even Anna, so stoic and strong, could not conceal her pain. Her eyes were filled with suffering and de Diego was full of joy. He held her firm and thrust, and each thrust was a conquest and each conquest held the thrill of great passion. He rode a fierce and savage ride. He was Cortés invading the golden land—Anna was his, his great golden treasure. Then, moaning excitedly and crying from pleasure, he convulsed into orgasm.

He pulled away. If he stayed near her, the insistent longing would start. His powerful sexual attraction to her filled him with dread. He got out of bed and went to the window. It was dawn. Through the gray mist, beyond the brilliant garden, was the bay. Everyone was asleep on their yachts. He went back to bed and lit a cigarette. He looked at his naked goddess and wished he were young, that they loved one another with the passion of youth. But he knew it was a dream and Anna would only come to love him through tears and abject pain. She was, after all, only a woman.

"The first time is always painful," he said matter-of-factly. "Tomorrow will be easier and when you know, instinctively, what it is like, I will not be able to give you enough."

"Teach me, Diego. I want to learn everything."

"You will, my sweet, I promise."

He brought her close and kissed her. Her mouth seemed like the sweet wild flowers of the earth. He was in paradise. He pulled away and said:

"You are still a child, *querida,* but you kiss with the skill of a great *puta.* In time you will make love with the same great skill."

Now Anna smiled and her eyes shone with the promise that Diego would enjoy all the sordid pleasure his depraved nature so desired.

If Anna knew she was a prisoner, she revealed nothing. The years under Madame's critical eye, the discipline, the deference, the cut of the stick for a breach of the rules, had taught her obedience. With a sixth sense she anticipated de Diego's whims. Within months she knew his tastes. She was master of his pleasures. When he was savage, she yielded. When he was the hunter, she was his prey; she outmaneuvered, outran, and outwitted him, and when her lover's strength began to wane, she gratified him in sweet surrender.

He loved her body, in the heat, glistening from sun, oil, and sweat. He ran his hand along her curves, felt the throb in his cock, the tingle, and rise.

One day she said, "Diego, I want to talk about Madame."

"Why don't you call her 'Momma'?"

"She is Madame. 'Madame' keeps us free. She is my teacher and I am her student. We are not sentimental."

"Women are sweet and sentimental." De Diego smiled. "It's not a crime."

"It weakens you."

"A woman's weakness is her strength," said de Diego. "You, *querida,* understand this. It is part of your talent."

"Please, Diego, I want to talk."

"I'm listening."

"You've heard of Andreyev. He was the greatest dancer in the world."

"I remember."

"Andreyev is my father!" Anna was suddenly shy. She quickly continued. "My mother was a good dancer but she knew she would never be as great as her ambition. She was determined her child would be. She became pregnant by Andreyev. She defected to America. I was her dancing prodigy. Except I wasn't. I dance, but I lack my father's gift. I do not fly. Madame will never forgive me."

"Poor *querida.*"

"Madame thinks I'm lazy. I'm not. I'm an ordinary dancer. She can't accept it. She dreams one day the world will applaud her Pavlova. Diego, darling, please help me."

Diego was silent. He knew Madame was a fanatic. He knew of the grueling lessons, the stick, but Anna's captivity under Madame's critical eye was part of his plan. He allowed Anna to dance at the Montezuma because Sandoval would protect her from an obstreperous or rowdy drunk. It amused Diego that Anna's beauty drove men crazy, and that Madame Rostov shut her away like a jack-in-the-box until he appeared to spring her out.

"Madame Rostov is a great teacher," said Diego. "There is no better in Mexico. You will continue the lessons."

"Listen, Diego—I'll do anything you want."

"My dear Anna, what do you do now?"

"Please don't joke."

"Nothing changes, *querida*. You will continue your lessons and everything stays the same."

"Diego, please!"

"Now listen, *querida*. If you take any liberties—I will treat it as any political offense, and you will be placed under house arrest. Now come here, my sulky beauty, and give your general a kiss."

He took her in his arms. Anna jerked free. The general smiled, but his yellow eyes were as friendly as golden daggers. He put his hand in his pants pocket. He pulled out a switchblade, flicked it open, and snapped the blade toward Anna's shoulder. It grazed the skin. She screamed, reached up her hand and felt a gummy droplet. Blood. She swallowed her fear, walked toward Diego, and took the knife from his hand. She dropped it on the floor.

"My *querida* is a brave one." The general smiled. "I like brave girls. Brave girls excite me."

"It was a scratch."

He moved his mouth toward the knife prick. He kissed it. "You wear my mark now, *querida.*" He paused. "Once I loved another. Not so beautiful as my *querida*. Not so brave. She became frightened of me and ran away. I had no choice. I gave orders to release the dogs. When my soldiers found her she was ripped open."

Anna knew there was one law: De Diego's law. You obeyed or were destroyed. She moved up against him. She lifted her head. She was soft and submissive.

De Diego felt his brain melt and his cock rise. Anna was no foolish child. She was as brave as any soldier. In that second, unguarded, de Diego was caught in Anna's arms. Caught! His most primitive fear had become a self-fulfilling prophecy.

Nastasia reflected bitterly on her own greed. How she had lent herself to the general's plan and how he had betrayed her, played Anna against her, fueled Anna's silent rage. She watched de Diego turn Anna into a glamorous slave with diamonds hanging from her neck, a sacrificial maiden he could offer to his gods. And Nastasia's shame was so great, she could barely face her daughter. She held the stick high. Then she broke it in half.

Anna watched and was silent.

"Now we're equal."

"We've never been equal."

"Anna, have mercy."

"Why? Did you have mercy? When I was small and scared and lonely, I used to lie in the dark and hurt from the pain. Did you ever come to my side? Did you ever hold me in your arms? Or think of what you were doing? When I danced and men came to bargain for me . . . was there mercy when you sold me like a slave?"

"Anna. Don't."

"I had no childhood. You robbed me. You stole it away."

Nastasia shuddered. Her body heaved with violent sobs. But Anna only saw vile self-pity.

"You never loved me, not for a minute, not ever."

Anna's hands turned into fists and she was pounding on Nastasia's chest, but it was as though she were pounding a rock. Anna looked at the pitiful sobbing wretch and she knew the love she longed for was not to be had. Nastasia cried because she could not love. Even if she wanted to, she was not capable. But Nastasia was her mother. And Nastasia needed her love. Anna's

fists stopped pounding and she opened her hands and she took
Nastasia in her arms.

"It's all right," she comforted. "We'll be all right."

And so they stood. The adult-child comforting the child-
mother. Anna had finally come of age.

In the late afternoons Sandoval took Anna for a drive. When
she walked along the bay, the black limousine shadowed her;
when she entered a shop, Sandoval was beside her. A passing
glance from a stranger, a nod of recognition or a hat tipped in
admiration, everything was reported to the general. On Fridays
he confronted her.

"But nothing happened, Diego."

"It's the way nothing happens that upsets me!"

"Why do you torment me so?"

"It's you, my *querida,* who enjoys torturing her Diego."

"I talk to no one but Madame. I do nothing but practice. You
can't deny me an afternoon walk."

"I would like to believe it is innocent, but I see you dance. I
watch the men. And I know. The devil dances in your legs."

Anna smiled. "This game of yours, that I belong to the devil,
gives you complete power over me. You don't need games, Diego.
Your power is absolute. I'm your Anna. I would never hurt you."
She held his face, looked in his eyes, and brought his mouth to
hers. She kissed him long and deep and hard.

De Diego trembled. He pulled her so tight, it hurt. His smile
had nothing to do with pleasure.

"No, *querida,* you won't hurt me. No woman has ever hurt
Diego. No woman ever will."

Nastasia still drilled Anna every morning and Anna finally satisfied the martinet.

"You are as graceful as a cat," said Nastasia.

"And my jumps?" asked Anna.

"Acceptable."

"You mean acceptable for a girl who cannot fly."

"Be generous, Anna. One cannot lose a dream overnight."

"Shall I tell you Diego's dream? He dreams he is Montezuma."

"What has that to do with us?"

"Listen, Madame. Cortés was a Spanish nobleman who came to Mexico with his soldiers looking for gold. Desire for gold made them brave, as brave as Montezuma. Within months they took him prisoner. His gold was theirs. You chose Andreyev for my father because you wanted it too. A golden girl who would leap up and fly. Well, your wish came true. Men adore me because gold is the passion of their lives and I am a golden girl. It is not in my legs, Madame, it is in my soul. Perhaps the love I yearn for is released by the audience. It is not important. What is important is that someone will watch me dance one night and will fall in love. The golden girl will blind him. He will be fearless and brave. He will help us both escape. Whoever this stranger is, we must be ready."

Nastasia looked at Anna dumbfounded. She was more primeval goddess than modern girl. If God danced through Andreyev, then he shone upon the world through Andreyev's daughter.

"And Sandoval," said Nastasia. "What about him?"

"He is human, Madame. A simple man."

"Anna, be careful."

"It is too late to be careful. It will happen. When it does we must be ready. This is the general's game. We are simply changing the rules."

It was late afternoon, but the Acapulco sun was hot. Anna lay beside the pool. Suddenly she stood. The slate burned her feet. She dived into the water and came up on the other side. She swam slowly toward the ladder and climbed out. A dark shadow stood behind a grating. It was Sandoval. She smiled at the half-hidden form. Through the lattice she saw his black gleaming eyes. She laughed, waved her hand, and went into the house.

That weekend, Diego had no complaints. Anna knew she had found an accomplice in this faithful watchdog. A look, a flirtatious smile, any gesture of affection, and he was silent. At some critical moment she would need his help. There would be a price, of course. There was a price for everything, and Sandoval's help was no exception. For the moment he was satisfied. Anna sighed a breath of relief. *There would be no more problems with Diego.* She had found a human link in his chain of iron soldiers.

It was a Friday afternoon in November. That night a full moon would hang over Mexico. It would bathe the country in an eerie light. The white adobe huts would glow. The gray cacti would glisten. The beaches would bleach like white bone. And the tides —the ancients had it a woman's pleasure was ever more keen, that her blood raced wild, when the tides are caught in the full white blaze of the moon.

General de Diego looked out the window of his luxurious office onto the Zócalo, where Montezuma's Palace once stood. On his downfall, Spanish Christian zealots erected a gallows and thousands of victims were hanged, their grinning skulls stuck on pikes. In 1478, the dreadful Spanish Inquisition was founded by Ferdinand and Isabella, and Torquemada, the first inquisitor general, burned thousands of sorcerers and heretics on flaming pyres. For crimes of a lesser nature the victims were strangled before being burned.

On any ordinary day the Zócalo was jammed with cars, trams, Indios in rebozos with their baskets of flowers and vegetables, lottery vendors, soldiers, beautiful women, the lame and the blind begging for pesos, the men who loved the bullfight. Today they were gone, replaced by bands of youths, screaming obscenities and dodging the general's mounted soldiers with their long-barreled guns. He looked down on this scum and felt the tedium of captivity. It had been a terrible week. This riffraff wanting more and more, while their leaders met with his deputies in endless negotiations.

It was the night of the full moon. All week long de Diego had yearned for Anna. Anna, dashing across the sand into the silvery water, and how de Diego would dive in behind her and match her speed, and how he would catch her and pull her close. How cool and wet and sweet she would be and how he would kiss her and she would break away and he would catch her again and drag her to shore. In the sand, under the full white moon, he would crouch above her and the animal within him would take over and he would thrust until her heat was as hot as the sun and then the phone was ringing and the general was wrenched back to the present. He picked up the receiver.

"*Sí, Presidente.* No, there will be no violence. You have my word. *Sí.* I have everything under control. . . . *Sí, Presidente, sí.*"

De Diego hung up the phone and looked out the window. All his life he had craved power. Now power kept him the captive of this dirty mob. The general was tired. He wished he were a peasant in a white shirt, a colored sarape across his back, walking beside his burro, on his way to the woman who would warm him in her love.

BOOK FIVE

FLAME
1970s

Nick was never exactly sure why he had Flame's blood tested for type, except that he was haunted by the violence of Jeannie's death and the thought of the endless and infinite strangers she lured into the dark. And though he loved Flame—in his head—as his own child, he had to know the truth.

Jeannie was a blood type O negative. Nick, too, was a blood type O negative. Flame was A positive. Indisputable proof that Flame was not his biological child. That night Nick went into Flame's room. He looked at her beautiful face framed by soft blond curls and he felt as if his heart were breaking. He spent the night beside the sleeping child. It was as if he were passing the eye of a crisis. Morning came. Flame opened her eyes and smiled at him and the ache that gripped his heart melted away. *My heart isn't breaking,* he told himself. *My heart is opening up.*

So the years passed and Nick became both father and mother to the little girl. They ate breakfast together, and afterward Nick drove her to school. Flame waved him off. She felt proud, very grown-up. Sometimes, after work, Nick drove her to the beach. He stood beside her on the merry-go-round. When she got the brass ring, she got a kiss too. They walked hand in hand in the sand and wet their feet in the cold surf and watched the sun sink away. They watched the scarlet streaks pass into dusk. Then they got into Nick's black Mercedes convertible and drove toward home. The wind brushed Flame's silky hair away from her face. Nick glanced at her profile, the oval shape of her face, the blue eyes fringed by thick black lashes, and he gasped. It was as if Jeannie were still alive in the blond sensuality of this beautiful child.

These times with Nick were the good times for Flame. The bad times were when pretty ladies came to the house and laughed at Nick's jokes and did funny things with their wet shiny lips. That was when she felt an uncontrollable anger. When Nick and the lady went outside to play tennis or swim, Flame opened her purse and stole a lipstick or a comb. On occasion she stole money.

The lady named Clair, still hanging around, annoyed her more than the others. Once Clair spent the whole day. Then she stayed for dinner. After that she kept hanging around. Around nine-thirty Nick said to Flame, "Time for you to go to bed."

"I'm not tired."

"I'll go upstairs with you," said Nick. "We'll talk for a while."

"No!"

Nick and Clair continued to talk. He smiled at Flame, but she knew the smile was a phony grown-up smile. After a while he said to her, "I think it's time."

"It's not."

"I see." Nick gave Clair a look in code and Clair stood up and Nick walked her to the door. Flame saw him kiss her. When Nick came back, she said:

"I hate Clair."

"Clair's a friend of mine," said Nick. "You're frightened I'll marry Clair and I won't love you anymore. I'm not going to marry Clair, and even if I were, I would still love you more than anyone else."

"Promise you won't marry Clair."

Nick laughed. "You're my silly little girl. You know that?"

"Promise, Daddy."

"Okay. I promise. Now, come on, let's go upstairs and Daddy will tuck you into bed."

When Flame was fourteen, Nick got a call from a journalist doing a series of articles on unsolved murders for the *National Enquirer*. Nick refused to see her, but the phone call upset him. He knew that sooner or later Flame would find out about her mother's death. If he didn't tell her himself, she might hear the grotesque details from idle gossip. But each time an opportunity presented itself, he hesitated.

About this time Clair received an award from the New York critics. She would fly to New York to accept. She asked Nick to go along. Nick asked Flame if his going upset her. Flame didn't hate Clair now because she knew Nick would not marry her. But she didn't like Clair either.

"You go with Clair," she said gravely. "But next month you'll have to take me to Arrowhead."

"I see you're a real Hollywood child who sees life as an endless negotiation," said Nick, and he smiled.

"Then it's a deal."

"It's a deal."

"Oh, Daddy, I love you."

"The feeling is mutual."

Nick and Clair left for New York on a late Friday afternoon flight. Flame went into Nick's bedroom. She lay on the bed and watched television. She had fallen asleep when the phone rang.

"Hello."

"Is Dr. Kahn there?"

"He's not here."

"When can I reach him?"

"He's in New York."

"I see." The voice was silent. "Who's this?"

"Flame."

"You're Dr. Kahn's daughter."

"Yes."

"Flame . . ." The voice hesitated. "I'm a writer. A journalist."

"What do you want?" Flame interrupted.

"I want to meet you. Talk to you. I don't know if your father told you but I'm writing a story about your mother."

Flame felt instant anger.

"I don't want to talk about my mother."

"My name is Miss Boise," the voice continued. "I understand how you feel. I think, however, when you understand the circumstances, you'll change your mind."

"My mother died when I was born," Flame said softly. "I didn't know her."

"Your mother was murdered."

Flame felt as if she had been punched.

"I know it's a shock. An awful thing to discover." Miss Boise paused. "I'm surprised your father hasn't told you."

"What do you want?" Flame said dully.

"Meet me tomorrow and I'll tell you what I know. What I want from you, in return, is that you answer some questions. I won't press you. If you don't know or can't answer, I'll understand."

Flame realized she hated what lay ahead, but she had to meet Miss Boise. She had to know what happened. She had to know the truth.

"All right," she said softly. "I'll meet you. Just tell me where and I'll be there."

They met in the park in the Beverly Hills flatlands off Beverly Drive. Miss Boise was wearing brown slacks and a red sweater. She sat on a bench. She carried a leather pouch purse.

"Hello, Flame. I'm Ann Boise. I'm glad you decided to see me." She pulled a tape recorder from the pouch and turned it on.

"What's that for?"

"I'm going to ask you some questions. I want everything correct."

"I told you I don't know."

"I don't want to know about your mother. I want to know

about you. About your life. My story is about the survivors of brutal crimes."

She quickly reached into the pouch and pulled out a manila folder. It held a sheaf of old newspaper clippings. She handed them to Flame and watched her carefully.

Flame read the headlines. She read the brutal details. She read the Ferris wheel attendant's description of the thug and the fortune-teller's prophecy of Jeannie's bad luck in love. She read of various sailors and dockhands who admitted making love to a pregnant stranger. It was too hard to understand, too painful.

She felt Miss Boise's cold eye on her and she knew she mustn't cry, mustn't show emotion. She must take a deep breath and not let Miss Boise see her hurt. She mustn't cry. Not a tear. She finished reading and handed the clippings to Miss Boise. She stood up.

"We had an agreement," said Miss Boise.

"You're hateful," said Flame. "Go to hell."

She turned and walked away. She felt Miss Boise's eye on her and she didn't look back.

Nick came home Sunday night. The house seemed empty.

"Flame," he called. "Flame."

No response. He went upstairs. Her door was closed. A sliver of light shone under the door. He opened it and saw Flame curled on the bed in a fetal position. He went to her side.

"You've been crying," he said. "What's the matter?"

She closed her eyes.

He reached for her hand. She pulled away.

"You're angry with me for going away."

She was silent.

"Tell me, darling."

"You should have told me."

Now Nick was silent.

"I saw a journalist . . . a Miss Boise," she blurted out. "She showed me the newspapers. The pictures of my mother in that cage . . . half naked . . . dead . . . I wanted to die."

"I'll kill her." His voice was a mutter.

"You knew I'd find out. Why couldn't you tell me?" Her eyes filled with tears.

"I wanted to." He hesitated. "Something, I don't know—I procrastinated. Listen, Flame. The newspapers made your mother look vile and cheap. The woman they wrote about isn't Jeannie."

"Who is she, then?"

"Your mother was a kind and loving woman."

"Sure. She went to bars. Picked up strangers. One guy said she paid him to do it." Her voice broke. "She was pregnant, Dad, pregnant. I was already in her stomach."

"Listen, darling, please."

"I wish I were dead."

"You must know the truth." Nick paused. "Sometimes people are sick with illnesses. Your mother was an unfortunate victim of a sickness that made her act like there were two Jeannies. The loving woman she was—and another crippling Jeannie against whom she was powerless. Helpless."

"Why didn't you make her well?"

"She hid her suffering." Nick paused. "She didn't trust my love. She was frightened that if I knew about it I would leave her."

"Would you, Dad? Have left her?"

"No." His voice was low and very gentle.

"I wish I was never born."

Nick reached over and stroked her head. She allowed his hand to comfort her.

"More than anything she wanted a baby," he said. "The happiest moments in her life were with you, holding you, singing you lullabies. No child was ever loved more."

"Oh, Dad, I can't stand it."

"I know." His voice still soft.

"I'm scared." She reached up and took his hand. "Suppose I grow up like that—like my mother."

Nick brought her close and held her.

"There's nothing to be scared of." He was stroking her head again. "It happened a long time ago. It's over now."

Flame sobbed on his chest. Nick continued to stroke her and hold her close.

George Warren was thirty years old and a walking fuck machine. His green eyes sparkled, his grin was irresistible, his six-foot body muscular and slim. He had a cleft in his chin and a tousled mass of dark blond hair. Cross Errol Flynn and Michelangelo's *David,* and it is clear why this rake's progress was such a happy event. A lover and friend to actresses, secretaries, students, dancers, waitresses, and Hollywood wives, women were his fix, his addiction, and acting in bit parts and commercials, an easy dollar to support his habit. His *habit* was his *talent,* taking a woman to the edge, stoking her and shooting her into space, a fireball, exploding in multiple orgasm as she crashed to earth.

He was virile and tender, and he gave to sex the illusion of romance, and the sharp danger of a gambler on a winning streak. It was afterward when he was alone and stripped of desire that George felt dead. To feel alive, he took another woman. When fucking no longer filled the void, George called Nick for help. "Pulling an orgasm from a woman once brought me luck. Like catching a falling star. Now it doesn't work."

Within a year, Nick helped George sublimate his sexual energy into his work, and George Warren led a world full of hungry women to the edge, filling their monotonous lives with the glow of desire.

Flame had seen all of George's movies. She had sat among his victims of romantic love, heard them pant and go all mooney, and thought it all very funny. Then, when she was fifteen, one Sunday night, under the moon and the stars, listening to the music, she saw George and felt it happen, a rush, a mysterious desire to be held, warm in his arms, enfolded by love.

In that moment, she was Juliet and George was Romeo. It was fated. Nick had helped George become a star. He had created

George for her. She had read of love's enchantment, but nothing had prepared her for its obsession. She fell terribly in love. Her days were filled with fantasy and her nights were filled with dream.

She entered her sixteenth then her seventeenth year in the grip of obsession. She fell prey to the deadliest boredom when her mind was off George. She believed her obsession to be passion and her passion to be real. One day George would marry her. Their marriage would have all the glamor of a Hollywood premiere. With a willpower even Nick would admire, she reined in her hysteria and emotion. She was cool, seemingly unmoved by George's good looks. She made fun of his womanizing. And George, attracted by her seeming indifference, ran fantasies of seducing this young, innocent sensualist. Unwittingly, he fell prey to Flame's bait.

Yet Flame had misgivings, a fear that he would never love her. If George sensed how much she cared, he would run far away. She knew about that from reading the great romances. Her passion became a torment and her torment made her ill.

"I need your help, Dad. And I want you to promise not to laugh."

"I won't laugh."

"I'm in love."

"Who's the lucky man?"

"George Warren."

Nick paused. "That's not too smart."

"I think it is."

"I see. George is handsome and famous and rich," said Nick. "A great sex symbol. But that's not the real George, is it, Flame. The real George is a sensitive, misunderstood human being who longs to be loved for his beautiful soul. And you're the one to rescue him from all those women who can't give him what he needs. You're wrong, Flame, George isn't there. He's a beautiful frame around a hole—a void that he keeps filling up with women. George can't love. He's not capable of love. George is a sexual tapeworm."

"I love him."

"And if you're not careful, you'll be hurt."

"It's too late."

"That's unfortunate."

"Why not accept that it's happened. I love him. Now, how do I make him fall in love with me? Dad, how can I get him?"

"I'm George's doctor. Not his agent."

"Okay, I'll do it alone."

"Good luck."

"If George is sexy, I'm smart. You always told me what a good head I have. All right, I'll use it. Don't smile that superior smile at me, Dad, I mean it."

Nick realized she had transferred her romantic dream about him to George. Perhaps it was for the best. An adolescent passion for a man like George would flush out her toxic notions of the great grand passion and she'd be ready, eventually, for real life.

It was another Sunday night and Nick's quartet was playing Mozart. The air was fragrant with exotic flora and musky women. Flame sat beside George. Her heart was pounding.

"George?"

"Shhh . . . later."

"Do you really like me?"

"Sure I really like you."

"I mean really really like me?"

"Is this another game?"

"No."

"All right. I like you ten."

"Ten's not an answer."

"Would you mind shutting up."

"Getting a ten is like getting an Oscar."

George smiled a big radiant movie-star smile. "It's a state of mind," he said. "For example, I'm a ten. Being a ten is my job. It makes me rich and famous. Don't mix me up with my job."

"Don't worry. Dad's warned me all about you."

"Yeah? What did he say?"

"Oh, just that you'll make me wildly unhappy and I'm stupid to fall in love with a man like you, and I said he was wrong."

"Can we discuss this some other time?"

"I also said I was strong and won't get hurt." George reached his hand over to cover her mouth.

"Do me a favor. Save it for Mr. Right."

Flame pulled his hand away. She looked deep into his eyes. "You don't get it, do you, George? *You're* Mr. Right. Mr. Right is you."

When Buck passed Wanda in the Titan halls, he remembered what a hot piece of ass she was and he thought he'd like to fuck her again, but Wanda was trouble. She got that romantic look in her eye. She'd run the fuck over in her head like a movie and gab gab gab about how great it all was. Then Buck remembered Jeannie, and how Wanda's crippled son stole Jeannie from under his nose. Not that he gave a damn. Not since Buck had read about Jeannie's death in the newspaper and suddenly everything made sense. Jeannie wasn't up in a cage with a stranger for nothing. She just couldn't get enough. He remembered saying, "You are a very hot piece of ass, sweetheart," and she'd answered, "I'm hot for you, baby," and he'd been schmuck enough to think her heat was for him. It made him laugh. The one time in his life he was in love and it was with a nympho. When he passed Wanda in the hall, he remembered and nodded his head and walked on.

Wanda said, "Hello, Mr. Herman," and smiled like a secretary. She wondered if Buck knew about her occasional visits to old Rose. She wasn't sure why she went through the pretense of friendship to a vulture she despised, whose shit of a son had destroyed her Mischa. She only remembered the Mischa of her youth, a dreamy violinist who wanted to make beautiful music. How kind he was, and decent. She must have been crazy! Destroying both their lives with some vision of glamor. Thinking life was some future fantasy, not knowing it was there, and all she had had to do was reach out and grab it. Well, she knew now. You lived life as it came along. And going back to Rose was a part of life—a piece of unfinished business. She didn't know why. She only knew instinct drove her—a fateful premonition that one day she would even the score. So she called Rose once a month and accepted her eager invitations for dinner.

She was dining with Rose tonight.

Wanda had won at gin rummy the last few months. No one won at cards but Rose. It was a rule of the game. Play to lose or your husband's job was torture. The orchestra wives never questioned the rule. Whatever you do, keep the old bitch happy. So Wanda's winning streak came as a shock. Rose would grudgingly write out a check for fourteen or fifteen dollars. Her check bounced once. Wanda didn't care. She could afford to win. She was a crackerjack secretary, she was loyal, her boss needed her around. Each winning hand, each winning game, was a dagger in Rose's heart.

Dinner was over, and the maid was dismissed. Wanda and Rose had finished two games of gin. Wanda was winning big.

"I ate too much," said Rose. "I don't feel good."

Wanda concentrated on her game.

Rose burped. "I feel rotten. Put a pillow behind my back."

Wanda put her cards on the table. She got up, puffed up a pillow from the couch, and placed it behind Rose.

Rose burped again. "I got a stomachache."

Wanda was silent. She picked up a card from the deck. The jack of hearts. She could use it. She laid down the four of spades.

"I don't feel good." Rose put her hand on her rib cage.

"Indigestion," said Wanda.

"What do you know about my pain?" said Rose.

"Sorry," said Wanda.

"I really hurt."

Wanda was silent.

"Go upstairs. Get my medicine. In the bathroom, on the shelf."

"Sure, Rose."

Wanda climbed the stairs. She went through Rose's bedroom, into the bathroom. She picked up a bottle of pills. That's when she heard Rose's screams. Rose yelling, "Bring my pills—quick! Bring me water! Quick, Wanda, my pills!"

Wanda stood still. Rose was begging for her medicine. Wanda looked into the mirror. A worn-out Wanda looked back at her, a Wanda robbed of her husband, a Wanda nursing a grudge. A Wanda directing her to pick up the pills and throw them into the toilet. A simple small act, but how it would ease the fury in her heart! Wanda lifted the pills. She poured them into the toilet. They hit the water with a splash. She flushed the toilet. The pills whirled around and were sucked under. Wanda faced Wanda. The rage was still there. A permanent scar. Rose was screaming hard. Wanda went downstairs.

"Gimme my pills," gasped Rose.

"They're gone."

"Gimme my pills!" Rose screamed. "Gimme the goddamn pills!"

"Gone," repeated Wanda. "All gone."

"Call Buck."

And Wanda suddenly understood; the Wanda of the mirror finally had her revenge. She watched Rose clutching her chest, her eyes bulging with terror.

"What's Buck's number?"

"Oh-nine-oh-two-one-three."

Wanda took the receiver off its cradle. She put it to her ear. She heard the dial tone. She put her thumb on the black bar. The phone went dead. She aimlessly dialed. Buck had robbed her of her Mischa—now she would take his Rose. Wanda watched Rose gasping for air, heard her heavy, spasmodic breathing, and thought, *an eye for an eye.* She hung up the receiver.

"Buck's not home."

"Help me!" Rose grabbed the table. She lifted herself out of the chair. She stood, swayed, and collapsed to the floor. She lay in a heap, shrunken and moaning. One last groan, a throbbing convulsion, and she was still.

Wanda watched the withered old woman enter the mysterious

moment that released her from pain. Rose had finally found peace.

Wanda stared at her numbly. She got up and walked to the French doors that looked out on the yard. The air was rich with the pungent scent of a tropical garden. The moon was white and full. The sky was full of stars. Wanda looked up to the heavens. Mischa was up there, somewhere.

Mischa, she whispered.

The night was still.

Can you hear me, Mischa? It's even now. The score is even between you and Buck Herman.

In a while she went back to Rose. She picked up the phone and called Buck. His maid answered. Wanda left a message that Rose had gotten sick and she was calling the hospital. Wanda called Cedars of Lebanon. She ordered an ambulance. Then she went back to the French windows, to the moon, to the night, and to her Mischa.

Wanda called Nick the next day, and they arranged to meet at his home at six-thirty.

"You heard about Rose," said Wanda. "I killed her, Nick."

Nick was very still. Finally he said, "What happened?"

"Listen, Nick. It wasn't Buck who destroyed Mischa. It was me. If I had let the boy I fell in love with live the life he loved, but no, some crazy part of me took over his life. This craving for life, it's like a sickness." Wanda was fighting back tears. "Mischa fell in love with me because I was so full of life and he was so sad."

"What happened with Rose?"

"I was upstairs. She was screaming for her medicine. I thought of Mischa. I thought of Buck and how Buck hurt him. I was holding the pills. Rose was screaming. Suddenly, it was all unfinished business—I must have been out of my head. I poured them in the toilet. Oh, Nick, I love him. I feel so bad."

"Go home, Mother. Get a good night's sleep. Tomorrow, go back to work. Work will ease the pain."

"Oh, Nick."

"It's a bad day for you. It will pass."

She was sobbing. "What happened, Nick? What happened to our dreams?"

"Our dreams came true. We just twisted them out of shape." Nick paused. "Go back to work, Mother. And trust in it."

"Good-bye, Nick. And thanks."

The chapel at Forest Lawn Memorial Park in Glendale was full of Buck's men and the orchestra wives. The bitch was dead! The shackle chaining them to her neurotic needs broken.

Buck, in the front pew, between Zelda and Danny, had never felt like this before. He ached with a dull emptiness. Rose had given up her life so he could go out into the world and make it big. She had loved him with her big coarse generous life. No one would ever love him like that again. His earthy adoring mother was dead. His eyes welled up with tears. The tears fell onto his cheek. The tears fell onto his suit. The tears were falling like goddamn rain. Hell, who gave a damn. He'd send the goddamn rag to the cleaners. For the first time in his life, Buck felt human grief.

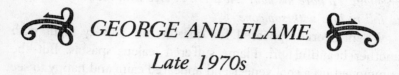

GEORGE AND FLAME
Late 1970s

For every able, ambulatory female, it was year-round hunting season for George Warren. George was pistol-hot, gorgeous, a star, and, most important, a heterosexual bachelor. One day he'd lose his balance and fall, and Flame knew she would be the one to catch him. *Adam fell from paradise. No one was exempt.*

"Hey, Georgie Porgie," she flirted, "it's over. I don't love you anymore."

"I read it in the trades," said George. "Yesterday's gossip. Flame's fallen out of love. George is finally safe."

"So now we can be friends."

"How did you reach this mature decision?" George asked.

"One night I couldn't sleep. Instead of sheep, I counted your women. By the time I hit a thousand I'd made my decision. I can't be in competition with every gorgeous bimbo in town."

"Look what you've missed—a man who can't love, a man in search of the perfect fuck. You're a very lucky girl."

"I am lucky. It would be hell. I'm much too smart for that. So you can stop running. I don't want you anymore."

If George suspected her game, he seemed indifferent. He confided in her and seemed to trust her. Before falling asleep at night Flame reviewed every detail of her brilliant performance.

Does he believe me? Of course he does. He'll marry me. He won't.
Why in hell do I love him. Because I do, I'm madly in love. He's
inside me and I can't get him out. I'll make him marry me. I'll get
pregnant. I'll have his baby. He'll fall in love with the baby. He's got
to fall in love with someone.

When George appeared for quartets on Sunday night with
another beautiful girl, Flame suffered jealous spasms. But she
summoned up a cool veneer and appeared calm and happy to see
him. She was obsessed and she carried on an endless inner dialogue in which she talked to George, thought of George, and was
drained of all energy not connected to him.

And out of her daydreams came a plan of action.

George was always complaining about the lack of good male
roles. If she learned to write a screenplay, wrote George a terrific
hero, a part George couldn't resist, wouldn't George need her?
Maybe Nick was right and George couldn't fall in love. But
George was an actor. He could fall in love with a script. Her
script. If George was to fall in love, then he needed a little push!

She drove up to the Pickwick Bookstore on Hollywood Boulevard, and with the help of an old salesman she bought up adventure and love stories in the public domain—books whose copy-
right had expired and whose plot could be lifted.

She read voraciously. In a month's time she found a love story
that suited George Warren.

She was ready to begin.

Again she returned to the bookstores, the big chains—Brenta-
no's in Beverly Hills, B. Dalton. She went to the shelves on film,
and bought books on screenwriting techniques. She plunged into
work. She broke the stories into scenes. She worked on three- by
five-inch cards. She arranged and rearranged the cards. A fierce
energy drove her. In six weeks she finished a crude first draft.
She slept for three days and nights.

Then she started again. This time she was more familiar with
the technique. She wrote less dialogue and more action. When
she had finished, she got the name of a professional typist from
Nick's secretary. Within two weeks the script was typed and

bound. Another week passed. She summoned the courage to call George.

"Guess what I've been doing?"

"I can't guess."

"I've written a screenplay. If you're my friend, you'll read it and tell me what you honestly think."

"That's terrific, Flame," said George.

"So you'll read it?"

"Sure, sweetie. Drop it off at the front desk and I'll get back to you in a week."

"Uh-uh. You'll give it to some dopey reader. Look, are you free Friday?"

"Working."

"When *are* you free?"

"Late Sunday afternoon."

"Swell. I'll pick you up at six on Sunday in front of the hotel." Before George answered, she hung up.

George lived in a bungalow behind the Beverly Hills Hotel, a pink palace on Sunset Boulevard. He was standing at the arc of the driveway when she drove up, her eyes bright, that defiant edge that so chilled and excited him. He opened the door and got in. She smiled. Her teeth were very white, very straight, very sexy. She pressed the accelerator. The car lurched forward.

"Hello, George."

"Where are you taking me?"

"Somewhere nice and safe."

"Can I trust you?"

"The point is, George, can I trust you?"

He looked at her face full of life and excitement and wondered if she could trust him after all.

She was speeding along Sunset. She was pretty, like a cat— high cheekbones, a spray of freckles, a perfect oval face—a cute cruel playful cat.

"Where in hell are we going?"

"Trust me, George."

"When my agent says 'trust me' what he means is 'fuck you.' "

Flame smiled.

It was pleasant driving along the Pacific Coast Highway, along the blue sea, pleasant to pass the million-dollar bungalows that hugged the shoals and cliffs, the people eating in taco and fish diners. Now they were at Malibu, with its weekend mansions for the rich, now flying past horse farms and fields of wild mustard.

She turned into Zuma, onto a promontory by the edge of the ocean. The sun was in its descent. She stopped in front of a Japanese cottage. Flame unlocked the door and they went in. There were paintings on rice paper and a Buddha in front of a fireplace. On a table sat a bottle of wine, a glass, and a script.

"Is this a seduction?"

"Read all about it. Famous star raped by ambitious young writer." She laughed. "We're friends, George. Remember!" She closed the door behind her. In a second, the car door slammed. George heard the skid of tires. He looked up. It was almost dark. He saw the moths banging against the window. Christ, he hated moths, hated the thud of their thick bodies smashing into the glass. What possessed him to trust this crazy girl? He began to read.

He finished the script in an hour. It was a love story. Amateurish, but she had talent. He knew suddenly it was her strategy for his capture. He stirred uneasily. She was like those goddamn moths. Crashing toward love. No matter what he did or where he went, she'd be there. If it wasn't a script, it'd be something else. She'd lay trap after trap, and one day he'd falter and she'd be there with the trap she called love. *Shit. He was doomed. A luckless male bucking a female force of nature. Shit!* He drank some wine. He heard the car door slam, the turning of the doorknob.

"Shut the door," he said. "You'll let in the moths."

She slammed it shut. "You're angry," she said.

"Hell, no." George lied with an actor's charm.

"You're mad because you know how I feel."

She moved up against him, her cat face with its spray of freckles, her hard blue eyes, her straight white teeth, her mouth parting for a kiss, caught him off guard.

"Fuck me, George."

Had he fucked her, a hard-driving fuck, relentless, pounding her into sexual pulp, Flame would have been like all the others, but George hesitated, and she knew it was from fear. She knew what she had always known. That she was the stronger, and he had no chance. She pulled against him. Her kisses were sweet and hot, and George held her close. She slipped off her dress. She brushed against him. He picked her up. He carried her to the bed. He lay beside her, pulling her nipples until her moans were more pleasure than pain. Now she was like all the others and he was in full heat, racing her the way he raced his Ferrari, for the flash and the thrill. Now she was just another girl, and George again felt safe.

"One day you'll have to fall in love," said Flame.

"Maybe. Maybe not."

"I'm crazy in love with you, George."

So many times had he heard this. So many hundreds and hundreds of times.

"Let's go back," he said. "I've got some work to do."

The ride back was quiet and sad. George wasn't sure why. He only knew he shouldn't have made love to this willful girl who said she loved him like crazy. Crazy love was a pain in the neck. It was for the movies—for the close-ups, the millions of lovesick fans. It was definitely not for real life.

"You've miscalculated," Nick said coldly. "George will never marry you."

"He'll fall in love with the baby, Dad. Then he'll change his mind."

"It's cold-blooded and calculating. He's got every right to refuse you."

"I'm glad I did it. I'd do it again!"

"Listen to me. The George you've fallen in love with is your own creation. It has nothing to do with George. If you saw George for what he is, you'd know it's pure fantasy—and you'll be terribly hurt."

"So I'll be hurt! Don't you understand, I can't live without him."

"It's not fair to George."

"What about me? Anyhow, I'm pregnant. And nothing will stop me from having his child."

After his initial fury, George began to watch his baby grow. Flame had done what so many others had threatened. But she was cold-blooded and without regret. In some cut-off part of his soul, he felt relief. Her way of getting what she wanted, her contempt for what he felt, excited him more than he dared admit. And Flame, sure of herself and optimistic, continued her offensive.

"You don't have to marry me, George. I know it's not your style."

"Aren't you ashamed?"

"Why should I be?"

"You're ruthless, Flame. You knew what you wanted and you went after it. Poor old George. I'm just a drone servicing the great queen bee!"

"You rat."

"Just honest."

"Suppose a miracle happened and you fell in love. Then would you forgive me?"

"Love solves everything for you."

"Everything. Dad says I'm cold-blooded. Suppose I am. You're a bastard with women. You can't help yourself. Neither can I. One day our child will make it all seem right."

"C'mere, bitch!" He reached over and buried his head in her breasts. He crowded out the fact that women were a fact of his life. His child within *her* stomach, her fierce boldness, blinded him to what he knew was not just habit but obsession: women. A woman's voice, her smile, a woman taking a cigarette, a woman walking, a woman naked. He looked into Flame's eyes and felt a second of panic. It was over. Sooner or later he would marry her. She had won. He couldn't be faithful, but his affairs would be quiet and covert. No one would know. He leaned back on the pillow and let her kiss him. "You realize the sacrifice I'm making."

"Oh, darling, tell me! Tell me, George."

"Okay, you crazy girl. I'll marry you."

"You won't be sorry. I promise. I'll make you the happiest man in the world."

George, as always, was ruled by his cock.

At first he slipped into an occasional hour of love. Then, like an addict, he returned to the life he had hoped to give up. An hour's pleasure—a form of oxygen. If Flame suspected, she turned her head in the other direction.

She was eight months pregnant when they were married. All the stars, the great power and talent, gathered at Nick's to celebrate his nineteen-year-old daughter and her impossible conquest. A civil judge said the words:

"I now pronounce you man and wife."

George bent over and kissed her. "Congratulations, kid."

"One day you'll love me, George."

But George thought he could make her happy without love. He wished with all his heart he did love her, but his heart was sealed to love, and when he said the words, it was a lie.

One month later, Flame had a baby boy. They named him Michael. George was an enraptured father. He appeared devoted to Flame. George and Flame bought a house on Bel Air Road. There were four cars in the garage, a housekeeper, a part-time maid, a gardener. It was the stuff of fairy tales. Wild Prince Charming and the Cinderella who caught him. What could possibly go wrong in this best of all Hollywood happy endings?

The powerful old and the cannibal young, a collective psyche, under Nick's care. He seemed to breathe fire, transform their lives from lusterless gloss to glittering gold. That is how they saw themselves, a golden elite leading charmed lives.

All but Nick, who was bored. Bored with his patients who

danced to his tune with a blind obedience. Bored with the controversy that raged around him. "A rogue and a fake," his critics charged. "A dedicated humanitarian, a genius!" his patients screamed back.

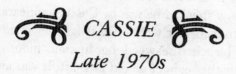

CASSIE
Late 1970s

Cassie sat on an unmade bed in the light green room with the peeling dresser. The sun zigzagged through the dusty venetian blinds and made a striped pattern on the floor. It was as cheerless as any cheerless rented room. Cassie coughed and brought up phlegm. She spit into a tissue and threw the tissue into a half-filled basket. She coughed and spit again and wondered if she would pull through. She had gone to the telephone three or four times and each time she resisted dialing. Finally, she summoned her courage and dialed Nick's office.

After one ring Nick's nurse picked up the phone.

"I'm Cassie Castle. I've got to talk to Dr. Kahn."

"The doctor is with a patient."

"Please tell him who it is. Tell him it's important."

The nurse hesitated. Something in the woman's voice. She buzzed Nick and a second later he took Cassie's call.

"Where are you?" he asked. "When can I see you?"

"I'm here, Nick. In Hollywood. I've rented a room on Yucca." She coughed a dry hacking cough.

"Are you all right?"

"No. Not really."

"I finish with my last patient at six. I'll pick you up and we'll have dinner."

She gave him the address and they both hung up.

They sat in Musso's, a few blocks from her room. Nick tried not to show how shocked he was by Cassie's appearance. She was small and shrunken, her wrists like twigs, her once golden curls dried out like bleached seaweed, her luscious mouth skewered by lines. Nick saw the seam of an old face-lift. It was awful. He took a deep breath and looked into eyes that had once sparkled with mischief.

Cassie reached up and patted her hair.

"I'm a mess, aren't I? Remember the girl everyone fell in love with?"

"Of course I remember."

"You loved her too, didn't you, Nick?"

"I loved her very much."

"I was so happy in those days, before *he* came along. He smashed our lives, though I didn't know I was smashed. I thought if I went away and changed my name I could start all over. I was a call girl for a while."

"I know."

"I met a guy who wanted to marry me, I thought marriage would solve everything. I shut my eyes and thought of space and just did it. I hated to sleep, I always dreamed of John Aherne, I'd wake up in a sweat. He'd get all worked up and want to screw and I'd say no . . . my husband . . ."

"I know who you mean."

"He started playing around. We got divorced. I got a job selling hats. I started coughing. A doctor put me in a hospital and I got better and went back to the store. The cough got worse, the owner was scared I was contagious . . ." Cassie twisted a curl. "I look awful, don't I?"

"No."

"You're such a liar. I'm glad. It makes me feel better."

She started coughing. Nick handed her a handkerchief.

"Thanks."

"I want you to go into a hospital. That's a nasty cough. They'll take X rays. Run some tests."

"I have no money."

"Don't worry."

"Oh, Nick."

"Afterward, you'll come to my place. You'll stay with me until you're better. I'll help you find work."

"You make me want to cry."

"Just use the handkerchief."

She sniffed and wiped away some tears.

Cassie was admitted into Cedars the next day and the doctors ran a battery of tests, took X rays, and performed a biopsy. The result was positive. A few days later a lung specialist opened Cassie up and closed her again.

"There's no point operating," the surgeon said to Nick. "It's like a pearl in tar. We'll never clean it out."

"What about therapy?"

"It could relieve the tumor. It might retard it. It won't reverse or cure it."

"How long has she got?"

"Can't tell. Couple of months."

"I want to take her home."

"She a relative?"

"She's a close old friend. I want her to be as comfortable as possible."

Nick took Cassie home with him. He hired a nurse to take care of her while he was working. After work, he sat beside her in the garden. One night he handed her a package from Saks. She ripped it open and pulled out a blue linen dress.

"You remembered!" she said happily. "Blue's my lucky color."

"Course I remember."

"When you look at me like that I get the feeling you think I'm still the girl in the off-the-shoulder blouse and huaraches."

"A gardenia in her hair."

"She's not me, Nick."

"She is, Cassie. She'll always be you."

She laughed softly.

"You're so sentimental. Will you kiss me, Nick?"

He leaned over and kissed her very gently.

Cassie stood up.

"I'll go and change into my pretty blue dress."

"And I'll take you to a movie."

"You got yourself a deal."

In a few minutes she returned. The blue dress fit her perfectly. Her hair was fluffed out. She wore mascara. When she smiled, for a brief instant, she was a gay and careless echo of a once beautiful girl.

"Well, how do I look?"

"You're a very lucky girl that I have this terrible yen for beautiful blondes with big blue eyes."

Six weeks later Cassie was taken to the hospital. She was put on intravenous feeding. Nick stood at her bedside.

"Hello, Nick . . ."

"I bought you a present."

He took a tape recorder from his pocket. He pushed a button. "Moonlight Serenade" filled the room.

"I remember." Cassie spoke softly. "That was the night I taught you how to dance. You were so shy then, Nick."

"You were dancing with Tom Flanagan. No one dared cut in. You danced by and said, 'You're next.' That night I knew I was okay. So what if I limped. The prettiest girl in the class wanted to dance with me."

Cassie smiled and Nick remembered the girl who knew all the boys were aching to dance with her—the smile of a sweet wild girl who had made his young heart pound with love.

"I always came back to you, Nick. You were the only one I came back to."

"Now you'll stay with me."

"It's over now. You were good to me, always."

"Cassie, don't . . ."

"I'm not sad, honest. It's beautiful, Nick."

She reached up her hand to touch his face. It was too big an effort.

"Nick . . . thanks . . ."

She closed her eyes.

"Cassie . . . Cassie . . ."

He laid his head on her breast and he wept.

A month later, heartsick and lonely after Cassie's death, Nick asked Flame and George to join him for a week in Acapulco.

BOOK SIX

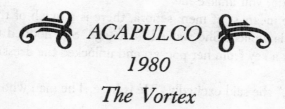

ACAPULCO
1980
The Vortex

Nastasia stood at the side of the room and watched the men in bright jackets and the women in silk flirting and drinking champagne. She saw George Warren. He sat still and silent, like a classical sculpture, breathtaking in his masculinity.

Luis Delgado stood nearby. He watched Nastasia with amusement.

"Handsome devil," said Delgado. "Look at them watching him. Even the great *putas* to whom sex is just a business, even they are not immune."

"He is like a Greek god."

"Very romantic, señora, but this man is no god. He is a womanizer—and notorious. The pretty woman beside him is his wife. *Pobre bonita.* What she must suffer!"

"The man with him. Who is he?"

"That is Dr. Nicholas Kahn. How shall I put it. He is not simply a famous doctor, he is a sort of Svengali . . . a magician men rush to to become a George Warren."

"Interesting."

"It is interesting, Madame. If you were superstitious, you could say he performs a kind of black magic, takes ordinary men and women and helps turn them into stars. Oh, there are plenty of stars, señora, they shoot to the top, defy gravity for a moment, and crash. The fall is very hard. Few recover. Dr. Kahn provides wings for that precarious flight."

"Delgado, you amaze me."

"In the meanest of men, señora, there is a touch of the poet."

Nastasia smiled. She walked backstage. She nodded to Sandoval, took a key from her pocket, and unlocked the dressing room door.

"Anna," she said excitedly. "He is here. The man who can save us."

"Who is he?"

"It will be easy to recognize him. He sits with George Warren and Warren's wife. His name is Nicholas Kahn."

"George Warren!"

"This man Kahn is a great doctor. Delgado says he is responsible for all the great stars. Anna, you must dance tonight as you have never danced before. Remember your father, Anna, and fly!"

Anna heard one thing: *George Warren.* The occasional hours away from the barre she had stolen into a movie house to see his film. His eyes, his smile, his strong lean body had filled her with excitement. This was the closest Anna came to happiness. Now, tonight, George Warren was here to see her dance. Madame had said he was married. Nastasia's words of so long ago came back to her: 'I have sacrificed two men to achieve my dream—nothing can stop me!' And Anna thought, *My legacy is not my father's genius. It is my mother's ruthless will. I have hated her all my life, but she is my mother, my teacher, she has taught me what I have to do.*

She looked at that alluring reflection in the mirror and she realized her great power. Her beauty had always been used in the service of others. Tonight she was its master.

She would fly, yes, but not in the service of Madame. She would fly for her life and all life meant—she would fly tonight for love! God had sent her Nicholas Kahn, yes, but as a messenger of love. It was through Kahn she would reach George Warren. She studied herself hard. What was all this beauty for except to get to happiness. She remembered Sandoval. It would cost her a small price, a bribe. Her heart pounded, yet she felt sure of her plan and ruthless in her desire.

"If you're thinking of the movie star," said Nastasia, "don't. Men like that are worthless. They only bring grief. Anna, don't be a little fool."

"Don't worry, Madame. I know what I must do."

Anna turned away from Madame and knocked on the door. In a second, Sandoval unlocked it. Anna's coppery mane tumbled over her shoulders, and when she smiled his cold heart flopped about like a baited fish.

This was no pretty puta. *This one belonged to the devil. No wonder the general was loco.*

Anna moved toward him, and his cutthroat heart was filled with sudden fear.

"What is it?" he muttered. "What do you want?"

"Tonight, a man will come to see me. I want you to let him in."

"You are loco, señorita."

"Two minutes alone with him, that's all. I promise, Sandoval, you won't be sorry."

"Loco! Loco!" He paused. "Do you know what the general will do if he suspects? His men will cut me up for meat for his dogs—except for my balls, señorita. De Diego will gild them in bronze, and each Christmas he will give plaster of paris copies to his men, a reminder of one who was disloyal!"

Anna looked into his eyes. She put his hand on her breast. When she smiled, Sandoval trembled.

"Sandoval, I beg you."

Anna had come to him with offerings. A kiss or two for a moment alone. Later there would be more requests, with richer rewards. Sandoval relaxed. He laughed at his fears. His imagination had carried him away. Anna was like all the others—a pretty slave girl yearning to be free.

Once Anna felt freedom, it would become a habit. Sandoval felt cool and detached. He knew what lay ahead. *He would share her kisses with de Diego, thrust his cock into her body with the same fierce lust. Yes! She understood he was the only one who could give her what she wanted. But she must pay the price. Sandoval was finally de Diego's equal!*

"No one will know," she whispered. "I'll make you happy, Sandoval, I promise."

The forbidden thrill of it, of Anna's being his *mujer* as well as de Diego's, almost deranged him. *She was right. No one would know. There was no one to tell.*

"Well, Sandoval?"

"All right," he said coldly. "I'll let the hombre in."

A pitch-black stage. Then a beam of white light, and in its center, Anna. She wore white. She stood motionless, a perfect human sculpture. The guitar throbbed. She clicked the castanets. Her feet cracked on the floor and it was like a volley of bullets. She leapt and twirled. She flew into the air. The crowd leaned forward. She whipped about in a flashy arc, a gossamer thread, sensual legs, a long, lean body, a heartbreaking face. Heavy heat filled the room as this goddess in white performed black magic.

It was pure raw chemistry. George felt his life change with a sudden violence, the way a bird that has been flying around his cage suddenly *smashes* against the bars. Yes! He had been flying around his twenty-five-room cage on Bel Air Road, flying in and out of rooms, and cars, and thousands of women. In his head he had been faithful to Flame, always flying back to *her* cage, *her* womb, *her* silent, stoic rage. Then, suddenly, in a strange land, on a strange night, he heard the siren song. And he was helpless. He felt immune against what passed between him and the dancer. He felt Flame's furious eye. For a second he thought he must protect himself. *Then he knew. It no longer mattered. Flame's claim on him was over. This mysterious girl had confronted him with his captivity. The cage door sprang open.* George knew that he would leave.

Come, Anna silently beckoned. *Come to me . . .*

I'm coming, he silently answered. *Nothing can keep me away.*

Flame looked at George and felt terror, swift and keen and

terrible. She couldn't touch or feel it, but it was there; the unbearable moment when a woman knows her husband is violently
drawn to another; when she knows whatever she says or does,
she can't stop what is happening. George's face was more radiant
than in his wildest moments of love. She knew he had other
women, but he conducted himself so scrupulously, she suffered
no pain—not from gossip, nor a feeling of loss. On the contrary,
his sexual excesses brought him back with an even greater ardor.
She accepted his "other" women taken in dimly lit hotel rooms,
stolen morning hours, or the afternoon heat. Women were a fact
of George's life. Hollywood said her marriage would never work,
but Flame looked the other way. She accepted George's promis-
cuity as the price she must pay for her marriage, and dulled its
pain with false laughter. But tonight her soul was dark. The girl
in white was the rider of a runaway horse and the runaway horse
was George. In that moment, Flame's few sweet years of romance and illusion were quickly snatched away.

The guitar stopped. Nick watched Anna face the crowd. She
lifted her arms. The force of her personality rolled over the
room, the mysterious moment when a performer holds commu-
nion with her audience, when technique is the voice of the soul.
A wild, brief, unplanned moment, but it shot through Nick with
primitive force. A twanging guitar and a beautiful girl in a skin-
tight dress, everything Nick had dammed up, everything he had
denied—the long-forgotten dream that haunted his life—came
together in one bright flame.

A quest for love.

He had it briefly in Jeannie's arms, but love had eluded him
then and all the years afterward. All the love affairs where Nick
had asked himself what he wanted rose before him. He had been
in some ephemeral pursuit of the beloved. What made him think
this dancing siren, a siren to her bones, could give him what he
wanted? Life was flying faster and faster. There had been too
many women and too many false dreams. No, he wasn't imagining it! She was sending him a signal, picking him out from the

others and willing him to her, relentless, coming at him again and again, in an unearthly siren song.

Nick, who had helped so many who had fallen victim to that great rash passion called Love at First Sight, in that instant fell victim himself. In that second Nick was the boy once again in touch with his dream and the siren was singing her song. Nick didn't ask himself *What am I looking for,* because he knew. She was up there on the stage, dancing, luring him on and love divine and love profane burned within him—one flame.

Nick glanced at George. He saw a face unfamiliar with romance filled with a romantic expression. Nick had forged George into a movie star the way a blacksmith forges iron. He forged a sexual hazard into a romantic institution. When George made love, love was a union between George and a hundred million women. George *was* love and love was a business that made George rich. But Nick knew George was man-made, an actor reciting lines, a supposedly reformed rake safely married; and watching him, Nick realized the yoke of marriage had never tamed him. George could no more resist Anna's allure than the tides can resist the pull of the moon.

Then Nick watched Flame. A strange anger on her face. She sensed George's attraction and was jealous. It was a charged and fated moment when lives fall into disarray. It decided Nick on a course of action. He got up, passed the cheering mob, and went backstage. A mean-looking brute sat in front of the dressing room. When he saw Nick, he stood up, unlocked the door, and went in.

So this is the secret lover for whom she risks her life, thought Sandoval. *Well, silence is dangerous. It could cost me my life and it will cost her more than a few girlish kisses.* Sandoval nodded brusquely and unlocked Anna's door.

Nick shut the door behind him. The excitement of this strange adventure made him feel like a boy, young again, and caught by the most beautiful woman he had ever seen. Her beauty was so startling, Nick gasped.

"You came," Anna said simply.

"Then I was right. You willed me here."

"Yes."

Anna moved toward him. She put her hands on his shoulders. She kissed him. Nick felt multiple heat-lightning flashes shoot off.

"When can I see you?" he asked.

"There's a small but good restaurant about ten kilometers outside of town. It's called La Luna. Meet me tomorrow at one o'clock."

"I'll be there," said Nick.

"Good-bye, Dr. . . . Nick."

"Good-bye, Anna."

Anna paced back and forth in her cramped little room. Nothing could stop her now. She would be happy, she had every right! One last obstacle, Sandoval. Her promised kisses would bind him to silence. Dare he tell de Diego, the greedy guard would be destroyed. She knocked on the door and Sandoval unlocked it.

"I'm ready," she said, "come collect your reward."

Anna stood before the mirror and looked at herself hard. Ordinarily she saw a face of sadness. Tonight she saw a face in love. She would will Nick to fall in love—he already had—and would ask her to marry him. Marriage to Nick would keep her close to George. They would talk—see one another without subterfuge—an ordinary family. She would pick up the phone and invite George and that wife to dinner, and slowly George would fall in love. She would make it happen. Nick was a small sacrifice for what she wanted . . . what she must have.

Nastasia unlocked the door. She came into the room.

"Quick," she said excitedly. "Tell me what happened."

"Well, he is very intelligent."

"Anna, don't tease me."

"He knew exactly what I was doing. 'You willed me here,' he said. I admitted I did."

"Then what happened?"

"Nothing. I meet him for lunch tomorrow. Tomorrow, the great Dr. Kahn will fall in love."

Nastasia looked at her incredulously.

"Yes," she said slowly, "I believe you can make it happen."

"I can and I will." Anna spoke softly. "All the years you talked to me of Andreyev, all the years you scolded and beat me because I wasn't like him, because I wasn't a genius. Do you remember you once told me how you sacrificed two men to get what you wanted? You said it was for art, for dance, a small sacrifice. My gift, my real gift, is not from my father but from you. It is my mother's ruthlessness. I had the most ruthless teacher in God's world train me to get what she wanted, what she thought was hers. She trained me well. There's no way I can fail. Do you understand, Madame? Failure is impossible."

"Anna, please . . ."

"It's all right, Madame. It's what you want too. You found him, remember? You pointed him out and urged me to dance. You didn't want me to dance, you wanted me to capture him and I have."

"Anna, be careful."

"I am careful . . . I've taken care of everything."

"Sandoval . . . If he tells de Diego, we are lost."

"He'll be silent."

"These are dangerous men, Anna."

"My talent is for danger. Ten minutes with Sandoval and you will see how dangerous I am. Now give me five minutes alone to rest."

"Yes, Anna."

When Nastasia left her, Anna continued to stare into the mirror.

"Yes, marriage to Nick Kahn would solve everything. No more de Diego. An end to Madame's power. A way to be near George Warren. A chance to have George for herself. Yes, marrying Nick had all the symmetry of great choreography, a human choreography, audacious and original, with each of the players dancing out his featured role. Like all great inspiration it seemed logical and terribly simple.

Anna took a long, deep breath. Another performance with Sandoval for a few hours with Nick. Sandoval's lust would bind him to silence. If he betrayed her to de Diego, he would be killed. Anna thought of the future with George and was all the more determined nothing would stop her.

Anna looked at the clock. Her next show would be starting in five minutes. She knocked on the door and Sandoval unlocked it. She took the cigarette from his mouth. She dropped it and smashed it under her heel. Her smile was radiant.

"Now what do you want?" he asked suspiciously.

"Tomorrow. I want three hours."

"You are crazy."

"Three hours," she repeated, and smiled again.

"You know how expensive three hours will be, señorita?"

"I think I do."

"You know if de Diego finds out it will be the end—for both of us."

"He won't find out."

Now Sandoval smiled and it was coarse and brutish.

"I am a fair man, señorita, a just man. I don't want to take advantage of your situation. Three hours with your gentleman will cost you three hours with me."

"Thank you, Sandoval."

"I want full payment in advance."

"Tonight, after the show, when you take me home, I'll see you're paid in full."

Anna turned and walked to the dance floor. Sandoval watched the way she moved—he watched the crazy sway of her hips and thought, *this* puta *is as diabolical as any man.* He spit. Women! They owned you through your cock. Well, he'd take care of this daughter of the devil. If she thought de Diego was her master, she'd learn differently tonight.

Flame was sitting on the edge of the bed. It was late. She wore
a satin robe. She crossed her leg and moved it against the other
leg. She had great legs and she knew how to move them. She
moved her leg back and forth and the sting of sex sprang up in
George's cock.

He hadn't fucked today. He wasn't sure why except for a yen
for something new. When he saw Anna swing her hips, he knew
why he'd saved himself. Then Nick stood up and went backstage.
Nick took his prize and George felt like a goddamn fool.

"She really got to you, didn't she, Georgie?"

"You're a jealous bitch."

"Jealous! Not me, George. I'm laughing, George. I think it's
funny."

"Yeah! What's so goddamn funny?"

"Why, the fact she must have known you were in the audience
and she didn't give a damn. Anyhow, you fell for the wrong girl,
George. She's not for you."

"She's not, huh?"

"I thought you noticed. Dad got there first."

Flame was still moving her leg back and forth like a goddamn
whore, smiling like a whore, getting up and moving like a whore.
And George, who never saved himself for anyone, much less
another woman, was reeking with sex.

He went toward her and kissed her and moved her toward the
bed and held her close and thrust slow and strong and steady
until he had her alive and pulsing—a current of sex—wired,
crazed, and moaning with joy. And once again they were partners
in what held them together, and when she screamed from raw
pleasure, he came with a fury. He lay on her, heavy and inert and
ready for sleep.

She felt his heavy breathing and wondered what she would do
if George ever left her. She'd have to face that awful fear: Was
she like her mother? As long as George was with her she'd never
have to face the fury that drove her mother to bars, to strangers,
to an inevitable death. George was sex, just sex, and each time

George fucked her he stilled the fear, and each fuck became love, the biggest and best kind of lovemaking, and life with George was finally a long sweet endless fuck that she pretended was love. If they didn't have much to say to one another—well, no marriage was perfect. Her marriage was like everyone else's—not quite perfect, except for the sex. And George had always come back to her for more.

George was right. She'd been jealous. She'd been like a wildcat. She must still love George more than anything else if she got that jealous over a stranger.

La Luna was a small and exclusive restaurant on the crest of a hill. It was filled with laughing, chatting tourists. A mariachi trio was wailing a song. The door opened. Anna entered. An electrical charge passed over the room. The maître d' led her to Nick's table and the current followed in her footsteps. When she smiled, strong men crumpled. The last of Nick's defenses were gone.

The waiter adjusted her chair.

"The staring. Does it disturb you?"

"No . . . I'm used to it."

"I guess you are."

"Dr. Kahn . . ."

"Nick."

"Nick . . . I'm sure you want to know—in your own words—why I lured you backstage."

Nick smiled. "Once, in olden times, men believed in gods and goddesses. The mythmakers tell us of a White Goddess, a sexual priestess. She was beautiful and cunning—a siren, a muse. She was Cleopatra—Delilah—she incarcerated Merlin. Men have feared her and worshiped her. She is irresistible." Nick paused. "You know you have these powers. Last night you used them. You danced for me. You compelled me to go back and meet you. Why?"

"Do you know who I am?"

"I know Nastasia Rostov is your mother. I remember her defection."

"Nastasia Rostov was an insanely ambitious dancer who knew she lacked the great talent. She got pregnant by the greatest dancer in Russia so her child would have his genius. His name was Andreyev and I am that child."

"I see."

"Since I was small, a little child, my mother trained me—punished me—to get what she wanted. We ran out of money. I was sold to cheap nightclub owners. Delgado saw me. I was sold to Delgado. To the highest bidder. To de Diego. Do you know about de Diego? Powerful, cruel. I am his prisoner. His dancing doll. I see no one else. I speak to no one but him. He has trained me to make his kind of love. I excite him. I torture him. I know his every desire. I make him happy. Do you begin to understand?"

"Go on."

"One day de Diego will get tired of me. He could marry me to one of his soldiers—it's his way. Or, if he is angry, jealous, I could die. I know it sounds crazy, but it's not."

Anna sat solemn and poised. Nick saw this strong-willed and fiercely sexual young woman was hurt and struggling with pain. He wanted to cry—not from pity but from admiration. She was magnificent in her strength and her desire to survive. A wild wild child, throwing herself upon the world to escape her agony. How he yearned to hold her, to dissolve her pain in his love.

"I heard you could change lives, like a magician. I used all my power to bring you to my dressing room."

"You have a bodyguard."

"Yes."

"Who unlocked the door for me."

"I bribed him."

"How did you arrange to meet me?"

"I bribed him again."

"This is a very expensive lunch."

"Yes . . . very."

"How can I help you, Anna?"

"Marry me."

"I'm very glad you said that," Nick said gently. "It relieves me of the awful anxiety of having to ask you."

"You mean . . ."

"Perhaps not marriage, but I was going to ask you to come back with me."

"Yes."

"When?"

"Now, as soon as possible. You can't understand how crazy he is . . . ruthless." She lowered her voice to a whisper. "If he finds out . . . you're serious . . ."

"Anna, you don't understand. This isn't pity. It's not charity. I fell in love with you last night. Today, sitting here waiting for you to come, I wondered if you were a mirage, a fantasy of my imagination. I wondered if when I saw you in the daylight, you would be different. You aren't. And I feel the same."

Anna felt a swell in her throat. She was using Nick as callously as her mother used Andreyev, to escape de Diego and make George fall in love. She had planned this, made it happen. So why did she feel this rise of tears, this congestion?

"I want to ask you something."

"Anything," said Nick.

"You say you love me. . . . You fell in love."

"I did . . . I do."

"If you didn't, if it hadn't happened, would you still help me?"

"Yes."

"Why?"

"If a beautiful little child came to me and asked for my help, wouldn't I help her?"

Anna smiled.

"Anna, it's not really about help. It's as if I'm listening, finally, to an old dream, a cry from my own childhood. Hearing it, Anna, and paying attention. I want to take care of you. I want to end your suffering."

"No one said how kind you are."

Nick took a handkerchief from his pocket.

"Wipe those tears," he said. "And let's get the hell out of this place."

In the foyer, beside the girl who operated the telephone, Nick said, "You'll need your passport. We'll have to go back to the hotel."

"I brought it along."

Nick grinned. "Pretty sure of yourself."

"I had no choice."

Nick told the operator to dial the Azteca. In a few minutes he was talking to Flame.

"Hello," she said.

"I've got a big surprise. Prepare yourself."

"Come on, Dad. Not today."

"I'm getting married."

"What!"

"That's right. I'm marrying Anna. Aren't you going to congratulate me?"

"I think you're mad."

Nick laughed. "Once you get to know her I think you'll understand."

"Just because you're crazy doesn't mean I have to make her my new best friend."

"We'll talk about it later. Right now I want you to book three seats on the first plane out of Acapulco. If there's no commercial flight this afternoon, charter a plane. Madame Rostov lives down the hill. Her house is covered with bougainvillaea. There's an official black car in the driveway. Tell George to go and get her. Have him wait for her. Tell her no luggage—just her purse and passport. If the chauffeur resists, have George make a ruckus."

"Will you tell me what this is all about?"

"Once we're home I'll explain everything. I'm going to go straight to the airport with Anna. Tell George to pay the bill. Get Madame Rostov—and get out of there as inconspicuously as you can."

"Dad . . ."

"Do as I say, Flame—quickly and quietly."

Flame booked three seats on the five-fifteen Mexicana flight to Los Angeles. She found George sunbathing by the pool.

"Prepare yourself," she said. "Dad is going to marry Anna."

"What?"

"That's right, George. He's going to take her back to Los Angeles and he's going to marry her."

"Jesus."

"He wants us on the first plane out," she said. "I made reservations on the five-fifteen flight. Nick wants you to get Madame Rostov. She lives down the hill in a house that's covered with bougainvillaea. There's a black car in the driveway. Nick says if the chauffeur makes trouble, start screaming."

"What in hell . . ."

"He'll know who you are, George. He'll shut up. He doesn't want trouble."

"What else does he want?"

"I'll take care of everything else."

George dressed. He told Flame to wait in the room. He rented a car. It cruised along, past the luxurious mansions on one side, and on the other, a drop to the sea. George saw the house shrouded by purple flowers. The black car was in the driveway. He had his driver wait. He rang the doorbell. A maid opened the door.

"I want to see Madame Rostov."

"Señora no aquí."

"Where is she? *Dónde está?*"

"Espera." The maid turned away. Within seconds she returned with Sandoval.

"You want to see Señora Rostov?"

"Yes."

"May I ask why?"

"It's a personal matter."

"The señora is shopping."

"Did she say where?"

"The señora is shopping," he repeated.

"When she returns, ask her to call me at the Azteca."

"*Sí*, Señor Warren."

Sandoval watched George drive away. He was confused. Last night, Anna had given herself to him like a *puta* in exchange for an afternoon with Dr. Kahn. Now the movie star was here and looking for the *madre*. *Something was terribly wrong!* He must find Señora Rostov. She would certainly know.

George returned to the hotel. If Madame Rostov called, Flame would arrange to pick her up. George would be back as soon as he could. He got into the taxi and directed it back into town.

Sandoval got into his car. Within seconds he was speeding down the hill. *Hijo de puta! Mierda!* He cursed Anna. He cursed de Diego. He cursed the goddamn sewers and the fucking politicians for tearing up the streets. *Phew! the stench!* He honked the horn as he crawled along. He passed a row of cafés. On the terrace of the Negrito, Nastasia was drinking coffee.

"Señora Rostov!" he yelled.

Nastasia looked around.

"*Aquí!* Señora! Quickly."

Nastasia stood up and walked toward the car.

"Where is Señorita Anna?"

A smile of contempt passed Nastasia's face, but she was silent.

"*Mierda!*" he roared. "Where *is* she? I must know or something *terrible* will happen!"

"What is more terrible than our captivity?"

"You do not know de Diego. When he finds that Anna is without a guard—the man is *bruto*, señora, *sangriento!*"

"De Diego is four hundred miles away."

"His men are everywhere, and no one—*no one*, señora—is safe. *Quickly, where is she?*"

"She is having lunch with Dr. Kahn."

"*Coño!* We must find her!"

Nastasia hesitated. She must warn Anna. She got in the back-seat. The street was choked with Indians and cows and chickens.

Mierda! Sandoval turned into a narrow side street, past small houses and old squares. He turned onto a highway. He pressed down on the gas. They shot ahead. The car picked up speed, honking, passing cars in its path. Ahead, a car was parked on a gravel shoulder. They passed it and it lurched onto the highway. Sandoval was racing like the wind. He looked through the rear-view window. The car was hard on his heels. It wasn't a black official car, but he recognized it as that of a colleague—a hit man. A bird of prey.

"*Mierda*. It's Ortez."

He was driving like a madman. A dog crossed in front of the car and he broke its back. Nastasia screamed. She covered her ears to drown out the yelps.

"You killed it," she whimpered.

Sandoval kept driving.

"You're as mad as de Diego!"

He was flying along.

"What's *happening*, Sandoval? I've got to know!"

"Your daughter Anna double-crossed me. Someone saw her with the doctor, and reported it to the general. You are no longer the general's guest. You are no longer welcome in his country."

"What will he do?" Her voice was trembling.

Sandoval reached his hand into his inside pocket. He pulled out a black revolver. He held it in his hand, on the wheel. That bird of prey, Ortez, was closing in. They were carrion now. Living corpses. Sandoval's foot, on the gas, reached the floor. Ahead, the headlights of an approaching car blinded him. *It was over. He had forfeited his life for a fuck. De Diego's fuck. It was pathetic. Loco!* He had blundered and blunder was death. *No escape. If he got away today, they would get him tomorrow.* The approaching car swerved in front of him. It cut off his path. Sandoval braked. The car behind him stopped. Ortez, carrying a gun, walked slowly toward the car. Nastasia screamed. Sandoval turned and pointed his revolver at her head.

"For God's sake, have pity . . ." She was crying softly.

Sandoval looked at her dully.

"We were fools, señora, and now we must pay. This way it is fast. If I leave you to those *coños* and their knives . . . Pray, señora, pray to God for your soul."

"Don't . . . Saanndo—" A bullet crashed into her forehead. Her head blew apart. She didn't feel the second bullet. Sandoval watched them coming closer, two in front and one from behind. He saw the gleam of their guns. He saw a silver dagger flash in the glare of the headlight. What did it matter? He put the gun in his mouth. He shut his eyes and pulled the trigger.

Two Indian boys playing in the cornfield heard the shots. They saw three men run toward their cars and drive away. The boys ran to the parked black car. They looked through the windows. In the backseat a woman's body sat slumped. A single sinewy thread connected her head to her body. In front, a body was lying, stomach up. The man's *cojones* were cut off and stuffed in his mouth. Human slaughter. The boys screamed. One boy vomited. The two boys ran away.

BOOK SEVEN

ANNA
FLAME
NICK
1980

A full moon shone down on the rich and ghostly mansions that sat like unused movie sets on Sunset Boulevard. From the hills above, music floated into the air. Nick was celebrating his marriage to Anna.

Lanterns fluttered in the jacaranda trees. A striped blue tent with golden tassels billowed over a wooden dance floor. Waiters in tuxedos passed among the guests, filling empty glasses with champagne. A dance band played old songs, and a balalaika trio strummed Russian melodies.

Anna's tight white dress hugged her hips as if they were a winding road. Her red hair glowed. She was fire. She was ice, a human comet hurtling through space. The crowd was keen on her every move.

All except George.

Flame was beside him. Flame danced in his arms. Flame talked and George listened and laughed. It is as if, Anna thought, I were invisible, as if I didn't exist. If I dance, the crowd will roar and George will have to notice me.

"I want to dance for them, Nick. Is it all right?"

Nick turned to the crowd.

"You've all met Anna," he said. "Now you'll see her dance."

Anna motioned to the balalaika player, who followed her onto the dance floor. She smiled a gorgeous half smile. She danced a waltz, so graceful and delicate, like a caress. The crowd went crazy and screamed for more.

George went crazy too. Anna's allure sent lethal shock waves up and down his spine. He felt helpless against her. He remembered how angry he'd been that first night he'd seen her, when Nick suddenly stood up to go backstage. How upset he'd been when he'd heard Nick was bringing her back to L.A. to get married. She was Nick's now, Nick's wife. He couldn't fuck Nick's wife. Of course not. He hated himself for the thought. But now that it had started, he couldn't stop it. *I'm a shit,* he thought, *a real bastard,* and having admitted to this defect in his character, he suddenly felt free of guilt. George watched Anna, glittery and sensuous, and felt a happy subversive thrill at the sweet adulterous adventure that lay ahead.

Within minutes he had everything planned. Yet an instinctive sixth sense made him turn and look into Flame's eyes. He saw jealousy, strong as poison, taking her over. George smiled his most radiant movie-star smile and put his arm around her shoulder and still he felt the poisonous flow.

Flame was smart enough to accept what George was and what George needed to survive. She'd put up with rumor and gossip by pretending indifference.

George's screwing around had nothing to do with her. She'd been smart about that. But this was different. Anna was different. She wasn't just another easy lay. Anna could be George's lover. She didn't know how or where or when, but she knew one day it would happen.

George knew how he'd wash away the poison—how he'd fuck her tonight and how Flame'd think it was love and she'd quiet down. It was his power over her—the way she translated sex into love. He'd counted on it and it had kept his marriage intact. Yes, he needed the safety of marriage to a woman like Flame—romantic to her core, and smart enough to understand it was George's way and to leave him alone. A rare quality in a woman, almost impossible to find in a wife. Well, Flame was smart, but she was human too. And George loved his home. He loved his son. He loved the sweet domestic comforts. He wasn't sure how long this fling with Anna would last, but it would be intense and that meant danger. He wasn't about to break up his marriage. He had to guard against jealousy, keep Flame busy, so preoccupied she'd never suspect.

Anna finished dancing. The crowd screamed for more. Anna put her hands to her mouth. She opened her arms. Her eyes fell on George. He quickly turned away.

"She wants you," said Flame.

"Sure she does," said George. "I'm a famous movie star. I accidentally blink and some dame faints from love. C'mon, baby, don't start imagining things."

"Okay," said Flame.

"It's too damned crowded in here. Let's go someplace and have a drink. There's something I want to talk over."

"What?"

George grinned. He squeezed her arm.

"Are you ever going to trust me?"

"Okay. I trust you."

"Good." He bent over and kissed her and quickly led her away.

They sat opposite each other in a booth in the Polo Lounge. It was wallpapered with large green silky leaves. Large pots held bright flowers. There was the cold-eyed festivity of actors, agents, and executives working one another over.

"Busy night," said Flame.

"That's why we're here."

"Why are we here, George?"

"Remember that afternoon you took me for a ride and asked me to read your script?"

She laughed. "Of course I remember."

"Well, I pulled it out and reread it."

"Why, George?"

"Because I liked it." He paused. "I've been reading so much shit lately—call it a hunch."

"What are you up to, darling?"

George grinned. "It's a good script. Good enough to spend some time and effort on. Six months work, Flame, and you can give me a script I want to make."

"Are you serious?"

"Dead serious."

"Well, why not get a real writer?"

"I want you. It's your script. Look, I'm not asking you to write *War and Peace*—I'm asking you to fix a love story. It's there, baby —everything. It just needs another draft. Well?"

George took her hand and held it.

"I could've taken you home and fucked the hell out of you and asked you to say yes then, but I didn't. I brought you here. I'm asking you here. Do you know why?"

"Why?"

"Because after I fucked you you'd say yes, but the next day you'd change your mind. I'd fuck you again and you'd say yes again and the day after you'd change your mind. I don't want you to say yes because of a great fuck."

Flame laughed.

"I want you to say yes because you want to do it. Say yes, baby. Tell me you want to. We'll have a great picture."

"You really are serious."

"That's why we're here."

George grinned. It came from his gut. He squeezed her hand tight.

"Let's go home," Flame said softly. "I want you to fuck the hell out of me. Then I want to say yes."

By 2:00 A.M. the party was over. Nick was outside on the terrace. It was cool. Anna walked toward him and Nick remembered his boyhood afternoons under the spell of the great movie sirens—how he carried their beauty from the movie house into his room, how he substituted the ecstasy of fantasy for loneliness.

And here was Anna, the same siren allure, an echo of a boyhood dream that once held him in thrall. Only Anna was real, vulnerable, this child-woman walking toward him, this beautiful lost girl.

And Anna, in Nick's arms, felt her anger against George melt away. When Nick held her like this, so tender with her, so gentle, everything she'd been denied, everything she'd longed for, sprang up within her heart. Her eyes were full of tears.

"I'm happy, Nick. Why am I crying?"

"Because you've never had a chance to be happy and the possibility is here. What you've wanted—a normal life, a happy life—it's yours."

"I almost believe you . . . about being happy. It scares me, Nick."

"It's all right, darling. Everything . . ."

She laid her head on Nick's chest. He stroked her head as he would a child's. He kept stroking it. It was very quiet. The still night, the sky, the clouds and the moon, and Nick holding Anna in his arms and stroking her head.

Six days a week at one o'clock Anna got into her red Mercedes and drove to Bedford Drive, where Bill Gull, a former Olympic champion, worked her out in his luxurious gym. Gull kept the most beautiful women in town in a state of perpetual youth, and their devotion to Gull's gym was as intense as that of the pilgrims at Lourdes.

A few days after Nick's party, Gull was working Anna out when his blond receptionist interrupted him.

"George Warren's on the phone," she said. "Says it's important."

" 'Scuse me," said Gull. "I'll be right back."

"Tell George hello," Anna said quickly.

Gull smiled and said, "Will do."

In a minute he returned.

"That's it for the day. Our mutual friend wants you to meet him outside. He'll pick you up in five minutes. Oh, he said to tell you he hates waiting."

"You're serious."

"Sure I'm serious. Better hurry, kid, you got four minutes left."

Anna rose from the mat. "You're a real friend."

"Hell, George is my buddy. He sent me half my clientele. I'm glad I can help."

"Anyhow, thanks."

He watched her walk to the door and even Gull, habituated to beauty as a business, caught his breath. *This dame,* thought Gull, *will really give that son of a bitch a run for his money.*

It was the kind of day where the smog cancels everything else out, but Anna stood on the corner of Bedford reeling from happiness. Finally, life was here. Her dream was answered. George's black Ferrari pulled up to the curb. She opened the door and got in.

"Surprised to see me?" he asked.

"A little."

"I wasn't sure you'd be out here."

"You're a liar."

"Yes I am." George grinned. "But it's a little white lie and that doesn't count."

"You know," she said, "the last few days I've had the funniest feeling. I can't explain it, like I wasn't alone."

"You weren't," he said. "I've had you followed. It was the only way I could find you. Am I forgiven?"

Now Anna grinned. "I forgive you."

George swung the car onto Maple Drive. Tall red-leaved trees were like sentinels before the vast houses.

George slowed down before a gray stucco house covered with purple wisteria. It was hidden from the street.

"See that house?"

"It's pretty."

George swung into the driveway.

"Whose house is it, George?"

"Mine."

"Your house!"

"Mine." George grinned. "It's a small town. You're married to my wife's father, who's also my shrink. You don't expect me to make love to you in a hotel!"

"Oh, George . . ."

They got out of the car and George unlocked the front door. They went inside. The large living room was painted white. It was empty except for a gleaming jukebox. George took a quarter from his pocket and gave it to Anna.

"Go on. Play something."

She scanned the titles and dropped the quarter in the slot. Sinatra was singing "My Funny Valentine." Once, on Highland Avenue, Nastasia had played it when she was lonely. Now Anna danced to the melody in George's arms. They danced slowly, wordlessly, and held each other close. When the music stopped, George kissed her. Loneliness was gone. Anna was helplessly in love.

George made love that afternoon with all the skills of a great lover. He was ardent. He was tender. He was reckless and romantic. He made love the way Heifetz played the violin, or DiMaggio ran, or Billie Holiday sang the blues. George didn't perform. He moved into Anna's soul. He took it over.

Anna looked at him, poised above her, ready to sink, slow, sweet, and sure into her love-filled womb. She took a deep breath. No artifice now, no glittery *puta* wiles. She was caught, swept up, alive with romantic passion. George looked into her glowing eyes and her rapture almost scared him. He shut his eyes and thrust . . .

Afterward she said:

"It's perfect, isn't it?"

"Perfect."

"When will I see you again?"

"Tomorrow."

"What about the day after?"

"Come here."

"And the day after that?"

"I'll be waiting."

"What about Gull?"

"Leave Gull to me."

"What about Nick?"

"I'll leave Nick to you."

"George, is there going to be a terrible price?"

"Listen, Anna, I'm not perfect. I've had a lot of women. Don't ask me questions, because I can't answer. I just know you're going to be my lover. You know it too."

"George?"

"What?"

"When you said you had a lot of women . . . that you're not perfect . . . I don't want you perfect."

George grinned.

"All I want is . . . well, let this house be for us."

"It is for us."

"I mean . . . don't use it with other women. Okay?"

George was silent. He had ruthlessly, yet instinctively, pushed this glorious girl over the edge, and as always there were consequences—possessiveness, jealousy. He'd been hoping for a miracle. Well, he had a miracle in his own home working her ass off so he could spend his afternoons fucking. He'd make it up to Flame tonight.

"George?"

"What?"

"Will you?"

"Is it an ultimatum?"

"A suggestion." She paused. "Well, will you?"

"Will I love, honor, and obey? Hey, I'm a married man, remember?"

"Yes or no."

"Yes," George lied cheerfully. "I won't bring anyone here but you."

"Seal it with a kiss."

"Listen, you greedy bitch, you got kissed better today than you've ever been kissed in your life, and tomorrow, if you're very good—that means no bullshit, no 'suggestions'—you'll get better than you got today. Now it's getting late, so get your beautiful ass into some clothes and I'll drive you to your car."

After George dropped her off at Bedford, Anna walked over to Rodeo. She stopped in at Giorgio's and bought Nick a shirt. Then she walked to her car, in Gull's lot, and drove home.

Every morning at eleven, Flame went into the downstairs den. She sat at an antique English desk that looked out on the grounds. She heard George upstairs, restless, heard him bound down the steps and go outside. She watched him dive into the pool and do his laps, his stroke so sure and strong, and she felt, as always, the old excitement. George, the master cocksman, had hooked her on his stylish sex, until she hid from life in an endless rerun of his last night's fuck. Flame often wondered where sex stopped and love began. It scared her that she might be like her mother. Except she only wanted George. She watched George swim and thought about last night's sex. She got up and shut the drapes. Now she sat in the darkened room, faced the typewriter, and still couldn't work. She sat for an hour, frozen and hopeless. She got up, pulled open the drapes, and saw George was gone. She sat down. After a while, she wrote a scene.

That night at dinner Flame asked, "What do you do all afternoon?"

"I make love to beautiful women."

"I hate your jokes."

"I hate your jealousy." George paused. "When are you going to learn how much I love you?"

"If you really loved me, George, you'd find another writer."

"I do love you, which is why I want you to do it."

"George, darling?"

"Hmmm?"

"Let's go upstairs and make love."

"After I finish my dinner, my love, I am going to take you upstairs and make you more crazy than you have ever dreamed was possible."

And he twirled the spaghetti on his fork and blissfully gulped it down.

When George was with a woman, any woman, he was sure there was no evidence: no lipstick marks, or telltale scratches, no stale scent of perfume. Despite his precautions, those times when Flame suspected him of adultery she was a wild woman, taking her pleasure like a demon lover. Her fierce response heightened his own, and in that moment she forgave him, abject beneath him, now his slave. Then, suspicions quenched, George was master of her body, and once again felt safe.

It was noon and Flame watched her gorgeous husband raise his arms and dive into the water. The movement of his body made her tremble. How much she wanted to be outside, sunning, swimming beside George, but she had promised she would get him a first draft and, dammit, she would. Instead she watched George. *Work,* she said to herself, *you've got to work.* She rose and closed the drapes and sat again and waited. After a while it would be easier. It always got easier after a while.

Hours later she finished her pages. She was all strung out. She got into her car and drove west. On Strathmore she turned left to Westwood Village. She passed modern high-rise buildings and low stucco offices. How much easier it would be to work away from home. She made another left on Wilshire. By the time she hit Beverly Hills, she'd made a decision. She parked in front of Rodeo Realty. She finally felt like the professional writer George wanted her to be.

Don Dresdon at Rodeo Realty was the undisputed master of the Beverly Hills monopoly board. He wore white linen suits all year round and he wore a year-round tan. He held his cigarette in a long ivory cigarette holder and he wore a cat's-eye ring. He was a failed but handsome actor who made redress for that sin by supplying the mansions of the once great stars to the fast-changing generations of Hollywood royalty.

"I need a real office," said Flame. "Where I can turn off the phone and just work."

"What about the house on Maple? Why not use it?"

"What house on Maple?"

Dresdon went pale. He had thought it odd that when George bought the house he hadn't shown it to Flame. George jokingly said he wanted a getaway. Now Dresdon understood. He wanted to get away from Flame. Maple Drive was for George's other women. Oh, shit . . .

"Has George a place on Maple?" She hesitated. "He has, hasn't he? A place of his own."

Dresdon was silent. This was a steel trap if ever he'd seen one.

"You've screwed up, Don. Made the biggest mistake of your career."

She wouldn't let him off the hook.

"So tell me, Don, when did he buy it, how much did he pay, and give me the address."

Dresdon continued his silence.

"If you don't tell me, I'll wreck you. You know I can do it. If this becomes gossip, you are through."

"All right," said Dresdon. "I'll tell you. George bought it about a month ago."

"Where is it?"

"On Maple, 947 . . ."

"What did he pay?"

"I'm not sure."

"Sure you are."

"Around a million."

Flame stood up. "Thanks."

"I'm so sorry . . ."

"Accidents happen."

But even Don Dresdon, insensitive to all emotion except the sound of a pen scratching a seven-figure check, felt rotten. He knew the cost of his blunder. Community property, after all, was an important part of real estate. No, what really bothered him

was, he had stupidly revealed Flame's Prince Charming to be the
son of a bitch he really was. She was being a damned good sport.

Outside, on the street, Flame leaned her head against the
white brick wall. A suntanned real estate agent flashing a cat's-
eye ring had broken her charmed and perfect life. She pushed
her head against the wall until there were marks on her skin. She
didn't feel the pain, nor the heat of the sun, nor the stares of
curious strangers.

George had betrayed her—ruthlessly, savagely, betrayed both
her and Nick. *Oh, George . . .* Her eyes filled with tears. She
wiped them away but they filled up again. She got into her car.
She drove to Maple Drive. The stucco house was hidden by
wisteria. George's car sat in the driveway and behind it was Anna's.

Flame had known from the first that Anna was different from
other women, but she couldn't face then what she must face now
—her marriage was over. Finished. "You bitch!" she sobbed, and
laid her head on the wheel.

That night she controlled her jealousy, pleaded a headache,
and went to bed early.

The following noon, Flame drove to the Beverly Wilshire,
parked her car, and rented a green Toyota. She parked down the
street from George's house. She wore sunglasses. A kerchief covered her hair.

Around one, Anna's Mercedes turned into the driveway.
George followed minutes later. Flame cried and she cursed.
Around three o'clock, the Ferrari backed out into the street and
George turned north toward Sunset. Flame wrote down the time
of his arrival and departure in a secretarial pad. In a minute Anna
followed. Anna recorded her departure on a separate page.

The next day she rented a red Porsche. She wore a hat and
changed sunglasses. George and Anna appeared punctually at
one.

Flame slunk down in the seat. What a dreamworld she'd been
living in, believing George's fucks to be love, playing out some
crazed fantasy that one day he'd exhaust himself and come back

to her for good. Some bad old movie she'd seen a thousand times. Well, this wasn't a movie. This was life. Something she'd never been able to face up to before. And Nick—what would Nick feel when she told him? She'd have to tell Nick . . .

But she didn't. Instead she rotated rented cars, changed hats and eyeglasses, and waited in the sun. Around three days later, the two lovers disappeared. They never came out. Three hours passed and then four. Four hours became five. Husbands returned from their offices. Children ran home for their supper. Around six o'clock, George and Anna came out of their house. They held hands. Anna pulled George close and kissed him. Flame gasped. She felt faint. George and Anna got into their cars and drove to their homes. Flame felt like she had received a blow to her stomach. She turned on the ignition, drove to Wilshire, parked, and called Nick's office.

"The doctor's in San Francisco," said the nurse. "He'll be back tomorrow."

Flame hung up the receiver. She had to tell someone. She put another quarter in the slot and called Wanda, who had loved her all these years in that special way that only grandmothers can.

Wanda lived alone in a one-bedroom apartment in an enormous old château in the hills above Franklin Avenue. She had lost her savage passion for life. She accepted each day as it came and was grateful she was healthy. Evenings she ate dinner with a friend or watched television.

When Flame was small, Wanda had been a frequent visitor to the house on Bellagio. Then, when Flame was thirteen, everything changed. Flame wouldn't see her. She refused to take Wanda's phone calls. Wanda insisted on knowing why, and Flame had told her.

"Nick's not my father . . . I don't care what he says, he's not. . . . And you're not my grandma. So don't lie to me, Wanda, just don't."

Wanda was silent.

"I know everything," Flame had continued. "I know all about my mother. Everything . . ."

"I know how you must feel," Wanda had said gently. "But I love you, Flame, I want you to know how much I love you."

"Don't . . . don't . . ."

"And I am your grandmother and I'll always be . . ."

But Flame had hung up. And whenever Wanda called after that, Flame refused her call.

It was only after Flame married George that she seemed finally to forgive Wanda. After Michael was born, Wanda had returned to the role she had played when Flame was a baby and lavished on him all the affection she had once given Flame.

"Are you free for dinner?" Flame asked. "It's important."

"Yes, of course I'm free."

"Good. I'll pick you up in half an hour. Where would you like to eat?"

"Let's go to Musso's. It's nearby."

Within the hour they were sitting in a booth with a red-and-white-checked tablecloth and a red rose in a small-necked vase. Wanda listened intently. Finally she said:

"You've got to tell Nick."

"I know. I haven't been able to."

"You've got to tell him. It's only fair that he know."

"I know . . ."

"You'll feel better once you do. He'll help you."

"What about Dad? Who'll help him?"

"Tell him, Flame."

"He'll be home tomorrow. I'll tell him then."

Musso's was Buck's favorite restaurant and he ate there every night. It was as close as he got to a home-cooked meal. God, he missed home cooking; a tender brisket or a beef and cabbage borscht. Some dishes you couldn't get in a restaurant—not the way Rose once made them. This was as good as you got.

He saw Wanda across the aisle and remembered what a great

lay she was and how he'd been a shit. What was her terrible crime, after all, that she was a passionate dame who fucked from her gut? That she'd fallen head over heels in love? He could use some of that passion today. He owed Wanda an apology. Buck took a puff on his cigarette and doused it. He got up from the table and walked toward Wanda.

Wanda's face was wrinkled now, but Buck looked into those bedroom eyes and remembered everything. He looked at that mouth that once blew him away. Old dames! Glenda Bruce was the best he ever had and Wanda would be as good or better.

"Remember me, Wanda? It's Buck."

"Hello, Buck."

Wanda looked at that dimple in his chin; she looked into those deep-set brown eyes rimmed by dark circles and felt a queer little shiver. After all these years the son of a bitch still got her going. Wouldn't she ever grow up? she wondered, and knew the answer was no.

"Good to see you," said Buck. "You still look great."

"You don't look so bad yourself."

"No, I mean it. Really great."

"Thanks." An awkward pause. "Oh, this is my granddaughter, Flame."

"It's a small world," said Buck. "You're a spitting image of your mother."

"So I'm told."

"Your mother once played in my orchestra."

"Oh, did she."

"Yeah. Pretty good violinist," Buck lied.

Flame didn't answer and Buck figured her as weird. Weirdness must run in the family, Buck thought, and congratulated himself for not wanting to call her.

"Look," he said to Wanda, "I'd like to call you. Take you out to dinner."

"I'd like that, Buck."

"You still at the same number?"

"I'm still there."

"I'll give you a ring. Well, I'll see you soon."

"So long, Buck."

After he left, Flame said:

"You're not really going to see him."

"Sure I am."

"Why?"

"Think of it as unfinished business."

"He turns you on. That's why."

"You're right."

Flame giggled.

"You think I'm a fool," said Wanda. "A foolish old woman. Well, let me tell you. Most women are fools . . . fools about love, romantic fools. You're born with it and you die with it. Buck Herman is my last big romantic fling and I wouldn't miss it for the world."

The following morning Flame called Nick at his office.

"I tried reaching you yesterday but you were out of town."

"I had a convention in San Francisco."

"Look, Nick, what I want—well, just bear with me."

"Tell me what you want."

"I want you to cancel your one o'clock appointment. I'll pick you up and have you back by two. No, you better cancel that one too. . . . You might not be up to dealing with a patient."

"What's the mystery?"

"Not on the phone. Look, I wouldn't ask you to meet me if it wasn't important."

"I'll see you downstairs."

"I'll be in a rented car."

Nick hung up the phone. He told his nurse to cancel both his one o'clock and two o'clock patients.

In another part of town Buck called Wanda.

"Hello."

"It's me, Wanda. Buck."

"Hello, Buck."

"When can I see you?"

A hesitant silence before Wanda said:

"Do you like brisket?"

"Do I like brisket! Does the pope like Rome?"

"I'm famous for my brisket."

"How about tonight?"

"No," said Wanda. "Not tonight. Brisket's best on the second day. I'll see you tomorrow."

"I'm not sure I can wait."

Wanda laughed and hung up. *Am I crazy?* she thought. *You're crazy,* an inner voice warned. *This guy is nothing but trouble—bad trouble.* But Wanda wasn't listening to inner voices with their dire warnings of imminent pain—she was burning once more with a passion to live . . . *just one night,* she told herself, *one last big fling and then I'll quit* . . . suddenly the phone rang.

"Hello," she said.

"Screw the brisket. I can't wait."

"I'll cook it anyway but it won't be perfect."

"Don't worry," said Buck. "It'll be perfect." And he hung up.

Flame was waiting for Nick in a blue Chevrolet. He got in beside her. He watched the grim set of her jaw. He kissed her on the cheek but remained quiet. On Maple Drive she slowed down and parked.

"There," she said. "That place on the left covered with flowers."

"Who lives there?"

"It's George's. A hotel is too public for George's adulterous activities."

Anna's car turned into the driveway and was hidden from sight.

Nick was silent.

"Now you know," said Flame.

"How did you find out?" His voice was cold and controlled.

"Don Dresdon let it slip. He sold it to George about a month ago."

Nick fell silent again.

"She's such a bitch," said Flame.

"She did what she had to."

"For God's sake, she's your wife. George is my husband. Why in hell don't you react like a normal human being?"

"I'm thinking about Acapulco . . . how she looked into my eyes over lunch and told me a sordid little story about her captivity. She asked me to save her." He paused. "She was brilliant in choosing me—because that's what I do, isn't it? I save and I rescue. She lured me on, except I wasn't the only one she was luring. She was luring George as well. She needed me to get away from de Diego and get back home. Mission accomplished, her next task was easy."

"George."

"George." He paused. "I suppose he's behind the staggering gym bills I get from Gull's."

"Gull is his old pal."

"It figures."

"I thought you'd go crazy when I told you."

"Not crazy—numb, bruised—that ache that comes with betrayal. I don't know what I feel. I only know we've got to face what's happened."

"How?"

"Stop the lies. I want you and George to come for dinner. We'll have it out . . . all of us . . . tonight. Here, use this."

He handed her a handkerchief.

"I never cry. Now I can't stop."

"Want me to drive?"

"No. I'm okay. Thanks."

She returned the handkerchief and they drove back to his office in silence.

Nick sat in his office and stared into space. He closed his eyes and saw Anna, arms outstretched and smiling, like an ancient mythic goddess. As a child, she had entered into his imagination.

Night after night he had dreamed of an Anna. He had wanted her so desperately to exist.

Then he saw her dance, all siren allure, and his boyhood dream rose up to haunt him. Dream and reality seemed one. The boy Nick, on his white charger, and the man Nick, rushing to save her. . . .

Oh, yes. He was Nick the rescuer. Nick the saver. Nick, Sir Galahad of Hollywood. He laughed mirthlessly. He'd come to believe his own myth.

For a long time Nick had been bored with his work, and restless, and falling in love seemed to bring him back to life. If he really did love Anna, why did he feel this profound emptiness, this numbness, this aloneness?

All his life he had studied to become the best doctor he could. He used the old ways and he used the new methods and now he was like a guru, a human god, treating the rich, the powerful, the exalted young who yearned to topple the old crowned heads and take over the movie business. Every day he heard a litany of greed and ambition. Once his work had served a purpose. Now it served a chorus of more—more—more.

Nick sat in his office and thought over his life. He thought about his work. He began to understand it wasn't numbness he felt—it was a personal despair. He picked up the phone. He told his nurse to cancel his afternoon patients. Then he put on a jacket and left.

Nick's car mounted the ramp of the Santa Monica Freeway. A breeze blew against his face. A strange force was pulling him eastward—as though he must return to another, more innocent time, a time of hope and courage lost along the way. At the Union Station exit he moved into the downtown traffic. Once, Foster and Kleiser billboards preached a high colonic cure while evangelists in white marble temples preached the divine healing. Now modern civic buildings rose into the air. He passed Olvera Street and the Union Station depot. The old county hospital stood before him, and memories of childhood: A small cramped isolation room, a cast-iron bed, the crowded ward, the suffering children with hearts full of hope. Nick remembered the first moment he saw his leg—a stick stuck to a splint—saw his foot, his toes, but couldn't feel. He was numb then, too, but his young heart had raged to live.

He walked u the granite steps and down the corridors. He was pulled along by memory. Now he was at the children's ward. The rooms had been modernized, but everything else was the same:

Damaged children.

Abused children.

Abandoned children unable to express their pain.

John Aherne was dead, but his spirit stalked the world and children were helpless against it. Nick had grown into manhood, but his heart embraced the terror and tears of childhood. He was of the children, at one with them, a part of himself never free.

He moved toward a small boy with dark, sad eyes.

"What's your name?" asked Nick.

"Victor . . . what's yours?"

"Nick."

"Are you a daddy?"

"I'm a doctor."

"Will you hurt me?"

"No. I'm your friend."

"Why are you my friend?"

"Because you're a good and fine little boy."

"My daddy hurts me. He hurts my mother. My mother throws things at him and he hurts her more."

"I won't hurt you," Nick said.

"Will you stay with me?"

"I'll come back tomorrow."

"Promise?"

"Yes, I promise."

The boy reached out his hand. The boy and Nick held hands and then Nick left.

Flame dropped Nick at his office. She was too angry to go home and face George. She decided on a movie. She sat in the dark and thought of George—of that hushed and mysterious moment before he bore down. She shut her eyes. She clenched her hands. Worse even than his betrayal was his imitation of love. A stab of pain shot through her. She stumbled from the movie house into the heat of the street. She drove over to Rodeo and parked. In Giorgio's she tried on a black blouse. She looked as if she were in mourning. In Charles Galet she tried on a Jean Muir dress. It hugged her body and made her feel better.

"It's you," the salesgirl exclaimed. "Absolutely you."

"It's nice," said Flame. "I'll take it." She handed her an American Express card.

"I'll have it wrapped immediately."

"Thanks."

Flame's eyes were red and puffy. She put on sunglasses. She combed her hair, freshened her lipstick. She noticed Anna looking at sweaters. She was simply radiant. Flame felt a queer dull rage—all the anger within her bubbling up like tar. *Careful,* an inner voice warned, *don't start a public scene.* But Flame wasn't listening to inner voices or caution or common sense. She felt the boil of her fury and she walked over to Anna and smacked her.

Anna screamed. She slapped her back. Flame grabbed Anna's hair and the two women were in each other's arms, impacted, scuffling, hitting, biting, and screaming obscenities.

A store detective rushed to the brawlers. God, he wished he had a camera. It wasn't every day a movie star's wife was caught in a cat fight. The *Enquirer* would pay a bundle for this. He wedged himself between them.

"Ladies . . . please . . . ladies . . ."

Anna shoved an elbow into his rib cage.

"Owww . . . you bitch!"

"Let me go."

Flame broke free of Anna's grip. The store detective grabbed Anna. The salesgirl handed Flame her package. Flame walked to the door.

"He's married to you but he's mine," Anna screamed. "He's mine. D'you hear? He's mine!"

But Flame was out the door and on the Rodeo sidewalk.

George and Flame were due at Nick's at seven o'clock. Flame dressed with particular care. The fit of her Armani sweater and slacks gave her a feeling of self-confidence and she needed all the confidence she could muster. Beneath her mask of composure was a little girl who wanted to hide. She had hidden so many years in an endless fantasy of sexual love, but it was over now and she felt wasted and ashamed.

She picked up the silver hairbrush engraved with her initials: *F.K., with love, Dad.* She remembered back to her fifteenth birthday and the morning she had unwrapped her presents. The first excitement with the matching set of silver toiletries, how she'd picked it up—this exact same hairbrush—read the inscription—and how all the adolescent fury within her had exploded.

"You're not my father," she'd screamed. "My mother was a nympho. She picked up strangers in bars. If you were my real father, you could prove it . . . I know all about it . . . I found out. If my blood type is different from yours, it's proof you're not my father. You've known all along, haven't you? But you pretend. Oh, God, if you'd be honest, it's my birthday, tell me the truth."

"The truth," Nick had said softly, "is if a man raises a child as his own and loves that child as his own, she is his child. I love you, Flame. You're my beloved child."

"Then help me. For God's sake, help me."

"Oh, darling," he'd whispered. "My darling sweet girl."

But when he'd reached toward her to hold her, she'd brusquely moved away.

It was soon after that, Flame had first seen George Warren and plunged into a frenzy of romantic love.

Flame finished brushing her blond silky hair. She put the engraved silver hairbrush on the dresser and went down the hall to get George.

George played with young Michael every day. They built towers with Lego blocks or played with tin soldiers or ran Michael's electric train. Tonight Michael was conductor and George his passenger.

"Toot toot. Here comes the train."

"Please stop in Glendale," said George. "I've got to see a friend."

"Can't stop in Glendale. Toot toot."

"It's important, conductor . . ."

Flame opened the door. George was on the floor with Michael. Michael's nurse was watching. Her eyes seemed glued to George's back. *George should be locked up in a museum,* thought Flame, *on display as human sculpture.*

"We'll be late," she said.

George stood up. He picked up Michael.

"Look, pal, tomorrow we'll go to Vegas. We'll play the slot machines. We'll hit the jackpot. We'll go to Wyoming, buy some horses, and start a ranch."

"Let's go now."

"Tomorrow, pal." George kissed his son and put him down.

He loves Michael, thought Flame. *It's the only part of him that's human.*

George backed the Ferrari out of the garage. The car twisted downhill. He glanced at Flame. She was still angry. Even after last night's fuck.

"Okay," he said. "You've been mad for days. What's wrong?"

"Nick will tell you."

"You're my wife. Suppose you tell me."

"All right, I'll tell you." She paused. "Maple Drive. Anna. Oh, don't lie your way out of it, George. Don Dresdon told me. I've seen the house. Watched you come and go. So has Nick."

George turned left on Sunset. They were part of a slow, steady stream of traffic. The line reshaped. The car sprang free of the bumper-to-bumper grid.

"You were brilliant, George. Keeping me busy with your goddamn script. There'd be draft after draft, wouldn't there? I'd never get it right—another scene, another way of making it better. Sure you were going to make a writer out of me. Until you got bored with Anna."

At Bellagio, George took a sharp left and zoomed up the hill.

"Hey, George, take it easy. . . . Okay, I tricked you into marriage, but I thought one day you'd come to love me. I swallowed my anger. My jealousy. I pretended I didn't know what was happening. Flame! The perfect wife—a small price, I thought, to be married to a world-class fuck."

"I love you . . . you've got to believe me."

"No, George. You need me. Nothing unpleasant will happen if you're safely married. I'm your protection against all those women who'd give a right arm to be the next Mrs. Warren. It's degrading, George, to be with a man who fucks you for protection."

"You've got it wrong."

"I doubt it."

"It'll be different. I'll change. I swear I will."

"You can't change. You're like some insect. You scrape your legs together and you're ready to do it. I don't want to be married to an insect."

Up ahead was Nick's place. It was all lit up. A sudden glare of white headlights leapt out from the dark. A black steel mass bore down. Flame screamed. She put out her arm to protect herself. George veered sharp left but not before an approaching car rushed by and cut into his tail. George's car jumped the curb. It banged into a wall. Flame was thrown against the dashboard and George was rammed against the steering wheel. He found the strength to press the horn. He kept blasting it until Nick appeared, running toward them from the dark.

Nick sat beside Flame's hospital bed. She'd suffered a broken arm, and cuts and bruises. Thank God no worse. He watched her sleep. The powerful attraction she had always held for him, held him still. He thought about the way he'd protected himself from his feelings in the love of other women. Love had been an escape, a grand illusion, and Anna, the grandest illusion of all. All these years he had denied his feelings. All these years he had struggled against his love. He kept looking at Flame and the whole of him —senses and soul—resisted no more. He took a long deep breath and let all the love he had denied take him over.

Flame opened her eyes. She saw Nick. A lock of silvery black hair fell onto his forehead. She reached up a hand to brush it away.

"Nick."

"Flame, dear Flame."

"George?"

"He'll be okay. He has a few broken ribs."

"You look so white. Is something the matter?"

"I was remembering. . . . When you were a little girl, in the evenings, we'd drive out to the beach. There'd be a sudden breeze, you'd open your arms to catch it, you'd laugh. I'd catch my breath; it was as if Jeannie were still alive—laughing, full of life."

"You still love her, don't you?"

"Let me finish. I want you to understand." He paused. "I'd look at you, at your eyes, your skin, the way you smiled—you were still a child. I was a grown man who had fallen in love. I tried to numb it, drowned you out with other women." He paused again. "When you fell in love with George, I sighed with relief. I'd be free, I thought, free of Jeannie's ghost—free of you."

"Until Anna."

"Until Anna. The damsel in distress. I fell under her spell, as all men do. She asked for my help. Well, rescuing is an old bad habit of mine, so of course I agreed. I was so self-involved, I didn't realize she was using me to get George. If Anna used me, I used her too. That night in Acapulco, I saw men fall in love with her so hard and fast, I knew George had finally met his match. Oh, I didn't consciously plan it, but fate was acting itself out, so I gave fate a little push. I brought Anna back to L.A., I even married her—to destroy your marriage."

Flame was silent.

"Are you very angry with me?" he asked.

"Oh, Nick. Do you remember how I used to love *Jane Eyre?* Each night I'd imagine I was Jane and you—you were Mr. Rochester. Night after night I'd play it out, this ritual, this beautiful love story." Flame smiled. "My mother craved sex, Nick. I craved love. I got sex and love mixed up. George got me crazed. It was like an inner wind. A kind of tornado whirling inside me. When I watched George with Anna, I thought my heart would break. It didn't, Nick. The fever broke. I passed a crisis. George fucked me, Nick, but he wasn't my lover. You've never touched me, but you've been my lover for as long as I've lived."

Nick reached his hand to her face. They were silent. Then they smiled at each other. After a while Flame shut her eyes and Nick sat beside her while she slept.

Anna decided to move into the Beverly Wilshire. She would wait for George there. When George came back from the hospital, she would move into the house on Maple Drive. She packed one suitcase. She'd get the rest of her things once she'd settled in with George.

The day after the accident George was semicomatose from the morphine. The second day he was sitting up. His eyes crinkled and he was smiling his radiant smile.

When Anna came in, he said:

"C'mere, you beautiful bitch. I missed you."

"Me too."

George pointed to his cock rising up from under the sheet. "He needs tender loving care."

"Suppose the nurse comes in."

"I told her my lover was coming and not to disturb me. If it's important, she'll knock."

"Oh, George."

But George's hand was on her head, pulling her down, while his other hand pulled back the sheet.

She slipped her mouth over the rim, took him deep in her

throat—and she was good, very good, a tireless virtuoso, except it began to feel like a workout, like those hours at the barre. She pushed the thought from her head. George had been without her for days—of course he was sexy.

There were three knocks on the door, a rest, then three more knocks.

"Shit," said George.

Anna pulled away. She sat in a chair. She patted her hair. A pretty blond nurse came into the room. She pulled a thermometer from its white plastic plug and stuck it in George's mouth. She looked at George as if he were a god. She pulled the thermometer from his mouth and read it.

"How about some lunch, Mr. Warren?"

"Make it lunch for two."

She looked at George as if she had heard from the Messiah. She left the room.

"She's hooked," said Anna.

"So am I. On you."

After they ate lunch, Anna played with George again. The barre was her rival for childhood. Her rival for George was his cock—his endless erection. *I'll feel better once we're home,* she reasoned to herself. She pulled away.

"Tired?" he said.

She nodded.

"I'm sorry, baby. I've used you for my monomaniacal needs and you've been a very good girl and humored me." George smiled his great movie-star smile. "You are good, baby. It makes us very special."

"Do you love me, George?"

"Sure I do."

"Then say it."

George hesitated, but said it. "I love you."

That night she fell asleep playing old tapes. George poised above her . . . the glitter in his eye . . . his deep, sure thrust.

She played his moans, his sighs, his sounds of love, and finally fell asleep.

A ringing phone aroused her. It was 9:00 A.M. She picked up the receiver.

"I want you to know I'm lonely," said George.

"Poor baby."

"And I miss you."

"I'll be there around noon."

"Too long. I can't wait."

She laughed. "I've got some errands to do. Be a good boy and I'll see you soon."

"Hurry!"

She kissed the air and hung up. She called room service and ordered breakfast. She ran a hot bath and sat in the steaming water. She thought this would be a good time for George and her to get to know each other. The hell with shopping. This was really important. She dressed and was at the hospital within an hour. George's door was closed. A DO NOT DISTURB sign hung from the knobs. She ignored it and pushed open the door. The pretty blond nurse was deep on George's cock. George pushed her away. The nurse saw Anna, gasped, and ran from the room.

"You bastard."

"I couldn't stop her."

"Don't, George."

"Okay . . . I'm a bastard. But you've got to understand . . . I'm a movie star. They go crazy . . . a bunch of groupies . . . I can't stop them. Anna, I'm only human."

"I'm human too."

"Then try and understand."

"How does Flame stand it?"

"She just does."

"Well, I don't. I won't. It would kill me if I had to."

"Anna, I promise. It won't happen again. Sweetheart, please. I'm sorry."

"What you said about Flame—it's important, isn't it, your being with someone who's not jealous?"

"I said it won't happen again and it won't. Okay? The subject is closed. Finished. Look, let's not spoil something very special. . . . C'mere . . ."

His eyes glittered. She had seen the glitter before—in the eyes of Pepe Faro before he killed the bull, in Diego's eyes, in the eyes of the men who howled when she danced—the glitter of the wolf, of men stripped to bare lust.

"If I ever catch you with another woman, I'll kill you, George. Now I've got to think about whether I want to spend my life in jail."

She walked out of the room without saying good-bye.

George leaned back on the pillow. He'd had a hard-on since morning. His balls were burning. He'd worry about Anna later. Right now he needed that nurse. He picked up the cord hanging beside the bed and pushed a button. Within seconds the door opened. It was the pretty nurse.

"Put that sign back on the door," he said. "Then make a sick man happy."

The nurse couldn't believe her luck. She'd make George Warren so happy, he'd never forget her. Tonight she'd tell her girl friends and watch them go green with envy. She hung the sign on the door, smiled, and walked toward George.

Downstairs, in a public pay phone, Anna called Nick's office.

"Dr. Kahn is with a patient," said his nurse.

"Please tell him it's important. I've got to see him."

"Yes, Mrs. Kahn." The nurse put Anna on hold. Within seconds she clicked back on. "Doctor will see you at one."

"Tell him thanks." Anna hung up and took a deep long breath.

Nick's office was furnished with a beige leather couch, two leather chairs, and a French Provincial desk. Medical degrees and honors hung on the walls. Framed pictures of Jeannie and Flame stood on the desk.

The moment Nick closed the door behind her, Anna started to cry.

"It can't be all that bad," said Nick.

She continued crying.

"Tell me what happened."

She wiped her tears with her sleeve.

"I went to the hospital . . . George didn't expect me. Yesterday, he said he loved me. . . . Today I found him with the nurse."

"Maybe George wanted you to find him with another woman —wanted you to know."

"Why?"

"Because you're going to be free soon. That means, sooner or later you're going to want to get married. I don't know if George is aware of what he did except it relieves him of the burden of your expectations."

"Why did he say he loved me?"

"I don't want to talk about George," said Nick. "All I'll say is that perhaps you do love him in a once-in-a-lifetime way and you're willing to suffer for the man you love. And perhaps you'll meet a more tender man who can love and even nurture this beautiful girl who lives for love. You don't have to make any decision today."

"I know."

"I want to talk about Anna."

"Okay."

"As a child, you were forced to dance. Madame was never satisfied. She was strict, punitive, a merciless taskmaster. You would have given your soul to be like other children. Instead you were sold. You danced for lustful men, danced to make them fall in love. You had no choice, you did what you had to do—dance or starve. But you made a vow you would never be what Madame wanted. This was your secret, your revenge." Nick handed Anna a box of tissues. "Here, wipe your eyes."

She wiped her tears. Nick continued.

"Despite her cruelty, despite your loneliness, you performed from a kind of inner joy. You stunned your audience, swept it away. You're a true creative force."

"I don't want to dance!"

"Of course not. It's dangerous, this strange power. It's brought pain and isolation—a world without love. You must protect yourself—destroy it if you must. Except, Anna, there's another side to it, a way this gift can bring you happiness. You can wake up in the morning with a sense of purpose—a sense of your own life. What seems a curse can become a blessing."

"Nick . . . I want to cry."

"Cry. You feel human. It's the best reason to cry."

"I feel better now."

"After a while you'll feel much better. You'll be free, Anna, for the first time in your life. You'll feel like a free human being."

It was a warm sweet day. Flame lifted a mirror and looked at herself. She fluffed her hair. Gosh, life was funny. She could have been killed. Instead, Nick was coming to take her home. The door opened and Nick came toward her. She felt a queer excitement—the thrill of loving him openly and freely, and of Nick loving her too.

Outside, they got into Nick's car. He turned the ignition. Within minutes they were on the freeway—flying westward.

"I want to show you a building," said Nick. "I'm going to buy it. I want your opinion."

"Why are you buying a building?"

"I'm giving up my practice."

"You're what!"

"That's right. I want to open a clinic. A hospital for emotionally disturbed children, poor children, children who need help and can't afford it."

"Nick?"

"What, darling?"

"You'll need help," she said quickly. "Someone smart—efficient. Someone with loads of energy."

"Like you."

She grinned. "Of course, I don't have experience."

"My dear girl. There are courses in hospital management at

UCLA. Given your brains and determination, I'd say you'll be ready to run the place by the time we're ready to open."

"It'll be very expensive," she said.

"State and federal funds are available. I'll have to match them, of course." He smiled. "That's where you come in."

"So it's my money you're really after."

"Think of it this way. You'll be returning some of what Josiah Rand stole from the poor." He paused. "You can start by selling a Picasso. That'll pay for the architect. That Renoir you're so fond of will cover the mortgage."

"I think my generosity deserves a big reward."

"Virtue, my love, is its own sweet reward."

Sepulveda hit Pico. Nick turned left. After a mile he parked in front of a four-story brick building.

"Well, that's it."

"Nick," she said, ignoring him. "What you said about virtue being its own reward. I think virtue deserves something—well, more romantic."

"Aren't you going to look at our clinic?"

"It's terrific." She smiled. She leaned over and kissed him.

"Happy?" Nick said.

"So happy it scares me."

Nick took her hand. The sky was glowing silver. Nick and Flame looked at each other and held hands and took a chance on being happy.

The Jeannie Rand Children's Clinic is open. Nick has lured some of the finest psychiatrists to work with him and his staff; even in these hard financial times, he is devoted to the clinic.

Nick is relentless—traveling to Sacramento and Washington to match private funds with federal and state aid, supervising the daily activities, tireless with his patients. The torment that gripped his life is gone. Here, in this building on Pico near the sea, Nick understands that in giving to others he gives to himself.

Flame has taken a crash course in hospital administration and now, under Nick's supervision, she organizes the chaos and keeps general order.

Wanda is Flame's secretary and helper. Despite her age she has unflagging energy. Those hours away from the clinic, she indulges in that sweetest of all pleasures, love in late life.

What Nick counted on—and he is right—are the wildly popular classes and workshops.

The most popular, of course, are George Warren's acting classes. When George is working on a movie he comes at night. But George is free now and he is there every day, teaching, leading workshops, advising the kids. He is bursting with plans. He wants Nick to buy a nearby building and start an acting school.

Nick thinks it's a fine idea.

"Help me raise the money, George, and you've got yourself a school."

George flashes his famous movie-star smile.

Down the hall in a large white room Anna teaches ballet and flamenco. She kneels to correct a badly placed foot. She straightens an arm askew. She smiles and encourages. She claps her hands in delight. After a class, she faces the mirror and leaps up —she flies. Half woman, half bird, she lingers in the air and lands in a perfect jeté. The kids go wild. No matter how bad things are outside, here, in this room, Anna helps them fly. The children crowd around their teacher and those up close see tears of happiness in her eyes.

One last empty room on the main floor serves as gymnasium and performance hall. It is here Buck Herman spends his afternoons. He has bought the children musical instruments from his own pocket—tax deductible, of course—and he stands in front of a wooden podium and cracks a baton.

The sound of "Embraceable You" comes from the horns— ragged and broken and not at all in unison, and then the violins take it up and it is hopeless—Hopeless! Buck looks out at the kids and thinks back on how he's had it all—the big career, the broads, the bucks, and how he's been miserable—a miserable son of a bitch except for the few short years with Glenda, and suddenly, out of the blue, Wanda, cooking him the dishes Rose once cooked and afterward making him feel like some young Turk . . .

Buck looks out at the kids and forgets Wanda and Glenda and all the dames he's *shtupped*. He feels funny . . . A kind of goodness. Bah! He's getting sentimental. But it continues . . . this feeling good . . . And then a horn breaks and Buck looks at the kid hard and cracks his baton on the stand.

"Bobby." He hears himself saying. "You're close to a terrific sound. So we'll just take it again, nice and easy, and I think you'll have it. . . ."

And the kid blows out the notes—thin and ragged and so goddamn out of tune, but to Buck it sounds like music . . .